Kregg P.J. J

CLUBS ARE TRUMPS

The Road From Plum Run

Outskirts Press, Inc.
Denver, Colorado

Clubs Are Trumps
The Road From Plum Run

v4.0

Outskirts Press, Inc.
http://www.outskirtspress.com

ISBN: 978-1-4327-7670-1

PRINTED IN THE UNITED STATES OF AMERICA

For the Tactical Tracking Operations School's Cadre; Good people, good trackers, and good friends.

The next dreadful thing to a battle lost is a battle won.'

-Sir Arthur Wellesley, Duke of Wellington

Chapter 1

Gettysburg, Pennsylvania-
Thursday, July 2, 1863

A haunting, piercing scream a hundred yards out on the field jolted Private Ben Nyhavn up onto his elbows and staring. The wounded horse was in an erratic race dragging its entrails and what was left of a ripped and bloody saddle beneath it.

Nyhavn watched as the panicked mount stumbled over the body of a dead soldier in the knee high grass, broke its left front leg in the fall, and then struggled wildly in a failed attempt to stand.

But the horse was only a momentary distraction and the seventeen year old soldier's attention was quickly drawn back out to the larger struggle along the Emmitsburg Road, where what remained of the Union Army's bloodied Three Corps was in a desperate fight to regain its own footing. They had failed to turn back the overwhelming rebel advance. Their battle line was gone, and they were now fighting in desperate groups and pockets as the numbers of the wounded and dead in both armies were growing well into the thousands.

"Keep your heads down, boys!" shouted Sergeant Mulligan as he moved behind the frontline of soldiers urging them to stay down behind cover.

Those other Minnesota Volunteers, who, like Nyhavn, had been up on their elbows watching the melee just south of their position, dropped back onto their bellies hugging the ground. The hail of incoming shrapnel and rifled musket fire bloodied the curious. Tested as most of them were, they were all battle hardened veterans who knew this but curiosity was still a powerful draw.

A shifting cannonade of rebel grapeshot shell and canister rounds sent waves of debris, concussive heat, and razor-sharp shrapnel flying into and over their ranks.

"Stay down!" yelled Mulligan again over the thundering booms of body rocking explosions.

It was sound advice from the big Irishman, but hard to heed, since it looked like every rebel in the world was coming at them.

The battle began in earnest just shy of four o'clock in the afternoon. During the opening salvo every big gun in the Confederate line had sent murderous cannon fire raining down on the Federal forces for a full thirty minutes. The objective of the coordinated artillery barrage was to weaken the Union line and create openings for the rebel infantry to push through. By six o'clock the tactic appeared to be working.

Three Corps was faltering and Two Corps didn't have enough troops to fill the bleeding gap, let alone hold the overstretched line.

"Steady boys, steady!" ordered Mulligan when Nyhavn and several others pushed themselves back up to see how close the advancing rebels were to their position. Just as he lifted his head, a shell burst sent a dark twisted object tumbling straight at him. He barely had time to duck and cover his head before it hit, with a dull thud, just inches in front of him.

Readjusting his forage cap, he found himself staring at a half-cooked chicken leg. It took a moment to realize that it was actually a severed thumb and a sizeable chunk of someone's left hand.

"*Faen*," he swore in Danish. The utterance carried all of the same startled surprise as damn did in English. What surprised Nyhavn most was just how clean and well cared for the thumbnail was. A pale quarter moon rose over a trimmed and manicured nail, in stark contrast to the bloody stump of splintered bone and torn tissue it was connected to.

He stole a quick glance at his own left hand; the thumb and fingers were grubby and the nails were chewed down to the quick, but at least they were still attached.

The dark eyed Dane rose up on his elbows again to see whose thumb it was and where it came from. Nobody near him was holding a hand, crying or screaming, and no one else seemed to have noticed it. Everyone around him was hunkered down trying to keep from getting hit by incoming fire.

"Jamie?" he yelled, nudging the soldier on his right. "Jamie?'

"What?"

The battle noise was deafening. He had to shout as he pointed to the torn thumb on the ground. "You okay?"

The soldier, a gap-toothed nineteen-year-old named Jamie Cobb, studied the severed thumb and then held up both hands for inspection, grinning. "Too small to be my pecker and I still got these two," he shouted, wiggling his thumbs.

Nyhavn started to jab at Al Frantzen on his left but stopped when he saw the big German Sharpshooter holding his rifle out in front of him with a steady two-handed grip. Next to Frantzen, Trigg Kinnunen had one hand holding his glasses while the he was using the other to rub sweat from his gun-smoke, tired, red-rimmed eyes. The severed thumb wasn't his either.

The young veteran loosened his grip on the stock of his rifled musket and stared down at his own hands again. God All Mighty, what can you grab or hold onto without a thumb? How can you button or unbutton your pants, let alone take a piss?

"They're turned!" yelled Frantzen drawing the younger soldier's attention back to the battle line.

"The rebels?"

"No," said a frustrated Frantzen, "Three Corps."

Nyhavn swore again, and he wasn't alone. Three Corps was now in full retreat. Some units were falling back in order, or as best they could, while others were fleeing in panic, stepping over, and sometimes on their own wounded or dead to escape the deadly onslaught.

Seizing the opportunity, Brigadier General Cadmus Wilcox's Alabama Brigade, over 1,000 strong, poured through the opening, howling and shouting as they came. Rattled as they were some Three Corps soldiers were flinging their muskets and equipment aside as they fled back across Plum Run creek towards the relative safety of Cemetery Ridge, the rebels fast on their heels.

Watching the scene unfold it looked to be a repeat of every previous major battle. The Confederate's strategy and their dogged determination were once again overpowering the larger Federal numbers. The emboldened rebel General Wilcox could see it, and so could the disheartened Two Corps Commander, Major General Winfield Hancock. Hancock's overstretched Corps would somehow have to fill the dangerous breach left by Three Corps' retreat.

The 262 soldiers of the First Minnesota Volunteer Infantry Regiment that Hancock was holding in reserve just above the battle were awaiting orders and could see it too. The rebel infantry was steadily moving forward. They were now just over 300 yards away with their skirmishers out front spearheading the attack. An artillery battery to the left of the Regiment was pouring it on the rebels but it wasn't enough to stop them.

Mulligan and five others from G Company had been pulled out to support the Regimental colors. They weren't alone in the shuffle. F Company, 'The Goodhue Volunteers,' had been moved further south to take on a deadly line of rebel skirmishers. L Company, the Second Company of Minnesota Sharpshooters, were sent out to support an Artillery Battery while C Company too, had been pulled away to guard rebel prisoners leaving the Regiment painfully short.

"Company sharpshooters up!" ordered an officer behind them. The command was being echoed by several junior officers and sergeants in the company line. "Tear into the rebels! Fire at will!"

Frantzen, a quiet and solemn man, was one of the best riflemen in the Regiment and went about his task with smooth, methodic proficiency. The big German searched the rebel line for an officer behind the iron leaf sights of his tube-fed Henry Repeater rifle.

The .44 Henry was said to be deadly accurate up to 1,000 yards but the big German knew there was too much of a drop in the bullet at 500 yards to prove effective, so he patiently waited until his target was within 400 yards before he fired.

With the enemy line now less than 200 yards away, and thirteen rounds ready to be jacked into the chamber one after another, Frantzen would be murderous.

Taking careful aim on a chosen target, he fired. The officer went down as Frantzen scanned for any other rebels with gold stars or braid on their uniforms, or holding swords. Those he took first. Five more fell before he set his sights on the rebel skirmishers out ahead of the main body of troops.

"Sharpshooters Hell!" muttered Jamie Cobb rising up on one knee and bringing up his rifled musket. "Even I can hit them from here." The farm boy turned soldier drew a bead on a rebel skirmisher and fired. The bullet caught the rebel high in the chest and sent him tumbling backwards.

"Ha!" yelled a satisfied Cobb, as he hurriedly reloaded his rifle, while trying to keep an eye on the ever advancing rebel line. A dark line of gun powder from the paper-encased charge he had just bit away, spilled down the right side of his mouth leaving a dark stained trail.

"Cobb, sharpshooters only!" yelled Sergeant Sean Mulligan. "You'll get your chance soon enough, boy. Keep down and stay ready."

Cobb couldn't help it. Like the others in the Regiment, who up until now had only been observing the battle, he was anxious to join the fight; the fight that began when General Sickles, the Three Corps Commander, disobeyed orders and sent his line forward to what he believed was better ground. But Sickles move had left the Union line vulnerable and the rebels capitalized on it. Now, with a little more effort, the battle would belong to the rebels. All they had to do was get through the small Regiment of volunteers.

The belching fire and roiling smoke from a storm of muskets and cannon was choking out what little was left of the day's thin light. Night was hurrying in and with it Nyhavn knew, came a much darker threat.

A cold shudder tore through his bowels like a pull from a saw-tooth knife as he remembered too many previous battles where rats, pigs and even dogs had come out to feast on the dead and helpless wounded left out on the battlefield after dark.

He recalled one soldier who had gone out to try to recover a wounded friend and had been shot down during the ill-fated rescue attempt. That night, his cries and pleas as the animals tore at him had only added to the horrifying cacophony that was etched into his memory.

"We'll stop 'em," Nyhavn said, squeezing the scarred wooden stock of his musket.

"Damn right we will!" said an animated Cobb, charging up his own confidence. "Clubs are trumps."

"Clubs are trumps," replied Nyhavn, echoing the Two Corps motto that had come to mean so much more than the words.

Rushed into position barely an hour earlier, the eight companies that made up the Regimental line were impatiently awaiting their orders to attack. Heads craned from the approaching enemy line to their own field commanders, but still no orders came.

With Three Corp fleeing in confusion, Cemetery Ridge was the weakest point in the line and the tactical opening the rebels sought. Anyone could see it. Take the Ridge and you flank the Union line. Flank the line, and you take the town and the victory. So the rebels were concentrating their fire on the Ridge as their reinforced line of Alabama infantry charged into, what surely seemed to be, one more, well earned, triumph.

The hysteria from the fleeing soldiers, the cries of the wounded still on the field and the advancing gray line were having an unsettling effect on those still occupying the ridgeline. The nervous glances, labored breathing, and fixed stares of his own people confirmed it for Sergeant Mulligan.

Mulligan knew how fear could paralyze even the best of his soldiers. He'd seen it happen enough to know what he needed to do, but knowing didn't make what he knew he had to do any easier.

"Ah, St. Jude, would you save me from my own self sometime?" he said. He took in a deep breath and slowly let it out to steady his nerves. As the Irishman got to his feet, to try to stop some of the Union soldiers fleeing through the Minnesotan positions, he knew he'd need the help of the patron saint of lost causes.

"Stop running and fall in behind us!" he yelled blocking the way for a handful of Three Corps soldiers who were racing up the slope. "Stop retreating!"

A few other officers and Sergeants in the Regiment were on their feet as well, trying to stop the panicked flight, but with little success. Nyhavn tripped one runner by grabbing his ankle, but the panicked soldier kicked himself loose with his free foot, and scurried off.

"Stay and fight you coward!" cursed Nyhavn, shaking his stinging right hand. Angered and smarting from the kick, he grabbed his musket and dropped down behind the iron sites.

"No. Don't!" Frantzen yelled as he grabbed Ben's arm to keep him from firing.

"I oughta shoot the son of a bitch!"

"He ain't our problem," added the big German, pointing back at the rebel line. "They are. Save your ammunition. We're gonna need it."

"Stay! Turn and fight!" yelled Sergeant Mulligan, man-handling another of the terrified soldiers. The man seemed lost in the fear that flooded his eyes.

"We can't stop them!" cried the soldier, trying and failing to break Mulligan's grip. The rebel line was just a little over one hundred yards from where they were standing.

"You can't if you run!" said the Sergeant. "Get back in line with us!"

"I don't want to die!"

"If you run, you'll only wish you had. Stay with us. For God's sake and yours, fight!"

The soldier's eyes darted from Mulligan back to the first line of rebels, who were starting down towards the dry creek bed below. It would only be a matter of minutes before they were here too.

"I…I ain't got a weapon," he said, unable to admit that he had thrown his own down.

"Then take mine," said the Sergeant thrusting his musket into the man's arms and making him take it. "I'll find another."

The soldier took the weapon and dropped to the ground in line, he leveled his new musket towards the oncoming rebel army. His hands were shaking as he gripped the rifle but he stayed in place.

Mulligan turned away from him, shouting something at the top of his lungs as he calmly walked up and down the Company line exposed to the rebel fire. He didn't have a weapon, but knew there would soon be one available, so he kept on walking back and forth, shouting encouragement.

"What'd he say?" asked Nyhavn.

"He said 'Hold steady!' replied Frantzen, and then repeated it loud enough for others around them to get the message. The former farmer stood several inches over six feet and had been 200 pounds of hard working muscle at the start of the war. His weight now hovered somewhere around 170. However, it was his unnerving calm, keen sharpshooter skills and self-assurance that made him someone his friends listened to. "Hold steady, boys!" Frantzen said, repeating Mulligan's order.

Ben wasn't even sure he could hold his piss in, let alone steady himself, as he watched the grisly bloodletting unfold. In two years of serving in the Regiment, in major engagements from Bull Run to this Pennsylvania ridge line, the battles hadn't gotten easier for him. The rubbery legs and stomach churning fear that came with each new fight had not abated in the least. If courage was fear going forward, as Kinnunen had once told him, then he had the grit that was required, stamina though, might be another matter.

"Why aren't we wading in at 'em?" asked an annoyed Jamie Cobb.

"We will," replied Frantzen, "soon, more than likely."

"Good. Let's get to it."

Nyhavn was nodding and agreeing with Cobb. His palms were wet and his chest was pounding. If they were going to do it he knew it had to be soon.

Fear could dig deep and take root because adrenaline only lasted so long.

Chapter 2

When the Regiment left Fort Snelling, Minnesota, in June of 1861, they left with a roster of one thousand men. In the two years of fighting that followed, their numbers were brutally hacked at and stripped away in battle or by dysentery or malaria. The cuts tore deep.

At Bull Run with Harpers Ferry muskets, their first engagement of the war, the Regiment fought well and held their line until finally ordered to retreat. Regimental losses were 42 killed, over 100 more wounded, and several dozen others that were reported as missing in action in the Union Army's humiliating defeat.

During the battle for Savage's Station in Henrico County, Virginia, they had lost another 50 men, killed or wounded. Outside of Sharpsburg, Maryland, at the bloodletting in the west woods that was Antietam Creek, their numbers fell again with over 150 more casualties. By the time they had reached Gettysburg, the thousand man roster had been whittled down to a little over three hundred.

The 1,000 Alabamans were now threatening to tear away a big chunk of what remained as was the Florida Brigade that was angling in to support them.

Watching the Three Corps battle line unravel, Nyhavn wanted to get up and run too, but he knew he wouldn't. Word had come down from headquarters that morning that any soldier leaving the ranks without permission would be shot on the spot. But that wasn't his reason for remaining in line.

No, he wouldn't run; he wouldn't leave his friends or shame his regiment. It was as plain, and as simple, and as agonizing as that.

A shell exploded behind them, taking down three of the fleeing soldiers. And, what the cannons failed to do with approximate fire, the rebel muskets were doing with better aim. Some of the Johnnie Rebs were using 'buck and ball' ammunition in their muskets. The combined three round buckshot pellets and thumb sized .69 caliber 'ball' in each load, fanned out as they left the barrel, spreading misery across a wide path. The field in front of them was an open slaughter house and a testament to the success of improved methods of wholesale carnage.

A number of the resolute Three Corps survivors who had fled the peach orchard and wheat field and retreated to the ridge, were regrouping alongside the First Minnesota Regiment, ready for another go at the enemy. Even so, it was simple math: the numbers wouldn't be enough. The momentum belonged to the Confederates and soon the ridge that the First Minnesota occupied would be theirs too.

Nyhavn watched as a stern-faced Major General Hancock road up in a hurry and leapt from his horse, just short of the Regiment's Commanding Officer, Colonel William Colvill.

The six-foot five, red-haired, Colvill, who had only been in charge of the Regiment since May, hurriedly saluted the much smaller Two Corps Commander. Their brief exchange was drowned out by the din of battle. Still, it didn't take much to figure out what was being said. He watched as Hancock adamantly pointed to the rebel colors in the field ordering something that was answered by a determined nod from Colvill. The Colonel saluted the General a final time, and then ran forward, shouting orders, as Regimental Officers and Sergeants jumped to their feet and converged on him.

Colvill was pointing back down towards the Plum Run creek bed, at the Confederate colors coming at them. Captains and Lieutenants followed his line of sight, nodding and then saluting the senior officer before hurrying back to their companies and barking orders of their own. This was it.

"Off your asses and on your feet!" yelled Sergeant Mulligan to his people.

"About time," Jamie Cobb said still spoiling for a fight.

The hole left behind by the retreating blue line had to be plugged and they were the only ones left to do it. Other Federal units were being shifted over to strengthen the line but it would be up to the Minnesota Volunteers to buy them the time needed to make it happen.

"Will you follow..." shouted Colonel Colvill to his Regiment.

"What he'd say?" asked Trigg Kinnunen.

"Wants to know if we'll follow," replied Frantzen, reloading his Henry rifle.

"Thought that's why we're here," said Jamie Cobb, annoyed again at what he thought was such a stupid question.

"Ours' is not to reason why,'" said Kinnunen.

"What?"

"It's a poem by an Englishman about the charge of a light brigade."

"The English are on the side of the rebels?"

"No, not quite yet."

"But the rebels got a light brigade, do they?"

Trigg snorted. "More like a full brigade, if you ask me," he said, studying their line.

Jamie Cobb knew that the sandy haired, spectacle wearing former Divinity School student was book smart and educated. He also knew that, as soldiers went, he wasn't the best of shots nor was he keen for battle. Still, he proved reliable in a fight.

Trigg Kinnunen had marched shoulder-to-shoulder alongside him and the others in every previous battle. Poor shot that he was Trigg often waited until they got closer to the enemy lines before he finally fired. Even so, accuracy wasn't his best suit. However, what he lacked in marksmanship, he more than made up for in resolve.

Although he was the only son of a Lutheran Minister, he had no immediate calling to the pulpit. Ever the ladies man, he drank, gambled, and figured he would find both redemption and ordination in due time, just not yet or, seemingly, anytime soon. And it was that randy part of Trigg that Cobb liked best.The book learning was another matter. He was just about to ask him what the hell he was talking about with the English and Light Brigade talk when a new order came down the line.

"FIX...BAYONETS!" Mulligan shouted, relaying the command from an unseen officer behind them. Although, the rebel cannon fire had ceased, it had been replaced by sporadic musket fire from the advancing line of southern skirmishers.

The main body of the Alabama brigade was fast on the skirmishers heels.

"Hurry it up!" barked an Officer to no one in particular. Excitement and fear bumped up the volume of their voices and their actions as the eighteen inch long blades scraped out of their scabbards.

Ben Nyhavn fumbled with the long bayonet but finally managed to seat it and heard it lock into place with a loud metallic click. It was properly seated but the young veteran soldier tested it anyway. He didn't want it falling off when he needed it most. He'd seen it happen to other soldiers so he checked it a third time just to be sure.

"We'll run 'em back to Richmond!" yelled a cocky and defiant Jamie Cobb.

"Yeah we will," said Nyhavn, more to himself than anyone else. He needed to believe the Regiment would turn the rebels. They had to.

Frantzen nodded, but said nothing. To those who knew him, his quiet resolve was clear and unmistakable.

"Five minutes are all we need, boys," yelled Mulligan. "Five good minutes."

Five minutes might be all they needed, reinforcements were already hurrying in to support them, but there wasn't a soldier standing who didn't know that those five minutes charging the Confederates would prove costly. Any victory, let alone glory, hard won.

Next to him Kinnunen laughed loud enough to grab Nyhavn's attention.

"What's so funny?"

"Well, one thing's for sure. With so many of them this close, this time I ain't likely to miss!" Trigg said, as he brushed dried grass and dirt from his thin wispy beard and stared out at the rebel mass.

Arne Hermansen, the big shouldered saddle maker's son from New Tonder, grimly laughed along with Kinnunen.

"Nope, ain't likely," he said stepping up beside him to even the rank.

The talk cut through the sweat soaked tension and had a temporarily soothing effect. It wouldn't last.

Nyhavn squeezed the stock of his rifle as Cobb shifted his weight back and forth on the balls of his feet like an anxious runner at a starting line. As Frantzen thumbed new rounds into his rifle, Kinnunen adjusted his glasses, while Hermansen checked his own bayonet.

Down the line to their right a soldier cried out when he was hit in the abdomen by a hurtling piece of shrapnel. A Captain in line ordered two soldiers in line to help the wounded soldier back to safety as furtive eyes enviously followed their retreat.

"Come on, you rebel bastards," yelled Jamie Cobb.

"Don't really think you need to encourage them, Jamie," said Kinnunen.

Across the field and to the right of Wilcox's Brigade, the Florida Brigade was moving quickly to support the Alabamans and press the advantage.

"SHOULDER…ARMS!" shouted Colonel Colvill as the Regiment complied with the order.

"I'm buying a woman tonight for any man who takes their flag!" yelled Sergeant Mulligan.

"How many do I get if I capture General Bobby Lee?" shouted Jamie Cobb, drawing nervous laughter from the soldiers around him.

They needed the laughter and the bravado. The charge would be suicide, but then, so was remaining in place on the ridge. Their only hope lay in shocking the overconfident Confederates and slowing their assault.

"FORWARD!" shouted Colonel Colvill, as the company officers repeated the command. It was soon followed by the order that would send their counter attack in motion.

"DOUBLE QUICK TIME…, MARCH!"

The Minnesotans started down the open, uneven ground with their bayonets leveled. Fixated on the rebel skirmishers, they made their way around flat slab boulders, through brush and over bodies as they went. Ben kept his focus on a rebel skirmisher in front of him, a stern faced lanky rebel who was yelling insults the Minnesotans. Ben would kill him first and then find another.

A rip of rifle fire from the rebel skirmishes greeted them and a number of the Minnesotans fell. "CLOSE THE RANKS!" Mulligan yelled over his shoulder and they did just that, racing to close the gap and keeping the Regiment charging forward.

With his eyes and attention focused on the stern faced rebel, Nyhavn was momentarily startled when he stumbled stepped over the torn chest cavity of a dead Union soldier.

"KEEP MOVING!" Mulligan yelled and Ben stepped over the dead man and picked up his pace. The rebels were jeering and shouting out oaths and curses while the Minnesotans remained eerily stone-faced quiet and deadly determined.

Just in front of Nyhavn another Three Corps soldier was on his back down behind a slab of rock, trying desperately to hold on to what was left of his face. The soldier's nose and left cheek were gone, shot away. There was a bloody trench where his right eye should have been showing ugly meat and jutting pieces of bone. His one good eye mirrored his torment.

"Help me…please," he pleaded to the advancing Minnesotans.

Blood was seeping through the man's fingers, but there was nothing Ben or any of the others could do to help. They were heading into the fight. Nyhavn tried not to look at the man and quickly stepped around him to catch up to his friends. He tightened his grip on the stock of his musket and stared forward.

"Hold on," he said to the soldier as both tugs of sympathy and guilt pulled at him. "Someone will be by to help you soon. Just hold on."

He hoped someone would soon be by to help the soldier, just as he hoped someone would be there to help him and the others, if they went down and weren't killed outright. Then it occurred to him that maybe being killed outright would be preferable to dying piecemeal or being torn apart by dogs or pigs in the dark. It wasn't much solace to Nyhavn, but it was all he had at the moment. After all, he still had his thumbs.

Chapter 3

The July heat was in the mid 80's and the sweltering humidity turned the roiling clouds of sulfurous cannon and gun smoke into a gritty yellow-gray fog. The battle cloud billowed over the battlefield in the crimson twilight like a sullied shroud. The foul haze tumbled slowly in the summer sun and mixed with the nauseating stench of the dead; it worked its way through Nyhavn's nostrils and settled in his throat. Dripping sweat spread dark rosettes across his arm pits and back. Beneath his tunic his blue striped cotton shirt was sticking to his skin.

Nyhavn was breathing through his nose to keep from vomiting. Cemetery Ridge, he figured, was a proper name for the place.

The day was proving to be an orchestrated slaughter. And all it had taken to bring him to this moment was a brass band and the promise of a new blue Army uniform with shiny buttons.

In early May of 1861 he had followed Frantzen, Kinnunen, Hermansen, Cobb and several other eager volunteers from New Tonder to New Ulm to enlist in the Regiment.

At nearly fifteen years of age, he was already six feet tall, broad shouldered, and sun worn from enough field work to make him look older than he actually was. Those that knew him described him as 'strong willed and determined' or, as 'a square headed stubborn Dane,' which probably explained why he wasn't about to be left behind when his slightly older friends and neighbors marched off to war.

The nearby town of New Ulm, Minnesota, was bustling with immigrants and sons of immigrants from the southern half of the state lining up to volunteer and show what good and loyal Americans they were. The New Tonder boys soon joined in the growing crowd of other volunteers. Why not? It was patriotic to enlist, the war would be a great adventure, and it wouldn't last all that long anyway. Everybody said as much.

Much to the dismay of his Lutheran Minister father, Trigg Kinnunen had returned home from Divinity School in Chicago in time to enlist with his friends. Standing in line with them and sporting a newly acquired goatee and stylish Prussian mustache that he unconsciously tugged on as he spoke, Trigg had other reasons for returning home too.

"Patriotism brought me back," he confided to the others. Al Frantzen, who knew him best, scoffed.

"Is that right?" he said with an arched eyebrow.

Kinnunen shrugged and said, "Well, that and the fact that I may have been asked to leave school unexpectedly."

"Unexpectedly, huh?"

"A little misunderstanding with a Philosophy Professor about his daughter..."

"Yeah, well, I bet I can guess why!" laughed Jamie Cobb, enjoying Trigg Kinnunen's latest escapade.

"Why is a wonderful and appropriate philosophic question, young Master Cobb. The simple fact is she was the Philosophy Professor's very lonely and wonderfully affectionate daughter, whom I deemed was in dire need of counseling. So I took it as my civic and charitable duty to counsel her," said Kinnunen as his friends chuckled and shook their heads.

"Counseling?" said Frantzen eyeing him with suspicion. "Is that what you're calling it now, are you?"

"Oh ye, of little faith."

"And how much or how little faith did the Professor have in your civic and, eh, charitable counseling?"

"Not enough, apparently," Kinnunen said, "For some reason he mistook me for a profligate..."

"A what?" said Jamie Cobb.

"Someone with less than honorable intentions..."

"Imagine that?" said Frantzen. The big German was stuffing a hand carved pipe with tobacco as he spoke. "He still looking for a horsewhip, is he?"

"Possibly," replied Kinnunen.

Of average height and looks, Trigg Kinnunen didn't necessarily stand out in a crowd, but for some mysterious reason, his friends couldn't quite fathom how, he held considerable sway over most women.

Ben's sister, Saffi, had once explained the Lutheran Minister's son's appeal to the local ladies this way: "He's funny, and he always seems genuinely interested in our opinions and what we have to say."

"Is that right?"

"It is, and, you know what?"

"What?"

"He's charming too."

"*Charming*?" said her surprised brother uttering a word he doubted he had ever used before or would again.

"Uh-huh."

"What? You saying you fancy him too, do you?"

Saffi nodded. "Ya sure, most of the girls in town do."

It was true. Kinnunen won them over with a flattering sincerity and disarming smile that even they knew wasn't all that sincere. It didn't matter. They liked him anyway.

It didn't hurt that Kinnunen could quote the Bible, Chapter and Verse, recite several sonnets of Shakespeare's, or poems from Shelley, and could make the social kind of small talk that young women seemed to enjoy. For those young women and well, any woman that responded to his advances, he was an always eager and willing participant. That some ladies would be attracted to a man in uniform he figured probably wouldn't hurt matters either, which was another reason why he decided to follow his friends to New Ulm.

The line of volunteers moved slowly up to a small field desk manned by a Corporal and several smartly turned out soldiers from nearby Fort Ridgley. Natty uniforms were a convincing enough calling card for rural farmers in sun-bleached and patched over clothes, and even the more well-to-do dandies. A brass band was blowing a lively tune keeping the recruiting drive festive.

After answering a few preliminary questions at the field desk, the Army Corporal pointed them towards several medical orderlies, who were conducting on-going basic physical examinations. The orderlies thumped on the volunteers' backs and chests, listening for signs of consumption, or worse. Then the volunteers were made to do a series of deep knee bends and kicks to make sure there were no serious mobility issues or problems.

Finally, their teeth were checked as were their eyes and ears. All of the poking and probing annoyed at least one potential enlistee.

"Why are you so concerned about whether we got upper and lower teeth?" asked the man, a bristled bearded Norwegian from Albert Lea. "You shopping for mules or fightin' men?"

"Just making certain we don't get a jackass or two," replied the medical orderly, not missing a beat. "Now kick your legs and see if you can prove me wrong."

Those who had passed the preliminary exam were sent over to a second table where Sergeant Mulligan would be the one to add their names to the Regimental roster.

"Name?"

"Bent Ole Nyhavn."

"Print it," Sergeant Mulligan said and Nyhavn did what he was told. When he had finished the Sergeant swung the roster around to inspect it.

"N-y-h-a-v-n?" he said spelling out the name. "Shouldn't there be a letter after the V and before the N?"

"No, it's correct," Nyhavn said while the Sergeant didn't seem all that convinced.

"And Bent? What kind of heathen name is that?" asked the Irish Sergeant staring at the name in large block letter print.

"It's Dansk...Danish," replied the farm boy defensively.

"Right," replied the Sergeant crossing out the T. "B-E-N. Ben."

"No, it's Bent."

"Yeah, well it's straightened out now, son. Move along," said the Sergeant pointing him over to the next line. "Wait! Hold up," said Sergeant Mulligan calling the volunteer back to scrutinize him more closely. The boy's patched pants were too short and fringed, his faded jacket was too large, and more than likely had once belonged to an older brother or father. His shoes too were lost souls. Tall and big shouldered as he was there was something more to him that told the Sergeant that Nyhavn didn't look to be of age.

"How old are you, boyo?" asked Mulligan tapping the ledger book with the pencil he was holding. He was ready to cross out the Volunteer's name if he didn't like the answer.

"He's eighteen," replied Kinnunen stepping up to answer for Nyhavn.

"Eighteen is it?" said the skeptical recruiter. They were all tall enough and with few exceptions many of them didn't look old enough to shave the few thin wisps of mustaches and beards they were tying earnestly to sprout.

"He looks young for his age," Frantzen said, which was another lie, but eighteen was the age you needed to be to enlist in the Regiment. Frantzen knew that Cobb was sixteen and figured that Nyhavn, who was a good head taller and a slight more sensible, had to at least be sixteen too.

"Is that right?"

"Yes sir," said Frantzen.

"That's yes, *Sergeant.*"

"Yes, Sergeant."

"So what year was he born then?"

"What?" Frantzen said momentarily taken back by the question just as Mulligan suspected he would be. Good lies, he knew, took work and most people just didn't put in the proper effort.

"Trouble with your ears, is it?"

"No, Sergeant," said the big German running the arithmetic in his head.

"Then quick, what year?"

"1840…"

"Actually, it was 1843," said Kinnunen offering additional support.

"Okay then, so which is it? 1843 or 1840?"

"Hell, I don't know. He came to join the fight."

"We all did," added Arne Hermansen. He's eighteen or close enough not to matter."

Mulligan snorted turning back to Nyhavn and asked, "Your Ma know you're here, son?"

"Yes Sergeant, all our folks saw us off when we came up to enlist. I plan on sending most of my army pay home to help them with the farm's mortgage."

The Sergeant stared at him, but didn't respond. President Lincoln had called for 75,000 volunteers and the new state of Minnesota was heeding the call. The Regiment needed one thousand men, and the Irish Sergeant was doing his best to make that happen.

However, even with the volunteers they already had, getting the daily numbers needed for the Regiment would still take some doing. The Irish Sergeant figured that if these boys were keen to join up, and if their families saw them off, then that was good enough for him and Minnesota.

Sergeant Mulligan scribbled something on a piece of paper and handed it to the gangly farm boy. "Take this and put it in your shoe," he said.

"What is it?" Ben asked staring at the paper that had the number eighteen printed on it.

"Something we occasionally use to verify what you're saying," he said. "It's so you can swear you are over eighteen when you take the oath."

"Yes sir," said Nyhavn grinning as he stuffed the paper in his right shoe.

"That's yes, *Sergeant*."

"Yes, Sergeant."

"Good, so I ask you again, are you *over* eighteen now, boyo?"

"Yes Sergeant, I am."

"There you go! Sign here," he said handing the boy a pen and pointed to the ledger book. "Welcome to the Regiment, Private," he said, adding the printed name 'Ben Nyhaven' to the roster.

"Thank you, Sergeant," said Nyhavn as the busy Non Commissioned Officer waved him away. Back to Kinnunen the Sergeant said, "And you, Mister 1843, what's your name?"

"Trygve Suomi Kinnunen."

Mulligan stared back at Kinnunen like he had been pole axed.

"Say that again."

"My name is Trygve Suomi Kinnunen, Sergeant."

"Kennen. T.S. Kennen," the Irishman said writing down the two initials and the altered name.

"Another 'en', Kinnun-en," said the smiling new recruit. "My friend's call me Trigg."

"Kennen, it is and I ain't one of your sorry ass friends," replied Mulligan ignoring Kinnunen as he turned his attention to the next volunteer in line. "And you?"

"Aalderk Uwe Frantzen."

Sergeant Mulligan wrote down the name as Frantzen slowly spelled it out.

"Next," said the Sergeant as Hermansen walked up to the table.

"Arne Bjorn Hermansen."

The Irish Sergeant lowered his head in his hands, took in a deep breath and sighed. "Oh, piss on Patrick's snakes!" he muttered. "And I didn't figure on making this a fookin' spelling bee neither. Just sign or put your mark and we'll sort out how to spell it or what to call you other than Private later. NEXT!"

"Jamie Cobb, Sergeant! C-O-B-B," beamed the volunteer.

"Finally, a proper name," Mulligan said adding Jamie's name to the roster. "And you're eighteen too, I suppose."

"1843 was when I was born too," lied the under aged youth. "When do we get our uniforms?" asked Cobb looking around, hoping to find somebody handing them out at another table.

"An officer will swear you in at Fort Snelling where you'll receive proper issue and training." Cobb's hope fell with Mulligan's response. He was hoping to get a new uniform to show off back home.

Minnesota had more than its fair share of Germans, Swedes, Norwegians and Danes and the Sergeant added the names of the new recruits to his roster in more anglicized terms. Under his hand and the hands of other recruiters the Hans and Johannes sometimes became Johns, Jurgens became Georges, Johansen's became Johnsons, and the thankful farm boy named Bent Nyhavn, became Ben Nyhaven or Newhaven to those who stumbled over the spelling or pronunciation.

Nyhavn was one hundred and sixty pounds of lean muscle when he enlisted but two drawn-out years of long marches in the summer's high heat, winter's shivering cold, thin rations and loose bowels from bad water and poor diet, had taken their toll. He couldn't keep his weight on. His weathered and worn uniform hung on his skinny frame like it was draped over a maple wood coat rack. Still, he wore it proudly even if he had punched three new holes in his belt to hold his pants in place.

By the time the Regiment had reached Gettysburg they were also battle hardened soldiers. But being battle hardened did little to alleviate the haunting understanding that this new battle would extract even more from the Regiment.

The six G Company soldiers were there to support the color guard for both the Regimental flag and gold-fringed Stars and Stripes that would become the focus and prize for the rebel army. If you captured their flag and colors, you shamed your enemy and brought honor to your unit. If you overran the enemy and held onto your own, then the glory was yours.

The Minnesotans advance momentarily slowed when the companies angling down the slope had to run to keep up. Once they had caught up Colvill shouted out his next command.

"CHARGE!" he yelled, even as the confused rebels stopped and brought up their muskets, less than twenty yards away, and let loose a volley. Scores of Minnesotans fell, leaving barely 150 still standing, to carry out the last command. Those who could were running and yelling at the top of their lungs as though to shout away the dying. Pent up anger, frustration and a strange sort of joy of battle propelled them.

With bayonets leveled at the rebel skirmishers there was no mistaking their intent. They would fire their muskets and then lunge, stab, and skewer the enemy down. An eighteen-inch bayonet would punch through a man while a twist and pull would leave him holding his innards.

Taking quick aim the advancing rebels fired again, the distance between the enemy soldiers less than fifteen yards. Holes in the Minnesota line opened up in a smoke-filled instant. When the soldier holding the Regimental flag fell, Trigg Kinnunen raced over and scooped it back up.

Just as Kinnunen lifted the flag Nyhavn saw him violently thrown backwards. His chest seemed to collapse under the impact of a rifle ball as he fell. Someone else behind Kinnunen grabbed the flag and raced on with the ever thinning line.

"FIRE INTO THEIR FACES!" yelled Sergeant Mulligan as most in his line let loose their own volley at the first line of rebels less than five yards away. Rebel skirmishers fell and those fortunate enough to have survived the salvo retreated to their second line in panic.

The Minnesotans slammed into the rebel line with a violent impact as their shouts, screams, and frenzied fighting were met with rebel yells, curses, and equal madness.

From one hundred yards away the enemy line was a gray mass, but this close they were a wall of angry faces. Ben's focus was fixed on a just as determined rebel in front of him who had his own bayonet leveled. He was ready to sidestep and parry the bayonet and run the soldier through with his own when a bullet the size of his thumb creased his jaw line and sliced through the flesh of his left ear. The bullet had the effect of a straight punch and drove him to his knees. Dazed, he fought to clear his head in the midst of the pandemonium. The earlobe was sliced in half and the skid mark crease burned as blood dribbled down his neck. Half an inch over and the bullet would have taken off half his head.

To his front Arne Hermansen bayoneted another rebel who was fixing to stab his fallen friend. But as Ben tried to get to his feet, Hermansen whirled around, and viciously slammed him across the bridge of his nose with his forearm. Ben went down a second time bloodied again by this latest blow. His nose was bleeding and his eyes were watering from the impact.

"Goddamn it, Arne!" he said to Hermansen. He felt like he had been mule kicked, but there wasn't time to stay down. The battle had become a brawl. Arne slammed the butt of his rifle into a rebel chin just over Nyhavn's shoulder as the young soldier got back to his feet.

"Help me find it, Ben," Hermansen said pulling Nyhavn back up as he searched the ground around him. "Help me find it."

"Find what?" said Nyhavn wondering what in the hell he was looking for when so much chaos was going on around them. Ben soon had his answer. Hermansen's left arm was missing at the elbow. Blood was pumping from the stump in spurts.

"Never mind the arm. Go! Get back to the ravine!" Nyhavn yelled to Hermansen who found and retrieved his lost arm, shoved it under his good arm and tried to retrieve his musket to get back in the fight.

To his left, a rebel soldier took quick aim on Hermansen and Nyhavn picked up a dropped loaded Rebel rifle and shot the man point blank. The muzzle blast sent the rebel sprawling backward and had set fire to the dying man's tunic.

"FALL BACK!" shouted a company officer on his right only to be cut down before he could repeat the order.

Another officer soon took up the command to retreat. "Fall back!" he yelled as those who were still standing began to heed the order.

"Go!" Nyhavn yelled to Hermansen reloading his own musket. "I'll cover you."

"I'm not leaving."

"Yeah, you are," Nyhavn said. "The officers already gave the order. Go! And cover me when you're back there, if you can."

With bullets buzzing around him Hermansen reluctantly turned back towards the ridge helping another wounded soldier as he went. Back on Cemetery Ridge other Union troops were stabilizing the line.

"MINNESOTA!" yelled Frantzen still charging forward, which brought Nyhavn back to what still needed to be done. If he tried to retreat now he'd have to leave Frantzen and several others in the company who were caught up in the melee, and that he wouldn't do.

On his right no more than a few yards off, Jamie Cobb went down and there would be no getting up. A musket round bored a hole through his left eye and splintered the back of his head. In the throes of death his body twitched as several more musket balls hit him again.

"SONS OF BITCHES! LOUSY SECESH SONS OF BITCHES!" Nyhavn yelled cutting and clubbing his way through the enemy line to join Frantzen. Bullets and blades came at him from several directions at once, but somehow missed their target. It was hand-to-hand combat at its most primitive and vicious.

Directly in front of him a rebel soldier brought up his rifle and fired. Ben juked to his left and the bullet missed him but hit his canteen instead. Ben was screaming as he returned fire. When the smoke cleared, the rebel was doubled over clutching his belly.

With no time to reload, he stabbed a second rebel soldier coming up and over the rebel he had just shot. He plunged the bayonet deep into the man's ribs, turning the blade and ripping out a lung. The man's eyes grew wide as Nyhavn yanked the blade out and then lunged again until the rebel finally fell.

Al Frantzen, who had somehow remained standing in the push and shove of the frenzied fighting, kept up his fire taking down three more rebels with the lever-action Henry rifle.

He took quick aim on a rebel officer who came at him with a sword in one hand and a long barreled Colt .44 caliber pistol in the other. The officer's mistake was leading with the sword as the big German promptly shot him through the mouth. Frantzen kept firing until he hit an empty chamber and then used the heavy rifle as a club, wildly swinging and yelling as he smashed it into the rebels closing in around him.

Just as Nyhavn had managed to free his bayonet from the dead rebel a burly Alabaman with a wild beard and even wilder eyes came rushing out of the gun smoke and bowled him over in a screaming fury. The attacker kept on screaming as he swung his rifle up in a wide arc and tried to bring his bayonet down on the young Yankee's chest. But just as he started to raise it up he was shoved from behind and thrown off balance. The shove also threw off his aim. The blade missed Nyhavn's chest but caught him high on the left shoulder instead.

It felt like he had been hit with a lightning strike as shocks radiated through his body when the blade burrowed deep into him.

He grabbed at the bayonet desperately trying to push it away, but with little effect, and only more pain. The sharpened English steel bit into his hand and momentarily slowed the blade before the attacker used his body weight to drive it deep through Ben's left shoulder, cutting through flesh and muscle before pinning him to the ground.

Ben cried out kicking at the attacker, only the rebel sidestepped the strike, and then heel stomped the boy's chest taking some of the fight out of him. The rebel pulled the bayonet from the Union soldier's shoulder with a mighty pull and brought it up quickly to finish him off.

Howling mad in anger, the rebel swung the bayonet down at Nyhavn again only to find that the Minnesota boy had somehow braced the butt of his rifle against the ground beneath him. It was enough to deflect the bloody blade. The attacker's bayonet scraped harmlessly down Nyhavn's rifle and dug into the ground just inches from the young soldier's head.

"You gonna die, blue-belly!" screamed the rebel with spit from the words sticking in his beard.

"You first!" yelled Nyhavn this time kicking the rebel's leading knee with every ounce of strength he could muster. The attacker's leg buckled while a second harder kick violently pushed the man's supporting leg backward causing him to fall forward. No stranger to wrestling the rebel went with the fall, lowering his head ready to head-butt the goddamn Yankee.

But as fell he saw the Yankee change the angle of the bayonet; the bayonet that was now aimed at his head. He tried to turn away but it was too late. The rebel was falling into the eighteen inch blade. The bayonet caught him just under his chin. The sharp tip and blade tore through his throat and tongue and lodged into the meat of his mouth. Gravity drove it in deeper.

He frantically clutched at the rifle barrel trying to extract the bayonet, only the frightened Nyhavn held the musket steady. The impaled rebel struggled to free himself but it was too late. Blood poured out over Nyhavn's hands, chest, and face, and the man's yell was reduced to a sloppy gurgle as he choked on his own blood.

Death tremors shook the rifle as Nyhavn held on and then shoved the body away giving him enough room to slide out from under the dripping mess.

The madness was still going on around him and he was suddenly without a firearm when yet another rebel soldier climbed over the bodies and charged at him. Grabbing up the dead rebel's rifle, Nyhavn flipped it around, cocked it, took a quick aim, and pulled the trigger. The buck and ball round tore into the rebel's chest and groin and sent him tumbling back the way he came.

The advancing rebel line was falling back as Union cannon fire from the twelve pound Napoleon's tore into their ranks. Close as he was Nyhavn ducked, covered his head, and rolled into a ball as the mix of shell and canister fire broke up the Alabaman's main assault.

The bloody ground bucked and trembled and Nyhavn bucked and trembled along with it. He was bloodied and battered, but he was he was still breathing. As the cannons thundered on, he closed his eyes and hugged the ground in pain, in fear, and giddy, giddy joy, happy just to be alive.

Chapter 4

General Hancock's improvised delaying tactic bought him the crucial time he needed to plug the hole in the Union line. As the First Minnesota Regiment was making their forlorn charge, the Two Corps Commander rushed in soldiers and secured the ridge line.

With their advance stalled, the rebels began falling back under the newly infused firepower that punished their retreat. Their opportunity at this part of the Federal line was lost.

However, those still caught out on the killing field, scattered about in tenuous positions and hugging whatever low ground they could find, would have to survive as best they could.

Down behind the dead in a small depression, and cringing in pain from his wounds, the physically exhausted and dry-mouthed Nyhavn searched the field around him for his comrades and friends.

Some survivors from the Regiment found temporary safety in the dry creek bed or, like him, were down, hiding behind the dead that littered the ground in a grotesque display.

Those Union soldiers caught without adequate cover were being picked off by rebels caught in their own small protective pockets. Nyhavn's curious head bobbing drew the attention and ire of several of the hunkered down rebels and bullets soon kicked up around him. A few more came from the Union lines as nervous soldiers back up on the line shot at shadows and anything that moved.

Frustrated, Ben lowered himself back down behind a small mound of the fallen as the incoming bullets thumped into the bodies of the already dead soldiers. Flecks of blood and flesh sprayed over him with each new incoming round. When he remained still, the shooters shifted their sites onto other available targets.

For the moment he was safe. Rolling over on his back, he gently peeled back his jacket and shirt. Tilting his chin to his chest he craned his neck trying to try to get a look at the bayonet wound. High on his shoulder the stab wound showed a nasty puncture. Pressing his palm on the hole to stop the bleeding, he could still feel a slow, and steady ooze running down his back from the exit wound. He couldn't lift his left arm, but he still had feeling in his hand and fingers. For now that was good enough.

Staying low he searched around him for anything he could use as a bandage. He snatched a haversack off the shoulder of the soldier he had gut shot and rummaged through it. The rebel had a gaping baseball size exit wound just below his right rib cage. Splintered bone glistened gold in the last light of the day.

The dead soldier looked to be a little older than he was, but not by much. Maybe eighteen, maybe nineteen, but not much older. He had badly barbered corn yellow hair, a scarred and pitted face from Smallpox, and to Nyhavn's surprise, he was barefoot. His feet were dirty and calloused and Ben wondered how long he had been fighting without shoes.

Finding a simple and reasonably clean and folded spun cotton shirt in the haversack, he ripped it in half, and then folded the pieces in small squares. When he figured they were the right size, he reached inside the back of his tunic and stuffed one of the make shift bandages over the exit wound. Then he did the same to the jagged hole in the front.

Hot as it was he re-buttoned his tunic to hold the make-shift bandages in place. The fight, the wounds, and the July heat left him spent and exhausted. He was parched well beyond thirsty and with his canteen shot away he searched around for another.

Spying the dead rebel's stamped tin canteen he reached across the dead man's right hip and then froze halfway as the dead man opened his eyes and blinked.

Scooting back on his butt, Nyhavn scooped up his rifle with his one good arm and aimed the gun on the badly wounded man who stared back at him through glazed over eyes.

"No...no honor in robbin' the dead," said the rebel in a choking whisper. Rivulets of dark blood spilled down the corners of his mouth. His hands and arms hadn't moved. "No honor at all."

"Ain't robbing," said Nyhavn. "Just looking for something to drink is all."

"Where's your'n canteen, Yank?"

"You shot it through and through, missed me though."

"Guess...guess I need to work on my shootin' some," chuckled the soldier. The small laugh soon turned into a harsh bloody cough. The soldier's body tensed as he coughed and his eyes glistened and welled over. "Go on, take the canteen," he said, finally.

When Nyhavn seemed reluctant to do so, the rebel made the offer again. "Go on now. Take it."

"You sure?"

The wounded Alabaman closed his eyes and sucked in short quick gasps of air, fighting off the hurt or trying to. When he opened them again he let out a thin, labored breath.

"Take...take it," he said. "It's only fair. I ruined yours."

"You sure as hell did!"

"I'd say I'm sorry, but I wouldn't mean it. Sorry my aim was off is more like it." The wounded rebel managed a small laugh that finished as a wheeze.

Nyhavn managed a half smile of his own as he reached around the soldier and retrieved the canteen carefully pulling the rope sling over the rebel's arm and shoulder. As he did he accidentally bumped the rebel's arm and blood flowed out of the wound at his side in a thick, dark stream. Nyhavn's hand came away sticky and wet.

"Sorry," he said and meant it. Any anger he had was used up along with his strength as a sudden weariness took hold of him.

"Funny, ain't it?"

"What?"

"That you gut shot me and now apologize for making me uncomfortable."

Nyhavn wasn't sure how to answer that since it just as easily could have been him who was gut shot. A cannon shell exploded nearby and Nyhavn flattened himself to the ground to avoid the deadly iron fragment spray. When the shell fire moved on, he propped himself back up, and took the cork stopper out of the canteen and took a quick drink.

"Jesus," said the rebel while Ben studied the retreating lines.

"Not unless he's one of your cannon cockers," Nyhavn said, turning back to the wounded man. "How about you, you want a drink?" He held out the canteen only the rebel didn't reply. The soldier was dead.

Placing the cork cap back on the canteen spout he surveyed the darkening battlefield around him. Cannon and rifle barrels now spewed fire and flames. Heated shrapnel flew in deadly orange fragments.

To his front the bulk of the rebel army was continuing to fall back. Behind him, maybe less than two hundred yards off, was the safety of the reinforced Union line. But with soldiers on both sides still trapped in the killing field and still sniping at each other the Union line might as well have been two hundred miles away.

The glint off a rebel officer's pistol barrel a few yards in front of him caught his attention in the gloaming. Keeping low, he crawled over and retrieved the handgun. In a close in fight against one or more attackers, the six-shot pistol could prove useful.

Crawling back to his hiding place, he wiped the blood and dirt off the pistol and then checked its load. Of the six rounds in the cylinder, four were capped and ready to fire while two had been fired.

"Good enough," he said as he stuffed the pistol in his belt and then went about the awkward task of reloading the Enfield rifle from the dead soldier's kit with his one good arm.

When he finally had finished he set the rifle aside and took another long pull on the canteen. Satisfying his immediate thirst he weighed his situation.

He'd been in enough battles to know that waiting until true dark was his best chance to get back to his lines without getting shot. The sporadic rifle fire confirmed it as he watched others who were caught out in the field, like he was, try to make a run for it only to be cut down by rebel rifle fire.

Union sharpshooters were doing the same to the fleeing rebels. It was tit for tat, shooting and sniping out of frustration and battle rage.

Dog ass tired and not wanting to be wounded again or captured, he eased himself back down and settled in to wait it out. As he did, he shifted the musket around in a small arc and pulled it in closer almost hugging the British made muzzleloader.

There was a noticeable change in the rifle and cannon fire as the battle lines shifted once again. The rebel army was hitting another part of the line. As the battle moved away Ben became aware of the sound of someone loading a musket nearby. A ramrod was scraping its way down a metal barrel.

Easing the rebel Enfield up in front of him, he slowly peered over the body of a dead rebel to investigate. Twenty yards out he found a small grass fire that had been ignited by the exploding artillery shells. The hip high flames were racing over a patch of summer dry grass and brush. The flames were pulsing orange and yellow in the fading day light and rising like a fiery wave. Ammunition pouches on fallen soldiers exploded in the intense heat of the wildfire.

Directly in the path of the growing flames sat a rebel soldier with ripped and twisted legs. Badly wounded as he was he couldn't crawl away from the rising wall of flame, so instead he was calmly loading his musket. Once done he turned the rifle around and stuck the barrel in his mouth.

"NO! DON'T!" Ben yelled rising up on his knees hollering at the soldier only the plea didn't stop what was about to happen. The shot rang out and the soldier fell by his own hand.

Both the shout and the shot brought up three other rebels who were trapped out in the battlefield just as Nyhavn had been. Seeing the Yankee holding the rifle and the head shot dead rebel's body twitching in the final throes of life, they bristled.

"MURDERING BUSH WHACKER!" shouted one of the rebels.

"I ain't murdering anyone. I…" he shouted back, trying to explain what had happened as one rebel came up on his knees and fired. The round missed him but not by much. Several more rounds quickly followed. Ben's protest didn't stop the incoming musket rounds and wouldn't.

"He's still moving!" yelled one of the rebels crawling on his elbows and knees pointing to the Union soldier's hiding place. "Get 'em!"

Nyhavn pulled the pistol and fired on two rebels who were coming at him in a running crouch. The first slug tore into the man in the lead, dropping him.

A second shot winged the other rebel but not enough to stop him. The determined attacker dropped and rolled away and kept on crawling forward, staying low. Ben rolled on his back, moved to his left, and waited.

When the rebel came up to where he thought the Yankee would be and didn't find him he turned and found him steadying his pistol. Before the rebel could bring his rifle around to bear Ben fired. The shot bored through the rebel's upper lip. Both attackers were dead or judging from the spasms and twitching soon would be.

Any elation though was soon gone when he caught sight of a third rebel coming up behind him. Nyhavn swung the pistol around and leveled the barrel on the man who was now only a few feet away. He pulled the trigger only to have the hammer fall on an empty chamber. The cold metallic click was the rebel's good fortune and Nyhavn's nightmare.

He dropped the handgun and before he could grab the Enfield the rebel was on him. The man kicked him hard in the balls buckling him before slamming the rifle butt into his face.

Nyhavn's head was spinning and bile was working its way back up his throat. Blood had spilled down a cut eye and he was having difficulty focusing. He felt around for a rock, something, or anything to hit the man with only to have the soldier stomp on his good hand. The pliant ground was the only thing keeping the hand from being broken.

"It's over, you goddamn bushwhacker!" the rebel said turning his musket back around and pointing the barrel inches away from Nyhavn's bloody face. He cocked the rifle and eased his finger against the trigger. "Let's see how you like it now, boy!"

An incoming artillery shell, short of its intended target and with a poorly timed fuse, exploded above them. Because he had been standing over Nyhavn, the rebel's body shielded Ben from the shrapnel. The rebel's head, neck and back were peppered with jagged scissor size splinters. While Nyhavn had escaped the shrapnel, he couldn't escape the heat and the concussion from the blast. The force from the explosion lifted him up off the ground and then tossed him violently back down. His lungs burned and he fought for a cool breath as his body shook with uncontrolled tremors. The battlefield was whirling around him.

Then there was nothing.

Chapter 5

It was a kick against his wounded shoulder that briefly brought him to. The booted toe-kick sent jagged slivers of pain seemingly into every nerve of his battered body. His mind screamed, but all he could manage to emit was a low, weak moan.

"This one ain't dead!" said a darkened figure leaning over him. A line of clouds in the thin moonlight left the night awash in vague shadows. Concussed as he was, what little Ben could see was blurred and out of focus.

"What?" said a second figure over the first man's shoulder. The battle, for now, was over, but since sound carried in the pre-dawn darkness, they spoke in low whispers.

"I said this one ain't dead," said the first man.

No, Ben Nyhavn wasn't dead. He was alive, but just barely. Besides the bayonet wound to his shoulder, the bullet groove in his cheek and split earlobe, he had a broken nose and a concussion. Spilled blood had crusted over his cut right eye and a line of dried blood from a broken ear drum that stretched across his throat making for a ghoulish mask.

"You sure he ain't dead?" asked the second shadow leaning over to see for himself. In the thin moonlight and sprawled among the other fallen soldiers from both armies, Nyhavn certainly looked dead.

"Sure I'm sure. Watch this," replied the first shadow as Nyhavn felt the boot prod his shoulder wound a second time sending another agonizing jolt radiating through his body. His back arched and fell in a terrible spasm and he groaned again. "See!"

"He a Johnny Reb?"

"Naw, he's got that white club badge on his jacket. He's one of those Two Corps fools, Minnesota more than likely."

"Well, then I suppose we'd better put him on the stretcher."

"Aye, but I'm thinking that maybe he's a little too heavy at this moment, what with all he's probably carrying in his pockets and all. We wouldn't want to put a strain on the litter canvas or ourselves."

"No, we wouldn't," said the second blurred figure with a chuckle. "Best we empty his pockets and make him lighter."

The two soldiers, who were sent out as stretcher bearers and were supposed to be helping to recover the wounded, had spent a good deal of time rifling through the pockets of the dead of both armies looking for anything of interest or value to steal.

On punishment detail for cowardice, they had been ordered out onto the dark battlefield to retrieve any survivors and weapons they could find.

The daylong fighting left thousands of dead and wounded strewn about the roads, orchards, and fields around Gettysburg where they had fallen. For some who had volunteered to go out and search for survivors the recovery process was an obligation and duty while for others, like the two pillagers, it was a punishment detail that was turning out to be a profitable enterprise.

Already on their third pass they had come away with a handful of gold rings, nearly $87.15 in script and a few racy French postcards. They also had a handful of Confederate bills that they could sell as war souvenirs.

Earlier the first soldier had found an engraved gold case watch with a heavy gold rope chain and jeweled fob that he had pulled from the headless torso of a Union Army officer.

"Don't think you'll be needing this," the pillager said snickering as he scooped it up from the dead man's vest.

"What is it?"

"Good watch on a chain."

"Lemme see!"

"Ain't nothing to see," he said, unhooking the chain and fob and tossing the watch to the second pillager. "Keep it. It's yours!"

"Mine?"

"Aye, but I'll take the next watch we find," said the first soldier.

"Done."

The first soldier knew the heavy gold chain and jeweled fob would be easier to sell without the engraved watch and besides he knew there were plenty more pickings to be had.

"Got some shinplasters!" he said going through Nyhavn's pockets and removing the seventy-five cents in paper currency script the wounded soldier had on him. "Wait! There's a pouch!"

"What's in it?"

"Hold on, hold on," said the thief the pouch's contents. "Oh hell, it's just some old letters, some coffee beans, and hardtack is all," added the disappointed thief. "Pitiful *shite*."

The thief was shaking out the pages of two old letters hoping to find currency but there was none. They were letters Nyhavn had received from Anna Lunde and had carried, read and reread until the cheap stationary sheets had become badly smudged and tattered with time. The soldier tossed the pages aside and searched the other pockets. Ben tried to protest, but all that came out was a prolonged groan.

"SHUT UP, you piss ant! You'll get us shot," snarled the soldier. "We're helping you."

"You check his teeth, Tookey."

"Why?"

"To see if there's any gold? Some of these rebel boys come from well-to-do families and I've heard they use gold when their teeths rot."

"I told you, he ain't a rebel."

"Maybe he's from money people."

The first shadow snorted. "What? You think if he came from money he'd be in this war, let alone be here as a Private?"

"I don't know. Maybe?"

"No maybe about it. If he was rich his family woulda bought his way out or woulda had him made an officer."

"Yeah, but Minnesota's out west, isn't it?"

"So?"

"So people out west found gold, didn't they?"

"In California, not Minnesota, you damn fool. But just to shut you up I'll look, and if there's any gold in his teeth, you gotta cut it out."

Nyhavn felt a hand grip his chin and lock it steady as dirty, grimy fingers pried open his mouth and pushed aside his tongue in the search. "See! What I'd tell ya? No gold," said the soldier and pushed the wounded soldier's head away as he wiped his hands on Ben's battle scarred jacket.

"Tookman? Hannigan? That you?" said a third voice along with the clear sound of a pistol being cocked.

"Easy, Sarge, it's us," said the first voice, "We got another survivor here."

The dark blurred figures unceremoniously rolled the wounded soldier on a blood-soaked stretcher. A white light of pain stabbed at him again.

"He one of ours or theirs, Tookey?" asked the Sergeant getting to the point of the unpleasant task.

"Ours. Well, one of the First Minnesota anyway. Two Corps."

"Le…letters," whispered Nyhavn. His voice was barely audible but still loud enough for the Sergeant to hear.

"Letters? What's he talking about?"

"Papers in his pocket is all," said Hannigan while Tookman frowned at Hannigan's stupidity. Why couldn't he keep his fool mouth shut?

"In his pockets?"

"Yeah, Tookey and me were just trying to find out who he was or is. Came across a few letters and some hardtack and coffee beans," said the soldier pulling the soldier's pouch from his own pocket.

"You took his things?"

"What?"

"The hardtack and coffee, Tookey," said the Sergeant a second time. "Hand it over."

The sullen soldier reluctantly handed the things over to the Sergeant who still wasn't satisfied. "The letters too."

Tookman grumbled a response and looked around and found the discarded letters.

"If I find out you Five Points thieves have been robbing our dead instead of doing what I told you to do it'll be your asses, you hear me?"

"We ain't robbing nobody."

"Yeah, well, maybe come sunrise I'll need to have a closer look at your pockets when we're done out here just to make sure," said the Sergeant tossing the pouch back to the sullen Private. "So help me, if I check on him later and find his things missing then I'll have both of you back out here at first light collecting the dropped rifles after the rebel sharpshooters have had their morning coffee and are aching to shoot at anything blue. You hear me?"

"Yes Sergeant."

"Carry him back," growled the Sergeant, handing over the letters.

"Yes Sergeant," said the sullen soldier while the second soldier nodded. Tookman dropped the folded letters and pouch on Nyhavn's chest. The two soldiers lifted the stretcher and started back to the safety of the ridge line. When the Sergeant broke away to find another of the recovery teams, Tookman swore.

"Rat bastard," he said, furious that they'd now have to hurriedly stash what they had stolen to keep the Sergeant from finding it.

"Water," Nyhavn whispered between parched lips.

"What'd he say now?"

"I think he wants water," said Hannigan.

"Well, he ain't goddamn getting any!" Tookman said turning his anger on the wounded Minnesotan. "What sort of soldier whines about losing hardtack and a few coffee beans, especially when he's being carried to safety! Ungrateful rat bastard."

"I got water," said Hannigan reaching for his canteen.

"Yeah, well you don't give it to him. You hear me? He's probably gonna die anyway, so he don't need it."

Tookman stewed on the long haul back to the ridge and the Taneytown road where a line of ambulance wagons were struggling in the dark with the crushing numbers of the day's wounded.

Many of the those soldiers who had been wounded earlier in the day still remained unattended as the harried hospital attendants were doing their best to properly see to the staggering numbers of the fallen.

"He alive?" asked an attendant.

"Barely," said Tookman.

"Put him there," said the exasperated Orderly pointing towards the end of the row of wounded soldiers.

When the attendant moved down the line administering to a badly wounded Major, Tookman led the stretcher over to a row of the dead instead. When he was sure no one was watching he tilted the handles of the stretcher and unceremoniously dumped the Minnesotan on the uneven ground. Ben landed hard on his already injured shoulder and his consciousness fluttered and once more began to fail.

"You didn't have to do that," said Hannigan.

"No, I did not!" snarled Tookman, "But thanks to this whiny little son-of-a-bitch we'll have to find a place to stash our loot before the Sergeant looks back in on us. Hold on a bit," he said to the soldier named Hannigan.

"Why?"

Tookman didn't respond. Instead he bent down and retrieved the soldier's pouch and letters from the wounded soldier. After taking another cautious look around he flung the pouch as far as he could throw it back out towards the battlefield, and then angrily ripped the letters into a dozen pieces and then sprinkled them over the wounded soldier.

"There!" he said leaning in closer so the soldier would hear him. "That's for your lack of fookin' gratitude, you rat bastard."

"What if the Sergeant comes back and checks on him like he said?"

"He won't," he said reaching down and yanking the Two Corps pin from his uniform and tossing it aside as well. "He don't know this fool from any of the others. Come on, let's hide our found things."

Chapter 6

Waking came painfully slow. Ben Nyhavn was a mess of discolored lumps, bruises and bloody cuts. His head was pounding with a pulse that reverberated in his ears. He moaned or thought he had. If anyone had heard him though, nobody noticed, or seemed to care.

He was lying on his left side in the harsh noon-day sun. Opening his one good eye, he was greeted with blinding sunlight that stabbed at him like a well pointed needle.

He brought up his good hand to shield the sunlight and to brush away the dried blood, pus and dirt that had caked over his eyelids. One eye began to find focus while the other was slow to come around.

Grimacing, he sucked in some air and reluctantly pushed himself up to a slightly swaying, sitting position. Someone had placed an old blanket on him and it hung on him like a poor man's shawl.

His face was tingling too, partially from the pain, but also from the ants and bottle flies that were crawling over his face. He cleared up some of the buzzing in his right ear with a half-hearted swat that dislodged and scattered most of the insects.

Ben coughed once and the tremor sent a burning stream of bile racing up his throat. He coughed again and a small stream of green spittle dribbled out over his chin. It spilled down his peach fuzz beard and further down the front of his torn and filthy uniform coat.

He was alive but knew it was going to be some time before he felt like it. The young soldier sat there for a moment taking his inventory. Besides the bayonet wound to his shoulder, his left arm was stiff from the puncture wound. Whoever had tossed the blanket over him had applied a bandage to the wounds while he was unconscious. Beneath the front bandage dressing his fingers found that the wound was weeping, and swollen and painful to the touch. His right ear lobe was split and his cheek had a blood groove showing the small trench the bullet had taken when it skinned him.

His nose was broken and at a new angle. There was little to no air coming through his right nostril while a thin opening of air somehow made its way through the left nostril. Broken as it was, he was forced to breathe through his mouth. Each labored breath seemed to roll around like an echo in his ears as he began to take stock of what was going on around him in the much too crowded farm yard.

The white clapboard farm, its once large and open yard, and its two rough hewn outbuildings, now contained several hastily erected canvas tents and were serving as a makeshift Union Army Field Hospital.

The trouble was, there was little to no room for the scores upon scores of wounded and dying soldiers that littered the grounds. Most, like him, were awaiting their turns with the Army Surgeons in the hastily erected surgical tents on slab-board operating tables.

A handful of medical attendants were doing what they could, treating and caring for most, covering others who had died, or moving some of the wounded ahead of the line to the surgical tents based on the basis of need or rank.

Next to the surgical tents a mound of amputated hands, arms, legs and feet were alive with the frantic dance of a swarm of black bottle flies. Just beyond the mound, several orderlies were loading the recently deceased into an open wagon bed. The bodies of the soldiers were stacked like split cordwood. Blood spilled over the tail gate of the wagon in a steady dribble while thicker sun-dried blood clung to the dropped gate of the over-burdened wagon like maroon colored pine sap.

Out on the road, in front of the farmstead, Ben stared at the seemingly endless stream of white-roofed Federal ambulances that were flowing past the farm in a tragic parade.

Thousands had already died, but the battle for Gettysburg was still undecided, as was the fate of those in the crowded farm yard, who were engaged in their own private battles. Soldiers who had survived the fighting were now dying of neglect.

A small benefit of the broken nose and his one working nostril, Ben could only get a thin whiff of the putrid odor emanating from the overflowing slit trenches, vomit, and festering wounds in the hot summer sun.

Hastily fashioned lean-tos made from shirts or uniform coats and support sticks brought relief from the heat to some while others, like Nyhavn, were left out in the open to the unrelenting sun that bore down on them on the congested and confused farm yard.

"Wa...water," said Nyhavn through parched and dried lips. His voice was hoarse and barely audible. He cleared his throat and tried again.

"Water?"

The soldier closest to him, a Corporal who was missing his right hand, reached over and pulled his tin and wood canteen selfishly closer to himself.

"Get your own!" the Corporal said, sullenly.

"Oh, give him a drink," barked another soldier, a gaunt, tired eyed Sergeant who was leaning on a haversack witnessing the exchange.

"What? Lend him a hand, you mean?" said the soldier, bitterly thrusting out his bandaged, bloodied stump. "Well, I don't got an extra hand or got any water to spare neither."

"Here," said the Sergeant handing Nyhavn his own canteen. A clean shaven man usually the Sergeant's chin showed a few days of dark stubble. He had made a kepi from a handkerchief and his forage cap to keep his neck from getting sunburned and seemed happily content leaning against his haversack. "Don't mind him," he added loud enough to be overheard by the soldier who had refused Nyhavn the water. "It ain't his wound talking. He was a miserable son of a bitch even before he got hit."

"You go to hell!" said the soldier.

"Already been there and it's a long road back, but you know what? I got a pistol here that can settle the question of who just might get there permanently, if you want to push it," replied the Sergeant, patting a captured Rebel Le Mat pistol tucked in his belt. The Sergeant's grin was anything but pleasant and his eyes bore through the other man's resolve with leveled certainty. "Anytime you want to bump up your departure schedule, friend, you just let me know."

The one handed Corporal started to say something more, thought better of it as the Sergeant stared him down, and the Corporal turned away, grumbling.

Ben took a much needed drink from the Sergeant's canteen. The water was warm and although it tasted of algae and bile, it was welcome. When he gulped down a second drink, the Sergeant cautioned him to slow down.

"Whoa, now!" he said. "It took me most of the morning to crawl over and fill it up." He nodded towards his legs and when Nyhavn lowered the canteen he saw why it had taken the Sergeant so long to do it.

The man's feet were gone from the shins down, the bone and muscle in splinters and tattered shreds at the ankles. Rope tourniquets tied at the thighs of both legs were held in place by pieces of a broken ramrod that he had probably applied himself. From the thighs down his pants were torn and bloodied and covered in dirt from dragging himself over to the rain barrel that sat at the corner of the farmhouse. The water barrel was just twenty yards away, but getting there with no feet, though the crowded yard, had been an effort.

"Maybe when you clear away some of the cobwebs from your head you can make the next trip seeing how you still got the legs for it?"

"I can do that," Ben said in a haggard voice he didn't recognize, all the while staring at the wounded soldier's bloodied stumps.

"See! Now that's neighborly!" laughed the Sergeant, wiggling his splintered legs and sending the accumulating bottle flies to momentary flight. Rosettes of blood spread out on the ground where his feet should have been and slowly pooled. He tightened the tourniquet.

"Rebel cannon ball," explained the Sergeant as he caught Nyhavn looking at the stumps. "It tore through two of their own ranks in front of us before it ground skipped over the stubble in the wheat field and rose up just enough to take off my feet. Ain't that a kick in the ass?"

The Sergeant laughed again and took a drink from a small brown medicine bottle that Nyhavn suspected was laudanum. The tincture of opium and alcohol explained why the Sergeant didn't seem to be all that concerned or bothered by the painful looking wounds. The laudanum was working.

To the Sergeant's left another soldier lay curled up in a fetal position quietly sobbing, far too gone in his own misery to care how he looked or sounded. The soldier was clutching his balled-up jacket against his torn abdomen and lap. A sharp shard of bone poked out from his hip. He had fouled himself and was forced by his injuries to lie in his own mess. He was dying and he knew it. Not shamed on the battlefield, death would shame him here, away from the fighting. Next to the dying man sat another wounded soldier who was casually brewing coffee.

"Doesn't seem to be much help to go around," said Nyhavn.

"There are a handful of saw-bone surgeons up in the main house doing what they can for those who need to be fixed up first. But it's more than they bargained for, I suspect. The Orderlies though have been making their rounds," the Sergeant said waving his laudanum bottle at Nyhavn's shoulder wound. "They came by earlier and left me this and put that bandage on you."

"They did that?"

"They did. Stuck their fingers inside the wound looking for the bullet that winged you. When they couldn't find it, they threw a patch on you instead figuring it would take the doctors to pry it out later."

"There was no bullet," Ben said.

"Shrapnel?"

"No, I got bayoneted and knocked around some."

The Sergeant nodded. "Make sure you tell them that when they come around checking our bandages later, otherwise they may go digging inside you again doing more harm than good."

Nyhavn said he would. He was still feeling a little woozy and sweating more than he felt he should, but at least he was upright. He pulled off his coat with difficulty and then laid it down beside him.

The sergeant pointed to the far corner of the farm house and the barrel as he took another sip from the medicine bottle. "If it turns out to be a scorcher like it was yesterday then I suspect the rain water's not gonna last the day either, if you catch my meaning?"

"I do."

"The name's Phillips, Sergeant Richard Phillips, 44th New York."

"Bent Nyhavn, First Minnesota."

Sipping on the laudanum bottle Phillips chuckled, "Your folks really named you Bent, did they?" he said, suppressing a smile.

"It's one of those old country names."

"Or maybe they had a premonition," he said and moved onto the more pressing issue. "Like I said Minnesota, things are heating up and too many men have been pissing in the creek up stream. The fact is I haven't seen much in the way of fresh water close-by other than that rain barrel. Can you take a few canteens?"

"Ya sure," Nyhavn said slowly getting to his feet. The damaged eardrum did something to his equilibrium and he felt like a drunkard. Steadying himself, he took the two empty canteens offered by the Sergeant and balled the leather straps in his fist. Fortunately, there was no straight way to get there through the mass of wounded so he slowly navigated his way around the crowded yard. Slow was the best he could manage anyway.

As he walked he looked around hoping to find a familiar face. But with so many wounded littering the farm yard trying to pick out his friends would take awhile so he tried calling out instead.

"Kinnunen, Trigg Kinnunen? You here?" Nyhavn called, searching the crowd. Raising his voice made his good ear ring and his words boomed in his head. Still, he had to try. "Frantzen? Al Frantzen?" Curious faces turned to see who was doing the yelling.

"You calling for Hagstrum?" said a soldier on his left beneath a small tarp. One of the soldier's legs, the left one, was gone above the knee.

Nyhavn shook his head and the gesture took something more from him. "Frantzen, Company G, First Minnesota," he said.

"Hagstrum's dead anyway," replied the soldier staring blankly off into the distance. "The peach orchard, yesterday. A rifle ball split his head." The soldier wiped a grimy hand across the top of his head demonstrating the path of fatal bullet. As the hand came down his voice lowered as well.

"Blugner, Edson died on the other side of him. Flynn and Jorgensen too, I think. They went down anyway. Head or gut shot. A lot of us went down, not too many got back up."

Not knowing what to say Nyhavn listened and nodded along. The soldier was ironing out what had happened and Nyhavn recognized the difficult chore.

"First Minnesota Volunteers?" Nyhavn called again looking around but no one answered. "First Minnesota?"

Along with the two empty canteens he found himself carrying a new burden as he wondered why he had survived when so many others had not. Each step he took seemed heavier than the previous. When he finally reached the rain barrel he stood staring into his own poor reflection in the stagnant water he didn't recognize the swollen face that stared back at him.

"You the one who's calling for the First Minnesota?" asked a tired looking Lieutenant who worked his way through the crowd to the wounded Private. Both the officer and a weathered looking Sergeant trailing him blanched when Nyhavn turned and they took in the full extent of the young soldier's wounds. The boy's face was a mess; his ripped and torn uniform was blood covered and filthy. He was standing, but just barely.

"Yes sir," he said, trying to stand at attention only to have the Lieutenant tell him to stand at ease. "Private Nyhavn, Company G."

"Newhaven?" said the Sergeant going over a make shift casualty list with a confused stare as he handed it to the Lieutenant beside him. "Ben Newhaven?"

"Yes Sergeant."

"You're listed among the dead," said the officer tapping the list.

"It feels like it, Lieutenant," Nyhavn said, managing a small laugh.

"Yes, I imagine it does," replied the officer."Most of our wounded are up at the Second Corps temporary Hospital at Rock Creek. You must have been brought up with the New York boys here by mistake. We'll get your name to Regimental Headquarters and let them know where to find you."

"Thank you, sir," Ben said, steadying himself against the rain barrel. "We stopped them yesterday, didn't we?"

"We did."

"Any idea on the numbers yet, Lieutenant?"

The Lieutenant was hesitant to reply. "We're still trying to get an accurate count," he said, skirting the question. "That's why we're here."

"Have you found any of our boys here besides me, sir?"

"Not yet, but as I said, most of our wounded are at the Second Corps hospital."

A roar of sustained cannon fire off in the distance interrupted their conversation as their heads and attention turned to the sound of the guns.

"Looks like the Johnny Rebs are going to try another go at it," said the Lieutenant. "Somewhere along the center, sounds like."

"I can still fire a rifle, sir," Ben said.

The officer held back what he was thinking. He admired Nyhavn's youthful exuberance and tenacity even with the touch of foolishness.

"You have enough to eat?"

"Had some hardtack," said Nyhavn, angrily. "But someone stole it from me along with my things after I was knocked out by a cannon blast."

The Lieutenant reached into his haversack and came out a cut of salted pork and half of a yellowed apple and added a small cloth filled with coffee beans.

"I'm told they'll set up a Mess tent soon," said the officer. "This should hold you over till then, Private."

"Appreciate it, sir," Ben said, pocketing the foodstuffs and catching the Lieutenant staring at his weeping bayonet wound and the flies that harassed it. Embarrassed, the officer quickly looked away.

"As I said, Private Newhaven, I'll get your name to Headquarters and let them know your condition and whereabouts."

"Thank you, sir."

"You get some rest, get healed up."

The wounded soldier wiped a line of beaded sweat from his forehead as the bile rose up from his stomach again. He didn't know it yet that the beginning signs of sepsis were setting in and the deadly toxins and body shaking, life threatening fever that would befall him was still a day or so away. He would be evacuated in the ambulance line to the rail head, and what would come back after that would only be remembered in brief flashes.

The two soldiers moved on to check the rest of the crowded yard for any others in the Regiment leaving Nyhavn to the task of filling the two canteens.

Scraping away a few dead bugs and a thin green film from the sides of the barrel, Nyhavn dipped the first canteen beneath the tepid water and watched the bubbles rush to the surface as it filled. When the first was filled he capped it and then pushed the second empty canteen beneath the surface. Behind him several other soldiers were lining up waiting to fill their own canteens. Sergeant Phillips was right. It would be another hot day. Most likely, by late afternoon the rain barrel would certainly be empty.

At the front of the white clapboard house he stopped to watch several soldiers unload a Sanitary Commission wagon as others set up a new tent.

Nyhavn saw several women from the Commission haul out pots, flour bags, food filled boxes and tins. With his mouth and stomach feeling as poorly as they did, soup or mush might be easier on him than hardtack and salted pork.

Although he hadn't eaten since yesterday afternoon, his rising nausea put aside any immediate pangs of hunger.

"Here! Thought you might like this," he said tossing the half apple to Sergeant Phillips on his return and took a necessary seat on the ground. He was sweating more than he should and the dizziness was back.

"You find any of your people?" asked Phillips.

"One of my officers told me our Regiment is up the road at the Second Corps Hospital."

Phillips nodded. "Once the battle is over it'll all get sorted out," he said. "He take your name for a roster report?"

"He did."

"Then, there ain't nothing more for you to do but wait to be treated."

"I saw some women from the Sanitary Commission putting up a Mess tent on the other side of the farmhouse," said Nyhavn.

"They gonna feed us?" asked the soldier who had refused to share his water.

Sergeant Phillips snorted. "Why? You gonna bring a plate back for the rest of us, you selfish prick?"

"They'll probably have something for us soon," Nyhavn said looking back towards the Mess tent.

"In that case, here you go," Phillips said handing the apple back to Nyhavn.

"What about you?"

Phillips held up the small brown bottle of Laudanum, shook it and beamed. Behind them on the road someone was yelling at a growing crowd of the walking wounded at the farm yard gate. Two guards were blocking the entrance to the farm.

"They keeping us in or them out?"

"A Doctor came out awhile ago and had the sentries posted after the last crop of wounded kept filtering into the yard with no let up. He told the guards to send them on down the road to the next collection point."

"They're turning them away?"

"Have to," replied Phillips. "There are too many wounded here already and too few of anyone to help."

In the distance the rebel cannon fire shifted and the rolling thunder grew increasingly louder. The battle was heating up again.

All around the farm yard soldiers turned uneasily towards the sound of the guns. Many were standing, or trying to, while some cowered and cried seeking unneeded cover.

"Must be the main assault," Phillips said.

"Ours or theirs," asked Nyhavn.

"Theirs."

"What do we do?"

"Not much we can do but wait and greet whoever comes up the road," said Phillips taking another sip of laudanum as he checked the load of his Le Matt pistol.

Chapter 7

They proudly marched off to war to the sound of boisterous cheers and rippling applause from the large crowd of well-wishers, family members and friends who saw them off from Fort Snelling. It was a raucous turn out.

As the long line of Minnesota volunteers boarded the steamboats *Northern Belle* and *War Eagle*, and went downriver, they were greeted again at the town of Red Wing, and once more at the town of Winona, this time by a slightly out of tune, but enthusiastic, brass band.

The glistening white steamboats framed against the limestone bluffs were their momentary war chariots taking them down the Mississippi to the rail line at La Crosse, Wisconsin. There they would board a series of trains that would take them to Chicago, and then further east.

At Winona two young women, girls really, in their early teens, had weaved and pushed their way through the crowd to get closer to the soldiers. They were trailed by a none-too happy looking ten-year-old boy. Parents and family followed or wisely watched from the distance.

One of the girls was Nyhavn's thirteen-year-old sister, Saffi. A lively, bright-eyed precocious blonde, who was as thin as a sapling, but just beginning to display her transition into womanhood. She was the first to spot her brother in the ranks. She pointed him out to the second young woman, a fourteen-year-old named, Anna Lunde.

True to her Norwegian roots, Lunde was a tall, big boned girl. Auburn hair complimented her high round cheek bones and her decidedly square dimpled chin. She had comfortably crossed the threshold to maturity and was well on her way to becoming a comely looking woman.

"There! Bent! Bent Nyhavn!" yelled Saffi, smiling and waving to her brother who shifted his gaze from the line of citizen soldiers in front of him to his sister and the equally excited Lunde.

"I intend to marry you, so you better come back to me, Bent Nyhavn! You hear me!" yelled Anna over the din of the spirited celebration, as Nyhavn's Company passed by. The young woman's bold proclamation drew a few hoots and guffaws from the crowd, and some of the soldiers in the ranks. The young soldier's face flushed with embarrassment.

"And I'm gonna be her Maid-of-Honor!" announced Saffi proudly to those around her where Jurgen, Ben's younger brother, disgusted by the girls' behavior, shook his head and lowered it.

"So you better come home to me soon!" Lunde wouldn't be easily dissuaded if the tone of her voice was anything to judge by.

"Tell the Lass you will," said Sergeant Mulligan as soldiers around Nyhavn hooted and laughed.

"I will," he said, flustered and flushed by the unwanted attention he was getting.

"Louder!"

"I WILL!"

"Good," said the Sergeant. "Now eyes forward and get in step, or I'll put a boot up your arse, and the little darling will be disappointed that her betrothed can't march, which will mean that you probably can't dance either, and where will that leave her on her wedding day?"

"I…"

"At ease, son. It doesn't require an answer. Just square your shoulders and make her proud."

The fourteen-year-old threw his shoulders back, puffed out his scrawny chest and looked more like somebody's little brother playing army than a real soldier. Still, in the newly issued Regimental uniform of baggy blue pants, red flannel shirt, black felt hat, and carrying a re-bored Austrian rifled musket on his shoulder, he marched in step with the others looking as stern and professionally adult as he possibly could.

He wanted Anna to be proud of him and she was. At that moment she loved him as heartbreakingly achingly strong as any determined teenage girl could, which was considerable.

Tears welled up in her leaf-green eyes and she found herself crying, both happy and sad tears, for the love and life that would have to wait until he came home. Saffi hugged her, soon to be, sister-in-law and began laughing and crying too, while Jurgen rolled his eyes very much wishing he could be anywhere else at this moment.

Anna's bold proclamation wasn't a surprise to Ben. If anything it was the affirmation of the mutual promise and proposal they had agreed upon earlier and she wasn't about to let him forget it. Anna Lunde had had a crush on Bent Nyhavn since she was nine. That was when she announced to her father, mother and sisters at the dinner table that one day she was going to marry the neighbor boy, Bent Nyhavn.

Then, the chubby little girl, with long braided pig tails and dimpled cheeks, was always sneaking peeks and glances at him in school, in church, and mooning over him something painful each harvest, when her father had hired Ben to help bring in the crops.

It was also painfully noticeable to the young boy who was more than a little annoyed by the adolescent fawning. At his mother's mild scolding though, he let it be.

"She has tender thoughts for you, so don't you dare hurt her feelings," warned Mrs. Nyhavn, scolding him after he had complained about it.

"But..."

"Uh-uh," said his mother holding up an out raised hand and cutting him off. "It is vat all little girls do to one boy or another at one time or another. It von't last," she said, prophetically knowing the usual fate of such things, even if her W's came out V's and her lectures in English carried a heavily accent-ed, Scandinavian lilt. "So you just be nice to her, you hear me, Bent Nyhavn?"

"Yes Ma'am."

"Good," said the mother, smiling over her son's annoyance. What she didn't tell him was that Anna, the youngest of three Lunde girls, would soon mature and if she grew to be anywhere near as good looking as her older sisters, then in a few years time it would be her son who would be doing the fawning. Ben's mother smiled to herself knowing that time and nature would solve the momentary annoyance, which eventually it did.

By the summer of 1859 the once bothersome and chubby little girl shot up to nearly six feet in height and she had blossomed considerably. At thirteen she had grown into a tall, gangly girl. But, just one year later she was transformed into a decidedly full-figured, youthful, Nordic Valkerie, with the kind of interesting comfortable curves and coy charms that brought on a number of interested suitors. Anna Lunde became a sought after prize.

Bent and Jamie Cobb caught a glimpse of the prize and more when they were heading out to go fishing and the two had heard shrieking laughter coming from the small lake that lay midway between the Nyhavn and Lunde farms.

Fed by a natural spring and a tumbling creek the small lake adjoined the two farmsteads and defined the property lines. Tucked behind a copse of shade alders and a ragged green curtain of cattails, and as isolated as it was, the lake was well hidden from view of either farm.

Following the laughter they soon caught sight of the water and the three Lunde girls skinny dipping in it.

"My, oh my, oh my," said Cobb pulling Nyhavn down to duck walk towards a thick stand of cattails and brush at the lake's edge for better concealment and a much better look.

"Maybe we shouldn't be here," said Nyhavn feeling slightly embarrassed and more than a little pleasurable guilt.

"Oh yeah, we should," laughed Jamie Cobb prying aside some of the cattails for a better view.

The two teenage boys settled in their hide and continued to spy on the water nymphs as the Lunde girls made their way back to the opposite shore.

"I think I'm in love," Jamie said as Anna's oldest sister, Katrina came out of the water first followed by Caroline who was one year Anna's senior.

"With who?"

"Well, at least two of them for sure," whispered Jamie as Anna was next to exit the water. "No, make that three. Oh my word, will you look at that!"

Nyhavn did look and as he open mouthed stared he knew he would never look upon Anna the same way again, at least not without grinning.

As the girls gathered up their clothing and got dressed one of the sisters noticed a fluttering movement in the tall weeds on the other side of the small lake.

"Down!" said Cobb and the two boys flattened themselves to the ground. They laid there and didn't move, remaining as quiet as they could for a long few moments. Ben's heart was pounding in his chest but not all of it came from the fear of being found out.

Only when he figured it was safe to take another look Cobb rose up slightly and carefully parted the thin stalks and leaves again. To his disappointment the Lunde girls were gone.

"Aw shoot," said Cobb. "They left. I was hoping…" only before he could get another word out, the thrown rocks flew at both he and Nyhavn in a calculated rain.

"OW!" yelled Nyhavn as a fist size stone struck his back amidst the flurry. The Lunde sisters were chucking rocks at the interlopers from only ten yards away with surprisingly good aim.

"Run!" yelled Jamie Cobb as both boys were up and moving as fast as they could, zigzagging to avoid getting hit again. The barrage of rocks followed their retreat only with little effect.

"You better run," yelled Caroline Lunde tossing a baseball size rock that just missed its intended target.

As soon as they were out of range Jamie Cobb suddenly stopped and wheeled back around. "Thank you! Thank you! Thank you!" he laughed as he made an exaggerated bow.

"I'm telling your Mama," yelled Katrina Lunde.

"Yeah, well I'm telling everybody I know," replied a much buoyant Jamie Cobb while Ben remained suspiciously quiet. The guilty grin still hadn't left his face or the image that he'd hold to for a long while afterwards.

An excited Jamie Cobb had related the account to his friends in town and before long some soon came sniffing after the Lunde girls, and predictably enough, so did Ben Nyhavn who had discovered a new found interest in the once irritating little girl.

One week later when he had finally worked up enough nerve to ask her if she wanted to go on a walk sometime, Anna agreed then immediately asked him if he wanted to make it a picnic instead.

"Picnic?"

"Uh-huh, at the lake."

"The lake?"

"Uh-huh, the lake," she said. "I'm sure you remember where it is."

"Oh ya sure," said Nyhavn, his pulse quickened and his mouth went suddenly dry. "That would be nice, don't'cha know."

"It will. When?" said Anna trying to pin him down asked when they would go on the picnic.

"When?"

"Ya, when do you want to go on the picnic?"

"I dunno, Sunday?"

"Okay then," she said, "Sunday noon, it is. Oh, and, by the way, my sister Caroline will be coming along with us."

"Caroline?" said Nyhavn barely hiding his disappointment.

"As a chaperone, of course," she said. "It wouldn't be proper without a chaperone."

"A chaperone...ya sure, of course," echoed Nyhavn.

The following Sunday, a little after twelve noon when he showed up at the Lunde's farm he found Anna sitting on the covered porch patiently waiting with her sister. A carefully packed picnic basket rested at Anna's side.

"Good morning, ladies," he said, nodding to the two sisters while Mrs. Lunde watched, smiling from inside the open doorway. Behind her the oldest sister, Katrina, scowled at him over crossed arms.

"Actually, it is mid-day, Mister Nyhavn," said Caroline with a less than enthusiastic greeting.

"Shall we go?" Anna said to Ben but it was Caroline who replied.

"Let's," she said and started off leaving Anna and Ben to follow.

They had crossed the Lunde's ploughed field west of the farm and were a hundred yards on and following a path through the brush when Caroline suddenly veered off in another direction away from the lake.

"You two go on," she said, excusing herself. "I'll catch up."

"Okay," replied Anna. "See ya soon."

"Ya soon," Caroline said without looking back as she hurried off.

"Shouldn't we wait?"

"No, she'll meet up with us later," said Anna ignoring the question. As they walked on Nyhavn periodically looked back over his shoulder. There was still no sign of the missing sister.

"She'll be awhile," said Anna, still walking on. "It's a pleasant day, isn't it?"

"Eh, ya sure it is. What do you mean she'll be awhile? I thought she was supposed to be our chaperone?"

"She is, sort of," Anna said.

"Sort of?"

"Uh-huh. She just has to meet someone first."

"Meet someone? Out here?"

"Close by."

"Who?"

Anna stopped on the path and turned back to the farm boy. "Promise you won't tell?" she said closely studying his face.

"I won't tell."

"I mean it," she said, adamantly. "You can't tell anyone."

"I won't."

"Promise?"

"Sure."

She was biting her bottom lip, still reluctant to confess. "No, say it."

"Okay, okay, I promise I won't tell anyone about who your sister went off to see."

That still wasn't good enough for the girl. "Or about leaving us alone?"

That promise would be easier to keep. "I promise," he said. "So, who's she going to see?"

"Jamie Cobb," she replied.

"Jamie?" Ben was stunned by her answer.

"Uh-huh."

"But she was doing her best to bean him with rocks at the lake for spying on you girls while you frolicked."

"True, but he at least had the courtesy to bow. She thought he was funny."

"I bowed too!"

Anna shook her head. "That wasn't a bow," she said. "You were just ducking rocks."

When they came out of the brush at the lake Anna picked out a small clearing in the shade at the water's edge. Wild flowers grew in a colorful green, white and pink display behind them.

Setting the basket down, she unfolded a small brightly colored quilt and laid it out on the ground and took a seat.

"It's pretty here, don't'cha think?" she said, patting the quilt gesturing for him to sit.

Ben took the cue, sat down beside her and after awkwardly working up enough nerve he had asked if he could hold her hand. Only, as their eyes met she leaned over and kissed him instead. That kiss blindsided him with Ben thinking that it went by far too fast. But the second kiss and long embrace that soon followed was warm and tender.

"Ya know, you're a better kisser than I thought you would be," she said as she turned her attention back to unloading the picnic basket. "Must have been all the practicing you did with skinny Beth Traumen."

"Beth Traumen?" said Nyhavn, feigning both innocence and ignorance in a tone that was hardly convincing. His blushing cheeks and fidgeting didn't help matters any.

"Ya, skinny Beth Traumen," said Anna as she sorted out the foodstuff. Beth had talked about it at school, how she and Bent had bussed and kissed after he had walked her home knowing it would irritate the Lunde girl who had a crush on the boy.

"I...eh,...I mean, we..."

"Yes?"

"It was her idea, you know, to see what it was like."

"To see what it was like?"

"Well...yeah..."

"Like your visit to Kelly's? Did someone else talk you into that too?"

"Kelly's?" said Nyhavn suddenly sheepish.

"Uh-huh," said Anna enjoying his discomfort. "My sister, Caroline said she saw you and Jamie in a tree peeking in a window at Kelly's with big fool grins on your faces."

Kelly's was a two-storied clapboard Roadhouse that sat on the south edge of the town. It was a Roadhouse, and of course, something more. The *more* everybody knew had to do with the three goodtime girls old man Kelly brought in from St. Paul.

Jake Kelly, who owned the two-storied establishment, figured that lonely farmers sometimes needed to plough more than fields and that his business would increase substantially with a little friendly social activity. He was right on both accounts. It was good commerce and served its purpose. No one harbored any illusions about what went on in Kelly's nor did they object too loudly to its presence. Germans and Scandinavians tended to be pragmatic.

"I mean, unless my sister was mistaken," Anna said, letting him off of the hook, only not before she gave it another good tug. "Just as you might be mistaken if you think I'll tolerate you kissing Beth Traumen again or say, running over to Kelly's after you're mine. You hear me, Bent Nyhavn?"

"Skinny Beth Traumen, you mean?" he said.

"Even if she puts on weight," said Anna punching his arm. "And no more visits to Kelly's Road House!"

Nyhavn nodded and before he could say anything else she leaned over, pulled him close to her, and then kissed him long and hard enough to make him wonderfully uncomfortable again. She was warm and supple in his arms and his mind jumped and swirled with happy hormonal revelry. The girl troubled him in ways he couldn't put into words, but in ways he definitely liked. Nyhavn leaned back on his elbows and said, "So what else do you hear?"

"I hear that you and some of the other boys are going to sign up for the Volunteers."

"Uh-huh," he said matter of fact. "Everyone's signing up for ninety days. Three months duty is all."

"Three months?"

"The war will be over by then. Can't last much longer than that, don't'cha know?"

Anna stared out at the lake as a slight breeze sent ripples across the glassy blue surface. "What if it isn't?" she said.

"What do you mean?"

"Well, what if the fighting isn't over in three months?"

The question gave him pause. He hadn't seriously considered that possibility. But then he soon shook it off, his youthful confidence overrode the thought. Of course, it would be over in three months time! There might be a few real battles, just to teach the rebels a lesson or two, but the talk and newspapers said there was no way the South could stand up to the might and will of the industrial Northern states in an all out war. Everybody knew that and said as much.

"No, it'll just be ninety days," the boy said certain of it. "You'll see."

She was staring out at the lake focusing on something he couldn't yet envision.

"I think we should build our home here on the lake when we're married," she said a little too cheery trying to hide the fear behind her eyes.

"Married?" Nyhavn was surprised by her boldness although this particular thought had crossed his mind a time or two.

"Well, not now, of course. I mean when I'm sixteen and of proper age. You do intend to marry me, don't you?"

"Sure, one day, but ain't I supposed to ask you first? I mean, how do you even know if I like you or not?"

Anna met his gaze again, smiling. Her eyes were lively with fun and mischief. "I already know," she said, brushing a lock of hair from his eyes. "Besides, if you don't ask me, then I'll ask you."

"Yeah well, how do you know I'll say yes?"

"Oh, you foolish boy, of course you will," she said with all of the cryptic confidence that only a young woman could possess.

"The water looks inviting, don't you think?" she said undoing her laces and stepping out of her shoes.

Nyhavn nodded glancing at the lake, it did look inviting. Summer had lingered well into September and the temperature was in the low 80s. A light breeze rippled off of the water making it a cool and pleasant setting.

He had glanced into the picnic basket eyeing a blueberry scone peaking out of a cheese cloth cover when his eye caught movement and he turned back around and found Anna walking to the water's edge.

She was loosening the buttons of her green floral dress as she walked and with one fluid movement she stepped out of it. His throat tightened as he watched her carefully fold the dress and set it on the ground beside her.

When she was done she turned back to Nyhavn in a thin cotton chemise, with her hands on her round hips, and brazenly stared back at him. The cream colored undergarment fit her like a second skin. His eyes were drawn to her full breasts and taut nipples and the outline of her long shapely legs beneath the thin cloth. He was appraising her in the way a young woman likes to be appraised.

"Well now, are you coming in with me for a swim or do you want to hide in the cattails again?"

"Eh, no…I mean, ya, ya…swim, okay," Nyhavn said with a suddenly dry mouth and pounding chest as he took in her curves and crevices again. He scrambled out of his own clothing leaving it in a heap where it fell.

She walked into the water until she was hip deep and then swam out to the middle of the lake in long, graceful strokes before turning back to meet him in the shallows.

In the clear water they could easily make out the shapes of the small fish darting in the shallows between them and as he turned to Anna he could see so much more of her in the wet undergarment.

"Your sisters aren't hiding in the cattails spying on us, are they?"

Anna laughed. "Oh, we considered it but I wanted you all to myself," she said. "At least until we get some things ironed out."

"Things like what?"

"Important things," she said, "like you coming home from the war so we can have a long and happy life together," she said pulling him into her arms.

"Oh, don't you worry," he said as earnest as he could. "I'm coming home."

"Good because three months, six months or however long it takes I'll be waiting here for you, Bent Nyhavn," Anna said coming to his arms. "I have everything you want and need to make you a good wife."

"I know," he said which only brought on another of her warm smiles.

"I know you know that too," she said and pulled him in closer. "Just like I know that you are going to love me forever."

He had no way of knowing then just how prophetic her words would be because in the quiet moments, especially late at night, when he would revisit the afternoon at the lake in his thoughts, the warm memory would briefly comfort him.

Chapter 8

It was a weekly ritual for some ladies from the local Philadelphia churches; Sunday, after services, they would visit with wounded soldiers at the Army's General Hospital on Broad and Cherry Street. They went there to talk, to help the soldiers write letters home, or provide bible readings for those confined to their hospital beds.

Often, the ladies arrived with bouquets of fresh garden flowers; red and yellow roses, lilies, bright orange poppies, and pink and white mountain laurels that almost masked the medicinal odors and putrid smell of the soldier's abscessed wounds.

Many of the ladies were sincere and well-meaning and their kindnesses were greatly appreciated. They would be thought of and remembered as, 'angels.' A few others though, who had reluctantly volunteered, so as not to look bad in the eyes of their congregations, viewed the visits as an exhaustive chore. They would be remembered, too.

The trouble for some of the bed ridden soldiers was that the visits, flowers, and the often somber Bible readings from several just as somber women, gave the convalescent setting the tenor and trappings of a prolonged funeral service.

The church women believed that the visits and especially the readings from the Scriptures would salve and soothe the wounded soldiers' physical traumas and misery. The visits and the readings though, didn't always have the effect that some had anticipated, at least not with Ben. Neither the doctors, medical attendants, nor the church women knew that the young Minnesotan soldier's most painful wound ran deeper than what lay beneath his bandages and had been inflicted long before the fateful charge at Gettysburg.

The battle had left its scars but it was something closer to home that had pierced his heart, leaving a slow and painful bleed. It had happened eleven months earlier when a small group of Santee Sioux Indians jumped their Minnesota River Reservation to forage for food, and attacked a family of settlers near Acton Township.

Some said they attacked the settlers because there was nothing to eat on the reservation and because a reservation official had told them it was 'too damn bad and that if they were hungry then they should eat grass or their own dung'. Others said it was because the soldiers were off fighting the war that the Indians chose to attack when they did. The *why* though didn't immediately matter to those caught up in the turmoil. That would be something for others on both sides to argue over later, when the memory and pain wasn't so close to the surface.

The initial raid had killed five white settlers and sparked an ugly uprising which claimed many more lives before it was over. By late August the rampaging Indians under the leadership of Little Crow, had poured over the Minnesota countryside attacking farms, townships, and settlements in their way. In what became known as the Dakota War of 1862, they laid siege to the town of New Ulm and nearby Fort Ridgely until they finally driven off.

New Tonder hadn't escaped the violence either. While the town had mounted a credible defense and only lost a handful of townspeople and buildings, the retreating Indians had turned their vengeance on the outlying farms. Of the 400 to 800 white settlers and their families that died along the Minnesota River Valley, two dozen were from New Tonder.

The brutality of the attacks shook many of those in the Regiment to their core. Names of those who were killed as well as the farms and settlements lost, stunned the Regiment with each report or newspaper story. But it was letters from home that personalized the loss. Hardened veterans, that had stoically stomached so much hardship and carnage in the war, sat down and openly wept over the news from home.

In the weeks and months that followed, those from New Tonder would hear how John Denison, the town Marshal, led an armed and determined group of townspeople in a hard fought, successful defense. It was Denison, who would later lead the search for survivors in the outlying farms, and officially document the atrocities.

It was in a letter from Frantzen's brother, Rolf, who rode with the rescue posse, that Ben learned the full extent of his loss. When Denison and the others had reached the Nyhavn farm they found his father dead in the yard. He had been shot in the hip, more than likely, when he came out to see what had riled the dog and what had stopped him with a yelp. A war lance left the father with deep stab wounds in his back and neck.

Just outside what had been the Nyhavn's front doorway where they found the half-burned body of Ben's mother, clubbed to death. His sister's body had been found a hundred yards down the county road, torn and bloodied. She had been beaten, violated, and then bludgeoned to death with a stone axe.

Later testimony from an Indian who had been captured by Denison's group said that a boy inside the doorway had gut shot one of the Indians in the raiding party who had dragged the girl outside. The boy, Ben's younger brother, Jurgen, was shot in the throat with an arrow in the return fire. Nyhavn had pictured his father's musket jerking his eleven year old brother's hands before he fell.

The marauders had left the boy where he fell as they ransacked the farm house before putting it to the torch. The Indian told the Marshal he couldn't say if the boy was still alive when the flames engulfed the home. He was pretty sure the white boy was dead, and Ben fervently prayed that he was.

Other accounts Ben had pieced together detailed how his neighbors, the Lundes hadn't fared any better. Caught unaware while they slept, the entire family had been slaughtered in their beds. Two farms down, Jamie Cobb's father and two brothers had been killed defending their farm. Their defense had bought time for Mrs. Cobb, her mother, and Jamie's sister to escape. They hid in the woods where the rescue posse, led by Reverend Kinnunen, and Jake Kelly, had found them and brought them back into town with other survivors before going back out with Denison to search for others and attend to the dead.

With the Indians menacing the countryside the Sixth Minnesota

Regiment was ordered back home from the war to put down the rebellion, which they did. Three hundred and three of the Indian ringleaders were captured and charged with murder and mayhem.

The court found all three hundred and three guilty and they were sentenced to hang. However, intervention by President Lincoln saved two hundred and seventy from the gallows. The remaining thirty-eight of the Indian marauders, who were considered the worst offenders, were hanged in Mankato in a mass execution to bitter applause.

For some in the Regiment though the bitterness entered a new phase. When mortgages couldn't be paid on the farms and lands, the banks foreclosed on them. Some soldiers, like Ben, who had lost their families, now faced the bleak reality of having nothing to return to, when and if they survived the war. Politicians made noise about looking into the unseemly land grabbing practice especially in New Tonder but little was done to remedy it.

Losing the farm and property though only compounded his grief. Since the Indian raids, there wasn't a night that went by when Nyhavn had beaten himself up over his decision to run off to war. He had been eager to go and fight under the guise of preserving the Union. But also knew he went for the adventure as well; a lark, and a desire to be something more than a simple farmer. He hadn't expected to lose everyone and everything in the process.

As he lay in the hospital bed Ben was heart sick and guilt ridden knowing that by running off to fight the rebels, he had lost what really mattered to him back home. In those quiet moments, he was haunted by the image of Anna standing knee deep in the water at the lake, his mind's picture as clear as a daguerreotype print. She was forever coyly smiling in the afternoon Minnesota sunlight and like a print, the picture and memory overtime would begin to fade.

She was gone and the heartache he felt, combined with the loss of his family, and close friends at Gettysburg, left him with a profound sadness.

The bayonet wounds were sewn shut leaving his left arm stiff, the muscles atrophied. Any strength and practical use, the doctors assured him, would come back with time. He just needed to heal.

The concussion he had received had diminished too. The bullet groove in his cheek had scabbed over and was healing. His left earlobe was now scarred and had been sewn back together. Some of his hearing in his left ear was lost, but he could still hear well enough in his right.

His nose was crooked, giving him a rugged prize fighter's profile. He could breathe through both nostrils and the assorted cuts were reduced to purple welts. The deeper wound though, would take more time.

"Good morning, young man," said a young, stern-faced woman loud enough to startle him from his thoughts. "You look to be in need of spiritual comfort."

The woman was tall, thin, and fair-haired beneath a tightly tied bonnet. Her black crinoline dress was properly buttoned to the neck so as not to be inappropriate, or to provoke lust. In her mid-twenties she had a long, pinched face with thin pursed lips and a demeanor that suggested a prudishness that bordered on prissy.

The dour woman clutched a Bible to her bosom, not so much from spirituality it seemed but more so to maintain a defined distance from the wounded soldiers, who she regarded as 'those poor unfortunates.' Her Sunday task was an obvious inconvenience that she didn't take many pains to hide from the other church women or the patients. She didn't feel a need to smile.

"Would you like me to read to you from the Scriptures?" she said with a politeness that seemed well practiced.

"The Scriptures?"

"Yes. Any particular passage that you would like to hear to help ease your burden?"

"TWO: SAMUEL!" shouted another patient slowly ambling up the center aisle of the ward, carefully skirting a pot belly stove. When the woman turned to the voice she found the freshly nicked face of a newly shaven patient grinning back at her. He was carrying a small brown package in his left hand and moving with difficulty. Beneath a cotton robe a thick gauze bandage was wrapped tightly around his chest. Looking slightly older and seemingly more confident than the boy in the bed, this wounded soldier wore a rakish smile that made her a little uncomfortable.

The soldier's glasses and once thin beard, stylish mustache and hair were gone. Much like his own, the soldier's hair had been shaved by the hospital attendants to rid them of lice. Nyhavn was thinking that other than looking a little stoop-shouldered, a little too thin and tired, Trigg Kinnunen looked surprisingly good for someone who was supposed to be dead.

"Pardon me?" said the woman.

"Two: Samuel," Kinnunen said again. "Chapter Eleven, verse two, my good sister. You are a good sister, I take it?"

"I am indeed!"

"Ah, more is the pity," said Kinnunen with a head bowed sigh. "I was hoping you were somewhat challenged in your virtues like the rest of us." Trigg turned and winked at his startled friend before turning his attention back to the woman. "Found it yet?" he asked.

His comment flustered her even more which was the reaction Kinnunen was hoping for.

"I freely admit that I am a troubled sinner badly in need of redemption," he said stepping within inches of her face and backing her against the bed frame. "It wouldn't do much good to try to save the already blessed, now would it?"

"No...but..."

"And your mission today is to bring us the comfort of the Good Book, is it not?"

"Yes..."

"Then please find the chapter and verse, so I can truly feel inspired again."

The rattled woman hurriedly brought the Bible up between them as she flipped through the pages searching for the requested chapter. When she finally found the chapter she ran a thin and busy finger down the page until she found the verse.

"Oh!" she said reading the words to herself and blushing. "Oh my!"

"Excuse me, but you did say 'any passage,' didn't you?" said Kinnunen with a hint of mischievousness in his tone.

"Eh...yes, I did... but..."

"Then put any doubt behind you, sister. It is the Good Book and I know my friend here would truly appreciate how King David enjoyed watching Bathsheba take her bath. I would too, for that matter. So read it aloud slowly, and with all the warm and sudsy feeling you can muster," he said. "Lather her up real good."

The woman closed the Bible with an audible thump, excused herself with a hastened apology and hurried off. "I'm sorry," she said.

"Me too!" Kinnunen said watching her walk away. "I was hoping for something to help lift my spirits!" Turning back to Nyhavn he said, "Well now, young Bent Nyhavn, don't you look like a pile of horse apples left in front of the pearly gates!"

It was true. Nyhavn did look like he was knocking on the Heaven's door while St. Peter was moving in a slow shuffle to answer it.

Seeing his friend alive and standing in front of him had momentarily shaken him.

"I…I saw you…fall…" he said sitting up or trying to. The stabbing pain from his shoulder made it a slow process.

"I did, but I got back up…well, eventually," replied Trigg admiring the swing on the woman's bustle as she walked away. He sighed again.

Kinnunen grinned as he retrieved a small flask from the robe's pocket, unscrewed the cap and took a drink before handing it to his friend.

"Here you go," he said.

"What is it?"

"Medicinal Irish whiskey..."

"Medicinal?"

"Well, certainly for the Irish. I know it makes me feel better with each drink," Kinnunen said, tucking it away before the hospital attendants caught him with it and confiscated the flask.

"Won it in a poker game from one of the Philadelphia boys. They have friends and family here in town who keep them comfortably supplied. Got this too when some of the boys snuck out to do some foraging in Ben Franklin's burg." Kinnunen handed him the small package.

Nyhavn's eyes lit up when he unfolded the loosely wrapped brown paper gift and found half of a meat sandwich on potato bread. After a little over two years of hard tack, fresh bread was a well received luxury. Peeling back the face of the sandwich Ben's face lit up when he found that there was mustard and newly churned butter on the sandwich as well.

"Figured you need it," Kinnunen said. "Hospital rations are pitiful, aren't they?"

Army rations at the military hospitals were, in fact, pitiful. The War Department had designated thirty cents for each meal for a healthy soldier in the field while rations for hospitalized soldiers were reduced to thirteen cents apiece.

At a time when those soldiers needed nourishment the most, the Army had reduced their food allowance, and with it diminished their overall chances for survival. In a little over a week Nyhavn was down eight pounds from his already thin frame. The thin, watery supper soups were hardly enough to keep meat or muscle on his bones. The half sandwich was much appreciated.

"Is it beef?"

"Naw, its scrapple."

"What's scrapple?"

"Don't know and don't care to," replied Kinnunen. "But it's a meat product of some kind and reasonably tasty. Oh, by the way, Frantzen's downstairs…"

"What?"

Kinnunen grinned and nodded. "Yeah, he's downstairs. He's bed bound from head and leg wounds and, he's maybe a little stir crazy too from not being able to get out of bed, but he should be up and running soon enough."

"Al's…Al's alive?"

"Yeah, but you know him. He doesn't talk much, so at times, it's hard to tell. A bullet tore into his calf muscle, another hit his head and skirted around that thick skull of his. He's got a trench along the right side of his head from a rebel rifle ball but with enough hair it will hardly be noticeable. In a rain storm I imagine it'll gutter nicely. His leg though still needs some mending."

"I…I thought both of you..."

Kinnunen's raised hand cut him off. "I know what you thought because at the time I thought it too." Kinnunen's smile faded as the battle roared briefly again behind his gray blue eyes. "One of those thankfully less than well manufactured Confederate soft lead bullets flattened itself against my sternum right here," he said tapping the thick bandage that wrapped around his chest. "Punched the steam out of me and I bled a lot."

"I can imagine."

"Broke some chest bones and collapsed a lung," he said, gritting his teeth. "I couldn't get a full breath till a few days ago. Felt like I was sucking air through a reed but you know what?"

"What?"

"I'm still here and so are you and Frantzen, which is something to celebrate!"

"Yeah, it is. I'm awfully glad to see you alive, my friend," said Nyhavn.

"Yeah, well I'm awfully glad to be seen."

For the first time in a long time Nyhavn laughed and despite the clenching pain in his shoulder there was a break in his melancholy too. "So, is that part true about King David watching Bathsheba taking her bath?"

Kinnunen's grin covered a large part of his face. "The Bible really is a good book, don't cha know?" he said. "Anyway, how badly are you hurt? You don't look like you're missing anything important besides common sense. With you Danes though, it's tough to tell."

"Shoulder wound got infected."

"Is that why they've been purging and bleeding you?" Kinnunen said gesturing to the scars on Nyhavn's arms.

Nyhavn nodded and said it was. "Wore me down some," he admitted.

Kinnunen snorted. He had seen several patients die from the bleeding process and didn't think much of it as a cure. "Al said he saw some rebel run you through with a bayonet. Thought you had bought the farm."

"Made a good down payment," replied Nyhavn. "Afterwards, I got caught out in the field. Couldn't get back. The rebels retreated, just not far enough to give me any running room."

"You wait until it got good and dark?"

"Tried to, but some rebel hold-outs had other notions."

"That what happened to your nose?"

"Uh-huh, rifle butt mostly," said Nyhavn. "One of the Alabamans just about finished me too until a shell exploded overhead. Don't remember much after that."

Kinnunen nodded.

"How did you find me?"

"Exercise," said Kinnunen. "Like I said, Al and I are on the first floor ward downstairs. I was climbing the stairs trying to build up my wind and strength again. Thought I recognized you from the end of the ward and figured I better save you from the Bible thumper."

"They aren't so bad, the visiting church women, I mean. Most seem to mean well."

"Seeming don't always make it so," said Kinnunen, making his point. "Like that one there. She just did her self-important rounds downstairs in a more than haughty and arrogant manner."

"She's here though, that's something."

"Maybe, but I got my fill of some of these hypocrites back at the field hospital before they brought us here."

"At Camp Letterman?"

"No, before that, at one of the farms they first took us too. It was a miserable shithole."

Nyhavn nodded as his own thoughts drifted back to his own farm yard field hospital experience."

"Wasn't much food, fresh water or shelter to go around," said Kinnunen. "We had to make tents out of blankets and anything we could find."

"We did too, to keep out of the sun," said Nyhavn.

"And then from the hard rain that followed," said Kinnunen of the torrential downpour and flooding the day after the battle that made the situation for the wounded even more dismal.

Nyhavn somberly recalled the drenched farm yard that was mired in mud and muck and how several of those badly wounded soldiers in the low areas had drowned in just a few inches of filthy run off water.

"Not long after the rain stopped, a group of good church people from Maryland came in by wagon to soothe our drenched and troubled souls."

"Good that someone came to help."

"Sort of," said Kinnunen. "They were reading scripture and praying for us too, until along about noon when they began setting up plank boards for a make-shift picnic table..."

"A picnic table?"

"And a heavenly feast it was! I mean, they hauled out wicker baskets filled with cured ham, biscuits with butter and honey, pan fried chicken, apples, pies, peach cobbler, coffee, and even a jug of fresh tea with sliced lemon."

Nyhavn's mouth watered just thinking about the dinner. "Boy, that must have been something," he said. "We had nothing like that where I was."

"It was something, only we had nothing like it either," said Kinnunen, confusing the young Private.

"What?"

"After they laid it all out right in front of us, they sat down and served themselves. I mean, they ate fat and happy like we weren't even there."

"You're kidding me?"

Kinnunen shook his head as a dark scowl covered his face. "Wish I was. I really do. However, the good and pious people didn't even offer us a crumb."

"No!"

"Yes, which is why I tore into them with chapter and verse," said Kinnunen. "I cited Matthew twenty-two for openers."

Nyhavn nodded, only not convincingly enough. His familiarity with the Bible ran to several of the key figures, a few parables, and a handful of Psalms, and Kinnunen knew it.

"It's about a rich man who told his servants 'Run out and bring back every poor, crippled or blind man to share a big feast in the name of the Lord," he explained.

"Nothing like hitting them where it hurts the most."

"Well, just to be sure, I mean, in case it didn't shame them enough, I called them selfish sybarites to boot!"

Nyhavn laughed along with his friend and then said, "I don't even know what a sybarite is, but knowing you, it can't be good."

"For your edification, my young friend, a sybarite is someone who lives a life of excessive luxury," he said. "These new sybarites, of course, took offense just not nearly enough in my opinion, so I pelted them with shit shoes..."

"Shit shoes?"

"Uh-huh. Bad off as most of us were, we couldn't crawl to the privy and didn't have the strength to dig a new slit trench or straddle an already filled one. So, when nature called, we took off our shoes, did our business in them, and then tossed them aside.

"The road to good intentions is paved in Hell. I was so damn mad I picked up a few well filled shoes and boots and tossed them right smack dab in the middle of their private little country picnic."

"You didn't!"

"Oh yeah, I did. I also told them if the Lord could chase out the money changers from the Temple, then I'd toss their phony, patriotic asses out of this new holy place. I told them those dying fields may not be sacred to some, but they'll always feel that way to me. Their private picnic was just their way of showing their contempt for us and I wasn't going to let them dishonor it, and those that fell fighting for them."

"Good for you."

"Yeah, well, shit-filled shoes tend to dampen the taste for peach cobbler, I can tell you."

Nyhavn was laughing so hard that his shoulder began to throb. He kept on laughing anyway.

"So, you up for paying a visit to the big German?" asked Kinnunen.

"Ya sure, but you might have to help me a bit," said Nyhavn shifting his legs over to the side of the hospital bed. "I'm still a little unsteady on my feet."

"Then let's get at it. Oh, and one more thing…"

"What's that?"

"Al doesn't know you're alive yet, so how about we give him a good scare? Maybe you can hide behind me and jump out and say 'Boo!' or something. Wouldn't be too much of a stretch since you look pale as a ghost anyway."

Kinnunen gave his friend a hand helping him out of the bed until Ben was on his feet. The movement caught the attention of a worried hospital ward attendant who hurried down the ward trying to stop them, his arms flailing in agitation.

"Uh-uh! No! No!"

"Uh-huh. Yes! Yes!" said Kinnunen, ignoring him as he continued helping Ben to his feet.

"What do you think you are doing?" asked the ward attendant. He was a small, timid soldier with nervous eyes.

"Convalescing," explained Kinnunen, matter of fact. "The boy needs a little exercise if your intent is for him to heal."

"He's not supposed to be moving about and neither are you."

"Actually, the Doctor downstairs said it's okay since those of us who are able will soon be sent back to rejoin our units."

"To the Regiment?" said a surprised Nyhavn. Even the ward attendant was surprised by this bit of news. He hadn't heard anything of the kind.

"Or what's left of it. I was told there was just forty or so still standing after the charge."

"Forty?" Nyhavn said shocked by the ridiculously low number.

"And less than that after the final rebel charge the next day. So they need as many of us as they can get. Those that can't stand up to muster will be sent off to something called 'the Invalid Corps.' And I'll tell you right now, that ain't us."

"No, it ain't," Nyhavn said, managing to walk with the help of his friend. He was light headed and his legs were stiff from too much time in the hospital bed, so he took short steps.

"If we can demonstrate we can walk and talk well enough for the Doctors in the next few weeks then we're going to New York City."

"Why New York City? I thought you said we're going back to our regiment?"

"That's where they're sending them. Seems there was some fighting up there with several hundred dead, thousands more wounded, and part of the city was set on fire…"

"Rebels?"

Kinnunen shook his head. "No, Draft riots or some such business. Our Regiment and a few others are being sent in to help keep the peace."

"I don't know if I'm up for fighting just yet," admitted Nyhavn.

"From what I hear there hasn't been any," said Kinnunen. "The Philadelphia paper, The Inquirer, said the rioting is almost over. There's an occasional dust up or shooting, but our boys tend to shoot back a little straighter and with more enthusiasm. Word is they're sleeping in good canvas tents on cots and folks will be bringing them fresh fruit and vegetables."

"Cots, fresh fruit and vegetables?" Nyhavn said, wistfully. That kind of luxury was unheard of for the average Infantryman, even in the hospital. "That's something, isn't it?"

"It is indeed and if the troublemakers want to mix it up then we'll handle them well enough. Besides, you wanna hear the best news in all this, something I'm sure you will appreciate?"

"Sure. What is it?"

Kinnunen grinned and said, "The rioters don't have cannons."

Chapter 9

It was another two weeks before their wounds had healed to the satisfaction of the hospital's chief surgeon. Then, a perfunctory physical evaluation would determine their fighting status before they were released from the hospital, and sent back into service.

However, what should have been a simple process became a drawn-out exercise in what Nyhavn thought of as the 'hurry up and wait' game. As long as they had been in the Army, they had been rushing off here and there, only to have a long wait, whenever they got to wherever the particular *there* happened to be.

They had hurried in a day long force march to get to Gettysburg only to be placed at Little Round Top before the battle. Then a little after midnight they were hurried down from Little Round Top to Cemetery Ridge, only to watch and wait for most of the day before they were finally allowed to take part in the fight. Then, they hurried into the fighting and afterwards waited to be evacuated.

From the temporary field hospital at the farm they were hurried to the newly erected Camp Letterman Field Hospital where they waited to be treated, hurried in line to eat and then waited to be fed, then hurried to the hospital and waited to heal, or waited to die.

This latest 'hurry up and wait' began after the physical exams when they were told to report to the Hospital's Quartermaster by 0800 to be issued new uniforms. Of course, once there they soon learned that the Hospital's Quartermaster didn't arrive to work until 0900.

"Here," said Kinnunen tossing several small metal pins to his friends as they waited.

"Two Corps badges?" said Frantzen as he pinned the club shaped trefoil decoration to his shirt. "Where did you find them?"

"A New York artillery man had some extras," replied Kinnunen. "He owed me a little poker money, so I settled on these. 'Clubs are trumps.'"

"Clubs are trumps," they replied, proudly.

Once they had their new uniforms the soldiers were sent over to the Paymaster's office for their back pay and travel vouchers to wherever they were going. For the three Minnesotans the *where* was Governor's Island in New York Harbor.

At the Paymaster's office they discovered that the Paymaster was a sixty-year old bewhiskered Captain who had served in the Seminole Wars and the war with Mexico. They soon learned too that the veteran Captain first had to collect the necessary funds across town, under Armed Guard, while they waited outside of his office. Upon his return an hour and twenty minutes later, the Officer began to pay out the appropriate sums to the appropriate people while the soldiers, once again, waited their turns.

"Found a place while I was out searching for new eye glasses that has some friendly ladies we can pay a visit to before we leave this fine city," said Kinnunen.

"By 'friendly ladies' you mean whores, don't you?" replied Nyhavn, as his friend frowned.

"I mean the only kind of ladies we are likely to meet or pretend to charm, given our present positions, and circumstance, Ben," he said. "Why? Does it bother you?"

Nyhavn thought about for a moment and shrugged. "No, not really," he replied, knowing Trigg was right about their likelihood for finding female companionship. "Probably not as much as it would bother me if you couldn't find them."

"Good, because once we get paid and sign out, we'll have time to go visiting before the boat leaves for New York."

"Might be nice to talk to a smiling woman again," said Ben, earnestly.

"Yep, that too," added Frantzen.

"Besides, it's spiritually medicinal," said Kinnunen.

"Is that right? Spiritually medicinal?" Frantzen said, waiting to hear him explain this one.

"Uh-huh," Kinnunen said to the big German. "The comfort of an attentive woman goes a long way to mend the damaged soul."

"How is it that you always seem to make sinning sound like redemption?"

Kinnunen blanched. "And how is it that you don't know that you can't be redeemed if you haven't done your share of sinning?"

As soldiers they had known their share of camp followers, the 'Doves,' 'Doxies', or 'Sporting girls,' as the prostitutes were better known. The enterprising women set up shop near the various army camps, plying the ancient trade to soldiers willing and eager for the purchase.

A dollar a poke was the going rate; early on Nyhavn hadn't participated, on principle, holding the moral high ground in a battle his friends knew, sooner or later, he was bound to lose, which he finally did.

The war was changing him daily, and if he hadn't noticed the transformation then Frantzen and Kinnunen did. The successive battles from Bull Run to Gettysburg had shaped and pounded him with the finesse of a ball-peen hammer. The loss of his loved ones back home had done their damage too. Gone was the somewhat naive farm boy, replaced by a hardened and tired eyed young veteran nurtured by war.

The Paymaster's line moved at a slow and steady pace. Still, it took another half hour before they had reached the Captain's desk. It took that long due to the large number of soldiers who were out-processing from the hospital, and because the officer had to find the name and amount of pay the soldier was owed, disperse the funds to the soldier, and then have him sign for it in the ledger. The Captain would carefully count out that sum and have the soldier verify the count, and sign for the money.

Frantzen was the first of the three to report to the paymaster. He took the position of attention and saluted until he was told to stand at ease. "Private Aalderk Frantzen, sir," he said.

The big German, who had let his beard grow since Gettysburg and now looked like a young Attila the Hun in Federal blue, momentarily startled the Captain.

"Sign here, Sergeant," the officer said to Frantzen turning around the pay roster for the soldier to sign.

"Sir?"

"Yes, Sergeant?"

"Eh…I'm not a Sergeant, sir. I'm a Corporal."

The Captain's face registered momentary confusion as he patiently went back over the names of the soldiers who were out processing from the hospital. "You are Aalderk Frantzen of G Company, the First Minnesota Volunteers, aren't you?"

"Yes sir, I am."

"Well, I only see one Aalderk Frantzen on my pay roster," said the officer peering up over spectacles. "Was there another Aalderk Frantzen in your Regiment with you?"

"No sir."

"Then it appears your Company and Regiment saw fit to promote you in rank," said the Captain. "Therefore the allocated funds you have just signed for will reflect your temporary pay increase. I suggest you sew on the chevrons of your new rank as soon as possible, Sergeant. By the way…"

"Yes sir?"

"Nice beard."

"Thank you, sir," Frantzen said, happily stuffing the money and travel papers in his pockets and saluting the Captain before going back out the door.

"NEXT!" yelled the Captain as Trigg Kinnunen entered and learned that he was now a Corporal, promoted in absentia. Ben Nyhavn had been promoted to rank of Corporal as well.

"Well, you did grab up the colors after the color bearer went down," said Frantzen to a still surprised Kinnunen after they had left the hospital and made their way through the thin and busy Philadelphia streets.

"Yeah, but, I didn't hold them for all that long."

"Long enough to get noticed, it appears," said Frantzen.

"Just as it would appear someone noticed you two as well," Kinnunen replied.

"Apparently they didn't notice how scared I was either," Nyhavn said. "Al took the fight to the Johnnie Rebs and all I did was try to stay alive. I don't deserve any stripes."

Kinnunen sighed.

"You want me to educate the boy or pass it over to you?" he said to the big German.

"No," said a mildly amused Frantzen. "This one's yours."

"Good enough," said the newly promoted Corporal. To Nyhavn, Kinnunen said, "There are two things you really need to learn from this... well, more than two but we'll keep this lesson simple for now."

"Simple's good for him," agreed Frantzen.

Nyhavn was annoyed at the fun they were having at his expense and it showed. "Younger don't always mean dumber," he said, more than a little defensively.

"That's true," said Kinnunen, "but you work harder than most to keep the two things intact..."

"In what?"

"Intact...together, and that proves my point. So, let's get back to the two things. First; and I want you to mark this well and pay close attention. Are you paying close attention, young Corporal?"

"Go to Hell!"

"Close enough," said Kinnunen. "Anyway, here is the first lesson: people seldom get what they deserve in life, good or bad."

"Yeah, but that don't make it right or fair."

"True enough, but fair seldom enters into the picture. Somebody, somewhere thought you deserved the Corporal stripes, so just say 'Thank you, sir,' salute, take the extra money that goes along with it, and move on, soldier. If it helps any, I was scared too. I suspect even Al here might have been a little frightened. You scared anytime at Gettysburg, were you, Al?"

"Nope, I was a shining example of calm and composure," said Frantzen eying some of the displayed hats in a haberdasher's window.

"Is that right?"

"Yep, even as the piddle was running down my shaking legs. Goddamn right, I was scared!"

"See? There you go," said Kinnunen. "Now take this new found wisdom and put it to good use. Got it?"

"Sure, sort of..."

"Sort of is good enough at times," said Kinnunen turning his attention back to finding some familiar city landmarks. "Oh, and Al, I'd appreciate it if you wouldn't say 'goddamn it' anymore."

"I can't promise I won't, but I'll work on it."

"Good enough."

As they walked the new Corporal was trying to get his bearings. Recognizing a familiar looking corner cigar store he smiled, pleased with himself. He turned onto a busy street, dodging a horse-drawn streetcar as his two friends followed.

"You said there were two things I needed to know? So what's the second thing?" Nyhavn asked coming up behind him.

"Ah yes, the second thing," Kinnunen said, taking them down a smaller cobblestone lane. "The second and most important thing for you to know is that rank has its privileges."

"Privileges?"

"Indeed. You see, Al here is an exalted Sergeant and you are just a lowly Corporal…"

"You're a Corporal too!"

"Yes, but who was promoted ahead of you, which makes me a *senior* Corporal…"

"Yeah, by only three minutes or so."

"Tomato, ta-mahto…"

"What's that supposed to mean?"

"It means that a Sergeant's mind needs to be free of everyday common and burdensome problems in order to properly determine how to best meet the needs of the Army. To this end as a Non-Commissioned Officer it is both his duty and mine, as your immediate superior, to delegate responsibility, so I'm delegating you to carry our bags."

"Carry your bags?"

"And smartly too, you bumptious lout. Don't dawdle."

"You two can carry your damn bags!"

"What'd ya know, insubordination?"

"That's a punishment offense, isn't it?" asked Frantzen chiming in on Kinnunen's side of the argument.

"Why yes, I do believe it is, Sergeant Frantzen, and, if I am correct, in a time of war, which makes it even more odious and offensive," replied Kinnunen. "But seeing how the offender here is still recovering from his battle wounds I think you should wait until he's fully healed before you have him placed up against a wall and shot."

"Tough on the firing squad if he's falling over," admitted Frantzen as they walked. "Moving targets being harder to hit and all."

"Excellent point! See, now that's a fine example of a thinking Sergeant who takes into consideration the best interest of his men. You should take note, young Corporal Nyhavn, if you ever expect to advance further in rank." One block on, Trigg found the establishment he was looking for down a side street. "Here we go!" he said aiming towards its entrance.

It was a three story brick building with a red door and polished brass fittings. Heavy maroon drapes hid the view through the windows. A sign next the entrance read: *The Fortunate Gentlemen's Club.*

Inside the doorway a small foyer with a beaded curtain opened up to a larger parlor room and a small, but well-stocked bar. A gilt-framed bawdy painting hung on the wall behind the bar. The painting was an odalisque; a nude, reclining beauty that left little doubt as to what went on here. A bartender, who was wiping down the bar as they entered, nodded to the three soldiers. Kinnunen returned it before turning his attention to several scantily clad sporting girls resting on a horse-hair settee on his left. He smiled and they returned the smile.

"Good afternoon, gentlemen." The voice came from a sultry, raven haired woman rising from a nearby table to greet them.

"Ah, the lovely Miss Paulette!" exclaimed Kinnunen with a polite bow. Miss Paulette had big brown eyes and a wide, sensuous smile. She wore a bright green crinoline dress with a tactically revealing neckline. An expensive gold and emerald necklace complimented her smooth, slim neck. The neckline and necklace drew attention to her ample cleavage. Freckles dotted the exposed flesh and Trigg was mentally enjoying connecting the dots. "I told you I'd be back," he said to the woman.

"That you did," she said. She barely remembered the promise, let alone the conversation, but recognized the soldier and his engaging grin.

"And I brought a few friends with me. Good as my word."

"They have money too? As you know, honey, words only go so far."

"We all just got paid," he said, pulling out a roll of fresh greenbacks from his pocket and fanning them out in display. "We're on our way up to

New York City to rejoin our regiment. Our boat does not leave for a few hours. I'm hoping a few of your ladies might be up for a social drink and a quiet backroom chat."

"A schooner of beer is ten cents, a shot of whisky is two bits, and the 'quiet backroom chat' will cost you two dollars a go," said Miss Paulette, setting the terms for the entertainment.

"What's a schooner of beer?" asked Nyhavn.

"A tall glass of beer, my handsome little soldier boy," said another of the ladies sidling up to Ben and taking him by the arm. "Buy me one too?" she asked, pulling his elbow into her warm bosom. Nyhavn grinned and said he'd be happy to buy her a drink.

Happy really wasn't the word for it. The woman was almost as tall as he was, smelled of perfumed flowers, and wore a naughty smile that carried well into her lively brown eyes. She was a little on the large side but gregarious, both attributes were fine by him. He liked his women womanly. There was a foreign cadence to the woman's voice, French maybe, thought Nyhavn recalling a shop keeper's wife back home who was French and who sounded just like her. However, the shopkeeper's wife didn't look anywhere near as good as this woman did.

As the bartender handed her a drink she thrust her ample bust forward into Ben's arm and canted one hip against his thigh in a maneuver calculated to make most men think more seriously about parting with their money. It had its desired effect on the young Corporal too.

"My, you really smell good," he said complimenting her with the second thought that had entered his mind.

"I do, don't I?" she said, beaming. "It's Bohemian Rosewater. Where are you from, sweetie?"

"New Tonder," said Ben, thinking he'd like to have his face where his elbow was.

The woman leaned back and eyed him with mild curiosity. "That back in the Alleghenies?"

"Minnesota," Frantzen said, answering for Nyhavn as another of the sporting girls rubbed up against the big German. The woman was a willowy brunette with long curls and a pleasing smile. It pleased Frantzen so he ordered two beers as well.

"What say we enjoy a drink or two and then go chat our socks off?" said Kinnunen suggesting the obvious to his friends.

"I ain't wearing socks," said a slightly confused Nyhavn. "The Quartermaster at the hospital didn't issue me any."

Frantzen almost choked on his beer as Kinnunen chuckled and shook his head while several of the ladies, in turn, wore bemused grins. "Ben, chatting our socks off has nothing to do with socks or chatting," Kinnunen said.

"Oh," said Ben in sudden understanding. His face reddened as a smile slowly began to emerge.

Kinnunen was smiling too as he turned back to the Madam. "Since we're in 'the City of Brotherly Love'," he said to Miss Paulette, "I think it is only fitting that we share some of it with its willing sisters."

"Money first and then we'll be willing," said Miss Paulette holding out an open palm and wiggling her fingers.

"Gotta love good commerce," Frantzen said reaching in his pocket for his own greenbacks. "Or even better commerce to celebrate my promotion. It's my treat, boys. I'm paying for the first round of drinks too. After that, you're on your own."

Miss Paulette waved over a sultry-eyed blonde and a grinning Kinnunen wasted little time with introductions. As she put an arm around his waist she whispered something in his ear that caused him to chuckle. Next to him Frantzen and the brunette were locked in their own conversation.

"How about you, sweetie? You up for a good chat?" said Nyhavn's Sporting Woman placing her right hand on Ben's crotch and gently squeezing it.

"Oh, yes ma'am. I am now," he said, grinning.

"Aren't you the polite one?" she cooed. "Call me Julia. What's your name, honey?"

"Ben."

"Well then, Ben, my cute, little soldier boy," said the woman. "You ready to mount up?"

"The Cavalry mounts up," said Nyhavn. "We're Infantry."

The woman chuckled while Kinnunen and Frantzen exchanged sidelong glances and pained expressions.

"He's not really as slow as he sometimes sounds," Frantzen said to Julia.

"Let's hope he isn't too fast either. I especially enjoy a drawn out chat," replied the woman with a wicked smile.

"Boys, the boat leaves in a few hours," said Frantzen, checking his pocket watch. Both soldiers nodded, although he wasn't really sure they had gotten the message, so he tried another tactic instead. "Ladies, the boy's here will pay you an extra dollar if you'll kick them out of your cribs in an hour or so."

"We will?" said Nyhavn.

"Seeing how I'm springing for your romps, you can toss in the dollar to keep us from missing the boat. So, to answer your question; yes, you will."

"Not to worry," Julia said tenderly patting Nyhavn's hand. When she smiled her eyes crinkled. "By then you'll be good and tired. In fact, you'll probably be able to sleep real well on the boat. Toss in two dollars more, and I'll show you how to please a woman so that she'll want to pay you."

"You talking love secrets?"

"Oh, *mon cher*, love's no secret," laughed Julia. "You just have to try to find someone who loves you as much as you love yourself. That's a tall order for some. No, I'm talking woman pleasuring secrets..."

"Pleasuring secrets?" said Kinnunen leaning back from the bar and taking interest into what Julia was telling his friend. "Like what?"

"*Un petite joie.*"

"The what?" said Kinnunen.

"Not a what," said Julia, "but a how, a very, very good how. *Un petite joie*, a little joy."

"Oh yes, it is," said the sultry eyed blonde at Kinnunen's side.

"Is that right?"

"Mmmm," said the blonde, dreamily which caused Trigg's imagination to dance with possibilities.

"You know, I think I have a few more dollars I can part with too," he said to the blonde, "So what do you say you teach me this...*zhurwha*...

"*Joie*," said Julia.

"*Joie*, this French joy thing."

"Sorry," said the blonde, "That's Julia's special little talent, not mine. She's really good at it."

"It's true, I am. Maybe next time you're in town and you look me up," she said to Trigg and then back to Ben she added, "Are you ready for a little schooling, soldier boy?"

Nyhavn held up two silver dollars. "Why yes, I am," he said wearing an unabashed grin.

"Oh honey, when I'm done with you any woman you entertain will tell you this is the best money you ever spent," she said lasciviously as she pocketed the two dollars and then led him by the hand towards the small cribs in the back.

Chapter 10

They reported to the military transient office for duty at Governor's Island in New York Harbor. Inside the single story brick building, behind a waist-high counter, and seated behind a blonde oak desk that would have made any teacher proud, they found a portly Ordnance Sergeant. The senior Non-Commissioned Officer, who had been eating his mid-day meal when they entered, was annoyed by the interruption. He grumbled something to himself stepping away from a half-filled tin plate of sausage and cabbage and a bottle of beer.

"Yeah, what do you want?" he said leaning on the counter as though the short walk over from his desk had been a great effort.

"We were told to report here to find our Regiment," replied Frantzen.

"Which Regiment?"

"The First Minnesota Regiment of Volunteers. They were sent here in July."

"Minnesota?" he said, consulting a roster and finding the Regiment's status on the list, tapping it with a food stained finger. "They're gone. They packed up their kits, marched down to the harbor and were loaded aboard a steamship a week or so ago." The Ordnance Sergeant turned back to his desk and meal.

"Gone where?" asked Kinnunen forcing the Ordnance Sergeant to turn back to him.

"Back to the war, back to Minnesota, who knows? It's not my concern."

The three Minnesotans stared blankly at the man unsure of what to do next.

"What? You have shit in your ears? I told you your Regiment is gone. You can go too," said the senior NCO.

"Where?" Frantzen asked. "Our travel orders are only good as far as New York."

"Who sent you here?"

"The Army Hospital in Philadelphia," the big German said handing over a copy of the travel orders.

What the Ordnance Sergeant read seemed to vex him. His lunch would have to wait and that he didn't like one damn bit.

The Ordnance Sergeant sighed. "How much time do you have left on your enlistments?"

"Seven, eight months," Frantzen said, doing a quick mental calculation.

The heavy-set sergeant grunted as he read over their travel orders a second time. Uncertain what to do with the three new arrivals and wanting to finish his meal, the Ordnance Sergeant took the problem over to a bored looking Captain in a corner office. A plate glass window gave him full view of the counter.

Reading over their papers while periodically eying the the three soldiers, the Captain settled the question with an imperious response that seemed to satisfy the Ordnance Sergeant.

The Non-Commissioned Officer returned to his desk, and with what sounded like considerable effort, set his food tray aside, pulled out pen and paper, and scribbled something in haste. Blotting away the excess ink and blowing on the ink to help it dry, he quietly read over what he had written and nodded at his work.

Seemingly satisfied, the Ordnance Sergeant folded the paper into itself creating its own envelope. Sealing it with a wax stamp, he rose from his chair, walked back to the counter, and handed it to Frantzen.

"You and your men will report to this address in Manhattan, Sergeant," he said pointing to the name and address on the outside of the parchment envelope.

"Where's that?"

"The city."

"New York?"

The Ordnance Sergeant looked at him like he was an idiot.

"That's right, in the city. Make your way to 156 Anthony Street in Five

Points. Give this to Captain O'Brian, the Officer in Charge," he said turning back to his lunch. Without looking up he added, "You're dismissed."

"And this Captain O'Brian will tell us how to find our Regiment, Sergeant?" asked Kinnunen.

The NCO bridled at the question. He didn't like it when lower ranking enlisted men questioned him after he had given them their orders or told them what to do. His look said as much.

"It is where I'm ordering you to report, boy. They teach you how to follow orders in Minnesota, did they?"

"Yes, Sergeant, they did," Frantzen replied.

"Good," he said, "Then get the hell out of my office and close the damn door behind you."

Outside Kinnunen said, "Pleasant sort of fellow, isn't he?"

"Not much of a welcome," said Frantzen, heading back towards the island's ferry dock. The shuttle boats that would take them back to the city ran on the hour.

"Were you really expecting a warm welcome?"

"Oh, I dunno, telling us where we might get something to eat would've been nice. I'm hungry and that old boss hog certainly looked like he knew where to find a trough or two."

"We'll pick something up in town. Come on. Let's go find this Anthony Street and find out where the regiment went."

In addition to serving as the transient station for arriving and departing soldiers, and a rendezvous point for new recruits, the Island's fortifications also housed several military prisons for captured rebel soldiers. Enlisted prisoners of war were sent to the round and imposing red sandstone Castle Williams, while the officers went to the more dismal star-shaped bastion that was Fort Columbus.

At dockside, they watched as armed guards escorted a line of dejected looking prisoners of war from the boat towards the gloomy walls of the prison. Much of the captured rebels' clothing was weathered and tattered. Good boots or shoes were a rare commodity among the gaunt and listless men.

"I kinda feel sorry for the poor bastards," said Kinnunen as they passed.

"I probably will too… someday," said Frantzen.

"Someday, huh?" asked Kinnunen.

"Uh-huh," replied the big German with a set jaw and hard stare, "Just not today."

It was a half mile back across the channel to the Southern tip of Manhattan and the city proper. The wind had picked up and the boat ride was rough, the water choppy. Shortly after they landed, Frantzen eyed a small café one block up from the wharf. 'There, we go!' he said and pointed them towards it, leading the way. Over coffee, biscuits and a thick, surprisingly tasty stew, they asked directions to Anthony Street and Five Points from the café's proprietor.

"Five Points?" said the man, registering obvious concern. "You sure that's where you're supposed to go?"

"It's where we've been told to report," he said. "Why?"

"It's a hardscrabble part of town is all," said the proprietor, a thin ruddy faced man with an accent that Nyhavn couldn't place. Scottish, maybe? "You're not from around here, I take it?"

"No," said Kinnunen.

"Then it would be wise to keep your wits about you," he added as he drew them a street map on the back of a scrap of paper. He handed the paper to Kinnunen who studied it with interest.

"Is it far from here?"

"Not in distance, no," he said cryptically. "Best be careful, lads."

"We will. Thank you," said Kinnunen as they paid their check before stepping back out into the busy street. The Minnesotans had to dodge and work their way around a line of dray wagons as they walked away from the hectic docks. Following the directions on the crude map the café proprietor had drawn, they soon found the main boulevard the proprietor had labeled, 'Broadway' and turned onto it.

And broad it was, as the city itself. The paved street was three times as wide as New Tonder's main dirt street with sidewalks broad enough for three to four people to walk side by side.

New York City was even more lively and populated than Philadelphia and more impressive. With 800,000 residents it was the largest city in the country, huge by any nation's standards, with a vibrant energy the likes of which they had never seen. Gas street lamps stood like sentinels over the broad cobblestone streets with its stately houses, large mansions and massive buildings that left them in awe. Shops, saloons, and stores of every kind and purpose also lined the sidewalk route they took north up Broadway. The grand boulevard was teeming with people seemingly from every social strata and class that the city had to offer, from beggars to well-dressed swells. They gaped as they walked, transfixed by the volume of people, large buildings, and lively air.

Broadway was a furious flow of vehicle traffic with horse drawn wagons, drays, carts, fancy coaches, carriages, hacks, hansom cabs, and mounted horsemen. The sidewalks too were crowded with a pedestrian mix of casual strollers and those walking with purpose.

A colorful omnibus with bold advertising and pulled by a team of draught horses offered a transit route up the man-made canyon-walled avenue. Still, they preferred to walk, taking it all in like the backwoods visitors they were. Even Kinnunen was impressed.

'You know something?"

"What?" asked Nyhavn.

"We really are small town hicks."

"Oh, I dunno," said Frantzen. "They have horse shit in their streets. We have horse shit in our streets."

"Horses' asses too," said Kinnunen. "Well, two more now that you and Ben are here in the big city."

"What about you?"

"I've been to Chicago," said Kinnunen, beaming. "I'm damn near a sophisticated thoroughbred."

Six blocks later, the new arrivals were stopped by a Policeman. "Hold up, there," said the beefy patrolman detaining them. He tapped a Billy club against his right thigh as he spoke and then pointed it towards the wall of a building indicating where he wanted them to stand.

"Yes sir, how can we help you?"

"You can start by showing me some travel orders that say you're not army deserters."

The policeman kept a cautious eye on the big German as Frantzen dug through his pocket and produced the papers as well as the envelope from Governor's Island.

"We're on our way to find our unit at Anthony Street," he said handing it all over for inspection.

"Anthony Street, is it now?" said the policeman, warily.

"Yes sir, we just got out of the Army Hospital in Philadelphia."

Somewhat pacified the policeman stuck the Billy club under his arm as he read over the official papers and studied the Five Points address. His defensive air and posture were soon replaced with furrowed brow confusion.

"You're Provost Soldiers then, are you?"

"No sir, we're Infantry. First Minnesota Volunteers."

Uncertain what to make of the reply, the policeman handed Frantzen back their papers and pointed them uptown. "Straight ahead then," he said reasonably satisfied with their explanation and papers. "Stay on Broadway until you get to Anthony Street then, go right until you wonder who it was you pissed off to have you sent there. Good luck, gentlemen. You may need it."

Dodging heavy street traffic they crossed Broadway and continued their trek. Four blocks further a second policeman stopped them as they turned onto Anthony Street, repeating the paper checking process and street interrogation until they were once again, free to leave.

"I take it they have a problem with deserters?" Trigg Kinnunen said to the others as they walked.

"And with Anthony Street too, I'm guessing," said Frantzen staring down the less prosperous street that led to the heart of Five Points. They soon began to see why the café proprietor and the policemen had questioned their destination.

The better part of town had given way to the dreary, seedier side of the city that eventually led depressingly down to the east river. Anthony Street was a busy, uneven corridor of dingy, crowded five to six storied tenements, store fronts, saloons, dancehalls, greengrocers, butcher shops, and questionable boarding houses. Noisy pushcart vendors hawked tired looking vegetables, used clothing, or other goods.

Behind the corridor of shabby buildings that faced the street, down ridiculously thin alleys, they caught sight of a second line of lesser dwellings. Some of those wooden tenements were tilting at odd angles and looked as worn and tired and desperate as the residents who listlessly peered from doorways or windows.

Here, those who had left Europe for the dream of a better life in America, woke up each morning only to find disappointment. It was a place that the visiting English author and social reformer, Charles Dickens, who had grown up in poverty and who himself had been forced to work as a child laborer, had labeled 'one of the worst slums in the world.' The rutted alleys here were narrow, filthy, and reeked with the stench of raw sewers, and garbage strewn about the squalid streets.

They passed a butcher's shop where a butcher and his blood splattered apprentice were gutting a pig over a large tub. The two gave scant notice to the soldiers as they went about their work. The tub collected the blood they would later use for blood sausages.

Dark and heavy coal smoke spilled down from chimneys and stained rooftops and hung over the streets and the lives of its residents like a cloud of despair. The Minnesotans didn't need a signpost to see where prosperity left off and hard times took over.

Ben Nyhavn watched as a woman came to an open window and dumped a day's refuse in the street below. A slumbering drunk, momentarily roused by the loud splat and near assault growled something unintelligible, and then went back to his drunken dreams.

On a side street several toddlers and a handful of slightly older, but much louder children, barefoot and dressed in tattered clothing, laughed and played next to an open stream of runoff water. Rag pickers hauling heavy bundles over their shoulders trudged on through their day seemingly unconcerned with anything but their loads. Further on they passed a busy and prosperous storefront with a large sign that read: *Crown's Grocery*. A half block down a dog was hunched over, shitting in the street. Crouched on its back haunches the dog studied the three soldiers with a mix of snarling suspicion and fear. It wasn't alone in its distrust.

On a nearby stoop, men with strange dialects and cynical eyes lowered their voices as the soldiers passed before they resumed their conversation.

"A swell looking place, wouldn't you say?" Kinnunen said, eying the scruffy buildings and even scruffier looking streets.

"Not to mention the kindly looking people," laughed Frantzen as they searched to find the address on the envelope.

"Hardscrabble is right," said Nyhavn. He looked around, taking in more narrow side lanes that led to poorer tenements where waves of laundry hung from drooping lines.

Through an open doorway he caught sight of a tired looking woman, bent over half-filled tub and washboard. She stopped to watch them pass. Several young children sat at her feet while a baby was coughing and crying behind her.

All this was punctuated by the sound of creaking carts and delivery wagons, a barking dog, and working saws and hammers from a carpenter's shop.

"It's a sore looking part of the city," said Kinnunen.

"Sore, hell!" said Frantzen. "It's a picked over scab!"

Three blocks further on Kinnunen spotted a newer looking, fortress-like building where a uniformed Provost sentry guarded its front entrance.

"A castle among the hovels," he said checking the address on the envelope and the pointing to the building. "That has to be it."

His assessment wasn't far off. It was a new and solid looking three storied building, a brownstone and flag stone construction. It made the surrounding clapboard or chipped brick tenements and well weathered streets seem even more destitute by comparison.

A polished brass plaque to the right of the double doorway read: *Sixth Ward Provost Company*. Its buffed shine proudly announced to passers-by who wielded influence and power here.

Starting up the front stairs they were soon stopped by the armed sentry who blocked their way.

"Whoa, now! And just where do you think you're going?" said the sentry. The soldier was a soft looking nineteen-year-old dressed in an oversized tunic that Frantzen judged was more filled with bluster than substance. The soldier held the rifle smartly enough, but still looked like a parade soldier regardless. The soldier wore a round green felt badge pinned to his collar and a smug smile that instantly grated on the big German.

A little tired from the long trip and the less than welcome greetings they had received thus far, Frantzen stepped up to the top of the landing, and loomed over the now intimidated guard, forcing him to take a stumbling step backwards.

"We were told to report here to a Captain O'Brian, Private," said Frantzen handing the guard the envelope. "He around?"

The Guard glanced down at the envelope, then to the Sergeant's chevrons on his sleeve, and then back to the big sergeant's unsmiling face. Over his shoulder he called for the Sergeant of the Guard who, thankfully for him, appeared in the doorway.

The Sergeant was the same size as Kinnunen but that's where any similarity ended. He had thick shoulders was heavily muscled, and appeared to have no neck. His nose looked as though it had been recently broken and wrenched back into place by a drunken doctor. There was scar tissue over his eyes which showed that the Sergeant was a brawler.

He eyed the three Minnesotans for a long moment before he turned his attention to the Guard, and the parchment envelope in his hand.

"So?" he said to the sentry.

"So, they say they were told to report here, Sergeant," said the guard, handing the Sergeant the envelope. The soldier studied the scrawl on the envelope with Captain O'Brian's name in bold print, and turned his attention to the visitors.

"Here?" echoed the Sergeant skeptically as Frantzen nodded. "Okay then," he said. "Follow me." Turning quickly on his heels he disappeared back inside the doorway not waiting to see if they were in tow. They followed him through a wet tiled foyer that smelled of lye soap and water. The Sergeant nodded to a soldier who was mopping the hallway and the soldier nodded back.

"When you're done here the First Sergeant wants you to go back over the front steps with the mop, Private McKay," he said.

"Of course he does," said the soldier leaning on the mop handle.

"No hurry, Kevin. Just don't let him catch you slacking."

"Wouldn't think of it."

"Wouldn't think of slacking or wouldn't think of getting caught?"

"Exactly," replied McKay as the New York Sergeant snorted in response as he turned and bounded up one flight of stairs with the new arrivals scrambling to keep up. On the second floor landing, the Sergeant led them through the opened door of a large office. Two-inch gold and black block printed lettering on the frosted glass door identified it as the Company's Orderly room.

They stepped inside and stopped at the cluttered oak desk of a tall, gawky looking senior sergeant. The face of the forty something year old, looked like it had been stretched over his skull and covered in dripped yellow wax. He didn't look up but instead held up the index finger on his right hand, indicating they should wait, while he kept reading the papers in front of him.

A wooden nameplate with fancy carved script on the desk identified him as 'First SGT. Lynch.' Gray wiry hair grew in tufts from his long lobed ears. He had a hawk-like nose and dark brown, almost black eyes.

Drake coughed and the First Sergeant looked up

"One minute," said the thin lipped NCO with a bothered sneer. Drake smiled as he went back to his reading. His lips moved slowly across the full page leaving the new arrivals time to take in the Orderly Room.

To Nyhavn the office was sparse and utilitarian. Besides the First Sergeant's desk there were several wooden filing cabinets against the wall on the left and a long wooden bench between two large bay windows on the right.

Behind the desk a closed oak door carried a polished brass name plate that read: *Commanding Officer*. To the right of the door an area map tacked to the wall outlined a portion of the city in red. Stick pins marked something of significance, but meant nothing to him. A company clerk, a short, skinny long-necked Corporal with feral features and bad teeth, had stopped his filing and stared at the Minnesotans with dull eyed curiosity. Nyhavn nodded to the soldier who didn't return it.

His roving glance brought him back to the First Sergeant. Even seated he could see that the man was all elbows, knees and angles. A bunched up pistol belt displayed a Walnut gripped pistol on his right hip.

"Okay then, what is it, Sergeant Drake?" grumbled as First Sergeant Lynch's black eyes scoured over the three new arrivals the way a chained dog views trespassers.

"They just showed up at our door, said they were told to report here," Drake said holding out the envelope to the First Sergeant.

"Here?" Lynch said, surprised as he snatched up the envelope, broke open the red wax seal, and slowly read over its contents.

"They gave you this at Governor's Island, did they?" asked the First Sergeant addressing Frantzen since he held the highest rank of the new men.

"Yes, Sergeant, they did."

"First Sergeant," Lynch said correcting him.

"Yes, First Sergeant. To tell us how to get back to our unit."

The First Sergeant chuffed, stood, and then walked over to the Commanding Officer's door. He knocked twice and waited.

"ENTER!" came the muffled response. The First Sergeant did just that closing the door behind him as he went.

"They joining us?" asked the dull eyed Corporal.

Sergeant Drake shook his head at the company clerk. "If you mean 'us,' as in here with you in this swank little office job, then no. They're real soldiers." The Corporal took the hint; red faced and embarrassed, he returned to his filing.

A few minutes passed before the door to the Commanding Officer's office opened again. "This way," the First Sergeant said from the doorway. "Move it!"

"Not you," Lynch said blocking Drake's way. "Has the load of coal for the boiler been picked up yet?"

"I sent Privates Roacher, Dean and Kirk for it a little over an hour ago."

"What? They bringing it back one lump at a time?" said Lynch, snidely. "Check up on them and make damn sure they're not slacking off. And don't come back with excuses," he added shutting the door in his face.

If Sergeant Drake was bothered by the obvious insult, it didn't show. He pivoted on his heels and started out of the Orderly Room. Out of the corner of his eyes he caught the company clerk smiling.

"Something funny to you, *Dumbshite*?" he said turning back to the soldier.

The company clerk didn't reply, wisely choosing instead to quietly keep on filing his papers.

"No? Well, I didn't think so," said Drake as he left the Orderly Room.

Inside the Commanding Officer's office, Kinnunen, Nyhavn and Frantzen stood at the position of attention just in front of the Captain's desk. An engraved nameplate read: *CPT. T. O'Brian, Esquire*. Nyhavn wasn't sure what an *Esquire* was, but at first glance, figured it must have had something to do with money.

The Captain, who left the soldiers standing at attention, looked up from the Governor's Island letter he had just finished reading, placed it down on his desk, and gave them the command to stand at ease.

"It would appear that your Regiment sailed away without you," said the Captain to the Minnesotans tapping the letter with his left index finger.

"Yes sir, that's what we were told at Governor's Island," said Kinnunen with the required and expected deference.

"Half a month or so ago, actually," the officer said swiveling in his chair and staring out his window while he considered what he should do with them. In his mid thirties the Captain was a bland and shapeless man with a trimmed mustache and a waxed and pointed Van Dyke beard that could not quite hide a weak chin and puffy facial features. His thin, black hair had the luster of pomade and a strategic coif. He had the look of a lifetime of privilege and of belonging to a lesser aristocracy that hadn't quite learned to conceal their disdain for those they secretly felt were the *underclass*.

He was dressed in an expensively tailored uniform and was seated behind a well polished mahogany desk that was much larger and more ornate than the First Sergeant's. Nyhavn was thinking that the Captain, quite possibly, was wearing the cleanest and best looking uniform he had ever seen.

The brass buttons gleamed in the sunlight coming from the large picture window, the gold braid of the officer's shoulder rank glistened on the natty tailored uniform coat that was made of fine cloth. A green sash was tied neatly in place around his waist. His white shirt was immaculate and the combined sartorial effect confirmed Nyhavn's nagging suspicion that the Captain had probably never served anywhere near a battlefield.

The First Sergeant, who was standing behind the officer and just over his right shoulder, scowled like the palace guard he was at the young soldier's gawking. Ben turned his eyes back to the office.

In stark contrast to the austere Orderly Room office, opulence reigned here. The office furnishings were substantial, moneyed. There was a long and expensive horse-haired settee near a brocade curtained window seat. The heavy curtains were dark blue with gold tasseled tie backs. Along one wall a book case held several shelves of fine leather bound books. A half-filled crystal Brandy decanter and two matching long stemmed glasses on a silver serving tray sat idly on an end table. On the wall behind the

Captain's desk there was an impressive oil painting of a black stallion rearing back and ready for a fight.

"Your Regiment is back into the fight, but judging from your injuries that won't apply to you three," Captain O'Brian said back to the soldiers.

"No offense, Captain," said Frantzen. "But we're fit enough now to join them."

"I don't doubt your pluck or your resolve, Sergeant...?"

"Frantzen, sir."

"Yes, Sergeant Frantzen," replied Captain O'Brian. "However, what I do question is your readiness as of this moment, as did the transient officer at Governor's Island. It seems you've been temporarily assigned to the Invalid Corps."

"Invalid Corps, Captain?" asked Nyhavn.

"For soldiers who were seriously wounded in combat and not deemed ready to return to their units."

"But we're not invalids, sir!" protested the young Corporal. "We're healed."

If the Captain was upset or annoyed by Nyhavn's outburst his face didn't show it. However, the First Sergeant was an easier read. He was irritated.

"Your strength back enough to do some ditch digging, log cutting or scuffling, is it?" barked Lynch already knowing the answer. "You up to snuff, are you, boyo?"

Their wounds may have healed, but their strength and stamina wasn't back to where it should have been, and they knew it.

"Maybe not yet, but it will be soon enough, First Sergeant," replied Kinnunen in a more conciliatory tone. He knew their role in the little drama that had very few speaking lines for the three new players. His words would take some of the focus off of Nyhavn who didn't seem to understand what was really happening here.

"And so, there's no chance of rejoining your Regiment until you are. Also, I'm told you signed three-year papers?" He said tapping the letter a second time.

"Yes sir," said Kinnunen. "We all did."

"When did you enlist, Corporal?"

"Shortly after President Lincoln called for volunteers, Captain."

"Spring of '61, I believe?"

"Yes sir, April," replied Kinnunen.

"April," echoed the officer. "Which means your three years are up this coming April?"

"Yes sir, they are."

"I assume then that you plan on doing your patriotic duty by re-enlisting?"

"No sir," said Kinnunen, matter of fact. "I've been in most of the tough battles since Bull Run. When my time's up, sir, I intend to go home."

"And you?" the officer said turning his attention to the big German.

"The same, Captain. I'm about done with the fighting unless the bastards march on New Tonder."

"Where?"

"New Tonder, Minnesota."

"Home, Captain," said Nyhavn finding better control over his mouth.

"And you too, I suppose?" O'Brian asked the young looking Corporal.

"Yes sir. We all joined up together."

The Captain grunted and drummed his fingers on the desk studying the three Minnesotans intently. He seemed to be making up his mind about something, and the slap on the desk that followed confirmed his decision.

"Then it looks like you'll be assigned here until you are discharged," he said. "The facts are these: I am short-handed and it would appear that the Army sent you here to temporarily help ease my dilemma."

"But sir...," interrupted Nyhavn only to have the Captain raise his hand, cutting off the protest.

"The officials at Governor's Island will inform the War Department who, in turn, will inform your Regiment. You'll be quartered here with good cots and good food. First Sergeant Lynch here will show you to your quarters and assign you your duties."

The officer rose from his chair, straightened his tunic with his stubby fingers. "With that said, let me welcome you to my command. Perform your duties like I know you will, and you will leave New York City the better for the experience. Good day, gentlemen," he said and they were dismissed.

"Come to attention, you country oafs!" barked the First Sergeant.

The three soldiers brought their feet together at the position of attention. Staring straight ahead they brought their hands down along the seams of their trousers until the First Sergeant came around the desk and ushered them out of the Captain's office.

"Outside," he said. "Go!"

First out the door, Nyhavn abruptly stopped and smiled at a young woman seated on the bench in the Orderly Room.

She wore a much faded brown dress and her shoes had seen better days. Tall and slender, she had brilliant green eyes, red hair, and a creamy complexion that brought a smile to the young Corporal's face. The smile though wasn't returned.

The young woman glared at him and then quickly lowered her gaze when the First Sergeant came through the doorway and moved the young soldier along.

"Move it!" he said ordering Nyhavn from behind with a shove to his back. Then noticing what had slowed the soldier down the First Sergeant turned his attention to her.

"You here for the housekeeping interview?"

The woman lowered her eyes and nodded.

"The Captain will see you shortly," said the First Sergeant. Back to the three Minnesotans he added, "Give me your attention here."

"But I need to speak with the Captain now if I could about these appointments," said the woman earning a snarl from Lynch.

"I said the Captain will see you shortly, missy. Have I made myself clear?"

"Yes," she said.

"So don't be interrupting me again."

The cowed woman nodded and retook her seat.

"I'll need your full names and unit designation," he said to the Minnesotans. "If you bumpkins can't write, then Corporal Dumshee, my Company Clerk here will put pen to paper for you."

"We can write," Kinnunen said, taking the pen and writing down the information the First Sergeant had requested.

"Judging by the little decoration on your uniforms I take it you are all from the same cabbage eating Regiment?" said Lynch pointing to the Second Corps trefoil club pins on their uniforms.

"Clubs are trumps, First Sergeant," said Nyhavn while Lynch stared at him blankly.

"And what in the hell is that supposed to mean?" he asked.

"It's the two Corps motto."

"Don't mean much here. Take them off," ordered the First Sergeant.

"But...," said Nyhavn, thinking he still had a say in the matter.

"But nothing, boyo! You deaf or just slow?" barked Lynch. "I said, take them off. You're part of this unit now."

The First Sergeant opened his top left drawer, pulled out three small, circular green felt patches, the same as the guard at the front entrance had pinned to his uniform collar, and tossed them across the desk. "Pin these to your collars, so you won't be confused for deserters," he said. The Minnesotans reluctantly removed the three cornered pins and stuffed them in their pockets.

"The green will identify you as my people, heathen little *shites* that you are. Corporal Dumshee?" yelled the senior Non Commissioned Officer back to the clerk.

"Yes, First Sergeant?"

"Get Drake back in here now."

"Yes, First Sergeant!" said the Corporal going out into the hall, yelling for the Sergeant who had delivered them to the Orderly Room. The shout echoed and reverberated off of the tiled floor and bare walls. Skinny as he was, the clerk could shout.

As they waited, Lynch laid out his expectations to the three new arrivals. "Here's how it is, so listen up," he said. "First, no more of that snotty back talk like you did in the Captain's office. Second; you do what you're told when you're told. Go against me and I'll bust your fookin' heads myself! You hear me?"

Both Frantzen and Kinnunen said that they did while Lynch caught Nyhavn smiling at the girl on the bench. With a surprisingly deft move, he reached over the desk and slapped him across the face. The open hand slap cracked like a shot from a rifle.

"Pay attention when I'm talking to you!" yelled Lynch. The slap surprised the Minnesotans, and rattled the young woman.

Meant to humiliate, the strike left a red mark on the right side of Nyhavn's face. His muscles trembled in anger. The young Dane wanted to drag the skinny scarecrow across the desk and bounce him off of the walls. Smarting as he was, he had the presence of mind to know his place, even if he didn't like it.

"That goes for the rest of you fookin' heathens as well. You hear me?" Lynch said to the others.

"You wanted to see me, First Sergeant?" Sergeant Drake said, coming through the doorway with the dull eyed clerk.

Lynch held up one finger motioning for the New York Sergeant to hold on a moment as he settled his focus on Nyhavn. "I said, DO YOU HEAR ME?"

"Yes, First Sergeant," Nyhavn said, finally.

"Good," said Lynch and then noticing Drake's impatience spoke to the New York Sergeant.

"Got better things to do, do you, Sergeant Drake?"

"Apparently not, First Sergeant, because I'm here."

"Well then, do something useful, goddamn it. See to these new men. They're pressed into your crew, at least until spring."

Back to the Minnesotans he said, "Sergeant Drake will be in charge of you while you're here. He's your squad sergeant. Corporal Dumshee is in charge of the company after duty hours. I don't give a rat's ass about what rank you heathens hold with the Volunteers or why you think you should be in charge, if you do. You will report to Sergeant Drake who, in turn, reports to me. Is that understood?"

The three Minnesotans nodded again.

"What bay will we put them in?"

"No bay," said the First Sergeant, "the canvas."

Drake balked. "The canvas?"

"That's right. They probably have lice. I don't want them spreading their infestations in my building. Besides, they won't be here long enough to need to get comfortable. Have them be ready for their assigned tasks after morning formation."

"Yes, First Sergeant."

"Oh, and one more thing…," added Lynch. "Put them on the burn."

"The burn?" said Drake, wondering what more he was going to pile on the new arrivals.

"You heard me. It's their job now," he said. "Have Private Miller show them how it's done. See to it."

"Yes, First Sergeant," said Drake. "Anything more?"

"If there is, I'll damn well let you know. Now get the fook out of here."

Chapter 11

The New York Sergeant led them down the stairs, through a long corridor, and out the back of the building. The back entrance opened up to a hard packed dirt courtyard that stretched to the high wooden fence with an open gate that showed a rutted alley beyond. A three story chipped brick warehouse across the alley stood over the yard like a rust colored cliff.

A bored looking soldier stood guard at the back gate. He was of modest height, wore his forage cap at a jaunty angle, and like Drake had the look of a scrapper.

"Anything new to report, Private Miller?" Drake asked the soldier.

"I can report that there is a drunk passed out at the end of the alley and that a delivery wagon went by about half an hour ago on the way to the slaughter house, and, if you'll notice, the proud and overworked equines pulling the wagon left a goodly amount of horse shite very near where I'm standing, which could very well be quiet commentary on this punishment detail, if that's what you mean, Sergeant," replied the guard.

It is not," said Drake, amused. "But if you like, Finn I'll pass that along to the First Sergeant to get his opinion on the matter."

"No, don't trouble yourself or him. I know he's a busy man, what with him being a bastardly son of a bitch and all."

"You know, if you hadn't smarted off to him you wouldn't be on his *shite* list."

"What? And miss an opportunity at one of life's precious little lessons?" said the Private taking in the new arrivals over Drake's shoulder. "Who do we have here now?"

"New replacements."

"They don't exactly look new."

"New to us," said the New York Sergeant. "They'll be quartered under the canvas."

"So I take it they must have irritated our fine First Sergeant too?"

"Just enough to have them assigned to the tents and the burn."

"The burn too!" said Miller. "Ah, fookin' brilliant!"

"Gentlemen, the Private here is Finn Miller, one of my wayward crew who managed to piss on the First Sergeant's shoes with what he thought was one of his clever witticisms. Say hello Finn before Lynch catches us blathering."

"Very pleased to meet you, you poor, unfortunate bastards," said Miller turning back to his guard post.

"Introduce them to the Sibley and give them instruction on the burn," said Drake.

Private Miller smiled again. "I'm being promoted, am I?" he said.

"Not likely. Lynch has me off to find some of our boys and the company coal wagon," said Sergeant Drake heading back towards the building as Miller took over his new assignment.

"In that case, gentlemen," he said leading the way, "follow me for the grand tour." Slinging his musket over his shoulder, he steered them around the yard.

The interior of the courtyard consisted of the company formation area, a large and seemingly neglected Sibley tent, an open coal bin and chute that led into the building's basement, and a large outhouse set back against the fence.

"We'll start with the glory holes," said Miller walking them around to the back of the clapboard crapper where he pointed to a hinged hatch panel. The panel was held in place by two wooden blocks that swiveled.

"To open it, you turn these blocks, lift the panel and use the piece of rope like this to hold it in place," he said, demonstrating. "As you can see there are four steel tubs beneath the latrine's four holes. See the paddles there?"

"Paddles?"

"Aye," replied the private pointing to several three foot long two-by-fours that were charred and stained on one end.

It was Trigg Kinnunen who voiced what the new arrivals were thinking. "What about the paddles?"

"Each morning you will remove the steel tubs from their holding place and drag them there," he said pointing to an open patch of ground near the coal bin. "Then, mixing in copious amounts of coal oil and using the two-by-four paddle, you will give the filth and coal oil mix a good stir. Once done you will ignite the mix, occasionally stirring the contents of the tubs, until the *shite* is burnt away and you feel like you've lost all your sense of taste, and smell, and hope for a meaningful future. It should take you no longer than an hour to complete the task."

"You want us to burn *shite*?" Kinnunen said, trying on Miller's pronunciation that produced a smirk from the Irishman.

"Apparently the First Sergeant does," said Miller. "And may I suggest you get it done before breakfast, if you wish to keep anything down."

"There's a thought," laughed Kinnunen while the Irish Private laughed along with him.

"And may I also suggest you stand upwind?"

"Good suggestion."

"The coal oil is kept in a drum in the cellar through those double doors next to the coal bin." Miller pointed out the doors. "There is a bucket next to the drum for the oil. Any questions?"

"Sure," said Nyhavn, "how do we get back to our Regiment?"

Miller snorted. "It isn't going to happen, boyo," he said. "And I don't suggest you consider trying to run off to find them either. If you do you'll be arrested for desertion..."

"And what? Get put on punishment detail burning shite?"

The New York private shrugged. "Or tossed in the Tombs," he said.

"The Tombs?"

"The Hall of Justice and House of Detention, a horrible place. Any time spent there will be added to your enlistments. By the way, how much time do you have left?"

"Seven months."

"Then do the seven months and go home," Miller said. "Now let's show you your lovely accommodations."

The accommodations, their new army quarters, would be the large, cone-shaped Sibley tent; the twelve-by-eighteen foot military teepee like structure with its square wooden base, topped with heavy canvas.

The walk-in tent was staked to the ground and was well weathered. Sections of the once off white canvas were now yellow or dust stained. Several pegs had pulled away from the ground and lazily flapped in the slight breeze. A lone pigeon sat atop a stove pipe at the top of the tent beneath a dried patch of bird droppings. The tent obviously hadn't been used in awhile.

Miller untied the straps to the doorway flap and pulled back the canvas opening. A wave of stale air and mold rose out to greet them.

"It's not much, but it has all the basics," he said as three heads craned to get a better look at the inside of their new home. "You'll draw blankets from the Supply Room in the basement next to the Arms room. I suggest you buy pillows, towels, and quilts as soon as you're able. Crown's store down the street has them and anything else you'll need."

"It'll do," said Kinnunen as they took in the lay out. A tripod with a mechanical crank held the center pole in place and served as the tent's support. Beneath the tripod rested a sheet iron conical shaped stove over a brick base.

Four wood and canvas cots were comfortably spaced out around the musty interior. Two large scratched and nicked chests of drawers were arranged back to back. A marble topped wash stand next to the chests held a chipped ceramic water pitcher and bowl. A tattered terry cloth towel hung off the side of the wash stand.

A serviceable wicker chair and open bench seat gave it more comfort than they had seen in a good while, musty or not. Several magazines and dime novels were scattered across the cots and on the warped wood planked floor. Nyhavn picked up one of the illustrated magazines that showed Kit Carson on the cover. In the illustration, Carson was holding a handgun in one hand and a knife in the other as he rescued a nearly ravaged woman from a handful of attacking savages. Other covers showed a Pony Express rider fleeing a band of Indians, and Texas Rangers in dramatic shoot-outs.

"Some use the Beadle's Dime Novels or other books to light the stove. The Frank Leslie's are for the crapper."

"Frank Leslies?"

"The Illustrated magazines," Miller said picking up one of the discarded publications. "Suppose you could even read 'em, if you're so inclined. Sorry about the accommodations."

"We've slept in worse," said Nyhavn.

"Maybe, but it can get cold here come the snow."

"We're used to that too," Nyhavn said, shrugging it off. The prolonged sub-zero winters that blew down from Canada into Minnesota made the two East Coast winters they had already endured seem mild by comparison.

"Appreciate the stove though," said Frantzen opening and inspecting its cast iron belly. Light glistened off of an elaborate spider web inside. "You say there's coal?"

"Aye, at the bin. There's some kindling too."

Frantzen nodded, stood and inspected the stove pipe. When he banged on its base an old bird's nest slid down to the stove's belly. A second hit dislodged the rest of the trapped debris creating instant kindling.

"Then, it should do just fine," replied Kinnunen testing the stretched canvas on a cot with his right hand before putting his full weight on it.

Frantzen stepped out of the tent and returned a few moments later carrying a handful of coal and wood scraps.

"Hand me one of those," the big German said as he placed the coal in the stove and tilted his head towards one of the discarded weeklies. Ben held onto the copy featuring Kit Carson and leaned over and picked up another, and handed it to Frantzen instead.

The big German tore out a few pages, balled them up in his fist, and then strategically stuck the loose wad of paper into the stove. Using the bird's nest as kindling, he lit a match and dabbed the match to the paper.

"Hand me another one of those magazines," he said as the smoke turned to flame. Nyhavn, who was still leafing through the pages of the magazine he had picked up earlier, reached down and handed Frantzen another of the discarded magazines with a less than interest grabbing cover. A poor reader, Nyhavn tended to like the stories with the dramatic action illustrations best.

"There we go!" said Frantzen as the fire took. Satisfied, the big German closed the stove's latch. With winter drawing near the stove would be their only source of heat. For now, in the late afternoon with a chill in the air, it offered a promise of comfort.

"Besides our morning shite cooking requirements what exactly are our other assigned tasks?" asked Kinnunen as the three began to settle in.

"Rounding up bounty jumpers and enforcing the Enrollment Act of Conscription," replied Miller, matter of fact.

Nyhavn looked up from the magazine with a questioning look. "Enforcing the what?" he asked.

"Conscription, the Draft," said the Private. "The riots are over but not the fallout from the lottery draft. When the names of those between the ages of twenty to thirty five were drawn and called up for service, they were required to show up for induction into the army at the enrollment office. The names of those who don't show on the lower East side are passed along to us. Our job is to go out and round up them up."

"That's it?" asked Kinnunen, seemingly pleased with the assignment.

"Or to collect the exemption fee from those who wish to avoid service, usually from swanky uptown addresses."

"Exemption fee? What? They can buy their way out?" said Nyhavn, outraged at the notion that someone could buy their way out of serving in uniform. He'd heard something of the practice but never paid that much attention to the talk since he never knew anyone who could actually afford it.

"Aye, for $300," said Miller. "Those that can pay are released from the obligation while those that can't pay are gathered up to serve. Some of them won't exactly be willing to come along with us. Seeing how you made it this far through the war I take it you can shoot reasonably well?"

"Reasonably," said Frantzen.

"You've seen combat, I take it?"

"A little since Bull Run."

"Antietam," added Kinnunen. "And Fredericksburg."

"And then Gettysburg before we got here," said Frantzen.

"Gettysburg too?" said the New York Private reassessing the soldiers. "The newspapers said you went up against five to one odds at Gettysburg."

Kinnunen shrugged. "Three to one's more like it."

"Charged into them and stopped them too," added Nyhavn.

"Seemed like the thing to do at the time," Kinnunen said. "Not much choice in the matter since they were coming at us anyway."

"Good enough, because we need reliable men who won't cower when we run up against some tough customers; some gangs who won't be happy that we're taking from their ranks."

"Gangs?"

"Aye, groups of organized thugs. The Draft thinned them some, but not as much as the rioting did. Lots of old scores between rival gangs were settled, while some opportunists carved out some new territory."

"It get bad during the riots?" said Kinnunen.

Miller nodded. "A thousand or so died, thousand more injured," he said. "Artillery was brought in and the cannon rounds persuaded the rioters to scatter."

"Artillery?" said Frantzen. He hadn't heard about the cannons. None of them had.

"Aye, the big guns cleared the streets."

"Must have been some powerful gangs?"

"Five Points and the Bowery used to be rife with them until most of the big gang bosses figured they could steal more in politics than they could with guns. Many became somewhat legitimate…"

"Somewhat, huh?" chuckled Kinnunen, liking the description.

"We're talking Tammany Hall politics here, so these days the real thieves wear fine cloth suits and silk top hats," Miller added. "Oh, and nobody openly uses the word 'gangs' anymore. Now it's all Fraternal or Benevolent Associations this or Friendship Societies that. But make no mistake; they'll slip back to the gutter fighting given the slightest provocation or opportunity, which is why tomorrow you'll be issued pistols…"

"Pistols? Not rifles?"

"Not enough room in tenement hall ways, stairwells, and alleys, which is why you'll be needing a good pocket-Shillelagh too," said Miller.

"A what?" Nyhavn asked.

"You know, a small head knocker, slung shot saps?" said Miller, and when he still saw the confusion in the young soldier's eyes he went on, "Spring-mounted lead bars wrapped in leather with a thong that goes over the wrist. They're good little head thumpers that fit nicely in your pockets."

"Blackjacks, you mean?"

"Aye, that's what I said, pocket-Shillelaghs."

"And we'll need them to do the job, will we?"

"Occasionally, you will. Some of the conscripts may need a little persuading and, depending upon where we're sent to find them, or how many friends and associates they have waiting to argue the point with us. The blackjacks you'll find will come in handy, especially in areas like Mulberry Bend or Thieves Alley," said the Private.

"Thieves Alley?" said an amused Kinnunen.

"Aye and there's a Murderer's Alley too. Uptown there's even a Hell's Kitchen."

"Hell's Kitchen? Now there's a pleasant sounding part of the city," Kinnunen said with a wry smile.

"It's a real Mick shantytown up around 34th that runs to the Hudson. You'll need more than blackjacks if we go there. Our work is mostly here in the Sixth Ward, but we work the Fourth Ward too, and go where we're ordered. After we get you your pistols issued we'll go down by the river and see how well you can shoot."

"And will these blackjacks be issued in the Arms Room?" said Kinnunen.

"No," said Miller. "Those you'll need to buy yourselves. I'll show you where."

"There's a store for head-bashers, is there?" laughed Nyhavn.

"In Five Points you can always find someone selling a little of everything at a price."

"Are we the only ones living in tents?" asked Frantzen staring up from the stove. The question was blunt, and so was the response.

"Yes, seems the First Sergeant views you as temporary help."

"Heathen, temporary help."

"You're Protestant, I take it?"

"Lutheran," replied Kinnunen.

"Ah, the chief Pro-testants! Lynch doesn't like Protestants. But then he doesn't like Jews, the Coloreds, Germans, Italians, Bohemians, anyone English, or all that many Catholics either, so you're in good company."

Kinnunen asked, "What about Sergeant Drake?"

"It's safe to say he prefers not to like people one at a time. Prove yourselves to Donnie Drake and he won't give a *shite* who or what you are."

Seemingly satisfied with the answer Trigg Kinnunen asked a more immediate question. "So where do we eat?"

"There's a small dining hall on the first floor. There's a mandatory five dollar a month charge that you pay to the First Sergeant…"

"Five dollars!" said Nyhavn, shocked at the amount. Five dollars was nearly a third of their monthly pay.

"Yeah, but it is well worth it. You'll see. We have an old woman, Mrs. McFeely, who's a keen cook."

"Keen, huh? That mean *good*, does it? For five dollars a month she better be."

"Tasty food and good portions too."

"I thought the Army paid for our rations?" said Kinnunen as Private Miller shrugged.

"They do, but here you'll need to get used to a new way of thinking," he said. "Breakfast is at seven o'clock. Dinner, if we're here, is at noon, and the evening meal is served from six to seven. Miss any of those designated hours and you'll be charged for the food anyway."

"And where do we drink? The Top Sergeant has a saloon, does he?"

Miller smiled. "Funny enough, he does allow us only one place to frequent. It's *The Thistle Down,* one block down on Orange Street owned and operated by one of the First Sergeant's business associates."

"Of course, it is" said Kinnunen.

"It's how it is," agreed Miller. "There's a mandatory one dollar a month charge for the beer kitty, and for that you get a growler of beer a night. Anything else is extra."

"What's a growler?"

"A good size mug that holds a couple of pints," said Miller. "The Captain tosses in a dollar a month for every reluctant draftee we bring in, but that won't apply to you until you actually prove yourselves. No offense meant.

"Oh, none taken," said Kinnunen, with more than a little sarcasm.

"This may be no Gettysburg but Five Points is a troubled place. Sergeant Drake has been stabbed twice, I've been banged with a club or pipe a time or two, shot at and missed, and even had part of my left ear here cut away with a broken bottle," Miller said pulling back his hair and revealing a nasty, purple welt.

"We're down to a six man crew, counting Drake. Two are in the hospital and won't be walking out anytime soon. Busted up badly the day before yesterday, they were. The First Sergeant put another in the hospital himself…"

"He put one of his own men in the hospital?"

"And on sticks afterwards, crutches. He busted the man's knees with an iron bar something terrible," said Miller. "In case you haven't noticed the First Sergeant is a belligerent sort on a good day. There are some men who like to leave their mark and others like Lynch who prefer to leave scars. You don't want to get on the wrong side of him."

"Ben here knows a little about that," said Kinnunen.

"How so?"

"He slapped him for no real reason, other than he could."

"That's right, because he could," Miller said. "Lynch more than likely wanted to demonstrate a point."

"That what? He's a son of a bitch who hides behind his rank?" said an angry Frantzen.

"Exactly," replied the New York Private. "Best to keep out of his way so that the rat bastard leaves you be."

"Rat bastard a popular saying here, is it?" Nyhavn asked peering up and over the open magazine.

"Uh-huh, why? You never heard it before?"

"No, I heard it," Nyhavn said. "Just wondering is all."

"You say there are six men working on your crew?" Kinnunen asked having a few questions of his own.

"That's right, and with you three that will put us up to nine, almost a full squad. Besides Sergeant Drake and myself there is Kevin McKay, Brian Roacher, Joe Dean, and David Kirk. Roacher, Kirk and Dean are out bringing in a load of coal. I'm not certain where McKay is."

"Mopping out the hall near the front entrance or was when we came in earlier," said Kinnunen as Miller nodded.

"What about the others?" Nyhavn asked.

"The others?"

"Uh-huh, the ones who eyed us from their windows upstairs when we were outside in the courtyard. They part of another street crew?"

Private Miller frowned. "Oh no, not them," he said, disgustedly. "Them little privileged sons of influence are our company toadies; clerks, front door guards, and message runners, mostly."

"How big is the Company?"

"Thirty seven total, not counting you three."

"And only one working crew?" said Kinnunen, more than a little surprised.

Miller snorted again. "Can't really have them do the *shite* jobs, now can we?"

"Like you and the rest of Drake's crew?" asked Nyhavn.

"Aye," said Miller. "We round up the conscripts and they escort them over to Governor's Island. We shovel coal, stoke the boiler, mop the floors…"

"Do the burn," added Kinnunen.

"It's how it is," dismissed Miller. "So where are you boys from?"

"New Tonder, Minnesota," said Frantzen.

"New what?"

"Tonder."

"Ah, New Tonder. I thought you said *thunder*."

"No, it's Tonder."

"And where would that be, exactly?"

"Just south of New Ulm and southwest of Sleepy Eye."

"Sleepy Eye?" said Miller failing to suppress a smirk. "Is that a real town or a visual ailment?"

"Sleepy Eye, Minnesota is a real town. It's just down the way from New Ulm."

Miller nodded but he had no idea where it was. All he knew was that Minnesota was far west of New York and rumored to be on the edge of the wilderness. "I hear it's really cold there, your Minnesota. I wasn't aware it had sleep problems?"

"It's not so bad once it warms up to freezing," said Kinnunen causing Miller to laugh again.

"You mentioned a saloon?"

"I did, *The Thistle Down*. It's a good German/Irish saloon..."

"German/Irish?" asked Kinnunen. "What's that mean?"

"An Irish style saloon doesn't have any tables or chairs, just a long bar and plenty of room to get drunk, dance, and brawl. The German/Irish just means there are tables and chairs to fight with. Of course, *The Thistle Down* does offer a bit of social entertainment with a right fine parlor house upstairs."

"Right and fine sounds appealing."

"Good slap and tickle," said Miller with a decided grin. "Just don't try slipping away without paying for the ladies' company."

"Someone tried sneaking off, did they?" said Kinnunen.

"One of the privileged boys upstairs," he said with a slow shake of his head. "He got caught by the saloon keeper; a mean, spiteful bastard named Hellman, who bit off part of his ear in the scuffle."

"Bit off his ear?"

"Aye, and tossed the little trophy and a few others in a pickle jar on the bar counter to serve as a reminder and lesson to other patrons. Gave the cheap Lothario a good beating too before he turned him over to the police who then gave him another thumping."

"The police?"

"Aye, they're paid to bring the violators back to the First Sergeant but the fool got mouthy with them. Caused a real Donnybrook, I can tell you. His father has some pull with Tammany Hall and didn't like the fact that Junior lost his ear and then took a beating. Anyway, after that the First Sergeant made the slap and tickle at *The Thistle Down* off limits to everyone but our crew. Lynch requires the sons of influence to frequent *The Irish Rose*, a slightly more upscale brothel closer to Broadway. Of course, it's off limits to riff-raff like us."

"So, the street crew is the black sheep of this family then?"

"Aye, the dark wool indeed, which is why we're left to *The Thistle Down*."

"Let me guess, both places though are owned by business associates of the First Sergeant?" said Frantzen.

"As I said, it's how it is. Oh, and speaking of ears," said Miller addressing them all. "If you don't want anything you say getting back to the First Sergeant then I suggest you keep your mouths shut around Dumbshite…"

"*Dumbshite*?"

"Dunshee, the Orderly room Corporal, he's the First Sergeant's ear."

"His ear?"

"Aye, anything you say to him or that he overhears gets right back to Lynch. Take that as a word of caution."

"Dumshee one of the sons of influence too?"

"It so happens that his father owns *The Irish Rose.*"

"It's how it is, right?" said Kinnunen.

"Aye, and now you begin to understand," Miller said, getting to his feet. "Get your things settled and I'll come back later and show you where we eat."

Finn Miller liked these new men. There didn't seem to be anything snooty or high handed about them. Although they'd proved themselves in combat, they'd now need to prove themselves in this broken part of the city that produced its own share of bloody casualties in some of life's seedier battles.

They would soon be tested.

Chapter 12

"Fall out!" yelled the company clerk sticking his head through the flap of their tent. "Fall out for formation!"

"Why? What's going on?" asked Frantzen without getting an answer as Dumshee's head disappeared from the tent flap just as quickly as it had appeared.

Outside, the soldiers in the Company were lining up in formation by the coal bin. With Sergeant Drake nowhere to be found, the three Minnesotans found Private Miller and fell in beside him. Two rows back they peered over the shoulders of the soldiers in front of them trying to see what was going on. At the end of the row Nyhavn leaned out for an unobstructed view.

"This isn't good," Miller whispered to the others.

"What?" asked Kinnunen only to have Miller shush him. The First Sergeant was leading the Private who had been mopping the front hall out of the building by the shirt collar.

Lynch shoved the soldier towards the coal bin's closed double doors where Dumshee, the Company clerk, was running one end of a rope through one of two iron rings that supported a protective awning.

"YOU!" bellowed the First Sergeant to Nyhavn. "Give Corporal Dumshee a hand!"

When Nyhavn hesitated Lynch shouted out the command a second time. "Move it, boy!"

Falling out of formation, Ben hurried over to the coal bin where the dull eyed Corporal handed him a second section of rope.

"Slip it through the iron ring," said the Company clerk. "And then tie it around his thumb."

To the man being punished Ben said, "Sorry."

"Ain't your fault that I might've called the First Sergeant a miserable fookin' bastard under my breath after he spit on my clean floor," replied Kevin McKay.

"You did," said the clerk. "I heard you!"

"True enough," replied McKay. "But I don't know how the First Sergeant could've heard me, what with him walking almost into his office and all? His hearing that keen is it, Corporal Dumshee?"

The Company clerk suddenly found new interest in the knot he was tying, avoiding McKay's stare. "You're a real piece of work, Dumshee," said McKay.

"Tie it tight!" the Company clerk said to the new guy, and just as Dumshee had done, Nyhavn tied the knot securely around the thumb with the remainder looped at the wrist. The pressure would be on the knotted thumbs while the loop around the wrist would keep the rope from slipping and hold the soldier painfully in place.

"Ready, First Sergeant," Dumshee said checking the ropes and knots.

"Do it," said Lynch and the two soldiers began pulling on the two ends of the rope through the iron rungs until McKay was up on his toes and wincing in pain, which seemed to satisfy the First Sergeant.

"Tie it off!" ordered Lynch as the two soldiers tied off the ropes, leaving McKay nearly suspended.

"Get back in line!" yelled the First Sergeant as Nyhavn returned to the company formation while the Company clerk took up his lap dog place at Lynch's side.

Lynch knew that Private McKay wasn't in real pain yet, but he soon would be. Sooner than later the balls of his feet and his toes would no longer be able to support his weight and he would have to go back down on his heels. Then the weight of his body would tug on the ropes until his thumbs would dislocate, or if he fought it, they would break.

During his time in the army Nyhavn had seen soldiers 'bucked and gagged'- hog tied and left outside on display for whatever transgression a soldier had committed. He had seen insubordinate soldiers or shirkers tied to spare wagon wheels or made to carry logs all day with signs announcing their transgressions as camp punishment, but this thumb tying business was something new to him.

"Hear me and hear me good!" yelled the First Sergeant in a rage as he paced before the assembled audience. "I will not tolerate insolence or insubordination."

McKay had arched his back against the wall trying to take some of the pressure off of the balls of his feet. For the moment it was enough but his leg muscles were straining under his own weight. Eventually, Lynch knew, they would buckle and the smart mouth son of a bitch would learn his lesson.

"Private McKay will learn to hold his tongue and he'll set the example for any other of you who have any notions about back talk or pissy remarks! Take a good look at this sorry piece of *shite* and mark my words."

The lesson was not lost on the Minnesotans or any of the soldiers in the Provost Company. Most seemed relieved that it wasn't happening to them. For a moment, the social separation between the street crew and the privileged soldiers was briefly bridged.

Grimacing from the pain the punished soldier's body began to tremble and slowly slip down towards the inevitable. Smiling, the First Sergeant seemed to take perverse pleasure in watching it happen. Nyhavn caught Captain O'Brian standing at a window on the second floor overlooking the courtyard witnessing the punishment. O'Brian gestured to the First Sergeant acknowledging that the spectacle was over. The emperor had given his nod.

"Company dismissed!" yelled Lynch ending the spectacle. Private Miller and the Minnesotans remained where they stood; something not lost on Lynch. "Private Miller?"

"First Sergeant?"

"You are now in charge of the punishment detail."

"First Sergeant?"

"You will not render any aid or assistance of any kind whatsoever to Private McKay. You are not to go near him, or let anyone else go near him, until I tell you otherwise. Is that understood?"

"Yes, First Sergeant," said Miller, reluctantly. With no choice or say in the matter, all he could do was follow orders.

"You damn well make certain of it. If I find out otherwise then you'll take his place. You hear me, Miller?"

"Aye, First Sergeant."

Lynch said something more under his breath to Dumshee before disappearing back inside the building. Standing at the back entrance, the Company clerk kept watch on McKay, Miller, and the Minnesotans.

"Shouldn't we do something?" Kinnunen said to MIller, who shook his head in frustration.

"Not much we can do until we're allowed to take him down," he said.

"When will that be?" asked Kinnunen.

"Hopefully for Kevin as soon as Sergeant Drake gets back from uptown and learns of it."

"Drake will cut him down, will he?" asked Frantzen.

"No," replied an exasperated Miller blowing air through his teeth. "But he'll convince the First Sergeant that we need him for tomorrow's crew work, and Lynch, knowing the work still needs to get done, will allow him to be taken down."

"So, until then?"

"We wait."

"That's it? Just wait and do nothing?"

"It is how it is," said Miller, watching as McKay struggled to get back up on his toes.

The punished soldier's stretched thumbs were painful, but not as painful as they would have been had the newly arrived soldier not shoved a lump of coal beneath the heel of his right boot. The single lump of coal the size of a small fist, would be enough to keep him supported without seriously damaging his thumbs. McKay didn't know the new soldier from Adam, but was glad for his help. And he would remember it.

Dumshee too, he'd keep in mind, and carefully plan a way to deal with later.

Chapter 13

The following morning after completing the *burn*, and after a surprisingly good breakfast of fried eggs and potatoes, fresh bread, and beans cooked in molasses, Sergeant Drake took the Minnesotans down to the Company Arms room where they were issued Starr double-action .44 caliber pistols and pouch holsters.

With ammunition and accompanying percussion caps in hand, Drake then led them out of the building and down to a neglected stretch of waterfront along the East River the company occasionally used for their target practice.

This early in the morning the open river front along Water Street was quiet, save for a working fishing boat out on the water, and the flock of noisy gulls that trailed it. Further down river a line of three-mast, tall ships and sloops lined the waterfront docks telling of good trade and commerce.

Searching the ground, the New York Sergeant found a small piece of driftwood the size of a plate, and tossed it into the water. It hit with a small splash seven yards away and bobbed back to the surface.

"Three shots each should do it," said the Sergeant, figuring it was far enough away to test their basic shooting skills. He checked the load on his pistol, pointed to the floating target, and then held out the firearm to the Minnesotans. "Who's first?"

Frantzen stepped forward saying he'd give it a try. Using a two-hand grip and sighting in on the floating piece of wood, he let out a slow, steady breath and squeezed the trigger. The first round chipped the right side of the small target, while the second and third rounds drilled the wood back down into the murky water. When it resurfaced, a foot or so from where it went under, light brown splinters and puncture holes glistened in the morning sunlight. The target was slowly drifting with the current, but not enough to make it any more difficult for the next shooter.

"Good. Who's next?" Drake said. Nyhavn went next. Following Frantzen's lead he fired and hit the piece of wood twice with one near miss.

"Pulled the last shot," he said.

"Good enough," Drake reloaded the pistol, checked the floating target that had turned in the current, and now moved a foot closer to the shoreline. "Your turn," he said holding out the pistol to Kinnunen.

Trigg studied the target bobbing in the water as though evaluating a complex problem. Straightening his glasses he placed his left hand behind his lower back, stood sideways with his gun hand outstretched as though he was about to fight a duel. He fired his first round, and when the pistol recoiled, he steadied the weapon and fired again. He fired a third round in quick succession with the same, precise method, but the floating piece of wood floated along undisturbed. The rounds hadn't even come close to hitting the bobbing target.

"I take it you're better with a rifle?" said Drake as Kinnunen's two friends guffawed.

"No, he's not," Nyhavn said while Frantzen howled.

"I'm a little better," said a slightly annoyed Kinnunen.

"Not much," laughed Frantzen. "Don't know for certain how many rebels he has shot since we started, but I guarantee he's scared the piss out of a whole bunch of them."

"I saw some fall," said Kinnunen, his feathers ruffled at their cawing.

"True, and fear has been known to make some folks pass out too," added the big German. Quite possibly, they fainted."

"Would you like to try it again?" Drake said offering the Minnesotan another go at the target.

Kinnunen shook his head. "Naw, I shoot better when it counts," he said.

"Let's hope so," replied Drake. "We'll stop at Crown's on the way back for the saps."

At the store they outfitted themselves with saps, pillows, blankets and other provisions before returning to the company. Drake gave them a few minutes to stow their purchases in the Sibley tent before reporting to the back gate.

There, they met up with other members of the street crew. Besides Miller there were three other soldiers eying the new arrivals.

"Finn, make the introductions while I retrieve the pick-up list," Sergeant Drake said as Miller nodded.

"Visiting heathens," said Miller turning to the Minnesotans to introduce them to the New York soldiers. "This is most of the crew; Privates Joseph Dean, David Kirk and Brian Roacher."

Dean was as tall as Miller, but wore a drooping mustache over a casual smile. He was the first to extend a hand. "Good to have you with us," he said.

"David Kirk," said a taller, red haired soldier while the third soldier in the group, Roacher, gave a chin up nod.

Roacher was a head taller than Miller and fifty pounds heavier. He had hunched shoulders over his heavy frame and seemed to have more of a visual interest in what he picked from his nose than he had in the greeting.

"You were in the war, huh?" he said to Kinnunen in place of hello. "Ever kill anybody?"

"Good Christ! That's a stupid fookin' question!" barked Private Miller.

"It's not a stupid question!" Roacher said defensively.

"You're right," Miller admitted, holding up his hands in mock surrender. "There's no such thing as stupid questions, just stupid fookin' people who ask them. Think on it a bit, you bloody wizard. They've just come from Gettysburg, which if you can read at all, the papers will tell you it was a bleeding nightmare of a fight. To add to that, they have just come from the Army Hospital in Philadelphia where they were recovering from their battle wounds...and let me answer your next stupid fookin' question before you ask it...no, you can't see their scars either."

Big as Roacher was, he didn't seem all that interested in taking on the more tenacious Miller, who seemed ready for a scrap. The exchange produced wry smiles from the other New Yorkers. They knew there was no matching wits with Miller, nor was there any denying that Brian Roacher was at times, an idiot. The word *lazy* often came to mind too when describing Roacher, along with a few other well formed observations with the same sentiments. Kirk and Dean both knew Roacher was of little help with the daily chores, spending more time and effort looking for ways to get out of work than he actually did working. If these new men were any kind of help at all, then they'd have more true value than Roacher and would indeed be welcome.

Sergeant Drake came out of the back of the building carrying a small canvas bag, and a list of conscripted soldiers who had failed to show up for induction. The list also included the names of those families that would pay the exemption fees.

"Private McKay won't be joining us today because of his injured thumbs. Seems they're not as bad as they could've been," Drake said momentarily eyeing Nyhavn and leaving it that.

"How many calls, Sergeant?" asked Private Kirk.

"Nine stops in all, some reluctant draftees and some families who will be paying to keep their precious little babies from wearing army blue. The first stop is on Mulberry Bend..."

"Jesus, Mary and carpenter Joseph! Not the Bend again?" cried Private Roacher earning him a scowl from Drake.

"Aye, the Bend, so stay sharp," he said.

"Pistols loaded and capped?" Drake asked as a chorus of 'Aye, Sergeant' came back at him. Drake received the same response when he asked if they had their saps. "Okay lads, then away we go."

The brisk walk took them into one of the poorest parts of The Points where few Police officers patrolled, and then only in twos during the hours of daylight. At night the Bend was on its own. If there was a weeping wound in the city, then Mulberry Bend was the site of its injury. The eight Provost soldiers made their way through filthy streets to find a crowded tenement, the first address on the list. This was no easy thing, since building numbers were scarce, and the few there were had been painted in a variety of hand drawn script.

"Keep sharp," said Drake eying the alleys and rooftops.

"During the Draft Riots some of the fine citizens here stripped and beat any soldier or Peeler they could find," said Miller to the Minnesotans as they walked towards the targeted tenement.

"What's a Peeler?" asked Nyhavn.

"A copper," replied Dean. "A policeman."

"You lose anybody?"

"Aye, Billy O'Keefe was grabbed up by a Mulberry mob," Miller said. "Pummeled him fierce and then set him on fire, they did."

"He die?" Kinnunen said, horrified at the prospect.

"No, but there were times, I suspect, he wished to God he had," replied Sergeant Drake. "So like I said, keep sharp."

"But the riots are over, right?"

"They are, but there are toughs who'll do it for sport. Pirates too, for that matter."

"Pirates?" said Kinnunen, skeptically wondering if the Sergeant was pulling his leg.

"Aye, some oyster fisherman who are not above plundering cargo from ships when they can and who don't like anyone in uniform to come nosing around in their nefarious doings."

"So, are there any good parts to the city?" asked Kinnunen, laughing. "With, I dunno, people who don't want to stab us or say, set us on fire?"

"There are, but few that we'll see this morning."

Because it was still early in the morning Mulberry Street was relatively quiet. Most saloons and whore houses weren't open for business yet so most of the neighborhood toughs were still sleeping off their late night drunks or raucous outings. However, the ice and fish mongers were hawking their goods from their carts and wagons, as were local produce growers with pushcarts piled high with fresh greens and vegetables. The Bend was coming to life, as was its informal early warning system. Shouts preceded the soldiers at every turn with heads craning from open windows trying to get a look at this latest intrusion by the authorities.

With a little doing Drake found the address they were looking for, a two storey tenement sandwiched between a flophouse on the street side of Mulberry and a cheap hotel on the street behind it. The New York sergeant stopped at the entrance to the narrow three foot wide alley they would have to use to get to the tenement.

"Rear tenement, second floor, apartment three," Drake said while the other New Yorkers fidgeted or swore.

"What?" Kinnunen asked Miller.

"Tight going in the tenements," he said, "Thin alleys, little sunlight, and plenty of good places for things to go wrong in a hurry."

"Finn, you and Roacher will stay here, cover the street," said the New York Sergeant laying out his plan. "Kirk, you watch the tenement entrance from the end of the alley. Shout out if there's a problem." To Private Dean and the Minnesotans he said, "Joe, guard the first floors while you three new men will come with me. Right. Let's get this done."

They moved quickly through the alley and into the building, taking the creaking stairs two at a time up to the second floor. Drake left Kinnunen and Frantzen at the top of the stairs while he and Nyhavn made their way down a dimly lit hall searching for apartment three. The hallway smelled of stale sweat, urine and boiled cabbage. In the tight confines of the hallway the fetid odors stung their eyes and noses.

"BRENDAN O'MALLEY!" Sergeant Drake yelled banging on the apartment door. When there was no immediate response, Drake banged again.

"BRENDAN O'MALLEY!"

There was some shuffling behind the door before it was suddenly yanked open by a stout man who filled the doorway. Behind him members of the large family peered out scowling at the soldiers. Pivoting to his left, Drake held the sap low at his side.

"Brendan O'Malley?"

"Who wants to know?" demanded the man in the doorway. In the shadows the man's face was dark, his big frame back lit by the flickering pale yellow glow of an oil lamp inside the crowded room. The small single room housed the O'Malley's, and Drake suspected, a handful of lodgers.

"Office of the Provost Marshal, and who might you be?"

"Timothy O'Malley, the father."

"Your son has been called up to service and didn't report. We've come to fetch him…"

"The Lottery Draft?"

"Aye, please produce the lad."

"It wasn't a fair lottery," said Timothy O'Malley. "So I don't think he'll be going with you."

The New York Sergeant smiled. "And I don't think you should be interfering with the performance of our official duties, so I say again, produce the boy."

At the far end of the hall another door opened and a hard looking man stepped out and just stood there staring at the soldiers. He held a club in his hands and his face was set for violence. Kinnunen squared off with the man with the club.

The sound of creaking stairs behind Frantzen brought his attention around as two more of O'Malley's people started up the stairs behind them. The two abruptly stopped at the sight and size of the big German.

A door squeaked open in the apartment directly across from O'Malley's and a thin bearded face peered out.

"Doesn't concern you," said Drake, back over his shoulder. "Go back inside."

The door closed, but didn't latch, something not lost on Drake or on Nyhavn, who was leaning with his back against the wall to the left of the door.

If Drake was surprised or even bothered by the reception committee, it didn't show.

His concern was for his three new replacements. He wasn't certain if they could handle this kind of work, but figured he would have his answer soon enough. The fight, if it came to that, would be close and fierce in the crowded tenement hallway.

"One last time, produce Brendan O'Malley," Drake said again to the father.

"He's not here," said a lanky lad over O'Malley's shoulder.

"And who are you to say so?" asked the Sergeant turning his full focus on the young man.

"Never mind him," said the older man pushing the youth back into the room and away from the doorway. "The boy's gone, Lord knows where."

Drake nodded. "And maybe you know too, I'm thinking," he said earning a sneer from O'Malley.

"What? You calling me a liar?" O'Malley said leaning forward to within inches of the soldier's face, trying to intimidate Drake.

The Sergeant's smile grew for a moment and then disappeared. "What I'm saying is that maybe if you would clean the bog water out of your filthy fookin' ears you might hear me better. I'm saying too, that I'm betting you that the boy there behind you is your son, Brendan, so what do you say?"

"I'm saying you'll be taking no one today, soldier boy," said the senior O'Malley.

"No problem. Then we'll take $300 in compensation costs to replace him with somebody else's son," replied Drake. "Now, if you will hand it over, we'll give you a proper receipt and be on our way."

"Just as it's always been," said O'Malley bringing up his right hand and jabbing the soldier's chest with a thick index finger. The poke had Drake taking a half step back. "Rich men buy their way out of the fight and leave it to the poor working man."

"Leave before we bloody you!" yelled the man with the club at the end of the hall. Behind Frantzen one of the two men on the stairs echoed the threat. The big German shifted his stance to keep a better eye on the two who seemed energized by their own slurs and curses.

"Look, Mister O'Malley, we're here to do our job," explained Drake, offering the man another way out of the tense situation before it turned worse. "There's a war on and your Brendan has to do his duty like the rest of us." To the boy behind the father he said, "Come with us, Brendan. There's no reason for this to turn ugly today."

"He's not going with you!" said his father. "And take that little head basher with you before I shove it up your *arse*."

"This?" asked the Sergeant holding up the leather encased lead bar sap.

"Aye," said O'Malley poking Drake's chest again with his thick finger.

"And there it is," Drake said, with a sigh. With surprising speed and deftness Drake grabbed the poking finger and bent it up and back, cracking it at the knuckle joint. As the big man screamed and buckled, Drake head butted him. Blood gushed from O'Malley's broken nose and he staggered back against the door frame to gather himself. Drake swung the sap back down hard and heavy against the inside of the man's left thigh and O'Malley slipped to his knees holding his nose.

The sap didn't break any bones, but it hamstrung the leg. It would leave the senior O'Malley sore and limping in pain for a few days afterwards. Behind Drake the unlatched door opened again and Nyhavn caught the glint of something metal in the thin light.

"GUN!" yelled Nyhavn swinging the sap down hard on the gun hand. The loud thump and agonized cry told of the damage done to the thumb and wrist as the dropped pistol skidded across the hallway and bumped up against the wall. The would-be gunman's wrist hung at an unnatural angle. Even so, the man scrambled to retrieve the pistol with his good hand only to receive a second slap this time across the back of his head as Nyhavn snatched up the handgun, pointed it back at the pain-racked ambusher and cocked it.

The would-be gunman cowered.

"No…don't! Don't shoot him!" pleaded a woman coming to the door behind the man realizing that the young soldier was about to squeeze the trigger. The Provost soldier would kill her man. It was in his eyes. She knew the look. In this part of the city, she had seen it far too often.

"Then get him back in there," yelled Nyhavn. "Shut the door and keep it shut!"

With the woman's assistance, the would-be gunman scooted back inside the doorway cradling his broken wrist, and kicked the door closed behind him.

On the stairs, Frantzen dove into the two toughs that were coming up at him. The big man's tackle sent them all sprawling back onto the stairwell landing. First to his feet, the big German went at the two men with a flurry of fists, elbows and boots.

"Rebel sons of bitches!" he yelled slamming his right elbow hard against one man's face, splitting an eyebrow, and sending blood spraying against the wall.

Back upstairs, the man with the club came running and screaming down the hall at Kinnunen. No stranger to enemy assaults, Trigg Kinnunen hit the man low, pushed up at the last instant, and sent the assailant flipping over his shoulder. The man landed hard on his back, let out a pained cry but came back up still swinging the club.

With no bayonets coming at them, or cannons booming, the Minnesotan soldiers took it to their opponents with what Drake would later tell others, was a strange, almost savage glee.

When the senior O'Malley fell, rocked and doubled up in pain, the younger O'Malley charged at Drake crying and swearing. And as he did the New York Sergeant set his stance, and sent a hard, left jab to Brendan O'Malley's throat, instantly stopping the attack. The short quick jab briefly cut off both the yelling and momentarily, the boy's airway. His eyes bulged and he made a gagging, mewing noise as he fell to his knees, clutching his throat.

The father was trying to get to his feet again when Nyhavn motioned him back down with the business end of the retrieved pistol.

"Uh-uh, stay down," he said. The senior O'Malley, knowing he was defeated, did what he was told.

Drake drew his own revolver and held it at his side as he took on the role of an interested spectator. From his vantage point he had a good view of the two remaining close quarter bouts.

On the landing between the floors, the big German kicked one attacker in the stomach, knocking the wind out of him before he sent another brutal kick to his balls, ending his role in the fight. When the second man tried to take him down, Frantzen reached in and balled up a handful of the man's beard with his left hand, and came down hard with his right elbow, giving three vicious blows to his face and head. The attacker was out. When he came to, he would tremble at how easily and effectively the soldier had accomplished the damage. But that would be later.

A loud angry grunt in the hallway brought Drake's attention back to where Kinnunen was still wrestling with his attacker in the hall. When the man tried to punch him, Kinnunen grabbed the man's right arm and yanked around his own neck. Then using every bit of strength he could muster, he pulled on the man's wrist and elbow until the man was choking himself out.

The man's eyes fluttered but he still fought. Trigg pulled harder until the man's eyes began to glaze over and lose their focus, his body went limp and he was out, unconscious. In the days that followed the man with the club might be able to take a full breath of air without his neck hurting when he did. There would be ugly bruising, and it wouldn't fade for a good while. But he would live.

Both Kinnunen and Frantzen sprang back up on their feet, looking around to see who might be coming at them next. They were ready for the next go. But there wasn't any next charge, this battle was over.

Ben couldn't help but notice that as Frantzen and Kinnunen were fighting, Drake seemed to be studying them with more than mild curiosity. The Sergeant could have stepped in at any time to help them, but didn't. And when he moved to help his friends, Drake held him back.

"No, leave 'em be," he said and Nyhavn knew they were being measured and tested.

Reasonably satisfied with the outcome, Drake nodded to Kinnunen before turning back to the senior O'Malley who was dazed and leaning against the doorframe.

"We'll be taking our leave now," said Sergeant Drake reaching down, grabbing Brendan O'Malley by the shirt collar and pulling him up to his feet. "Walk boy and you'll avoid further trouble for you and yours." To the senior O'Malley he said, "He'll be at the transit camp at Governor's Island. You can reach him there."

The sulking and subdued draftee did as he was told and the soldiers cautiously backed out of the hall and down the tenement stairs. "Pistols at the ready," Drake said, taking the lead. More doors cracked open as they went and they were met with a barrage of insults and epithets, but little else.

At the bottom of the stairs they found Private Dean struggling to get to his feet. He was holding his head in his hands. Blood seeped through his fingers from a deep gash over his left ear. A blood trail spilled down his face and neck.

"Can you walk, Joseph?" asked Drake. Private Dean nodded that he could.

"They came up behind me," he said, as they helped him stand. Drake inspected the wound and found a deep two inch tear. "I bloodied one good before the second hit me with a brickbat."

"Give him a hand," Drake said over his shoulder to Frantzen. The big German nodded, slipped his arm under Dean's arm, and easily hefted the smaller man up right.

"Nothing but a scratch," Drake said, dismissing the wound for the soldier's sake. "A few stitches and you'll be good as new."

"Doesn't feel like a scratch," said a glaze-eyed Dean.

"They never do at the time, do they?" To the others he said, "Keep your eyes open and watch the roofs as we go. They sometimes like to send us off with rocks or bottles."

Hurrying out of the tenement and into the alley, they found Miller, Kirk and Roacher on Mulberry Street facing off a small crowd of street toughs that had gathered. The Mulberry thugs were goading the three soldiers. There were a dozen in all and all wore the slicked back hair, long sideburns, checkered frock coats, wide legged pants, and the sturdy hob-nail boots that identified them as Bowery B'hoys, a gang Drake was more than a little familiar with. Fueled with alcohol and belligerence, the toughs claimed their sections of the Sixth Ward one street corner at a time.

Sergeant Drake and the Minnesotans came out of the alley with pistols drawn. As they emerged the startled toughs stepped back to a more strategic position. Three soldiers were one thing; five more brandishing pistols were something else. Injured as he was, Dean had a good grip on his pistol. There was obvious relief on Roacher's face as the others rejoined them while Miller and Kirk just nodded a welcome.

"Bloody English bastards!" yelled one of the gang members.

"Actually lads, we're right fine Irish bastards, thank you," Miller yelled back at the thug, somewhat confusing the gang member.

"Aye and happily bloodied at that," Dean said as they moved.

"Fook the Provos!" yelled one gang member looking to another thug who stepped out in front of the group towards the soldiers to become the spokesman.

"Took a bad beating, did you?" said the tall, bunch-shouldered thug who wore a cocky smile on a pugilist's face. A half smoked cigar that looked more chewed than smoked, hung from the right side of his mouth.

"Just as you will if you don't get out of my fookin' way, you piss dribbler," replied an angry Miller until Drake stepped out in front of him, locking his eyes on the obvious gang leader, taking his measure.

"Any trouble from you or them, any trouble at all, and I'll personally put you on crutches. You hear me, boyo?"

When the mouth for the group of toughs smiled at Drake's threat the New York Sergeant stepped to within kicking distance of him. "The name's Drake, Donnie Drake, but I suppose you already know that, so I can only assume that you're looking to test me."

The thug offered an insincere smile. Drake's reputation was well known in the Points and beyond while the tough was still establishing his own.

"They say you were a hard man back in the day," said the thug, flexing some verbal muscle along with his chest and arms. He shifted the cigar from one side of his mouth to the other. "That was awhile ago, wasn't it?"

"Aye, it was, and I was as tough and dumb as you are now," said Drake, talking a half step back. "But with time comes some wisdom, and you know what else came with it?"

"No, what?" laughed the thug enjoying his role in the street theater.

"The ability to shoot a whole lot better," Drake said, raising his pistol to the gang leader's face with an effortless ease the thug hadn't anticipated or imagined. Drake held the pistol steady and aimed in on the thug's nose. He had cocked the pistol on the way up with his thumb and had his right index finger resting on the trigger. "The army gives me a whole lot of time and ammunition to practice. Care to test me on that either, fella?"

The tough's eyes showed fear that the rest of his face fought to hide. There was no mistaking Drake's meaning or resolve.

"Just asking is all," the tough said slowly raising his hands palm out and backing away.

"Nothing wrong with good social dialogue," replied Drake easing the hammer back down and lowering the pistol. "If you'll excuse us we have to be going."

Two blocks on he told the others to put away their pistols.

"Let's have a look at that little trophy of yours, young Mister Newhaven," Drake said wanting to take a look at the handgun retrieved from the tenement.

"It's Ny-havn, Sergeant," the young Corporal said handing him the weapon. "Nothing new about me since Bull Run, Sergeant."

Drake studied both Nyhavn and the pistol with new interest. "No, I suppose not," he said. The pistol was a Model two, .32 caliber Smith & Wesson, a bullet cartridge hole-puncher big enough to separate a breather from his last breath, and its new young owner didn't seem to have any qualms about using it.

"How old did you say you are?"

"Seventeen…eighteen come April."

"Seventeen?" said Drake, clearly surprised. The soldier had seemed older. "And you've been in the war for nearly three years?"

"That's right, since April of '61."

"Making you, what, fourteen at the time you enlisted?"

"Fourteen and a half…"

If Drake was surprised, then so was Frantzen who stared at the younger soldier dumbstruck. "You mean to tell me you were only fourteen when you joined up?"

"Uh-huh."

"My God, I thought you were sixteen!"

"Yeah, and you told the recruiter that I was eighteen," said Nyhavn.

Frantzen was speechless, but Kinnunen wasn't. "Well, that explains a lot, I suppose," he said.

"What's that supposed to mean?" growled Nyhavn with his hackles up. "I soldiered right along with you, didn't I?"

"That you did, but only because you weren't tall or talented enough to be a drummer boy."

"Tall and talented enough now to thump you like a drum."

"My, how the boy has grown," Kinnunen said to Frantzen who chuckled along with Miller.

"Here you go, Corporal," said Sergeant Drake handing the pistol back to Nyhavn. "Use this to thump this little shite if he tries to run," he said canting his head towards the young O'Malley. "You have my permission to shoot him too, if need be. You have a problem with that, do you?"

"None at all," Nyhavn said, matter of fact.

A shaken Brendan O'Malley shot sidelong glances to the Sergeant and the hard looking soldier. He was sure the Corporal would shoot him if he ran off and that the others would let it happen.

"He shoots well too, so don't test him," added Drake.

"Is it like this all the time?" Kinnunen asked Drake as they moved on to the next name on the list, "The street crew business?"

"No," Drake said, wiping the blood on several scraped knuckles into his open fist and then shaking away the sting. "Sometimes it gets bad."

Chapter 14

It was Private Dean's slurred speech that worried the New York Sergeant, and when the soldier started vomiting, Drake suspected it was more serious than the man was letting on. He was having trouble keeping his balance and staggering like a drunk.

"Take Dean back to Company and get Doctor Steen to look at him," Drake said to Private Miller.

"No need," protested the bloodied Private. "It's just an annoyance, is all. Besides, Lynch won't be happy if we miss the rounds."

"True enough, but I'm not worried about your head," replied the New York Sergeant. "I just can't stand to see you mess up a perfectly good uniform. Go on, Finn. Recruit O'Malley here will give you a hand."

"Why can't I go back with them?" said Private Roacher, irritated that he wouldn't be the one to take Dean back to the company.

"Jesus, did you really just ask me why?" Drake said, letting out a heavy sigh.

Roacher, sensing the Sergeant's annoyance, didn't answer.

"I hope to hell you didn't because then I'd have to fookin' remind you that I'm in charge here and I make the decisions, unless, of course, you're just trying to bust my balls. Is that it Private Roacher? You trying to bust my balls?"

"No, sergeant. I was just offering to help is all," he said but Drake knew better.

"Good, then you and Kirk here will help me and the heathens. We still have more calls to make. We can't leave the new men to do it since they don't really know Five Points now, do they?"

The question didn't require an answer. The three Minnesotans didn't know their way around the city, let alone the lower East Side. They would have to remain with Drake to find their way back to the company.

With the soldiers splitting up, Brendan O'Malley, the reluctant draftee, was considering another option. His darting eye movements in the nearby alley caught Drake's attention so the New York Sergeant confronted him. "Don't even think about running off. You understand me, boy?"

"I...I wasn't thinking of it."

"Good, because Private Miller here is not the shot the young Corporal is. He'll probably just cripple you."

"True enough," said Miller. "I'll aim at your head and probably will shoot your balls off instead."

If there was one deciding factor for O'Malley, then that was it. "I'm not running off," he said, but Drake had known his answer before he offered it.

The remaining eight stops went off without serious incident or casualties. Working their way through the rest of the list the First Sergeant had supplied, there was some more name-calling and verbal attacks against the soldiers' lineage, a high assortment of glares, scowls, and nasty comments, but no more displayed weapons, head butts, kicks, or thrown punches.

Two of the calls gathered up several draftees and came to little or no real trouble. Another call took them to a dismal backstreet Fourth Ward address that was poor even by the Lower Eastside's standards. The housing here was a mix of blighted shacks, shanties, and overcrowded flophouses.

At the sight of the armed soldiers most gawkers disappeared inside doorways, moved along, or stepped aside giving the soldier's a wide berth.

"Here!" said Drake turning down a rutted dirt lane that led into a dismal cul-de-sac of clustered shacks. In what had once been horse stables, there were six separate connected cabins with battered and patched over Dutch double doors. Small windows had been added to a few but there had been few changes to the large stalls that once housed horses.

A goat was tethered to a post in front of one of the scarred doors, while an addled old man was tethered to a second post. The old man was stabbing at something between the spaces in the porch with a stick. The old man took no notice of the soldiers and was enjoying himself immensely.

The closer they got the soldiers could see why. He had dropped food scraps as bait and was poking at a few curious rats beneath the porch. When he would stick one, the rat would squeal and the old man would laugh loud and long enough to let them know that he was addled.

There were no addresses on the doors, so Drake gave a name to a woman in an open doorway, who pointed out the third run-down dwelling from the end. The small window showed little of value through thin and tattered curtains. The New York Sergeant knocked on the door and a young, willowy, woman in a well-worn dark blue dress answered the door. She had raven, dark hair, sky blue eyes and a frown that showed she wasn't pleased with the soldiers' visit.

She stood behind the partially opened door. The frown soon turned to a scowl when she saw the soldiers in the yard staring at her, especially the fat one, whose opened mouth leering couldn't conceal his thoughts. Unfazed by her indignant look, Roacher kept lustily staring at her anyway.

Two of the three Minnesotans were more subtle about it while Nyhavn had lowered his gaze when his attention was drawn to the heel of the woman's left shoe. The heel was split and tacked together with a bent brass tack that glistened in the sunlight.

Drake spoke to the young woman alone on her doorstep in hushed tones while the others watched on and waited. Ben noticed that there was a familiarity between the two, but if there was any friendship, then it was strained.

When the young woman glanced over Drake's shoulder in their direction Frantzen flashed the woman a friendly enough smile, and nod that was returned with a defiant glare. It was the same response Nyhavn had received from the other young woman in the Orderly Room the day before.

"Friendly sort of city they have here," he said dryly to Kinnunen. "I smiled a civil smile at the woman and she snubbed me cold. That's the second one in as many days."

"You ever think that it is possible that the women here have standards, Al?" Kinnunen said.

"You ever think you're an asshole?"

"Frequently," said Kinnunen. "And I'm reasonably certain I can document it too, if you like?"

"I'd be more than happy to swear to it before a judge too, if you need a witness," said Nyhavn which earned him an appreciative nod from Kinnunen.

"It's always good to have supporting documentation,"Trigg said, laughing.

Their attention was soon drawn back to the porch when the woman briskly stepped back inside the small cabin and slammed the door behind her.

"That went well," laughed Kinnunen. Drake rejoined them and kept walking. He had his list out and was reading it over as he made his way back down the rutted lane and out into the busier street. He stopped, swore and then whipped back around.

"I forgot something. Wait here," he said and disappeared back down the thin lane back towards the string of cabins. He was in a sour mood and no one seemed interested in irritating him further.

"Ben, keep an eye out for him," Kinnunen said to Nyhavn. "Watch his back."The young soldier nodded and followed the New York Sergeant but stayed in the shadows of the thin corridor. The darkened vantage point allowed him to keep an eye on Drake while safely covering the doorways, windows and rooftops.

Drake was at the woman's door again talking to someone inside the darkened doorway. Ben couldn't hear everything that was being said but could plainly see that it was getting heated.

"Do it and I'll fookin' kill you myself!" threatened Drake only to have the door slam on him again.

The New York Sergeant stood at the closed door for a long, few moments before he wheeled around and started back towards the street. He stopped when he saw the Minnesota Corporal standing in the shadows.

"I thought I told you to wait on the street," growled Drake.

"You did but someone needed to watch your back," said Nyhavn tilting his head towards the faces in the open windows above him.

Realizing his mistake, the New York Sergeant gave a quick nod.

"Let's go," he said.

Back out on the street Kinnunen and Frantzen were questioning Roacher and Kirk about the stop.

"She looked a little young to be a draftee's mother, wouldn't you say?" asked Frantzen to the two New Yorkers in the crew.

"A wife, actually," replied Private Kirk.

"What then? The drafted husband's not at home?"

"No, he's there."

Frantzen was confused. "So, it's the Conscription fee instead?" he asked. "They don't really look like they can afford it."

"They can't," Kirk said. "It'll be housekeeping work for her."

"Aye, housekeeping," echoed Roacher rolling his eyes.

"She's working off the fee?" asked Kinnunen but before he received an answer Drake and Nyhavn emerged from the rutted route.

"No time to tarry," said the New York Sergeant. "We have more stops to make."

"Ah, and even more chances to appreciate the friendliness of you fine city folk," said Frantzen.

"We soldiers are what we represent," Drake said. "And to some, we're the sons of bitches we seem."

The remaining calls proved to be money stops uptown where they collected the $300 commutation fees from those well-to-do families in posh neighborhoods that spoke elegantly of money; money that they were, at times, reluctant to part with.

"This isn't Five Points, I take it," said Kinnunen in a more upscale part of town. Trees lined clean paved streets in a neighborhood of fine houses, big yards, and carriages.

"No," replied Drake. "The more genteel citizenry here tend to respond more favorably to our calls simply because we are from the Points."

"What? They don't have their own Provost office?" echoed Nyhavn.

"They do, but we've been given the task."

"Nice to be appreciated," Kinnunen said.

"It is how it is," said Drake.

They found the final address on their list; a fine, three storied brownstone with expensive and artistic wrought iron railing leading up to an even more impressive looking heavy oak door. Beveled glass panes spread out in a fan over the door frame. Using a polished brass door knocker, Drake knocked, and waited.

A chestnut-haired, middle aged housekeeper answered the door. "Yes?" she said.

"We're here to see Mister Charles Kenwick," said the New York Sergeant.

"Regarding what, if I may inquire?"

Drake smiled knowing that the housekeeper knew exactly what it was about, but decorum dictated the social subterfuge.

"The exemption fee for young Master Kenwick."

The housekeeper nodded, said 'Just a minute, please,' and closed the door behind her. A few moments later the door was opened again this time by a well-dressed, stately looking man in his mid-forties.

"Yes?" said the man as a woman, possibly his wife, crowded in behind him.

"I take it, sir, that you are the father of Charles Kenwick?"

"I am."

"Splendid," said Drake. "We're here to collect the exemption fee for your son, sir."

"Exemption fee," scoffed the outraged father. "Its extortion is what it is!"

"It's the law," replied Drake.

"It is plain and simple robbery."

"Tell you what, sir," said Drake offering him a simple alternative. "You can keep your money if you give us your boy. Your choice? What will it be?"

If the father had any notion of considering the swap, the terrified mother didn't. "Take the money, please!" she pleaded, her eyes shooting barbed darts at her husband, who angrily reached for his bill fold and counted out the greenbacks.

"I will insist on a receipt!" demanded the husband and father reluctantly handing over the money.

"Good as done," Drake said. He wrote out the receipt, and handed it over to the father before depositing the fee in the collection bag. "There you go, sir, all properly signed and accounted for."

The man closed his fist in token defiance around the paper and, in what was becoming an all too familiar act to the Minnesotans, slammed the door behind him.

"This city has some pretty strong doors," said Kinnunen.

"Keeps out the riff-raff. Let's move it," said Drake stuffing the collection bag into an inside pocket of his uniform. "We need to be at City Hall no later than five o'clock."

"City Hall?" asked Kinnunen.

"Aye, at the temporary Provost central office. We're to meet First Sergeant Lynch there. Privates Kirk and Roacher will drop these new volunteers off at the company while the rest of us will go meet up with Lynch. Does that suit your schedule, Private Roacher?"

"It does, indeed. Thank you, Sergeant."

"No more whys."

"None, Sergeant."

"Then, there you go."

Drake explained that five o'clock was the tally time for the collected conscription fees. Each company level office across the city, reported to the temporary central office, which in turn, reported to the Tammany liaison office located in City Hall.

"So what if we're still across town or something and can't make it on time?" asked Frantzen.

"That's the thing," said the New York Sergeant. "We don't miss the five o'clock. Lynch won't allow it."

"Won't allow it?"

"No."

"So whatever we're doing..."

"We stop doing it and make sure we get to the central office in time for the count."

"It's how it is?" said Kinnunen while Drake nodded. Kinnunen caught on quick.

"It's how it is."

Drake and his three Minnesotans were waiting at the central collection office when Lynch arrived by horse drawn Hansom Cab. The convergence of the various crews at the central collection office came and receded in Federal blue waves as the collected currency was delivered, counted and recorded, before the collection crews were sent on their way for the day.

Stepping out of the cab and ignoring the new men, he told the coach driver to wait. The First Sergeant then approached Drake and held out his palm for the fees and receipts bag. "Let's have it," he said impatiently. Drake handed over the small cloth bag.

"Wait here," ordered Lynch calmly before he entered the building and left the soldiers standing on the busy city sidewalk.

"We wait," said Drake taking Lynch's rude demeanor in stride.

Not that it was a long or even a bad wait, since there were a number of attractive young ladies who passed by on the busy avenue in this better part of the city, something not lost on Trigg Kinnunen who actually seemed to be enjoying the delay.

"Ladies," he said, doffing his forage cap to a cluster of fashionably dressed women in large hats, who returned his gentlemanly gesture with courteous nods. Several of the young ladies had actually smiled at him as they passed, and Kinnunen and the others watched them walk by with quiet appreciation. "New York's looking better and better," he said staring after them.

When one of the ladies glanced back over her shoulder, Trigg tipped his cap a second time with a grin and a wink. The woman chuckled. "Yes, definitely a nice looking city," he said and then urged Nyhavn on. "Okay Ben, your turn. Make the most of it."

As two more women began walking towards them arm-in-arm Nyhavn stepped out and doffed his uniform cap. "Ladies," he said. He smiled and kept smiling as he locked his eyes on one of the women's considerable bosom.

"Indeed!" said one of the women with an audible huff. "How vulgar!"

"And rude!" admonished the other as they stormed past the young Corporal, leaving the soldiers howling and hooting at Nyhavn's misfortune.

"That's the trouble with him being a farm boy!" laughed Frantzen.

"How's that?" asked Drake.

"Every time he sees big udders he has a strong desire to start tugging on them!"

Drake guffawed along with them and Kinnunen offered the young soldier a little helpful advice.

"Ben, the thing is you have to learn how to disguise vulgar."

"Disguise it?"

"Sure," he said. "All men are vulgar and all women know it. That's no surprise to them at all. They just prefer that we hide it better. As you tip your cap you can glance at their charms on your way back up to meet their eyes but you've got to be subtle. Look. Here come a few more ladies heading this way. This time why don't you start with their eyes and offer a simple smile and a polite, 'good afternoon.' No staring at their teats."

Armed with this new advice, Nyhavn tried again.

"Good afternoon, ladies," he said trying Trigg's approach. His tone was cordial, his eye contact appropriate.

While he didn't receive an inviting smile the women weren't offended or outraged by the greeting either. They returned the greeting in kind and walked on.

Emboldened with new found confidence the young soldier tried a third time and achieved the same result, earning a return nod, and a generous smile from another passing young woman as a bonus.

"You know, I think this town is growing on me too," said the much pleased Nyhavn.

"That it will," agreed Drake.

Twenty minutes later First Sergeant Lynch came out of the central collection office accompanied by another Senior NCO. They were locked in deep conversation as they came down the stairs and started towards the waiting cab. Lynch glanced at his street crew but otherwise ignored them until he got to the curb and finally addressed his sergeant.

"Sergeant Drake!" barked the First Sergeant.

"Yes, First Sergeant?"

"I've got matters to attend to. You and your people are dismissed once you collect the tally receipt. Someone will bring it down shortly. Give it and the collection bag to Corporal Dumshee when you get back to the Company."

Lynch started off, but turned back a second time.

"Oh, and one more thing," he said motioning for Drake to follow him to the coach for a private conversation.

As this was happening, a soldier appeared in the building's main doorway holding up a receipt and the crew's collection bag. "You from the Five Points crew?" he asked, not recognizing the Minnesotans.

"The very same, boyo," Kinnunen said, mimicking the man's brogue while pointing to the green felt on his collar.

"And you are?"

"T.S. O'Kennen."

"I don't know you," said the soldier, warily.

"We're new. We're with Donnie Drake's crew," said Kinnunen pointing to the New York Sergeant who was locked in conversation with Lynch.

"Okay then," said the soldier handing Trigg a receipt and the now empty cloth bag. "There you go."

Kinnunen immediately shoved it off on Nyhavn. "And there you go, junior Corporal," he said eyeing another group of ladies parading down the street. "Put the receipt in the bag."

"Junior Corporal?" said Nyhavn.

"It is what it is."

As Nyhavn folded the receipt to fit in the collection bag he gave a quick glance at the tally figure just as the First Sergeant and Drake were finishing up their conversation. Slightly confused he stuffed the paper inside the bag and buttoned it up as Lynch and the Sergeant Major rode away in the coach.

"The First Sergeant wanted to know how you bumpkins did on your first time out," he said rejoining his people. "I told him you did well enough to earn a well deserved beer at *The Thistle Down*."

"So, does that mean no more lovely burn details?"

"Not hardly," he said. "So a beer it is. We'll leave once we get our paperwork."

"You mean this?" said Nyhavn handing him the cloth bag.

"What about the receipt?"

"I put it in the bag, but I'm not sure we got the right one. The numbers seem off," he said as Sergeant Drake opened the bag, read over the receipt, reclosed the bag and tucked it in his coat.

"No, it's the right receipt."

Ben nodded unconvincingly, so the Sergeant added, "There's city charges and fees or as the First Sergeant likes to remind me, 'it's none of my fookin' concern.' if you take my meaning."

"It is how it is, right?"

"There you go," said Drake. "Now it's time we celebrate a good day's work."

Good wasn't exactly the word Nyhavn had in mind for the day's work they had done or for the accounting job demonstrated on the receipt. They had taken in fees on four calls. They had collected $1,200 in all, but the tally sheet only showed $600. So what happened to the rest?

He was reasonably sure that Drake hadn't taken it, considering that he had seen him stuff the money, and receipts in the bag, and then handed the bag over to the First Sergeant once they arrived at the central office for the count.

And since Lynch handed out their schedule for the collection route that told Ben that the First Sergeant knew what the central office expected to find in the bag. If the count was off, then Lynch would have been aware of the shortage shortly after he turned it over.

Maybe there was another explanation for the discrepancy. Maybe the central office had another method of tallying the count or maybe he misread the numbers and since Drake made it clear enough that it wasn't his business, he kept his suspicions to himself.

However, by week's end, and with a few more cautionary looks at the receipts Ben found that the collection numbers were consistently off. And it also told him everything he needed to know about Lynch, and maybe how business was done in the Company, and the pecking order that went from Five Corners up to Tammany Hall.

New York was a city of big and bigger streets, broad avenues and even broader ambitions. All over town, the Provost Companies were making daily collections and taking in commutation fees. He wondered how many other company counts were off.

Ben though held both his thoughts and his tongue. Voicing those kinds of suspicions only invited trouble, especially from the First Sergeant who was prone to violence in a neglected part of the city where violence and corruption reigned. He told himself that there was no need to stir up a stinking mess, unless of course, you were burning it.

Either way, he knew the smell wouldn't be all that different.

Chapter 15

The first week set the routine for the work days that followed. There were more fights and physical confrontations; more kicks, cuts, bloodied and bruised knuckles, and noses, and a fair number of sore or torn muscles from sudden wrestling matches and brawls. And through it all, the three Minnesotans proved their worth to the crew. They also proved to be a welcome addition to the crew's after hours activities, joining Miller, and a few others for drinks At *The Thistle Down* several nights a week.

The saloon was long but narrow with a stand up bar that ran the entire length of one wall while ten to twelve tables, with accompanying mis-matched chairs, were spaced out thirty feet along the opposite wall. The bar was dark wood with a brass foot rail. Sawdust covered a wood floor and soaked up the spillage, blood, and spit.

Behind the bar several rows of assorted whisky and liquor bottles were arranged in front of a large mirror, and gave the appearance of more bottles than there actually were. A bawdy painting of three dancing nymphs hung to the right of the mirror, strategically at eye level.

At the back of the bar a stairway led to the rooms upstairs where a number of working girls plied their trade. Business was good, several of the women that worked in *The Thistle Down* were attractive enough to warrant even sober notice, while a few of the others looked considerably better after a few drinks. It wasn't as nice or as upscale as *The Fortunate Gentlemen's* bar in Philadelphia, but it was larger and a whole lot livelier, and served the same purpose.

Overseeing it all was the bar owner, John Henry Hellman, who was as blunt and angry looking as the nail studded mallet he kept just beneath the bar, and frequently pulled out when customers got out of hand. Always ready for a scrap, Hellman kept a watchful and wary eye on his usually loud and busy domain. Behind Hellman, and prominently displayed on a shelf, sat the pickle jar with a yellowed severed ear.

If that wasn't enough to discourage troublemakers then the hulking figure seated at the saloon's entrance offered additional incentive.

"That's Barney," explained Miller on their initial visit to the saloon. "He's strong as a plough horse, but not quite as smart. Hellman uses him to help break up fights and to keep an eye on the free lunch down at the other end of the bar."

"He keeps as eye on the free lunch?"

"So long as you're drinking it's free. Keep in mind that Barney doesn't have sense enough to realize that unless he sees you're holding a glass. Oh yeah, and once he's charging in on you the only one who can call him off is Hellman. Although he has to give him a good thump from his club occasionally when his words don't work. Pay your way and don't start trouble and Hellman and his lummox will leave you be."

"And what, our ears won't end up in a pickle jar along with the boiled eggs on the free lunch counter?" asked Kinnunen.

"Not to worry, the eggs are fresh enough; The ears he keeps as trophies."

"Of course, he does,' laughed Kinnunen, "He's a proud sportsman."

This night, like many others, they were sitting at their usual table near the stairs. A nearly drunk Nyhavn was staring into his half empty mug of beer, brooding. He was bothered that they had actually gotten good at their job of helping the crew collect the reluctant conscripts and the fees, and knowing that if Lynch and the Captain were stealing money, then he and the rest of the crew, were part and party to the theft.

The trouble was that his face was an open book, which made him a lousy poker player, and an easy read. Frantzen was the first to notice that their young friend was unusually quiet, another tell-tale sign, at least to Al, that something was bothering him.

"So, what's with you?" he asked the much too quiet Dane.

"What?"

"You drunk or just coming down with something?"

"A touch tired is all," he said. "It's nothing."

The big German nodded, and for the moment, let it be.

"Or maybe you just haven't had enough to drink yet!" said Kevin McKay getting to his feet. "Come on, Finn! We'll get a round of growlers for our resident heathens."

"Of course, *we* will your worship," said Miller. A bothersome mystery though, don't you think?"

"What mystery?"

"That Mister Lincoln emancipated the poor unfortunate slaves and yet you continue to think of me as your servant."

"I'm not asking you to pay for the beer, you bleedin' little peat eater. I'm just asking that you help me carry the damn things."

"Ah well, in that case I must insist on acting like your most humble and always obedient servant."

While the New Yorkers went to retrieve the drinks Frantzen picked up where he left off with Nyhavn. "Okay," he said, "so what's this nothing that's really bothering you and don't tell me nothing again. That excuse just won't wash."

Unable to dodge the question, Ben took in a deep breath, and let it out slowly, as he laid out his suspicion about the discrepancies between the amounts collected and what was on the official tally sheets to his two friends. When he had finished Kinnunen sat back in his chair, steepled his fingers, and said, "Well, that's an interesting twist."

"So you really think the First Sergeant and the Captain are stealing the money?" said Frantzen.

"Yeah, I do," said Nyhavn. "I've snuck enough looks at the receipts to know that the numbers don't add up. They're stealing it all right."

Kinnunen didn't seem to be as bothered by the revelation as Frantzen was. "Doesn't surprise me," he said.

"It doesn't?"

"No, not really, considering it's Lynch we're talking about," he said. "How much you think they're taking out of the collections?"

"Gotta be at least three to five hundred dollars a week."

"Which makes them thieves, plain and simple," Frantzen said.

Trigg Kinnunen shrugged. "Maybe not so simple since it plainly makes us surrogate thieves too." Before Ben could ask what the word surrogate meant, Kinnunen quickly added, "Substitute thieves."

Nyhavn sat back in his seat and took a long pull on his beer. "That ain't the worst of it either," he said, wiping the beer foam from his mouth with the back of his hand.

"What, there's more?" said Frantzen, wondering what else he had missed.

"Uh-huh. Have you ever noticed when we make our rounds, how Drake seems to hold private conversations with some of the better looking sisters and wives of soldiers who were scheduled to be conscripted?"

"A fair amount, sure."

"And they don't really seem like they can afford to pay the commutation fees?"

"Yeah, so?" said the big German.

"So, there seems to be a lot of unhappy looking young housekeepers coming and going from the Captain's Office, like the one who was sitting on the bench in the Orderly Room the day we got here…"

"The one that Lynch smacked you silly for not paying attention to him?"

"Uh-huh. She had that wiry red hair and apple green eyes."

"Don't recall the color of her eyes but I suppose you had reason to."

"I did," added Nyhavn. "Anyway, yesterday, I was mopping down the entry way and stairs to the Orderly room, when she was being escorted to the Orderly Room by Corporal Dumshee."

"You sure it was her?"

"Yeah, it was her all right," said Nyhavn. "Anyway, I'm just finishing up with the front hallway when they came in. She starts to tip-toe around where I'm mopping only Dumshee takes her right across through to the stairs. It was nasty out so they tracked in some mud and muck from the streets. She apologized while Dumshee just seemed to think it was funny."

"Of course he did," said Kinnunen. "He's a dumb *shite.*"

Frantzen laughed at the remark. Kinnunen's Irish accent was getting better.

"So Dumshee's escorting her up to the Orderly Room and on the way up the stairs I see him pat her on her ass…"

"Dumshee?"

"Yep and she turned and slapped him a good one."

"Good for her!"

"Damn near made him cry, so then it was my turn to laugh."

Frantzen snorted and said, "So, he got what he deserved."

"Yeah, he did. Anyhow, because of the mess they made coming in, I had to tromp back down to the basement to change out the mop to go over the entry way and stairs one more time.

"Half an hour or so later when I'm almost finished, I see her coming out of the Orderly Room and down the stairs looking more than a little disheveled. I nod and say, 'Hello,' only now she seemed too shamefaced and embarrassed to acknowledge me."

"So?" asked Frantzen.

"Do you know how to ask a question without using the word 'so'"?

"Why yes, I do," said the big German before adding, "So?"

Nyhavn shook his head and continued. "So, I think the dandy Captain is taking favors…"

"In lieu of the fees," added Kinnunen working it out. "Which means he's pokin' them?"

The younger soldier nodded. "Most likely," he said. "What I can't figure out is why the women would do that?"

"Because they love their husbands, brothers or fathers," said Kinnunen, evaluating what he had just heard.

"Yeah, well then why would their loved ones let it happen?"

"I dunno," Kinnunen replied, "maybe because the husbands, brothers or fathers don't love them as much in return."

Nyhavn chewed on it for awhile before he replied. "Tell me something, *pards*," he said, a little louder than he had intended. "When exactly did we become thieves *and* pimps?"

"Easy, Ben," said Frantzen, noticing Miller turning back to them from the bar with a handful of small beer buckets.

"Why? It's not like folks around here don't know what we're doing. You ever think that's why we get some of the receptions we do? I'll be damned if I wouldn't toss bricks at us from the rooftops too!"

"Ben, look at me," said Kinnunen facing the younger soldier. "Ben? Hey! I said, *look at me*!"

"Yeah, okay, I'm looking."

"You're a little drunk."

"What? Like being sober is gonna make it sound any better?"

"Probably not, but that kind of talk, especially that kind of loud talk in public, can lead to trouble..."

"And just what trouble would that be?" said Miller, just over their shoulders holding an armful of beers.

"I'll take one of those," said the big German trying to change the subject.

"Me too," added Kinnunen while Nyhavn was still brooding in his chair. Miller set the buckets down and took a seat in front of them.

"This 'no trouble' of yours have anything to do with our boy Ben's louder than necessary talk about us being thieves and pimps?" Miller asked pouring the beer from one bucket into their glasses.

Trigg figured that since the cat was out of the bag, there was no need to pretend it was still comfortably purring. Miller wasn't a fool and had shown that he could be trusted. He deserved an honest answer, so Kinnunen gave him one.

"Okay then, as a matter of fact, it is," he said, and then laid it all out much the way Nyhavn had. When he was done, he waited for Miller's response.

"It is how it is," Miller said nonchalantly as he filled his empty beer glass from one of the new beer buckets. "So don't go looking to see if it's right or wrong. That doesn't matter."

"So this 'it is what it is' business is supposed to make it all right?" countered Nyhavn.

"No, but it is how you leave it," replied Miller. "And let me tell you why: the fees that are collected go uptown…"

"Minus a cut of the pie, maybe for Lynch and the Captain?" asked Kinnunen.

"More than likely, and certainly headquarters gets their cut too before it climbs up a rung to the bosses in Tammany…"

"Minus another cut of the pie," added Frantzen.

Finn Miller nodded. "Aye and I would expect that by the time it reaches wherever it finally needs to go, everyone else in between found it tasty."

"But that's still stealing," protested Nyhavn staring into his half-filled beer glass.

"No," Miller disagreed. "That's just the business of New York politics."

"Shouldn't we report it?" said Nyhavn.

"What? Turn somebody in, you mean?"

"Uh-huh."

"A noble thought," replied Miller with a smirk. "And like most noble thoughts, it is just as stupid to try to take it to fruition. Think about it a moment. Who would you report it to, exactly? To the First Sergeant? The Captain? No, because they're the men Tammany put in charge to run their profitable enterprise. They're Tweed men."

Nyhavn shot him a questioning look. "What are Tweed men?"

"You know, Tammany's Grand Sachem, Boss Tweed."

"The grand what?"

"Sachem," Miller said, "The chief."

"That another of your Irish words, is it?" asked Kinnunen trying to track the flow of the power structure and who was what and where.

Miller shook his head. "No, Indian," he said.

"Good lord, Irish Indians?" said Trigg with a chuckle. "Okay," he said, "Let's try this again. Whose boss is this Boss Tweed?"

Miller said, "Everyone's or soon will be. Boss Tweed controls all of the Municipal jobs in the city."

"The police too?"

Miller nodded. "Did you know some buy their jobs? Usually about $300 just to get hired and a *shite* load more for promotions after that."

"Did Lynch buy his job?"

"More than likely with Tammany's say so," he said.

"What if someone took the story to the newspapers?"

"Not a good idea for someone to do. Boss Tweed's a power on high who can rain down a *shite* storm or even smite you in an instant should word get back to him that someone- say someone here from Nowhere, Minnesota- wants to shed some light on something he prefers best left in the shadows."

"So what about Sergeant Drake? Is he in Mister Tweed's pocket too?"

"In a way..."

"In what way?" asked Kinnunen troubled by Miller's reply. He had wanted to believe better of the Sergeant.

"Donnie Drake is a good bag man and they know it. He brings in the money. Does he know what's going on? Certainly, but is he in a position to do anything about it? The answer to that is 'no' and here's why: Drake is Lansdowne Irish from Kenmare. The family came over when he was a wee lad, courtesy of Lord Lansdowne and Mister Trench..."

"Important friends, I take it?"

Miller snorted and cocked his head to the side. "Heartless bastards, actually," he said. "Even before the Potato Famine, the poorest of the Irish poor came from the Lansdowne estate. His tenants were farm workers and laborers without good farm land or any real jobs, so many went into Lansdowne's poorhouse, which the good Lord had to feed. Then, when he decided he could save money by emptying out his poorhouse, he had them loaded on boats in Cork and sent them to America."

"Not by choice, then?"

"Not really and not much better. It was a one way trip without adequate food or water for the thirty nine day voyage..."

"Good God," said a distressed Kinnunen.

"Not to those who were on the boat, he wasn't," replied Miller. "A good number of them died on the voyage over, or soon after. Too weak, you see. Drake's Da..."

"Da?"

"His father. He died on the 15th day at sea along with his older sister, Rosaleen. The ship's Captain said some words and then dumped their bodies and a few others overboard and then dumped Mother Drake, and her ten year old son, Donnie, and dozens of others on the docks in New York, where they were all left to fend for themselves. They followed the other unfortunates to the Points, and like so many others, they made do as best they could. Growing up in Five Points Donnie Drake became one of the top head bangers for the Bowery B'hoys gang..."

"And what? He found the error of his ways?"

"No, he found one too many jail sentences. A judge offered him a choice between the Army for the duration of the war, or a long term stay in the Tombs. He chose the army."

"And Captain O'Brian?"

"Ah, the Squire," sighed Miller. "Our dandy Captain is uptown, lace curtain Irish..."

"What's lace curtain Irish?" asked Kinnunen.

"Moneyed people," Miller said rubbing his fingers together. "The kind who see the rest of us as barely tolerable servants or those to be used, like the women Lynch brings him to be his 'housekeepers.'"

"Do any of them actually keep house at his home, his real home?"

Miller shook his head. "Don't think so," he said. "Each night he goes to his fancy home in a fine part of the city, to his beloved wife and darling little kids, who probably don't have an inkling of what an ungentlemanly fook he really is. No, his 'housekeepers' here will never be anointed or elevated by him to even clean his commode."

"And what about Lynch, he another product of the Points?"

"No, He's bottom bog Irish, or worse. He was a spiteful *shite* in the old country, who became a bigger *shite* once he floated ashore here five years back."

"And by 'old country', you mean Ireland?"

Miller gave him a sideways glance. "And what other 'old country' could there possibly be for such a contentious Gaelic son of a bitch?"

"But you're from Ireland too, right?"

"Different County, better class of sons of bitches," replied Miller. "Anyway, my heathen Viking friend, as an outsider, Lynch has no allegiance to the Points, which is why he does what he does..."

"What do you mean?"

"Simple. He's not swayed by family or gang associations. He keeps a room here but spends most nights on Mott Street with the Chinamen's pipe."

"The Chinamen's pipe?"

"Opium, which is why his face looks like dried horse piss. And since he has no ties to the Points, he's free to take as much as he can from it."

"Ah!"

"Ah, indeed, and so long as Tammany gets its tribute and Lynch and the Captain pay a little something to the police, they can do what they want, undisturbed."

"You talking company business now, are you, Private Finn?" said Kevin McKay, coming back to the table with two more buckets of beer. He had heard enough of the conversation to register concern on his face.

"Just educating our country cousins, is all, Kevin," Miller said to McKay. "They've earned that much, haven't they?"

The three Minnesotans looked to McKay who stared back at them as he considered his response. "Aye, I suppose they have," he said setting down the drinks. "So, where were you in the telling?"

"Uptown in Tammany," replied Miller, "where wisdom and divine light shines back down to our blighted lives, in return for a small plate offering to the First Sergeant and Company Commander."

"How many Provost Marshal's offices and plates are making their offerings?" asked Kinnunen. "How many crews like us are we talking about?"

"Around the city?" McKay said.

"Yeah."

"A couple dozen at least, and several more in some fancy neighborhoods where the pickings are better, and the other nephews, sons, or sons of bitches are all adding to the pot."

"Then it's organized stealing and everyone is in on it, are they?"

"Oh, it gets better," said Miller. "Can I tell them why the privileged ones in the company don't work on the street crew?"

"Sure," McKay said, "why not?"

"They're bounty boys," Miller said, smiling.

"Bounty boys?" said Frantzen. "You talking about enlistment bonuses?"

"I am indeed. They received $300 each to enlist, of which $200 went into the Company welfare fund…"

"What Company welfare fund?"

"Precisely," said Miller. "And there's at least twenty five of them who were bounty boys, which makes at least $5,000, if you country oafs are capable of basic addition," said Miller. "Then to make sure they remain in the city, and don't accidentally get sent off to the war, they each contribute $5 of their pay each month."

"Five dollars? You mean, above what they're already paying for food?"

Miller nodded.

"You too?"

"The enlistment bonus, yes, but not the monthly charge. Lynch doesn't take it from the working crew," said McKay. "We need it for stitches, bandages, and such. He has to keep us relatively in good shape for his enterprise to work."

"Damn *Gedekneppers*!" said Nyhavn.

"The what?" asked Miller.

"*Gedekneppers.*"

"And what exactly does that mean in your heathen tongue?"

"Goat lover."

"Goat lover, huh?" said a skeptical Miller.

"Sort of," Nyhavn said, with a snort.

Miller nodded, comprehending what wasn't being said. "Isn't education a grand thing?"

"It is," McKay said. "But talking too much or too loud about the business of the commutation fees and where it goes isn't wise either, nor safe, if you follow my meaning."

"Okay, so maybe it's not my concern either," said Nyhavn, reluctantly coming around to the practical. "Maybe all I really want to do is do my time and go home in the spring. If pretending I don't know what's really going on gets me closer to that, then that's what I'll do."

"A wise plan," agreed Miller.

"And not a bad plan for the rest of us either, Ben," added Kinnunen. "By the way, did you call us '*pards*'?"

"He did," said Frantzen.

"Pards?" asked a confused McKay.

Nyhavn stuttered his reply, "It…it means…"

"What it means," laughed Kinnunen, "is that you've been reading too many of those dime novel Pony Express stories, is what it means, *pard*."

"The Pony Express is more than stories," countered Nyhavn. "It's a real job."

"What? That you're considering as employment?"

Nyhavn shrugged. "I can shoot and I can learn to ride."

"Okay, so what about the Indians?"

Nyhavn wasn't put off. "I don't see them being much different than the rebels we faced or getting ambushed in some back alley tenement. In fact, working in Five Points has probably schooled me some when it comes to ambushes. I don't think the Indians are much better at it than the Irish," he said giving a nod to Miller and McKay.

"That's a compliment, is it?" Miller asked mid drink.

"It is."

"Always nice to be appreciated," Miller said to McKay who held up his beer glass. Miller toasted him with a nod before they both took a drink.

"So I think I'll look into the Pony Express once my time here is up."

"No point," said Miller, setting down his glass and following it with an audible belch.

"Why's that?" said Ben.

"The Pony Express is no more."

"Since when?" said Nyhavn, clearly dismayed.

"Since a year or so ago actually. But if you're thinking of learning to ride for your future job prospects, there's better ways to start. Hey Maggie!" Miller said turning to one of the Sporting girls on the back stairs. Maggie was a plump red haired woman with whisky red eyes and a well practiced smile.

"What is it, soldier boy?"

"You and your lady friends got time for riding lessons for my friends and me?"

"Always willing to serve our fine men in uniform…so long as we see the money first."

"Ah, patriotism," said Miller digging into his pockets while Maggie walked over and sidled up to young Nyhavn. She playfully ran her fingers through his hair.

"You're the one who does that French thing, aren't you?"

"Yep, the little French Joy," replied Nyhavn.

Maggie smiled and took his hand. "That's right, the French Joy," she said cooing. "You're coming with me, sweetie."

"Let's go, ladies and gents. It's time to mosey," laughed Miller partnering up with another of the sporting girls.

"*Mosey* a good word, Ben?" laughed Kinnunen picking up on Miller's comment. "Did we get that right? There's so much to your cowboy lingo I just don't know, pard."

"Like the French Joy too, I suppose?"

"That's right."

Nyhavn grinned as Maggie led him towards the stairs to the rooms upstairs. "Good," he said smiling back to his friend. "Then you can add that to your list too."

Chapter 16

They were working their way through the pick-up list along the East river waterfront in early November, when two fishermen in a rowboat at the waterline were yelling and wildly waving, trying to get their attention. One of the men was standing in knee deep water holding the boat on the shoreline while the second fisherman was balancing himself in the boat, using an oar to keep some floating debris tightly wedged against the boat gunnels. A light layer of morning fog hugged the surface of the water matching the grey sky overhead.

Several irked seagulls circled and screeched over the fishermen and their catch. One of the birds dove towards the two men looking for more scraps to rip away from the buoyant bounty, only to be angrily shooed away. It was their feast that drew the fishermen to the floating debris.

"Hey!" called the man in the boat as Sergeant Drake held up the crew to see what was the matter. "We need some help here!"

Drake started towards the rowboat and then stopped short when he caught sight of what the two men were trying to haul in.

"Found her out in the water," said the man holding the oar, "Drowned." He had wedged the oar under the woman's left arm and used leverage to push the bloated body to shore. The cold water lapped against the young woman's lifeless body as a constant drumming to the tragedy. The river water had diluted the blood on her torn dress and undergarments but couldn't diminish the color of the crime.

"Murdered, it looks like," said the second fisherman staring stared at the victim's hands and feet that had been tightly bound behind her. His face was ashen and he was visibly shaken.

"Haul her in," Drake said to the fishermen, and when they hesitated, he turned to the Provost soldiers. "Boys, give them a hand."

Together they pulled the body to shore. The woman's face had been bashed in, and what wasn't beaten, was bloated and unrecognizable. Her dark dress with a light trim was ripped and torn, showing signs of a terrible struggle. Her left shoe was still on her foot while the right shoe was gone. The woman had been in the water for several days. Her distorted face was a bluish gray and her left eye was missing where a seagull had plucked it out.

"Kirk, run and fetch the police," Drake said. The tall Irishman nodded, and raced off. A small crowd of curious on-lookers began to wander over and cluster around the body.

"Anyone know who she is?" asked Drake turning to the gawkers for an answer. And when no one responded he tried again.

"Anyone recognize the girl?"

Several of the less timid on-lookers leaned in for a closer inspection, but few lingered.

A disheartened Kinnunen turned away wondering how anyone could recognize her. He whispered a silent prayer. He had seen far too many dead in the war to relish the notion of looking at another one, especially a young woman.

Most of the others in the street crew soon joined Kinnunen at a short distance. Nyhavn though remained beside Drake staring down at the dead body.

"Poor thing," said someone from the crowd while several of the older women snuck quick peeks and then crossed themselves. "May she rest with the angels."

"Amen," murmured Kinnunen.

"Just like poor Mary Rogers," said the fisherman who was holding the boat in place with his oar.

"Murdered too," said an angry man in the small audience as more oaths were muttered. Drake called for calm as Frantzen repeated the order more forcefully quieting the crowd.

The big German's voice boomed. "The police are on their way. They'll figure it out."

Anyone know her?" Drake said a third and final time.

"Probably just another Five Points whore," said a laborer who was staring at the dead woman like she was just a bag of garbage.

"Or maybe someone's mother, wife or sister, maybe yours," Drake said, bridling at the remark, his glaring stare daring the man to challenge him. "You certain your loved ones are at home, are you?"

The man was saved from the soldier's wrath when Kirk and two Police officers hurriedly came around the corner and made their way over to the small crowd gathered around the body. In the brief time they had been there, the numbers of the curious had grown to a little over a dozen. Someone claiming to be a reporter for Horace Greeley's Tribune tried to pull Drake aside to ask questions, but the Sergeant ignored him. He didn't like muckrakers.

The reporter wisely backed away and listened in, taking notes.

"You Lynch's people?" asked the policeman in the lead, a barrel-chested man.

"We are," said Drake. "We were rounding up Conscripts and came across this."

"You found her?" asked the Policeman, warily.

"No," said Drake, "they did." He gestured with his chin tilted towards the fishermen. "We just happened along, and helped bring her out of the water."

"Anyone knows who she is?" said the policeman to the crowd. "Anyone recognize her?"

Drake chuffed. "If they do then no one's saying anything," he said.

The Policeman frowned. "Around here most people don't," he said. The small audience was growing into a good size crowd. The newspaperman had pushed his way through the mix and standing over the body he was quickly scribbling his notes and looking pleased with himself.

"If you don't need us, then me and my people need to finish our rounds. If you know First Sergeant Lynch, then you know he doesn't want excuses, only results."

"So I've heard," agreed the Policeman. "You're Donnie Drake, aren't you?"

"I am."

The Policeman stared at the Sergeant trying to reconcile the soldier in front of him with all that he had heard and known about him. He was surprised that Drake wasn't taller. "If you hear anything on your rounds, you'll tell us, yeah?"

Drake said he would but the Policeman knew better. Drake wouldn't hear anything, or if he did, then the former gang member probably wouldn't pass it along. After all, this was Drake's neighborhood too.

Another murder in this part of town wasn't all that unusual anyway. They averaged one or more a day, although Nyhavn noticed that this particular victim seemed to have an unsettling effect on the New York Sergeant.

"Something on your mind?" Drake said when he caught Nyhavn looking at him out of the corner of his eye.

"No," Ben lied. "Thinking about the dead girl is all, wondering who did it."

"And why?" said Kinnunen.

The New York Sergeant cut them off. "That's police business. Not ours," he said, gruffly. "We've got work to do. Let's get to it."

Badly beaten as she was, Nyhavn may not have recognized her face, but he had a guess who she might be. For the moment though, he kept his suspicions to himself.

It was only when they had finished their rounds and were back in their tent that evening before he brought the matter up again with the other Minnesotans.

"The drowned girl," he said. "The one who was beaten…"

"Yeah, what about her?" Frantzen said, tending a pot of beans, sausage chunks, and molasses that he had heating on the stove.

"I think I recognized her."

"With her face the way it was I doubt if her own mother could recognize her," said the big German. "So how are you so certain you can?"

"Well, I mean I didn't *recognize* recognize her, but I have a pretty good idea who she is."

"Then, let's hear it," Kinnunen said looking up from his Bible. "How do you know her?"

"I don't know her, but I think I saw her, in fact we all did."

"Saw her where?" asked Kinnunen.

"Our first day working on the crew," Ben said. "The fight in the tenement on Mulberry Street with what's his name's people? The O'Malley's?"

"That's right, the O'Malley's," said Kinnunen rubbing the scar on his arm. "She was there, was she, in the tenement?"

"Not then, afterwards, she was the woman in the run down shack on that skinny dirt street that went nowhere."

"Skinny dirt street?"

"Yeah, you know, the one with the goat and the crazy old man tied to the porch?"

"Oh yeah, the one that was poking the rats with a stick," said Kinnunen, nodding and smiling.

"Uh-huh," he said. "The stop where we didn't get a draftee or the conscription fee..."

Kinnunen tried to recall the woman's face, but only came away with a vague recollection. He remembered that she wasn't all that tall, was reasonably good looking, and had dark hair. He also remembered that she wasn't particularly happy to see any of them, especially Drake, most of all.

"You saying the dead woman was one of the Captain's 'housekeepers?'"

Nyhavn nodded. "Aye, I think she was," he said, lowering his voice.

"Ben, this may not necessarily come as a secret to you, but you might know I really like the ladies," Kinnunen said, admitting what his friends already knew.

"So?"

"So, if I'm not so certain I can recall too much about her then how can you be so sure it was her?"

"She was wearing a dark dress like the one the dead girl had on."

"New York's a big city. I imagine there are a lot of women here who have dark dresses just like that."

"Okay, but what about her shoes?"

"What about them?"

"Her left show had a split heel..."

"A split heel?"

"Uh-huh."

"Weren't we all standing in the street when Drake was talking to her?" said Frantzen.

"We were," agreed Kinnunen.

"Right, so how could you notice a split heel on her shoe?"

"It was held together with a bent brass tack. The bent tack caught the sunlight and it struck me funny that someone would repair a heel that way."

"A bent brass tack, that's it?"

"Uh-huh, I think it was the same as the dead girl's."

Frantzen looked up from the stove and said, "I thought all shoe heels had brass tacks?"

"They do," Kinnunen replied.

"They do?" Ben said, somewhat surprised.

"Yep. So, are you still sure about the shoe?"

"Well…no," Nyhavn said with a little uncertainty.

"Did you tell Drake about it?"

Ben shook his head. "No, not yet," he said.

"Because you're not really sure it was the same girl?"

"Yeah, I suppose," lied Nyhavn.

"Then tell Drake about the bent tack and let him look into it," Trigg said. "If there's anything to it, you heard him, he'll pass it along to the police."

Ben nodded and said he would, but he knew he wouldn't tell Drake because he also remembered that the girl slammed the door in his face after he threatened her.

In the days that followed, Nyhavn read the newspapers' sensationalize-daccounts of the crime with keen interest. The Tribune and The Mirror kept the story alive, in large bold print on their front pages, for three mornings straight before relegating it to the inside pages. Ben read the Coroner's ruling that the young woman had been severely beaten, then strangled before she was dumped in the river. "It's a sad and tragic crime," said the Coroner.

It was also a shocking and salacious story that sold newspapers, so the editors kept it in the public eye for the rest of the week with follow up articles. They ran lurid leads that paperboys shouted from street corners and sold for two cents a copy.

Several newspaper editorials speculated about possible gang involvement, while others suggested that, horrible as it was, the killing might have been little more than a lover's quarrel gone wrong. Another daily paper suggested that perhaps the unidentified woman could have been in a family way, and died after a blotched procedure.

Whatever it was, it gnawed at Nyhavn until he made up his mind that he needed to find out for sure if it was the same girl. If it was, he might be able to leak her name, and if it wasn't, then at least he could put it to rest. So, a week and a half after the event, on a Sunday morning, and his only day off, he put on his civilian clothes, tucked his pistol in his waist band, and then made his way back to the Bowery.

There were few toughs on the street corners this time of day, but the few there were gave him hard looks and glares. However, the exposed pistol and a returned hard glare of his own allowed him undisturbed passage and dissuaded any real trouble.

After a few false starts, some backtracking, and several turn-arounds down side streets and alleys, Ben found himself following the thin, dirt lane into the familiar dingy cul-de-sac. The tethered goat was gone, but the addled old man was still tied to the post on the porch. Someone had taken his sharp stick away. He was sitting on the porch talking nonsense to himself and laughing.

Ben waved a hello to the old man who just ignored him.

Since he wasn't sure which door belonged to the woman he took a guess. Thinking that it was somewhere near the middle he tried the third from the left. When he knocked and no one answered, he knocked again, and waited. After a few minutes he moved on and tried the next door over with the same result.

As he moved on to the next door in line, a rail thin woman with dark rimmed eyes and sunken cheeks opened the door before he could knock. She was probably in her late twenties, but looked a whole lot older. Life had not been kind, and because of that, she eyed him with more than a little suspicion behind the partially opened door.

"What do you want?"

"Pardon me, Ma'am," he said addressing the woman. "I was wondering if you can you tell me about a young woman who lives in one of the rooms here? Thin, dark hair? I think it was that one there," Nyhavn asked the woman pointing to the first door he had tried. Behind the woman, four shoeless children peered out from the shabby room.

"You're one of Provost Soldiers, aren't you?"

Nyhavn reluctantly admitted he was.

"Then maybe you should be asking your people about Molly Neal instead of coming around here where you're not wanted, threatening trouble for me and mine." A surly looking man slipped in behind the woman and sneered at Nyhavn.

"What's he want?"

"He's asking about Molly Neal."

"We don't need your trouble," he said, eyeing the pistol in Nyhavn's waist band.

"I'm not here to make trouble," replied Nyhavn, closing his coat.

"Sure you're not," said the woman with a cynical edge. "I already told that Sergeant of yours I'm not saying a word to anyone, so leave us the hell alone." The woman disappeared back into the room and her pitiful existence leaving the man and several of the older children still standing in the doorway.

"Who? What sergeant?" asked Nyhavn.

"We saw nothing so piss off!" the man said and slammed the door behind him.

Chapter 17

A tainted beef scare at a slaughter house in the city stole the newspaper headlines and much of the remaining public's interest away from the mystery woman's murder. It was briefly revived in a follow-up article when she was laid to rest in Potter's Field, a communal pauper's plot on Ward's Island, along with dozens more of the city's destitute. On a gray, rainy day the plain wooden coffins were stacked three deep in a rain soaked hole the size of root cellar.

Other than the grave diggers, a volunteer Chaplain, and several teamsters whose job it was to transport the dead from the city Morgue to the burial site, there were few mourners at a funeral ceremony on a gray, rainy day for those without means.

A newspaper reporter had been sent out to cover the story because the editor knew that a heart tugging account of the murdered young woman's funeral could still sell newspapers.

The reporter didn't disappoint his editor when he wrote, *'If the meek inherit the earth, then they do so in cheap pine coffins on days while the city goes about its everyday business and takes little to no notice.'* The article then rehashed the grisly details of the crime, touched on the lawlessness of certain parts of the city, and scolded the police for not coming up with any new leads in the investigation.

The day after the mass funeral, Sergeant Drake split up his work crew, sending Kinnunen, Frantzen, Miller, Dean and Roacher to pick up several bounty jumpers while he kept Nyhavn and Private McKay with him.

"The two men you're going after frequent The Joy House on Orange

Street," Drake said to Miller. "Go fetch them and we'll catch up later in front of Delmonico's."

"We dining with the swells afterwards, are we?" asked Miller, already knowing the answer. "Maybe mix with those from the Astor House?"

"Don't think they'd have us, Finn," said Drake.

"Pity that, they'll lose out on some interesting conversation."

"Their loss," replied the Sergeant, taking off with his two remaining men in tow. Compact as he was with tree trunks for legs, both Nyhavn and McKay worked to keep up with him. They headed west out of the Points towards Broadway, and then down the grand avenue until Drake spied a stately looking building and started towards it.

It had an entrance portico with impressive stone columns and was surrounded by a high iron rail fence. The New York Sergeant bypassed the entrance and turned into an alley that led to the back of the building where they found a high stone wall with large double barn-like doors. A high iron arch over the doors held a night lamp. A posted sign on the left door read: *Receiving*.

"Wait here," Drake said, rapping twice on the closed double doors, the barbarian at the gate. There was the scraping sound of an iron bar sliding out of its hasp as one door opened slightly. Drake exchanged a few words with someone inside, and the door opened just wide enough to admit him. The door closed and locked behind them.

"We picking someone up?" Nyhavn asked staring at the double doors.

"Sweet Jesus, I hope not," said a wide eyed Private McKay. "This is the Dead House."

"The what?"

"The Dead House, the city Morgue," said McKay. "Drake has to identify the body from a draftee who died last night in the Bowery." A Catholic, the soldier quickly made the sign of the cross.

"This where they brought the drowned girl?"

"The one from the East river?" McKay said giving the young Minnesotan a troubled look.

"Yeah."

"Ben, you've been here, what? A few months or so now?"

"About that," said Nyhavn. "Why?"

"Because that's enough time for you to know that there are some questions better not asked or answered."

"What are you saying?"

"I'm saying that the First Sergeant strung me up by my thumbs for calling him a name he couldn't hear, but someone else did, and told him about it."

"Dumshee?"

"Aye, Dumshee, but he's only one set of ears in a town of many ears and many eyes. You were seen visiting the Bowery yesterday."

"So?" replied the young soldier trying to hide his surprise that McKay had known about it.

"So, Sergeant Drake asked me if I knew where you went and why, I told him you went gambling."

"No, I went…"

McKay held a hand up, cutting him off. "No," he said, adamantly. "Stupid as it was you went gambling and had a miserable time of it. You lost more than you wanted to, and you're pretty certain you were cheated, so you won't be going down there again anytime soon."

Nyhavn took the hint and nodded as McKay continued.

"If anyone asks, that's what you tell them too; so that there won't be any more concern about what else you were doing there, or what you were looking into, if you take my meaning."

Nyhavn said he did. Before he could ask who else was concerned, the loading dock door opened and Drake emerged. Once again the door closed behind him followed by a scraping sound of the iron bar being shoved back in place.

The New York Sergeant was lost in his thoughts and when he looked up he and caught the Minnesotan staring at him, he said. "Go on."

"Go on and what, Sergeant?"

"Go on and ask why we're here."

"I figure its company business," said the Minnesotan trying to play it off, only Drake wasn't buying it.

"It is, or was," Drake replied. "One of our reluctant draftees, Brian Neal, got good and drunk last night, *shite*faced he was when he stood up on a chair, slipped a knotted rope around his neck and then kicked the chair away. I came to identify the body."

"Neal, from the Bowery?"

"Aye, but how would you know that?" asked Drake reeling in his suspicions.

"Because..."

"Because you recognized the drowned girl too," Drake said pointedly.

"I...I thought I did. I wasn't all that sure, not at first."

"Her name was Molly Neal, the dead man's wife."

"His wife?"

"Aye, and she deserved a better man than what she got." Drake went silent again and then changed the direction of the conversation.

"You were told that you only have *The Thistle Down* to visit for our social entertainments, like gambling, whoring, and what not," Drake said eying Private McKay who suddenly found new interest in the tops of his shoes. "Do you recall that, Corporal Nyhavn?"

"Yes Sergeant, I do."

"Do you know why we tell you that, what purpose it serves?"

"No Sergeant, not really."

"It's for your own fookin' safety," Drake said. "Because if you go sticking your nose into places where you're not welcome, snooping around in other people's business, terrible things can happen, and you could very well end up here. You take my meaning, do you?"

"Yes sergeant," replied Nyhavn.

"Do you?" Drake said holding his stare to make certain that the Minnesotan understood the gravity of what he was saying.

"I do," Nyhavn said, properly intimidated.

"Good," Drake said following the alley back to the busy street out front. "Now, let's catch up with the others. We have work to do."

As he walked Nyhavn wondered why Drake still hadn't said anything about who killed Molly Neal or why. He wondered too how come if he recognized her or suspected who she was at the river, then why hadn't he said anything to the police?

As he and Private McKay hustled to keep up, Ben also wondered if what Drake had just offered was truly advice after all, or perhaps, a not so veiled threat.

Chapter 18

Winter blew in out of the North Atlantic like an open-handed slap to the city's face. It stung the exposed skin of those caught in it and had its red faced victims bending low and shivering as they clutched their hats, scarves and collars, and moved quickly to their destinations.

The first severe storm hit in late December and dumped several feet of heavy wet snow on the city. Throughout the first two weeks of January, more snow and freezing rain continued to fall and accumulate, bringing the city to a near standstill. Snow drifts, as high as their thighs, compounded their daily duties and they went about their routes with cautious steps on slippery paths.

Even with the lousy weather the job still had to be done. Exemption fees still needed to be collected, bounty jumpers, and those who had been called up and failed to show, still needed to be rounded up and brought in.

For the Minnesotans, cold as it was, it was nowhere near as cold, or as bad, as the winters back home. There, bitter storm fronts howled down from the vast and open Canadian plains and sent temperatures plummeting, and leaving the Gopher State well below zero for months on end.

First Sergeant Lynch and those who figured that the Minnesotans would whine and complain about their canvas accommodations were surprised when the three made do with little fuss. They took their winters in familiar stride.

Each morning after taking care of their outhouse chore, and before heading out on their rounds, they banked the hot coals in their stove, covering them with a mound of protective ash. They counted on the blanketed ash to keep the hot coals smoldering until their return later in the day. Most days, it worked.

But when the work day ran late, the protective ash wasn't enough and the covered coals went out, they struggled with numbed fingers and Lucifer matches to light crumpled paper and kindling, to carefully bringing the stove back to life.

Cold, wet boots were dried on a make-shift rack near the stove while chilled feet were covered with several pairs of warm, wool socks and positioned towards the stove.

From late November to mid March, they fed buckets of coal chunks into their stove to keep the Sibley tent, in what Kinnunen told Drake was, 'reasonable comfort.'

To Frantzen, that included the radiant warmth of the stove, a good meal, and a tobacco filled pipe on the worst of nights. To make sure they had something to eat when the work day ran long and when they missed their dinner hour, the big German kept a covered kettle of sausage and beans flavored with molasses nestled in the snow. In the cold, it would keep.

Next to the pot of food he also kept an always filled coffee pot. As the coffee and the beans were thawed and reheated, the tent was filled with a pleasing aroma, and 'reasonable comfort' was maintained and well appreciated.

'Reasonable comfort' left room for the odd icy gust of wind to slip through the tent flaps, or having to knock away the build-up of ice on the canvas walls to keep the tent from collapsing.

On nights when the bad weather kept them away from *The Thistle Down,* Privates Miller and Dean would stop by to play cards bringing with them brown, longneck bottles of beer and a flask of, what Miller claimed was, 'proper' Irish whisky.

"Proper, is it?" asked Trigg, grinning.

"It will leave you screaming like a Banshee unless you sip it properly," he said, on his first visit to their make-shift card table.

"What's a Banshee?" asked Kinnunen.

"My sister, but she bore two lovely and glorious little girls..."

"You have two nieces?"

"Three, but the older one's a horrible, mean little shrill like her mother, a Banshee in training," Miller said, pouring himself a small glass of the bottle's golden content before passing it around to the others.

"To dull your heathen wits, so drink up, deal the bloody cards, and feel free to make as many drunken, foolish bets as you can."

On other nights the Minnesotans would take care of their mundane chores; mending holes in their shirts or socks, stoking the stove, cleaning their weapons and boots. Frantzen began his winter project of carving an elaborate new bowl for his pipe out of a wood burl, while Trigg could usually be found deep in his Bible earmarking and making notes on several chapters and verses. Despite his occasional lapses in moral judgement, he was still planning on getting ordained.

The cold nights and oil lamp turned young Ben into a devout reader as well, but not the Bible. His reading interests were found in the growing collection of Illustrated Weeklies and Beadle dime novels that he stored in a wooden crate beneath his cot. In the flickering light from the lantern, he could be found entrenched in Wild West adventures. He would read, well into the night, of bold escapes from blood thirsty savages, heroic saves of helpless, and well illustrated shapely young women, or remarkable gun play from keen-eyed marksmen. Whenever he encountered words he didn't know, Kinnunen or Miller would serve as his dictionary and mentor.

Not all nights though were spent in the tent or at *The Thistle Down.*

One benefit of the dismal weather conditions was that it occasionally offered up some reduced rates on other city entertainments. On less blustery nights or off duty hours Miller pulled them out of their tent to visit P.T. Barnum's American Museum on Broadway and Ann Street, assuring them that they'd enjoy themselves.

"What kind of museum is it?" asked Kinnunen uncertain whether he wanted to make the trek uptown.

"There are good shows and curiosities, and you know, awhile back I even saw Jenny Lind there."

"The Swedish Nightingale?" said Kinnunen, warming to the idea of a visit.

"The very same," said Miler. "She had the face and voice of an angel."

"Will she be there tonight, you think?"

"Probably not but you'll still find Barnum's interesting for the .25 cent admission charge."

Miller was right, of course. Barnum's American Museum was interesting and slightly bizarre. It was a huge five storey building adorned with colorful signs, panels, and flags on its exterior and more visual distractions inside. In good weather they were told that an out of tune band played on a second story veranda over the entrance to attract business. On their first late afternoon visit though, the band was playing indoors. After paying the two bits admission they found what Miller had promised, along with an entertaining flea circus, a bearded lady from Europe, and a well worn tree trunk that Jesus's Apostles sat upon as they pondered their gospels.

Trigg, of course, was skeptical about the authenticity of the tree trunk as well as another of Barnum's curiosities, '*The FeeJee Mermaid*,' that looked more like the top half of a small female monkey had been sewn on the bottom half of a large fish.

"What? You don't think she's real?" Ben said to Kinnunen leaning in for a closer inspection.

"Naw," he said. "Fish breathe water, women breathe air. Besides, if mermaids were real, I'd spend more time fishing."

However, one of the entertainers at the Museum that Trigg and the other Minnesotans found impressive was General Tom Thumb, who stood less than three feet tall and gave an interesting, and entertaining performance. After the show and on their way back to Five Points it was all they could talk about.

"He's got to be the smallest man I ever saw," Nyhavn said as they trudged through the snow.

"That's a fact," said Frantzen. "Talks funny too."

"Hey waiter! Bwing me a Welsh Wabbit!" said Miller, mimicking Barnum's General.

The group of soldiers guffawed.

Nyhavn had another question. "Whose army do you suppose he was a General in anyway?"

"Can't say," replied Miller.

"What do you suppose he did in the army? I mean, with his being so tiny and all?"

"Small unit tactics, most likely," said Kinnunen bringing on a new round of laughter.

By late March, when the cold weather had finally released its grip on the city, their anticipation of going home began to bud and blossom along with the first signs of spring.

By early April, after seven months in New York, the Minnesotans' three year enlistments were finally coming to an end. Two days before their official release date Miller informed them that the First Sergeant wanted to see them in the Orderly room.

"Donnie Drake told me that you've been summoned by the man himself. Ten o'clock sharp," he said.

"The good First Sergeant or the Lord of the Manor himself?" replied Kinnunen in a fine Irish brogue.

"Both actually, my country cousins," said Miller.

"Did he say why?"

"Perhaps you've heard me say that why is never big on the First Sergeant's list of philosophical fookin' questions. Could be because the Captain wants to let you bask in his greatness one last time."

"We heathen baskers now, are we?" asked Kinnunen.

"Or something like that. "Could be because the Captain will try to talk you into staying on."

"Staying on?" Trigg said, waiting to see if Miller was kidding him. "You're joking, right?"

"No. It seems we're short on heathens..."

"No offense meant, Finn," said Frantzen. "But short or not, I'm not staying on. I'm going home."

"None taken. It's a sound idea. A few of us didn't think you would be staying on which is why we're planning a proper send-off for you at *The Thistle Down* later tonight. If you can't make it, we'll celebrate without you."

"You're a good man, Mister Miller," said Kinnunen.

"Ain't I though? Now get to burning your morning *shite*, so you have the proper aroma to greet the good First Sergeant."

At five minutes to ten they had reported to the First Sergeant in the Orderly Room, and at ten, they were standing in front of the Company Commander's desk.

It was only the second time since they arrived that they had been invited inside the plush and comfortable confines of the Captain's office, and just as with their first visit they were not offered a seat this time either. After the First Sergeant took up his customary position as Praetorian Guard behind the seated Patrician, the Captain addressed them.

"Stand at ease, men," said O'Brian with uncharacteristic joviality. "Stand at ease. Your time here has passed swiftly, hasn't it?"

Because it was a rhetorical question and didn't require a response, they gave none, and instead waited for the Captain to get to the point of the meeting, which he would, after some lofty posturing.

"Sergeant Drake tells the First Sergeant that you are good, reliable men who have been invaluable to his crew," he said.

Kinnunen suspected that the Captain knew the exact value they had provided, right down to the penny. They all did, but they wisely remained quiet.

"With that being said, I would like to offer you an opportunity to extend your enlistments and remain with us here awhile longer. There would, of course, be certain incentives and proper inducements to do so."

"What kind of incentives, sir?" asked Nyhavn showing interest that surprised even his friends. He sounded genuinely interested.

"Well, for one, we'd move you into the barracks. That tent was only meant to be a temporary accommodation until certain renovations upstairs were completed. How are the renovations coming along, First Sergeant?"

"They're almost done, Captain," assured the First Sergeant carrying on the lie. "We'll find them room."

"Good, good," said Captain O'Brian. "In addition, I'd like to offer $100 bonus to each of you in return for a one year extension here with the Company."

The officer offered a practiced, benevolent smile as he waited for their answer. It was Frantzen who was the first to decline. "It's a tempting offer, sir," he said. "It really is. But speaking for me, it has been a long war, and I intend to head back home, sir."

"And I, as well, Captain," added Kinnunen, leaving the Commanding Officer to redirect his attention to Nyhavn. The young Corporal at least still appeared to be interested in the proposition.

"And you, Corporal..."

"Newhaven," said Lynch, mispronouncing his name.

"Yes, Corporal Newhaven," echoed the Captain. "How about you? Will you consider the offer?"

"I'd like to think on it some, Captain, if that's all right?"

"Yes, of course, certainly," said the officer, somewhat rebuffed. "I can promise you that there's much to be gained by staying on," he added. But when not one of the Minnesotans had asked for any elaboration on what exactly would be gained by staying on, the Company Commander cut the interview short, along with his jovial tone.

"Well then," sniffed the officer with a sudden air of formality. "I suppose we're done here. Corporal Newhaven, I look forward to hearing your answer. Gentlemen, I thank you for your service. The First Sergeant will see to your separation papers," Captain O'Brian said and then turned back to Lynch. "First Sergeant?"

Lynch nodded to the Captain and hurried the three soldiers back out into the Orderly Room.

"You two can turn in your side arms and issued equipment to the supply room. Be back here at one o'clock for your travel and separation papers and any pay you have coming to you," he said. Then, pointing to Nyhavn the First Sergeant said, "You! Hurry up and make up your fookin' mind."

Without another word, Lynch did an about face and went back into the Captain's office for a private discussion.

"Know what?" laughed Nyhavn. "I think I just did."

"Don't tell me you were you serious about staying on, Corporal Newhaven?" asked Frantzen.

Nyhavn shook his head and said, 'Naw,' only the big German knew better. Of course he was giving it some serious thought, and Frantzen knew why. He had nothing and no one to go home to. Had Lynch not been his usual, miserable self, it was likely he might have stayed on. But it didn't matter now.

At a little before one o'clock they reported back to the First Sergeant and found him seated at his desk, hunched over his ledger book. As usual, Lynch let them stand there for a bit before he finally acknowledged their presence.

When he did look up, he opened his top right drawer, and pulled out a small stack of papers and several pay packet envelopes. "Before I release you from duty here, there are still a few outstanding accounts that need to be settled," he said holding onto the papers and pay envelopes.

"Outstanding accounts, First Sergeant?" said Kinnunen wondering what this latest play was about.

"That's right, for the coal."

"The coal, First Sergeant?"

"That's right," Lynch said checking his ledger book to verify the amount. "The coal you used to heat your tent. That's a dollar a month you owe," he said. "According to my records, you were here seven months, so that's seven dollars…"

"Seven dollars?"

"Each."

"But you put us in the tent!"

Lynch lip curled up in a feral grin. "You want the separation papers or not?"

With little choice Frantzen and Kinnunen recognized their only real play here and took it. Arguing with Lynch amounted to pissing on your own boots.

"Go ahead and take it out of the pay we're owed."

Lynch tossed over the papers along with the brown paper packets. "I already did, so now you're free to go back to your back wood hovels and wallow away your pig *shite* lives," he said, just as a young woman entered the Orderly Room, balking at the sight of the soldiers.

"You the Fallon girl?" barked Lynch.

"Aye, Bridget Fallon," said the young woman. "I have an appointment with Captain O'Brian." She was clutching a worn cloth handbag to her abdomen and staring at her best and scuffed shoes. The woman- a girl really- was perhaps seventeen or eighteen years old, and too thin to be called slender. Her long straight blonde hair fell flat against a wan face and displayed a wide forehead while her tired brown eyes chronicled disappointment.

"Your appointment was for twelve-thirty. It's one o'clock. You're late," said Lynch momentarily ignoring the Minnesotans.

"I'm sorry, but I was…"

"Late is what you are," growled Lynch. "No excuse."

The First Sergeant stood and escorted the woman over to the Commanding Officer's door. He knocked twice, cracked open the door, and leaned his head in the office. "Your afternoon appointment is finally here, Captain. You still have time to see her?"

"Send her in," said the Captain. "And please, no disturbances."

"Yes sir."

"Let's go, missy," said Lynch, impatiently waving her forward. "We don't have all day."

Once done Lynch turned his attention back to the three soldiers standing at his desk.

"You made up your mind yet, Newhaven?" he asked of the young Corporal.

"I have, First Sergeant," Ben said. "I'm going home too."

"Yeah well, I thought as much," he said retrieving Nyhavn's separation papers and pay packet, and shoving them towards the young Corporal. "Turn in your issued…"

"Already have, First Sergeant."

"Then, you three are officially dismissed. You have twelve days to report to your headquarters in Minnesota. Take any longer than that and you'll be absent without leave and arrested, and brought back here in shackles," he said. "Now get the hell out of my building." Over his shoulder, he yelled, "Sergeant Dumshee!"

"Yes, First Sergeant?" said the dull-eyed clerk.

"See them from the premises and make sure they don't steal anything when they go."

"Will do, First Sergeant," said the Company Clerk.

"But our train doesn't leave till tomorrow, First Sergeant," said Frantzen.

"Not my problem now, is it?" Lynch said gruffly. "Get out and close the door as you go."

They were halfway down the stairs when the pistol shots rang out behind them. The first loud boom was followed by two more in rapid succession, with a fourth, more deliberate shot a moment later. The shots thundered out into the hallway like focused lightening strikes.

Dumshee was down on his knees clinging to the rail while the Minnesotans were already bounding back up the stairs towards the Orderly Room.

The door to the Company Orderly Room was partially open, but blocked by someone seated against it. The frosted glass of the upper half of the door showed little of what was going on inside. Hugging the wall and easing up to the doorframe, Nyhavn drew his captured pocket pistol from beneath his jacket, and took a quick peek through the narrow opening. He knew better than to rush into a room where shots had just been fired until he had a better idea of what kind of trouble might be waiting for him on the other side.

He tried nudging the door open with his left foot, but it didn't budge. Whoever was leaning against it was taking in labored breaths. The Minnesotans were soon joined by Kevin McKay who had a pistol ready. Since he and McKay were the only two that were armed, Nyhavn motioned for the others to stay back while he and McKay took the lead.

"Hello the room!" he called and when there was no response, he tried again. "Hello the room?"

"In…in here," came a raspy reply. "Here…"

"Cover my play," said Nyhavn and McKay nodded.

The Minnesota Corporal leaned his shoulder into the door and shoved. He went in low to the left with his pistol ready while McKay went in high to the right.

"Bollocks!" cried the First Sergeant. "Be careful, you clumsy oafs!"

Lynch, who had been seated against the door, shoved it back with a prolonged groan and a flurry of profanity. He was sitting up with difficulty with his legs stretched out in front of him. He was holding a pistol in one hand and covering a bullet hole in his chest with the other. Blood oozed out between his fingers, and his face was pale and losing any of its remaining color. Both soldiers lowered their pistols taking in the bloody scene.

Bridget Fallon, the thin and tired looking blonde who had arrived late for her 'housekeeping' appointment, was lying dead in the open doorway of the Captain's office. Next to her hand lay a small Derringer. There was a bullet hole in the girl's thin chest and a second bullet hole through the top of her skull. Fired from less than ten feet away Lynch had had an easy kill shot.

Further on Nyhavn could see the splintered hole in the Captain's ornate desk showing where the bullet to her chest had punched through her frail figure and into the dark wood.

Behind the desk, Captain O'Brian was slumped back in his chair, a look of surprise locked in his unmoving eyes. The Derringer's bullet had entered his face just below the right eye. Brain matter, blood, bone, and tissue were sprayed across the back of his chair and on the expensive drapes and wallpaper behind him.

"The...the stupid little bitch...she...she killed the Captain," Lynch said in a hoarse voice. His breathing was raspy and forced from the lung wound and getting worse, his words blood wet. "Shot me too!" Pink blood bubbles were foaming and popping at his nostrils. "Don't...don't just stand there, you halfwit," he said to McKay. "Get me some help."

Nyhavn shoved his pistol in his pocket and used one hand to steady Lynch and pry him forward to free up the door, much to the First Sergeant's angry displeasure and pain.

"Goddamn it!" he yelled, but Nyhavn ignored him as McKay leaned back out into the hallway.

"The First Sergeant and the Captain have been shot," McKay said to the others. "You!" he said fixing on the frightened Sergeant Dumshee who had inched up behind the others and was trying to see what had happened in the Orderly Room. "Run and get some help."

The company clerk peered around the shoulders of the others in the doorway, and as he caught sight of the dead girl and the growing pools of blood, he froze.

"Dumshee! I said go and find some help," McKay said again to the stunned company clerk.

"Wha..., what happened?"

"The girl killed the Captain and lung shot the First Sergeant. He needs a doctor. Run and get some help."

"Listen to him, Dumshee...," groaned a weakened Lynch. "Go. Get the police too." The still shaken clerk finally acknowledged the request and did what he was told. Lynch sat back against the door and it closed under his weight.

More soldiers in the company had begun to gather on the landing near the Orderly room door, but still kept a wary distance. When Sergeant Drake came bounding up the stairs a few minutes later, he barked his way through the small crowd.

"Step aside!" he yelled. "Move!"

At the door, Kinnunen tilted his head towards the Orderly Room. "We heard gunshots and came running," he said. "Ben and Kevin are seeing to the First Sergeant. He's been shot."

Drake shoved open the door to gain entry only to have Lynch cry out again. "I SAID GET ME SOME GODDAMN HELP, NOT KILL ME!"

A bewildered Drake stood stock still.

"We sent Dumshee for a doctor," explained McKay. "The First Sergeant's wounded. The Captain and the girl are dead?"

"Dead?"

"Yeah, the housekeeping girl," Ben said.

"The housekeeping girl shot them?"

Ben nodded pointing to the dead woman in the Captain's doorway.

"You shot her?" Drake said to the First Sergeant who, stared at him angrily from the floor.

"Damn right...I did! She...she murdered the Captain...and then tried to murder me too...but I...I put her down," he said pointing to the girl with the barrel of his pistol. "I put another round in her just to be sure."

"Here now! Give me that," Sergeant Drake said reaching down and taking the pistol from the First Sergeant's bloody hand. Lynch started to object, but the searing pain in his punctured and torn lung turned his mind to more immediate concerns.

"Where's...where's the doctor?" said the First Sergeant.

"He's on his way," said Drake, tucking the hand gun in his belt. "Help's coming."

To McKay and Nyhavn Drake said, "We need to move him away from the door. Take his feet."

The First Sergeant groaned loudly as they lifted him up and moved him just to the right of the doorway. Drake opened the door and said to Kinnunen and Frantzen, "Keep everybody out who doesn't have any business here. We don't need an audience for this bloody mess."

Kinnunen and Frantzen nodded and took up their positions.

"And let me know when the doctor or the police show up."

"Will do," Kinnunen said before Drake closed the door again.

"Good Christ, it hurts," moaned Lynch when the sergeant took a knee beside him.

"Little wonder," said Drake taking another glance at the dead girl who he knew would be blamed for the shooting. "The bullet's punctured one of your lungs, air's escaping, and blood is flooding in, drowning you. Hear it?"

Lynch's eyes suddenly went wide in fright as he leaned his ear close to his chest and heard the faint gurgling sound coming from the bleeding hole.

"Sit me up! I can't breathe on my back."

"I've seen wounds like this before. You're dying," Drake said. "In fact, you'll soon be dead."

"The Hell you say!" rasped Lynch, struggling to sit up.

"No," Drake shoving him back down on the floor, "To hell you're going!" He brought his right knee down hard on Lynch's bullet damaged chest and pressed his weight into it.

What little air that was left in the shattered lung, and what air remained in the good lung, was quickly being squeezed out.

"This is for Molly Neal, the girl you put in the river," said the New York sergeant.

Lynch struggled to sit up, only to have Drake slap his arms away and violently shove him back down. The First Sergeant fought to push Drake's knee from his chest without success.

"She was with the Captain's child. That's why she was killed."

"I…I didn't kill the girl," protested Lynch. "It was her husband. He… he did it."

"Aye, and you made it so," said Drake.

"No…no, I didn't. Get off of me…I…I can't breathe."

"Neal whored out his wife to the dandy Captain. And when he couldn't take the shame of her being with another man's baby, he got drunk, and choked her, maybe by accident, maybe on purpose. Then, to cover it up he beat her so that no one would recognize her before dumping her body in the river. Her blood's on your hands and so is this poor girl here, you fookin' pimp."

Lynch roared, or tried to as he clawed at the Sergeant, but any strength he had remaining was diminishing from the blood loss. Drake easily pinned the First Sergeant's arms to the floor.

"It's Judgement Day," he said throwing his full weight over the knee and pressing harder. "So just die and go piss on brimstone."

The First Sergeant bucked violently but Drake held him down until a final rush of blood wet air wheezed from his damaged lungs and his eyes rolled back and his body went limp. Drake kept his knee on Lynch's chest to make certain he was dead before he slowly got back to his feet. He calmly straightened his uniform as he studied the faces of the two soldiers who had witnessed the act.

"The First Sergeant died from his horrible, gunshot wound," he said. "Bled out."

Nyhavn and McKay, who had watched and done nothing to stop it, agreed. "Nothing we could do to save him," said Private McKay, taking the hint.

"Nothing at all," added Nyhavn, "A real shame."

The matter was settled.

"When the police get here I'll handle it," said Drake as he reached to open the Orderly Room door. "Stick around; they'll probably want to ask you both a few questions."

"Afraid there ain't much to tell," said Nyhavn. "It is what it is."

"Aye," said Drake turning his gaze back on the dead Fallon girl, "but no longer how it will be."

Chapter 19

The first police officers to respond sealed off the Orderly Room and the building to keep the soldiers in and the press out. The two Detectives, who were conducting the investigation, went about it in methodical fashion.

After a cursory examination of the murder scene, they noted the placement of the bodies and the weapons, before interviewing the doctor who responded to the call, and the city coroner. Then, while one Detective talked to McKay and Nyhavn, the other interviewed Donnie Drake before comparing their notes.

Their conclusion, as they would report it, was that it was what it appeared to be, nothing more.

They were just about finished when a troubled looking Police Captain appeared in the doorway, brushed by the policeman at the door, and made his way over to his Detectives.

The Police Captain, Big Jim Flannery, was a bulky, ruddy faced Irishman with bloodhound eyes that had tracked one too many brutal crimes in the Points, and left him wearing a cynical disposition towards his fellow man and a constant scowl.

As his Detectives filled him in on what had happened, and the Coroner went back downstairs to send his people up to retrieve the bodies, Flannery did a quick survey of the crime scene and shook his head, disgusted by what the Detectives were telling him and what he could see. His eyes stopped briefly on Drake before settling back onto his two Detectives.

When the lead Detective had finished his assessment, Flannery said, "So, who's in charge here, then?"

The Detective pointed him towards the Provost Marshal Sergeant.

"I know you," said Flannery, crossing the room. "You're Drake."

"Yes sir, Sergeant Donnie Drake."

"You run the street crew."

Drake nodded and Flannery said, "Don't suppose maybe you can tell me what really happened here?"

"Not much to tell, really," said Drake. "I was downstairs when I heard the gun shots. I came running up the stairs, and found the First Sergeant slumped against the door..."

"Dead?"

Drake shook his head. "No, not then," he said, "But bleeding badly. We sent someone for a doctor and for your people."

"Lynch able to talk before he died?"

"Aye, he said that one of the Captain O'Brian's housekeeping appointments, the girl there, shot the Captain..."

"Housekeeping appointments?"

Drake shrugged. "The Captain, it seems, had worked out, eh, special arrangements with some women in the ward who couldn't afford the commutation fees for their sons, husbands or brothers that were drafted..."

"Worked what out? What are you talking about?"

"Favors, instead of payments, and a promise to keep them out of harm's way."

The Police Captain's flushed with anger. "Good Christ! And Lynch knew about these appointments, did he?"

"He set them up."

"The dumb sons of bitches were lucky they didn't get shot sooner," Flannery said, fuming at the arrangement.

"Lynch wasn't in his right mind, what with him being an opium smoker and all," said Drake.

"Opium?"

"Yes sir, this fell out of his pocket," Drake said handing the Police Captain a small ball of brown tar in crumpled paper. "There's a pipe in the top drawer of his desk."

As the Police Captain slowly shook his head and swore to himself Drake went on.

"Lynch said the girl shot the Captain, and then turned the pistol on him. Close as she was, she hit him once in the chest, but he said he managed to get off a few shots of his own."

Flannery's gaze went to the dead girl in the doorway and then back to Drake, his face mirroring what he was thinking.

"What a bloody cock up," he growled, rubbing the late afternoon stubble on his prominent chin. Drake wasn't sure if the Police Captain was talking about the shootings or the attention from the newspapers that the incident might bring. The press would have a grand time with this. "Where's the First Sergeant's clerk, Corporal Dumshee?"

"He was in a panic so I sent him to let our headquarters know what had happened here. After all, we still have a Company to run."

"Yes, that's right, you do," replied Flannery. "Good thinking, what with tomorrow being the second Friday of the month and all."

"Second Friday, Captain?"

"I take it then you're not aware of the existing arrangement between this office and the Sixth Ward's Betterment Association?"

"Existing arrangement, Sir?"

"Bi-weekly donations to the Association that your Captain had worked out with the Alderman. It goes to benefit the needy in the Points, all perfectly proper."

And there it was, thought Drake. The sudden shift from the shootings to the business side of things wasn't even subtle. Drake though, played along.

"No sir, I wasn't aware, but once Dumshee gets back I'll make sure he briefs me, and I'll personally see that it is handled."

"You do that," replied the Police Captain.

Drake knew now that it wasn't just the killings that brought the Police Captain down to the crime scene. It was that, and, of course, to ascertain just how much damage had been done to their tidy little enterprise.

"Consider it done, sir," said Drake who now saw an immediate opportunity and went for it. "I mean, unless headquarters decides to send some other uptown dandy down here who doesn't appreciate the local Association, and what it does for us here in the Points. The Captain wasn't a Points' man, you know, and neither was Lynch. If they were, they would have known better than to do something this stupid. Lynch should have never let it happen."

"No, he shouldn't have," said the Police Captain.

"It wouldn't if I was the First Sergeant," added Drake as the big Police Captain reappraised the plucky street crew Sergeant. It was a moment or so before he spoke.

"You saying you could handle things here the way Lynch did?"

"No sir," Drake replied, matter of fact. "I'm saying I'd handle things better."

"Better, could you?" said the Police Captain, skeptical of the soldier's claim but waiting for his next response.

"Yes sir."

"And how would you do that?"

"Well, for one thing I wouldn't allow any new Captain who shows up here to have any 'commutation appointments.' That's money that's not going into the proper hands. It's bad business, and bad all around."

"That it is."

"It wouldn't hurt to put another crew on the street either."

"Another crew?"

"Aye," Drake was thinking about the 'privileged soldiers' who needed to earn their keep. "We could double our collections…"

"Double them?" echoed the Police Captain working the numbers in his mind. His eyes glistened with possibility and, of course, greed.

"Yes sir, from the soldiers I already have here on the roster. There are some that got a pass from Lynch for the collection work. If I had Lynch's job I'd put them to work, and any who say that they can't serve the ward, I'd take out back for a sensible little talk."

"If they still have a problem with that, you just bring any of the little whiners by my office and I'll straighten them out as well."

"You saying I have Lynch's job, Captain?"

"I'm saying I'll tell the Alderman that things here are temporarily in good hands. The Alderman has some influence with your headquarters regarding those who are assigned to the company. Who knows? If things run smoothly here, then maybe we'll see about making this your full time job."

"Good enough, Captain," Drake said knowing he would make it work. The first thing he'd do when Dumshee returned would be to corner the little weasel to find out where the rest of the company records were kept.

He'd found one ledger in Lynch's desk, but only the one that listed and tabulated the company's official expenses. It was the second ledger that he knew that Lynch kept and kept hidden that would provide the real tally.

From that book he would find out just how much of what they took in was siphoned off before they passed along to Headquarters, where the money went, and how much was delivered to the Police Captain and the Betterment Association.

Although Drake had never heard the Latin phrase, *Quid Pro Quo,* something given in return for something else, the street wise Sergeant readily understood its meaning as did Captain Flannery.

"Stop by the precinct at eleven o'clock tomorrow," said Flannery. "Ask the Desk Sergeant for me personally. I'll tell him to expect you."

"Eleven o'clock it is."

"Good," said Flannery, who then told the detectives to find out what was taking the Coroner's people so long to retrieve the damn bodies. "They're starting to stink up the place." Pointing to the dead officer, he said, "And for God's sake, someone pull up the piss ant's trousers!"

The tall, lanky Detective turned to the uniformed Policeman standing guard in the doorway. "You heard the Captain," he said. "Take care of it." The policeman reluctantly complied. Rank had its privileges.

"The dead girl have any relatives?" asked Flannery and the lead Detective nodded.

"A brother, we found a telegram in her purse informing her that he'd been killed fighting somewhere in Virginia," the Detective said.

"No other relatives then?"

The Detective shook his head and said, "None that we can locate."

Flannery weighed what he had seen and heard and then said, "Okay then, here's how it plays. There is a mob of newspaper reporters outside, so when the Coroner and his people carry her out to the morgue I want the gun in her hand. Nobody here talks to the newspapers about this, and I mean nobody. You hear me?"

"Yes sir," came the reply from those in the room.

"I'll handle the reporters," he said. "And you," he said turning back to Drake, "I'll see you in the morning."

"Eleven o'clock sharp, Captain."

Flannery nodded. "I'm sure that the Alderman will want me to pay a call to your Provost Headquarters afterwards and tell them to send a replacement officer who knows how to keep his pecker in his pants," he said. The Captain looked back at his detectives and asked, "We done here?"

"All done, Cap'n," said the tall detective.

"Let's wrap it up. I've got better things to do."

And with that, the official investigation was over.

The Captain's impromptu press briefing on the front steps gave the reporters their stories. The morning newspapers would carry sensationalized accounts of how the woman, distraught over the recent conscription and subsequent death of her only brother in battle, had shot and killed the two valiant Provost Marshal soldiers.

O'Brian and Lynch, of course, would be honored for their dedicated sacrifice while serving their city and nation in a time of war. Captain Flannery would make no mention of Captain O'Brian's trousers being found down around his ankles. Nor would he mention the sordid arrangement that the First Sergeant and the Captain had forced the young woman and the others into, let alone suggest any hint of wrong doing or impropriety on their part.

Black arm bands would be distributed, and the Mayor would eulogize the two, publicly mourning their passing. Meanwhile, Tammany would scramble to find some new crony to fill the vacancy and keep the Five Points office up and profitable.

Later, when Sergeant Donnie Drake joined the Minnesotans at *The Thistle Down* for their going away party he filled them in on the rest. Miller, Joe Dean, and Kirk were with them, and between the six soldiers, they were doing a decent job of celebrating. Their eyes and speech tallied the number of drinks they had consumed.

"Here you go," Frantzen said handing him a shot glass of whisky, while Nyhavn poured him a beer chaser from a half-filled bucket.

"Much obliged."

"Figured you'd need it," Nyhavn said.

"I do indeed," Drake said, dropping the shot glass into the beer mug and downing it. Once done he set the mug back down hard on the table and wiped his mouth with the back of his sleeve. "The Police came and went in no time. Blamed it on the girl, of course."

"A shame that," said Miller with genuine dismay.

"Another shame is that Headquarters will be sending someone from up town to take over for Captain O'Brian."

"Another dandy?" asked Kinnunen.

"Certainly someone whose hands have never known a callous," said Miller with a snort.

"More than likely," added Drake. "We'll see."

"And what about Lynch's position?" asked Kinnunen. "They sending in another wretched sort to replace him?"

"They already have."

Joe Dean frowned. "Well that didn't take them long to drag the gutters to find some suitable piece of *shite*," he said.

"I've been called worse," Drake said as heads turned towards him.

"You?" said a pleasantly surprised Dean as Drake nodded.

"It seems I've received a temporary promotion," he said.

If he was looking for a protest from those seated at the table around him, he didn't find it. The others seemed genuinely pleased.

"The Company is better for it," said Kinnunen congratulating him by holding up his beer mug, as did the others in salute. "Hear! Hear!" he said with the soldiers repeating the toast. They downed their drinks.

Frantzen was refilling Drake's glass when Miller lowered his head and swore. "Damn my drunken Da! With you in charge I'll be walking punishment guard till Judgment Day!" he said with an exaggerated sigh.

"Worse, since you and Dean will be taking over your own crew, Corporal," Drake said.

"Corporal? Me?"

"Aye, since it will now be your job now to break in the lads from upstairs on their new duties as assigned."

"What? You mean the precious little ones will finally be getting their hands dirty!"

"Kev has Dumshee and a few others cleaning up the Orderly Room. He and Roacher will by later. Dumshee's about ready to *shite* himself."

"Like I said," Kinnunen said with a chuckle. "The company's in good hands."

Drake offered a chin up nod in thanks. "So, when are you heading out?" Drake said, changing the subject.

"Tomorrow noon," said Kinnunen.

"Can't say I'll be happy to see you fellows go. You heathen berserkers are good in a scuffle," laughed Miller. "Almost good enough to be Irish!"

"What's a berserker?" asked Nyhavn.

"From the word *berserk*. You know, crazy? It's one of your people's words," Miller said.

"My people?"

"Yeah, from the maniac Vikings who charged off into battle screaming and yelling and terrorizing the good and decent civilized folk. What? You don't know your own history, boyo?"

Nyhavn shrugged. "I guess I don't," he replied. He knew that his family had come over from Denmark when he was maybe five or six and that he had a vague recollection of a crowded, foul smelling, lower deck of a ship. Fragments of the less than joyous ordeal were well etched into his memory. He had heard his mother and father talk about the old country from time to time, but the fact was, he only knew a little Danish, and even less of the country itself, let alone anything about the Vikings, other than they were good fighters.

"Berserk is one of the words you Vikings introduced to the Irish shores."

"You're not fooling me?" said Nyhavn taking a drink of his beer.

Miller shook his head. "No, your heathen ancestors rowed up to our beautiful peaceful emerald isle, ambushed our men, burned our villages, and then ravaged our slowest and ugliest women. Those they took to settle in England, France or home to create a long line of homely miserable little bastards. Much like yourselves," he said. "No offense meant, of course."

"None taken," said Kinnunen, "Hard to argue with Irish history."

Finn Miller held up his beer glass in response. "Ah now, isn't education a grand thing?"

Chapter 20

The going away celebration at *The Thistle Down* carried on well into the night. The saloon was noisy and crowded and the New York soldiers and the Minnesotans added to it in loud and boisterous fashion.

Beer and whisky flowed amid cigar smoke and more toasts. The soldiers were drinking, flirting with the sporting ladies, and enjoying themselves immensely. Miller noticed Nyhavn chuckling to himself as he kept eying a soldier who was standing at the bar. The soldier, who wasn't part of the company, nor anyone Miller recognized, was locked in conversation with several other men and took little to no notice of the going away party. He was a slope shouldered Army Private with a waxed tipped mustache that couldn't hide a ruddy, pock marked face.

"What's so funny, Ben?"

"Ah, better and better," announced Nyhavn, sitting up straight and straightening his tunic.

"What is?"

"I think I know that soldier over there," Nyhavn said canting his head towards the bar.

Miller turned his chair for a better look.

"That fellow there," Nyhavn said pointing to the soldier, "The one with the fancy mustache."

"He's not in our company," said Miller, trying to recall if he had seen the soldier before.

"Who?" asked Frantzen, overhearing part of their conversation and turning in his chair out of curiosity to see who they were talking about.

"The soldier with the squirrel's ass for a mustache," replied Miller turning back to the table to resume drinking.

"He someone from downtown?" asked Frantzen.

"No," Nyhavn said getting to his feet. "Gettysburg."

"Is that right? He one of those New York boys who took part in the charge with us?" said the big German.

"No, not the charge…later," Nyhavn said taking a moment to steady himself. Two hours of casual beer drinking made him a little wobbly. "I'm gonna go on over and say hello."

The young, semi-drunken soldier eased his way around a few tables and made his way over to the bar. As he got closer he turned his right ear to listen in to what the soldier was saying to those around him, and after a moment he was certain of the voice.

"I'll be damned! It is you!" he laughed stepping up and slapping the soldier on the back by way of hello. The slap was a little harder than he intended and startled the man. The soldier broke into a confused smile, as did two of the civilians he was with at this sudden reunion.

"I'm sorry, but do I know you?" asked the soldier.

"Sure you do. We were at Gettysburg together," replied Nyhavn. "In different units, I mean, but we were both there." Tipsy as he was some of his words carried a little spray as he spoke, much to the soldier's mounting annoyance.

"A fierce battle," said the soldier, first to Nyhavn and then to the others. "A touch of hell, it was."

"And hell afterwards too. But you know that, all of the dead and dying around us."

"Horrible, it was."

"Tookey, isn't it? Your name, I mean?"

"Brian Tookman, but yes, my friends call me 'Tookey.'"

"Friends like Hannigan?"

"Now there's a name I haven't heard in a long while."

"Me too," said Nyhavn, leaning back and then hitting the soldier as hard as he could. The punch came in low from his side and carried behind it all of the weight he could muster. Tookman reeled from the blow and fell back against the bar. Nyhavn kicked the man's feet from under him, sending him sprawling to the floor. He was cursing all the while he was putting the boot to him. Ben was causing some real damage until Frantzen raced over and pulled him off.

"Let me go! This no good snake in the grass robbed me!" yelled Nyhavn trying to break free. He almost succeeded until the big German readjusted his grip.

Realizing what else was about to happen, Drake ran around the table to intercept the bar owner, who came bounding over the counter, wielding his wicked looking club. Close up the nails that were tacked into the much dented and scarred end showed a terrible history, and intent.

"Hear now! There will be none of that!" yelled Hellman starting to move on Nyhavn as Drake waved him off.

"No, leave 'em be!" Drake said overriding the bartender's call. "It's a personal matter." To better emphasize the point, Drake held open his coat and rested his hand on the grip of a pistol tucked in his waist band. Hellman froze.

"Lynch will have your fookin' heads on a pike when I tell him about this," he growled.

News traveled fast in Five Points, but it seldom traveled true. Word had it that there was a shooting at the Provost building, but there were few actual details.

"Perhaps you haven't heard. Lynch was shot this very afternoon. He's dead," Drake said. "And perhaps you also haven't heard that I'm the new Lynch."

That bit of news surprised Hellman, who in turn stopped Barney, his big, slow-witted lout from charging in to quell the fight from his seat near the free lunch counter.

"Hold on, Barney," said Hellman, grabbing the man's arm and momentarily restraining him. Barney, who was eager for a fight, reluctantly did what he was told.

"If it starts to get costly I'll break it up myself," said Drake, offering a reasonable compromise to the bar tender.

Hellman wasn't happy with it, but he reluctantly agreed. This was now a business matter, and for some, a little light entertainment. A number of patrons were on their feet cheering on the fight. They wanted more.

"No breaking of furniture or glassware!" bellowed Hellman, but Drake had no intentions of letting it too far out of hand. He knew it was in his own financial best interest to minimize the damage.

From Lynch's second ledger Drake learned the full extent of the First Sergeant's illicit activties or other earnings. The numbers revealed just how much of the siphoned off funds went to Tammany Hall and the local police. It also detailed how much the two had taken for themselves, and which banks they had stashed the Captain's money. When he found the second ledger in Lynch's room Drake also found a small can of Chinese opium and $7,000 in cash the First Sergeant had squirreled away. The ledger devoted several pages to Lynch's private dealings and interests in several establishments, including *The Thistle Down*; interests that Drake would now manage, something not lost on Hellman.

"He's lying," said a defiant Tookman getting to his feet. "I didn't rob anyone."

"Yeah you did, you rat bastard!" yelled Nyhavn still trying to break free to get at him.

"You sucker punched me, boy, but try me now," said Tookman taking a Prize Fighter's stance.

"You up for it?" Drake asked Nyhavn and when Ben nodded, Drake yelled, "let him loose." The big German did just that.

Tookman came in with two quick left jabs followed by a right hook. The jabs missed but the hook caught Ben on the left side of his face. He staggered but stayed on his feet. Ben was clearly no boxer. But Five Points had taught him to be a scapper.

Tookman came at him again with a series of straight punches, and as the thief set his left leg for a left hook that would finish the little bastard, Nyhavn kicked the man hard in his leading leg. The kick caught Tookman in the left shin and caused him to lose his balance and stumble-step. That's when Ben hit him with a left hook of his own. Tookman raised up his arms to block the punch so Ben kicked him in the balls.

Tookman was doubling over in pain when a third kick caught him on his upper lip. A chunk of tooth flew across the sawdust covered floor as the thief slumped back against the bar, down and dazed. Nyhavn was about to kick him again when the New York Sergeant nodded to the big German, who once again stepped in and scooped the young soldier up in a bear hug.

Having made wagers on the outcome, several of the saloon's patrons were egging on the fight.

"Leave 'em be," yelled a disgruntled customer. "I've got a fiver says the boy will win!"

"Enough now!" yelled Hellman over the noise. "Enough. He's done."

Tookman wasn't getting up off of the floor to carry on the fight. He barely managed to right himself, sitting with his back against the bar trying another ploy instead.

"What's wrong with you goddamn people? He attacked me for something I didn't do! I want this man arrested," he said, looking to Hellman, and the others for support, but found none. His plea wasn't convincing enough to draw any sympathy, let alone assistance.

"Yeah, you did!" yelled Nyhavn, twisting in Frantzen's grip, but was unable to free himself.

"He rob you, did he?" said Drake stepping in to calm him down.

"The night of the charge, he did," Ben said. "They spoke their names. He and another soldier named Hannigan were robbing those who had died or those of us too wounded to do anything about it. He took everything I had."

"No, he's mistaken," Tookman said from the floor. "We were helping to bring back the wounded, risking our lives, and this is the thanks we get."

"You were helping yourselves to anything we had in our pockets!"

"Did he now?" said the Sergeant stepping in and hovering over Tookman, who was still adamantly denying the allegation from the floor.

"It's…it's a lie!" he said, a little too unconvincingly. "I swear it."

Tookman hadn't yet caught on that it didn't really matter to Drake. He was on Nyhavn's side regardless.

"You're done with this thieving piece of *shite*?" he said to the riled up Corporal.

Nyhavn gave a reluctant nod.

"He squared up with what he owes you?" Drake said to the bar owner as he reached down and helped Tookman to his feet.

"Aye, he's paid up," said Hellman.

"I don't deserve to be treated like this," the beaten man said, wiping the blood from a nasty looking swollen and split lip.

"Yeah, you do, so I suggest you leave now and don't come back," Drake said, and with an afterthought held him there in place. "Only before you go, I think you need to pay back what you took from my friend. How much was it, Ben? How much did he steal from you?"

"It wasn't just money," replied a still fuming Nyhavn. "I didn't have much money."

"Okay then, what was it? A family watch, maybe?"

Nyhavn shook his head still glaring at the thief. "Hardtack," he said, finally.

There was an awkward stillness in the room from the crowd as Nyhavn's reply sank in.

"Hardtack?" said Drake as laughter slowly grew in volume. It was too ridiculous for it not to be true. "Army crackers?"

"And some family letters and a few coffee beans too. He took it all!"

Drake looked to the bartender who rolled his eyes and let out a snort deferring it to the Sergeant. "Well then, taking everything a wounded soldier had on him, that's something different now, isn't it? Let's see what he has on him to compensate you for his robbery. Oh, will you look here!" said Drake, rifling Tookman's pockets and coming up with two five dollar gold coins, and some other assorted loose change. He stuffed one of the gold coins and loose change back in the injured man's pocket but kept the second gold piece. "This will do," he said.

Tookman protested or tried to. "Even if I did what he says I did, no hardtack or coffee beans are worth five dollars gold." His words whistled through his fat lip and broken tooth.

"Probably not," said Drake. "However, if you like, you can take it back up with my friend again. You still up for another go, Ben?"

"Ya sure, you bet'cha I am!" roared Nyhavn.

"There you go. Your decision," Drake said to Tookman, even though Drake already knew the man's answer.

As the thief limped out of the saloon, Drake flipped the gold coin to Hellman. "For the inconvenience," he said with a nod to the bartender, who managed a chin up nod of his own.

"But no more trouble from him," Hellman said pointing a cigar stained finger at Nyhavn who was rubbing his bruised fist that was beginning to swell.

"He's had his justice," Drake said as Kinnunen led Nyhavn back to their table.

"A right fine Biblical solution too," Trigg Kinnunen said, refilling the young soldier's beer glass. "I don't know about the eye for an eye part. However, I definitely saw a tooth go flying. By the way, did I hear you call him a *snake in the grass?*"

"I did and he is!"

"More cowboy talk from your illustrated cowboy stories, is it?"

Nyhavn started to deny it but couldn't. "It's as good a description as any," he said, defending the term.

"Yeah, it is, *pard*," Kinnunen said taking another drink, "Especially for a polecat bush whacker like him."

"Our keen eyed hero here stood valiant and true," said Frantzen, getting in on the ribbing.

"I'd say he rode off on his horse, but there seems to be enough horse *shite* here already filling the conversation," Miller said as the table erupted in laughter.

With calm restored, and money and drinks flowing freely once again, several working ladies closed in on their party.

When soldiers had money in their pockets, alcohol and lust produced lucrative results for both the women and the saloon. As the sporting ladies conducted their negotiations, Drake made his way over to the bar for a private word with the slightly mollified bar owner.

"Let's talk," he said, moving down the bar so they could hold a private conversation.

Unsure of just what Drake knew about the business arrangement Lynch had with him, Hellman chose to play his cards close to the vest. Drake expected as much, so he laid out his own hand.

"Lynch had a sixty-forty split for the soldiers he sent your way, both to the saloon and brothel, isn't that right?"

"Yeah, we had an arrangement," said a suspicious Hellman. "What of it?"

"Well, since I'm charge of the men in the Provost's company now I'm thinking it's time we renegotiate the agreement," Drake said.

"Could be you're just temporary," countered Hellman, "So maybe I should just wait and see if anybody else comes along?"

"Could be," admitted the Sergeant. "But you know Big Jim Flannery, don't you?"

Donnie Drake knew he did and waited for Hellman to acknowledge the obvious. The bartender gave a slight nod. "I know Flannery, sure."

"Yes, well… could be he thinks I'll be in charge of the Provost Company for a good while. But you can take the matter up with him, if you like?"

There was no way the bar owner would take anything up with the Police Captain, unless he wanted to lose more of his profits. Hellman was a lot of things, but he was no fool.

"What kind of terms are you thinking?" said the annoyed owner.

"I'm thinking a split more along the lines of seventy five-twenty five."

The bartender's eyes narrowed as a thin cord of muscle in his neck began to twitch. "You looking to press me harder, are you?"

"Not unless you won't be satisfied with the seventy five?"

Hellman's surprise was immediate. "Me with the seventy five?" he said leaning back from the bar, quizzically staring at the Provost Sergeant. After a moment of trying to figure Drake's angle, he gave up. "Since I don't believe in the goodwill of my fellow man why don't you tell me what you're really after?"

"What I'm after is a more honest working relationship," Drake said. "I suspect you held out some of the take with Lynch…"

Hellman started to take exception to the accusation, but the Sergeant held up a hand cutting him off. "I have his book. I've seen the numbers and let's face it; I've seen the business you do here too. It was a lousy split to begin with," he said. "I would've done the same. An honest twenty five's good enough for me, just don't short me or we'll have a problem."

Hellman held his tongue and temper. He was well aware of Drake's reputation.

"In addition, I would like you to run a tab, like say for some table drinks and some company from the ladies. It's for my friends there who are leaving us in the morning."

"A tab, tonight?"

"Uh-huh, a running bill that you take off against the twenty five percent for the soldier's I send your way."

Hellman rubbed his whiskered jaw still trying to figure the play. "A suspicious man might ask why you're being so generous and settling for less."

Drake smiled. "A suspicious man might not understand that since I plan on sending more business his way, what I lose in the split, I'll make up in numbers."

"Numbers?"

"That's right," said Drake. "Lynch decided where his people could drink and socialize in their off hours so he sent them over to *The Irish Rose*. He said it was because you chewed off the ear of one of his uptown soldiers..."

"I didn't chew the damn thing off," countered Hellman, "My club cut it so I just ripped off what was hanging."

"Yeah, but that was his public excuse. What he kept private was, about that time, he bought half interest in *The Irish Rose*."

"I figured it was something like that."

"If you're interested, I'd like to sell that half interest to you at a decent price."

Hellman didn't need to ask Drake how it suddenly was his to sell and instead asked, "What's decent?"

"A little less than what he paid for it. I'll show you his numbers and what he pulled in each week and you decide. The simple fact is I'm a soldier, not a businessman."

Hellman could argue that point with the Army Provost Sergeant as well but so far liked what he was hearing.

Drake added,. "Of course, if you're not interested, then I can always send all my people to *The Irish Rose* and stay with the agreement that Lynch put in place with you."

What Drake was offering was a good deal and Hellman knew it. "So, what kind of tab are you looking to set up?" he said.

"One for only me and a selected few of my boys. After all, you still have a business to run. I'll let you know who gets put on a tab in advance. So, do we have a deal or what?"

"Aye, we have a deal," agreed Hellman. He spit in his palm, Drake did the same, and they shook on it. By Five Points standards the deal was sealed. Greed had a way of making Hellman happy.

"We've paid for our drinks up to now, so put the rest on the books for my table."

The bartender nodded and did just that reaching down and retrieving his ledger and making the necessary notations before waving over the house madam who was standing at the end of the bar.

"A moment, Kate?" Hellman said to the long legged doxie with auburn hair who sashayed towards the bar smiling. As Hellman explained the new arrangement to Kate the woman kept her playful eyes on the New York Sergeant.

The Brothel madam was dressed in a pleasing low cut cream colored bodice and a short black ruffle skirt. She wore black stockings and maroon high topped boots and an impish smile that promised a whole lot of fun at a price.

"Oh, and one other thing," said Drake before rejoining his people. "Would you remind your girls not to rifle my boys' pockets, especially my backwoods cousins over there?" Drake pointed to the Minnesotans. "They're leaving in the morning. They need their money for the journey, so no pilfering."

"Wouldn't think of it," Kate said with a glint of fun behind her Celtic blue eyes. "Well, not now anyway."

Chapter 21

A barking dog in the alley below brought the big German awake. Turning his head on the goose down pillow towards the bedroom window, he was met with a sharp shard of sunlight that cut through the parted curtains and stabbed at his eyes. Frantzen squinted as he brought a hand up to shield him from the glare. Turning his head, he sat up on his side of the bed, scratched, yawned, and then stretched out a few kinks.

He smiled at his pocket watch on the night stand. It was a little after nine and in a few hours he'd be boarding a west bound train heading home. The big German smiled again as he reached down and pulled on his trousers and boots, and retrieved his shirt. Even with a head pounding hangover, it was a good day, maybe even a great day.

"You paid till noon," said the woman who was watching him dress. "No one's saying you have to leave."

"Got a train to catch, sweetie, but I appreciate the offer. I truly do." Frantzen pulled out an extra dollar from his pants pocket for a tip and laid it on a nearby washstand. "Enjoyed myself considerably, thank you," he said, patting her blanket covered rump. "Oh…don't suppose you know which rooms my friends are in, do you?"

"The other soldier boys?"

Frantzen nodded. "The Minnesotans anyway," he said. "We'll let the others sleep."

"Which ones were they again?"

"The clever, book smart one with glasses..."

"Can't say. Maybe Megan or Kate..."

"And the younker..."

"Younker? You mean, the young one, the fighter?"

"Aye."

"He was pretty drunk so I think he's with 'Once Blessed Moira.'"

"'Once Blessed who?"

"Moira. Last door on the left. If you change your mind, you know where to find me," said the woman rolling back over and going back to sleep. She wasn't expected to be downstairs until late afternoon, and it was still way too early to be getting up.

Out in the hallway Frantzen knocked on Nyhavn's door, and then on a few others until he found Kinnunen two rooms down on the right. "Nine o'clock," he yelled through the closed doors. "Best be getting up and ready. We don't want to miss the train!"

Grunts and groans acknowledged the call as did a string of curses and insults from others during the finding process.

Carrying his sackcoat and cap, the still smiling big German made his way downstairs to the now empty saloon and took a seat at a table to wait for his friends. Other than an old swamper who had swept away the sawdust and was mopping out the bar, *The Thistle Down* was deserted.

The saloon wasn't much to look at, but in the evening light it held an illusion of promise. Chipped upended chairs sat atop scarred tables. Old, creaking floor planks smelled of soap, stale beer, tobacco, and vomit. In the more honest light of day the promise was long gone.

Outside, Five Points was already alive and bustling and the noise and bright sunlight that came through the window left him squinting and searching for some much needed coffee.

"Any coffee?" he asked the swamper who shook his head.

"None here," said the old man, "but they got some at Brennan's bakery down the street. They've been open since dawn."

"Good enough," Frantzen said as Kinnunen slowly made his way down the stairs to join him. Trigg looked much the way he felt, which was more than a little worn from the long and loud night. After a quick visit to the privy closet, he was ready to find the coffee too.

"Where's our young Kit Carson?" he asked, brushing away the sleep from his eyes.

"On his way," replied Frantzen, but after ten minutes more when Nyhavn still hadn't shown, they decided that maybe they needed to go back upstairs to fetch him.

"Which room?" asked Kinnunen staring down the darken hall.

"That one, best as I can recall," replied Frantzen, pointing to the last door on his left and then corrected himself remembering which way he was facing. "No, your other left."

At the door Trigg knocked and yelled, "Ben, you ready?"

When they received a mumbled response they entered and found Nyhavn still nestled in the arms of a partially clad woman. The woman's back was turned to them and both Kinnunen and Frantzen found themselves staring at the body of a goddess that was 'Once Blessed Moira.' Her legs were long, shapely, and led up to a heart-shaped backside and a beautifully tapered waist. Her hair was the color of honey, soft and shiny as expensive Chinese silk, and cascaded down cream colored shoulders.

When she craned her neck to see who the interlopers were, Kinnunen's eyes immediately locked onto what he would later swear were the most perfect breasts he had ever seen. They were large, firm, and wonderfully inviting. 'Once Blessed Moira' was well-blessed.

However, when he finally made his way up to her face, Trigg Kinnunen physically blanched. Any blessings had suddenly stopped at the shoulders for 'Once Blessed Moira' had the face of a horse. Her face was long, thin and blunt, on a much too long neck. Her nostrils, like her eyes, were a little too far apart, and good gravy, she even had large horse teeth!

"Go away! He doesn't want to go with you," she said, while a still drunk and semi-asleep Nyhavn seemed content with the idea as he nuzzled back into her soft, warm flesh.

"Yeah, he does," said Kinnunen, yanking back the covers. "He just doesn't know it yet. Come on, cowboy. Time to go home."

"Gaw...way," Nyhavn mumbled trailing the talk with unintelligible gibberish as he pulled the bed cover back over himself and settled into a fetal position.

"How much did he drink?" Kinnunen asked the woman as he scooped up Ben's trousers, trophy pistol, and shirt from the floor.

"Plenty and he still owes me for the bottle of whisky," she said, pointing towards an open bottle on the wash stand.

"But it's still half full?" said Frantzen picking it up and shaking it.

"Doesn't matter," she said. "Once it's been opened, it's been bought."

Trigg leaned over and shook Nyhavn's shoulder. "Come on, Ben," he said. "There's a train to catch, remember? We're going home," Kinnunen pulled back the bed cover and thrust the young soldier's pants and shirt into his hands. He held onto the pistol. "Now get up and get dressed, Corporal Newhaven!"

The bleary eyed Nyhavn sat up, bundled up the offered pants and shirt in his hands, pulled them into his chest, and then eased back against the woman.

"Oh, no you don't! I said, let's go!" yelled Kinnunen nudging his shoulder a little harder this time. "MOVE IT!"

"In a minute…" said Nyhavn, without moving his lips. His eyelids fluttered briefly and then closed again.

Looking around the room, Kinnunen found a partially filled water pitcher atop a marble-topped wash stand. Realizing what he was about to do with the water pitcher, 'Once Blessed Moira' scrambled to free herself from the young soldier's drunken embrace, just as the intruder dumped its contents on him. Nyhavn sat up in bed sputtering from the wave of water.

'Once Blessed Moira,' who hadn't been fast enough to get out of the way, was once splashed in the process and didn't appreciate it one bit. "There's no call for that!" she said, as she started around the bed, ready to fight.

In her hurry she banged the big toe on her right foot against the bed frame. She let out a cry, swore, and then sat back down on the edge of the bed, clutching her injured foot.

"Sorry, but the boy has gotta go," said Kinnunen.

"What?" said the bleary eyed Nyhavn, staring at Kinnunen trying to figure out what was going on. "Is it the rebels?"

"No rebels, Ben. Train's leaving. We gotta go."

Behind him Frantzen was happily cataloging the scene. 'Oh, this is good,' he said more to himself than the others. The woman's body was jaw droppingly beautiful but her face proved that Heaven blessed gifts required a hell of a cost. Unattractive as she was, both men watched appreciatively as her breasts bounced and jiggled like a pair of frisky, warm nosed puppies in the thin, diaphanous robe she was barely wearing as she massaged her bruised big toe.

"He says he loves me and wants to stay," she said. "You want to stay, don't you, honey?"

"I…I do. I love…her..,"

"Yeah? Who?" asked an amused Frantzen.

"Her!"

"Her, huh?"

"Yeah, her."

"Okay, then what's her name?"

"Moira, honey," she said to Nyhavn as Frantzen pulled his legs off of the bed and handed him his shoes.

"That's right, Molly Hunley," Nyhavn replied, looking to the woman and then back at the big German nodding.

"Moira Connelly," said the woman correcting him. "Besides he paid up till noon."

"I'd say you gave him his money's worth and then some," said Kinnunen.

"Oh, I did and he's welcome to stay. The boy knows how to please a woman, especially with that French Joy thing he does."

That little admission surprised his friends, especially Kinnunen who was dermined to know what it was exactly and how and why it worked women into a joyous frenzy. Later, he'd ask him about it again but with a train to catch there was no time to waste. "What's he owe you for the whisky?"

"Two dollars."

"For a half bottle?"

"Then make it one dollar. But the bottle stays."

"Molly can come with me…" said Nyhavn, buttoning his pants and struggling to get into his shirt through blood shot eyes. Bile from the night's drinking was churning in his stomach, threatening to heave.

"Moira," said the woman correcting him.

"…can come with me…you wanna come with me, Molly?"

"To your ranch, sweetie? Sure, maybe I will. Tell me about it again."

"Actually, it's a farm," said Kinnunen. "And did he tell you its way out in Indian Country?"

"Indian Country?"

When Kinnunen nodded the woman stopped rubbing her bruised big toe and began paying closer attention to the conversation. "At least it was a farm until the Indians killed his people…

"Killed everyone," Ben said staring at the wall in front of him and seeing more than striped wallpaper. "Savage sons of bitches."

"Stole everything worth taking and then burned it down," said Kinnunen.

"Sons of bitches!" growled the young soldier.

"So it'll take some time and money to make it reasonably comfortable again. He's got the time but not the money. Hell, not the farm either. The bank took it."

"The rat bastards!" said Nyhavn. "But I'll get it back. I ain't afraid of hard work."

"Backbreaking work," added Frantzen to the woman, without much in the way of exaggeration.

The sporting woman's eyes narrowed as she began to rethink her retirement strategy. What had sounded promising last night abruptly began to wane this morning.

"I…I love her!" said Nyhavn and turned back to the woman. "You!"

"He's still drunk, but maybe he does love you like he says, so you are welcome to come along with him, if you want," said Kinnunen. "But you'll have to make up your mind in the next few minutes and pack a quick bag because, like I said, we have a train to catch."

"No ranch, huh?", 'Once Blessed Moira' said to Kinnunen.

"Charred ruins."

"I'll build us a sod house," Nyhavn said, reaching for his black leather brogans and falling over against the wash stand. The fall knocked the water pitcher off of the stand, and when it hit the floor, it shattered into a dozen pieces.

"That'll cost you too!" yelled the woman. Hellman burst into the room to see what the noise and commotion was about. He had a truncheon in his meaty hands and appeared eager to use it.

"Everything okay here?" he asked the woman from the doorway, seemingly unconcerned about the soldiers or the odds that were clearly against him.

Kinnunen dug into Nyhavn's coat pocket and found his separation pay. He counted out four dollars and handed it to the woman. "That should cover the whiskey, the water pitcher, and then some. We good to go?"

"You are now," 'Once Blessed Moira' said snatching up the money. She limped over to Nyhavn who was still trying to get into his shoes. Leaning over she grabbed his head in her hands and bounced his face between her perfect breasts. Kissing him on his forehead, she said, "Goodbye, my love! I'm afraid it's over."

"Over?" protested Nyhavn. "What? Why?"

"You'll have to go home without me."

"Without you? But I proposed to you!"

"Yes, you did," said the woman. "And I'll be heart broke about the decision for a long while to come, but somehow I'll manage, and eventually, so will you."

"Come on, Ben," Frantzen said, helping Nyhavn up on his shoulder and half dragging him out of the room.

"I won't forget you, Molly!" said Nyhavn over his shoulder.

"Ah, but you already have."

"Oh, don't you worry," said Kinnunen, "because in case you do, I can assure you that Al and I won't let you forget this anytime soon either."

"Thank you, Trigg."

"Oh, you are more than welcome, Romeo!"

"Who?"

"Another young tragic-comedic figure."

"What?"

"Nothing," laughed Kinnunen. Because all's well that ends well."

Chapter 22

It took a series of trains, several unscheduled delays, and two drunken nights in Chicago to get them as far as La Crosse, Wisconsin. Along the way Provost soldiers, town marshals, or city police had stopped them to check their travel orders before allowing them to proceed.

The delays and trip took ten days to the rail line that ended at the Mississippi river. The next part of their journey home would come by boat and then coach after that.

Their plan was to take a paddle wheeler upriver to St. Paul, debark at Lambert's Landing and then make their way up the bluff to Fort Snelling. There they would officially out-process from the Volunteer Regiment and once done, they could at last make their way home. But that would come later, and judging from the number of boats and barges tied up at the Wisconsin waterfront because of heavy fog, it might very well prove to be much later.

The train had squealed to a jerking stop in La Crosse a little before sunset, and after retrieving their baggage, they made their way over to the waterfront on Pearl Street.

At the quayside Steamboat Line ticket office, they learned that the *Northern Belle*, the very flat-bottomed paddlewheel boat that brought them down from St. Paul three years earlier, was moored and waiting as well. Like the other boats and barges hugging the river pilings, the *Northern Belle* wasn't going anywhere.

"Fog got us locked in, huh?" asked Kinnunen, making conversation with the ticket agent.

"You see Grand Dad bluff from here?" said the ticket agent pointing off in the distance behind them. The three soldiers turned and saw nothing, but cold, thick, roiling clouds blanketing the countryside.

"Big as life right in front of you when it's clear. But then, there you go," said the ticket agent. "A thousand boats go upriver every year but none today. The fog's swallowing up the upper Mississippi and most of northern Minnesota and Wisconsin. Nothing's moving on the river, at least till noon tomorrow. Where you boys heading?"

"St. Paul."

"Fort Snelling, huh?" said the ticket agent "You got your travel papers? We're not supposed to sell you tickets unless you have your travel papers."

"Yes sir, we got them," Kinnunen said handing his over as the others did the same.

"Well, if it clears up any, the *Belle* will go, but can't say what you might run into further upriver. You might get as far as Winona or Red Wing, if it fogs up again."

"Well that gets us closer."

"That it will," said the ticket agent, handing their papers back. "Could be it'll take you all the way to St. Paul tomorrow, could be a day or two, if it doesn't lift."

"We're optimists," replied Kinnunen. "We'll take three tickets."

They were up against the clock and calendar to get back to Fort Snelling, and a day or two of delays would make it a close call. Lynch had purposely only given them twelve days on their travel orders knowing that if they didn't make it home on time, then they would be held as deserters by the local authorities, and turned back over to the army until the issue was resolved. Given all that had happened they hadn't thought about having the travel orders amended or even suspected it would be a problem.

The best solution was to get to Fort Snelling. If all went well in the morning then the trip north would only take a day which meant they had a day to spare.

However, fog as thick as raw cotton made river navigation impossible for the passenger boat, as well as the freight-hauling river traffic. It was overtaking those streets closest to the river with a decided chill and soon it would be rolling over a large portion of the town.

"It was clear for awhile this afternoon, so it's likely to do the same tomorrow too," added the ticket agent handing across the boat tickets. "If you can't afford cabins I can let you sleep in the main parlor on the boat for a dollar more. There are tarps and blankets."

"Is the kitchen open on the boat?"

The Ticket agent said it wasn't, telling them that any meals while the boat was docked would have to be found in town.

"Any place you would recommend? Someplace with good food at a good price?" asked Kinnunen. The ticket agent nodded and pointed them back towards the street that paralleled the river.

"Three blocks up Front Street, next to the hardware store, there's a small café run by some Dutchies," said the agent. "Good food and plentiful for the price."

"You feel like eating some German food?" Kinnunen said to Frantzen. "Do you, Dutchie?"

"Oh, only for going on three years now," replied the big German, dryly.

With growling stomachs they hurried off to find the cafe. They paid the extra dollars to sleep in the boat's parlor, figuring they could kill some time at the café over a hot meal, and maybe kill some more time over a few beers at a saloon.

It was the table noise and inviting aroma of sizzling seasoned meat that steered them through the cold to the crowded cafe. Well into the supper hour, the café was busy with a mix of what looked to be locals and a handful of better dressed steamboat passengers. The proprietress, a tall woman in her late-forties greeted them just inside the doorway and pointed them back to the last remaining table near the batwing doors of the kitchen.

"There!" she said with a thick European accent. The 'there' came out 'dare' and produced a small smile from Frantzen. The German pronunciation was fine with him, and comfortably familiar.

Weaving their way around the tables and chairs, Nyhavn and Kinnunen took their seats, while Frantzen remained standing. He was offering a significantly friendlier smile to a younger version of the hostess who was making her way out of the kitchen with a tray full of food orders. The obvious daughter was as tall and sturdy as her mother. The resemblance was clear. Both women were big boned, had bright blue eyes and pleasing smiles. The mother's once blonde hair had been dulled and grayed by time, while the daughter's hair was the color of woven wheat. A handsome woman to some, Frantzen though, was mesmerized.

The daughter caught the big man staring and blushed as she brushed away a lock of hair from her face. She held his stare and then returned his smile. The mutual attraction was immediate.

"Please," said the older woman walking over to their table, pointing to the day's menu that was neatly printed out on a chalkboard on the wall. The older woman's accent made Frantzen smile again.

"*Sind sie Deutsch?*" he said, asking the older woman if she was German in her native tongue. The big woman broke into a broad grin and then tore into the language at a fast clip. In an instant they were both laughing and locked in an old world conversation. Nyhavn and Kinnunen listened, not really understanding much except for the word 'beer,' and maybe something about apples as Frantzen apparently gave their orders to the woman, who left to fetch them.

"What was all that about?" asked Kinnunen.

"Intelligent dialogue in a civilized tongue," replied Frantzen to his two companions. "By the way," said the big German turning back to his friends. "I ordered us some fried potatoes, sauerkraut, and baked pork slices with apples. Beer too, lager beer."

"Beer in any language is civilized," said Kinnunen. Ben agreed.

When the older German woman brought their drinks, their guttural conversation continued until her attention was drawn away by customers looking for coffee refills, to place their orders, or to pay for their meals. If that hadn't kept her busy, taking away the cups and dishes, and wiping down the tables afterwards, did. Shorthanded, the mother and daughter shared the café tasks at a hectic pace.

Before she excused herself, the older woman said something more to Frantzen in German, laughed and patted his shoulder as she went off to wait on the other customers.

"Well, you've seem to have made a friend," said Kinnunen leaning back in his chair. "And judging from the silly grin on your face, it looks like you wouldn't mind making a friend of the younger one over there either."

Kinnunen glanced over at the woman only to have the others follow his gaze.

"That's one comfortable looking girl," Nyhavn said, admiring her.

"The German word for that, Ben," said Frantzen, "is *zaftig*."

"Good looking too," admitted Kinnunen.

"Beautiful, actually," replied Frantzen. "The older woman is Frau Gonsenheim and that's her daughter, Margot. Seems the mother's husband died of consumption last winter and the daughter's husband was killed in the war a little over a year ago."

"A widow, huh?"

"Uh-huh," said Frantzen. "And they've both more than likely struggled since, but, it looks like they managed to make a go of it with the cafe."

"You got all that just ordering our supper, did you?"

"Time waits for no man."

"Well, you wasted no time getting down to business, and speaking of the obvious, business here seems good," Kinnunen said looking around the diner. The eight tables and three bench seat booths were filled with customers, who appeared to be enjoying the food.

His survey of the café momentarily stopped on three hard cases seated in a corner booth. The three were river men, roustabout boatmen or freighters, most likely. From their loud, irritating voices and mouthy tone, it was evident they had been drinking before they decided to get something to eat. Most of their conversation was laced with profanity, much to the annoyance of a timid couple seated at a nearby table. The couple tried to ignore the river men, but couldn't. When they rose from a half eaten dinner to pay their check and leave, one of the men muttered something crude to the woman, and then guffawed over the woman's embarrassment, and the man's sheepish discomfort.

"Decorum, gentlemen, decorum," said a well dressed, older gentleman seated a few tables away from the river men.

"Oh, shut up, old man. We're just having a little fun," said one of the river men, a hatchet faced little man who laughed at the customer until he was forced to turn away.

A second boatman, a burly, round-shouldered bull of a man with a gray bushy beard that had the color and look of wet, dingy moss, was making more than his share of grumbling. Their behavior frustrated Frau Gonsenheim, but there was little she could do about it, and they knew it.

"Hey, Dutchie! Bring me more goddamn biscuits!" boomed the big boatman from across the room, as Frau Gonsenheim was serving the soldiers their drinks.

"One moment, please," said the heckled woman.

"Not you!" laughed the river man, "The young one with the big tits."

Frantzen's head shot up and his back stiffened as he turned towards the loud mouth. Without a word he stood, and walked over to the café's small counter where the young woman was preparing the basket of biscuits.

"Here, let me take those," he said taking the basket from the young woman who had just started around the counter. "Let me help."

When the young widow hesitated, Frantzen insisted. "Please let me. You're a little busy here." The young widow passed him the small basket. Frantzen smiled at her again before it faded when he turned back to the task.

As he passed the mother, Frantzen said something to her in German. Frau Gonsenheim glanced at the river men and slowly nodded as she excused herself to see to the older, well-dressed gentleman who was holding up his hand to get her attention for his bill.

"They're a little short handed. I think I'll help out," Frantzen said to his friends as he passed their table.

"This our concern, is it, Al?" asked Kinnunen already knowing the answer.

"As good as any we've seen so far," replied Frantzen.

"And I suppose you're just going to talk to them, right?" Kinnunen said, suspecting he knew the answer to that question too, but asked it anyway.

"Depends on how well they listen."

"Of course, it does."

"Angle off as you go so I can keep a better eye on them," Nyhavn said, pushing his chair back and resting his right hand on the grip of his trophy pistol. The Smith & Wesson stock felt comfortable in his hand.

"Will do," said Frantzen starting off, only to have Kinnunen grab his arm.

"You're not doing this, say, maybe to impress the comfortable looking daughter?"

"Maybe that too," said Frantzen. "Is that a problem?"

"No, not really," said Kinnunen as he slid his hand into his pocket and brought out his New York blackjack bone breaker, tapping it once against his free hand. The heavy lead weight bounced on the spring inside its leather closure. "Always good to know why we're fighting and what cause we're serving."

As he approached the river men Frantzen kept his focus on the smaller, hatchet-faced man with the worrisome looking knife sheathed at his hip. Hatchet-face looked up from his plate when he saw the soldier making his way towards the table, and elbowed the burly man to his left to get his attention. The burly man with the bushy beard turned in his chair to face the soldier. Because his back was turned the third river man hadn't seen Frantzen walk up behind him and was startled when he looked up from his food and found the big German standing at his side.

"You ordered more biscuits, did you?" asked Frantzen.

"Not from you we didn't," said bushy beard. The big German ignored him choosing instead to keep his eyes on Hatchet-face. The knife, he knew, presented the real threat.

"Wisconsin's best serving tables these days, are they?" said Hatchet-face smiling a chipped tooth smile as Frantzen set the biscuits on the table.

"First Minnesota Volunteers, actually," he said, correcting him. "Things are a little busy around here, so I just thought I'd help out some, especially with you being so damned impatient and all. I'm told that between the three of you, you boys owe a total of $2.25 for what you've ordered."

Hatchet-face's nasty grin disappeared when he saw the other two soldiers at their table staring back at him, ready to jump. The young looking soldier had a serious expression and a just as serious grip on the pistol in his waist band. A second bookish looking soldier seated beside him was holding a head knocker of some kind, or maybe even a small gun.

"There's no cost for these biscuits that you're taking with you," said Frantzen, friendly enough as he kept close watch on the man's hands for any sudden movement. Trouble, he knew, would come from the hands.

"Maybe we ain't done yet, soldier boy," said bushy beard.

"Yeah, you are," he said and filled his left hand with the man's hair and slammed him face first into the table. Bushy beard's nose exploded with blood as it bounced off the hard wood surface. The café went suddenly quiet with the exception of Hatchet-face who had started to rise out of his chair.

"There's no call for that!" he yelled.

"Not now there isn't, no," replied Frantzen, still watching his hands. If Hatchet-face thought about taking on the big man with his knife, a quick glance at the younger soldier across the room made him change his mind. The boy had his pistol drawn and ready.

"You friends of these goddamned Dutchies?"

"And a goddamned Dutchie myself to boot, if that don't beat all," replied Frantzen. He held a stare and didn't blink. "Pay for your food and go," he said, and then waited until Hatchet-face and the third river man dug into their grimy pockets and counted out the coins to pay the bill.

The still dazed freighter was holding his bloodied, broken nose as a goose egg began to sprout from his forehead. He was a little weak in the knees too when his friends helped him to his feet. He may have been a hair taller than the German, but nowhere near as formidable, much to the annoyance of Hatchet-face. His man wasn't just hurt, he was cowed. He'd give him hell later.

"The food wasn't all that good anyway!" said Hatchet-face to the rest of the diners.

"Then you won't mind leaving," the big German said escorting them out of the door.

Heading back to his friends, he smiled when he caught sight of a stern faced young widow holding a cast iron frying pan in a tight grip. Frantzen nodded his thanks to the woman who returned the nod and went back to work.

Within moments the café soon was back to normal, or what passed for it. Nyhavn kept his hand on his pistol and his eyes on the cafe door for a good while afterwards, watching and waiting. It was a habit that had served him well in Five Points and he saw no reason to abandon it now.

The older, well-dressed gentleman, who had initially tried to calm the rowdy river men, made his way to the soldier's table just as Frantzen sat back down to his meal.

"Gentlemen, I'd like to thank you for the way you just handled the situation with those ruffians," he said, only to have the big German wave it off.

"No thanks necessary," said Frantzen. "Decent folks don't need that kind of trouble."

"He was glad to have us help him out," said Kinnunen, as the man held out a small white calling card.

"John Bishop Gaul, sir," announced the well dressed man. An impressive diamond stick pin adorned his cravat while a gold watch was tucked into his vest pocket beneath his expensive great coat.

"Trigg Kinnunen, Mister Gaul," Kinnunen replied reading over the card, wondering what he was supposed to do with it. "Sir Galahad here, is Al Frantzen, and the Kit Carson looking shootist there is young Ben Nyhavn."

"Pleased to meet you, gentlemen," said Mister Gaul. "And I apologize for intruding upon your dinner. I won't keep you. But did I hear you say you had served with the First Minnesota Volunteers?"

"Yes sir, we did," said Nyhavn.

"You were at the battle of Gettysburg, Pennsylvania?"

"The second day of it anyway."

"Then may I shake your hands?" he said, extending his hand and shaking theirs with palpable glee. "What your Regiment did at that pivotal battle was truly heroic."

"We just did what we had to," said Nyhavn with a shrug. "That's all."

"You're being too modest, young man, because I can tell you that what you men did was a bold and gallant accomplishment that will be heralded along the lines of Leonidas at Thermopylae."

"We were lucky. We fared slightly better," said Kinnunen, wondering where Gaul was going with this. Although he knew who the Spartans were, this was still Greek to him. "What can we do for you, Mister Gaul?"

"I am a Procurement Officer for the Pacific Transcontinental Railroad," he said. "We are looking for qualified men like you to accompany us as we move west."

"West?" said Nyhavn, his curiosity spiking.

"That's right," replied Gaul. "With the Pacific Railroad Act authorized by Congress, we'll soon have a railroad that stretches all the way to California, young man. When your military time is up and if you're interested, then I'd be honored to offer you good and steady employment."

"Our service time is up," said Nyhavn. "We're on our way back to Fort Snelling to be discharged. If you don't mind me asking, sir, what kind of work would it be?"

"We need stalwart men such as yourselves to serve as outriders and scouts for the survey teams, to watch over them…"

"From the Indians, you mean?"

"Yes, and to hunt game. I can assure you the food is good, but the pay is even better. We are going to have a mighty railroad across this great land of ours and I would welcome you to become part of this noble enterprise."

As Gaul laid out what Trigg Kinnunen thought was a recruitment pitch about the railroad, he politely smiled and nodded. Frantzen though, was still under the spell of the young German widow. When she brought over a complimentary basket of oven fresh rolls for their table, along with a small bowl of honey butter, the big German was lost in her blushing smile.

"*Danke*," he said, thanking the woman.

"*Bitte*," she replied, and in broken English added, "Please, your meal enjoy."

"I most certainly will," he said.

The eye contact between Al and the girl was brief, but long enough for any onlooker to see that both were interested in much more than biscuits.

Watching it happen, Kinnunen chuckled at his dumbstruck friend, interrupting the railroad man, and embarrassing Frantzen.

"Gentlemen, I beg your pardon," apologized Mister Gaul. "As I said, I don't mean to intrude on your meal. In fact, I insist on paying for it!"

Gaul dug into his frock coat pocket, pulled out several greenbacks from his wallet, and laid them on the table. It was enough money to cover the cost of their meal a few times over.

"No, that's all right, Mister Gaul," protested Kinnunen, his right hand raised to stop him. "You don't have to do that."

"Indeed I do! And I do hope you will consider my offer of employment."

"Out west, you say?" asked Nyhavn.

"That's right, son, all the way to California. The war will be over soon and we'll be sending out more surveying teams searching for the best route to the Pacific."

"How do we reach you, say, if we're interested in signing up?"

"I'll be in Council Bluff, Iowa on the Missouri River through June. If you wish to contact me there, you can send a telegram to me at the Grandview Hotel. Again, it has been an honor," he said. Mister Gaul, the railroad man, tipped his hat, excused himself, and exiting the cafe. Kinnunen and Nyhavn read over the calling card while Frantzen's attention was still very much focused on the young widow behind the counter.

"Good pay always sounds good," Nyhavn said to Kinnunen who took in a deep breath and then slowly let it back out.

"Ben, you worry me at times," he said. "You really do."

"Why's that?"

"Did you somehow forget that the pay seemed good before we joined the Army and then marched off into rebel cannons?"

"Indians don't have cannons."

"Yeah, well they've managed to do pretty well against the armies we send against them."

"We've done pretty well against the best the rebels could send against us too, you know."

"So there's no talking you out of it, I suppose?"

"No, not really."

"Well then here you go," said Kinnunen, handing Nyhavn the railroad man's formal calling card. "I will not deny you your destiny or fascination with the west, if you are so inclined. Al?"

"What?" said the big German, taking his eyes and attention away from the young widow for the moment.

"How about you womp our thick-headed younker a good one to knock some sense into him?"

"He can't," replied Nyhavn. "He's too taken with the young widow, who by the way, seems to be fascinated with him," said Nyhavn, grinning at Frantzen who ignored him, or tried to.

"She's probably lonely too," added Kinnunen. "I mean, she'd have to be to take interest in him."

"Very lonely," agreed Nyhavn. "Probably doesn't get out much. Could be poor eyesight too."

The big German frowned. "Why don't you boys go and see if the river's still there and maybe leave me be for a bit," he said.

"Alone, but not for long, I'll wager," Kinnunen said taking the hint. "How about we leave after we eat? And, what say we use some of that supper money the railroad man gave us for the saloon?"

"If that will get you two gone then, by all means, you can use my share," he said.

The two soldiers made fast work of their meal while the big German took his time. "If your romancing doesn't work out then you can find us up the street at the nearest saloon or parlor house," said Kinnunen with an outstretched arm, pointing in the direction they were going.

"A bar or a brothel? God knows there's a surprise."

"God also knows that man is weak, which is why He only made Ten Commandments. Anything else that isn't covered by the Ten I figure he left open to interpretation."

"Interpretation?"

"That's right."

Frantzen sat back and chuckled. "Why do I think that when you're ordained you're going to have a large flock of followers who are nothing but sinners?"

"Who better to save, Al?" replied Kinnunen, grabbing a dinner roll and putting it in his sackcoat pocket for later. "Who better to save?"

Chapter 23

The fog rose off of the river and spilled into the low lying streets and alleys that buffered the Mississippi. As Trigg and Ben left the café it had rolled around them in tumbling cold, gray waves.

The street was empty but there were loud hoots, laughter and lively piano music coming from what sounded like a saloon further up Front Street. Brightly lighted as it was, the fog reduced the saloon window's glow to a pale yellow haze. The raucous noise though was easy enough to follow.

"There we go," said Nyhavn, taking the lead.

"Good enough," said Kinnunen as they headed towards the revelry. The soldiers appeared as apparitions floating through the low and wet billowing clouds. Half a block on, Kinnunen's attention was drawn by several painful grunts and a muted cry coming from the end of a thin alley they had just passed.

"Ben, hold up a minute," he said.

"Why? What is it?"

"Gimme a minute."

The young soldier shrugged. "Gotta piss anyway," he said as Kinnunen stepped into the alleyway and made his way towards the commotion. His right foot kicked away an empty bottle in the dirt and mud path. The space between the buildings was narrow and cluttered.

Because of the fog, Trigg couldn't quite make out what was happening at the end of the thin lane, other than a flurry of shadowy movements that brought on the disturbing grunts.

Forty feet on the alley opened up to an abandoned boathouse on the river. Empty crates and the weathered spine of a broken rowboat blocked the route to the south while a keelboat was moored to the open and old wood pilings to the north. A warped wooden plank served as the boat's gangway.

Moving closer the soldier recognized the burly profile of one of the freight haulers they had ejected from the café. Next to him, the hatchet faced river man was standing over someone who was on the ground and desperately trying to defend himself from the vicious kicks Hatchet-face was giving him. The third freighter, who was supposed to be keeping watch, was instead, standing by watching the beating.

"What's going on here?" said Kinnunen, bringing out the blackjack from his pocket and holding it low at his side. Caught off guard, the freighters whipped around towards the interloper.

"Damn it all to hell, Jed. I told you to keep watch on the alley!" Hatchet-face said chewing out the third freighter as he did quick scan over the soldier's shoulder, immediately pleased that no one was behind him. The soldier was all by himself. Hatchet-face smiled.

"You soldier boys just can't seem to mind your own business, now can you?" he said as Bushy beard, the man that Frantzen had slammed head first into the table, positioned himself behind Kinnunen cutting off any possible retreat.

Trigg put his back to the wall to keep a better eye on the three river men. The man on the ground was the railroad man who had paid for their dinner and had offered them jobs.

"This my business, Mister Gaul?" Kinnunen said. The bleeding man nodded and received a boot to the ribs from Hatchet-face as a consequence.

"I'm gonna stomp you till your ears bleed for what your friend did to me in the cafe," Bushy beard starting towards the soldier only to have Hatchet-face call him off.

"No, Billy, not before I cut him up some first, you ain't," he said, drawing his knife from its grimy sheath. Bushy beard wasn't happy, but he wasn't all that put out either.

"So long as you save a little of him for me," he said.

"What ain't cut," promised Hatchet-face, "You can stomp."

The knifeman came at Kinnunen in a practiced crouch. The reversed grip he had on the handle showed scarred knuckles and the spiked hilt of the deadly blade. The river man was comfortable with the coming knife fight, while Trigg Kinnunen was not. With his escape route blocked, he brought the head basher up and ready.

"I'm going to tear your belly open, *Minnysoda*, and feed your innards to the bottom fish," laughed Hatchet-face as his two accomplices urged him on.

"Cut him, Tyrone," laughed Bushy-beard. "Cut him good."

"Hurry it up though," added the third river called Jed. "I'm cold."

Hatchet-face angled in slowly, and with a surprisingly agile move, he leaped forward with a quick series of jabs, bringing the knife within inches from Kinnunen's chest. When he stepped to his left to parry the strike, Hatchet-face swung the blade up in a high arc, and then violently back down and across the back of Trigg's right forearm. The sharp blade sliced through his jacket's sleeve and into tissue and muscle. Blood rose out of the wound in a slow, steady spill and brought on a growing dark pool on the sleeve. It wasn't deep, but it was a painful, annoying cut.

However, as Hatchet-face began to dance away, Kinnunen shifted the head basher to his left hand and swung the sap back hard at Hatchet-face's head. The lead bar missed the river man's head by a hair and scraped down his right shoulder instead. The bludgeon felt purchase. Hatchet-face tried to shake it off laughing as he went but he had taken a lick and he knew it. He would move in more cautiously next time.

"That's close, Army boy," he said, bolstering his own nerves. "But close don't count, 'cept in a game of horse shoes. So, how 'bout we count all the cuts I'm gonna give you instead? That's one."

The knifeman sniggered as he danced back in wildly slashing at Kinnunen's neck. Trigg swung the sap up to knock the blade away only to have the knifeman reverse the direction again. Kinnunen's strike missed while Hatchet-face's blade did not.

The razor sharp knife tore through the front of the soldier's coat and shirt and the stomach flesh beneath it. The blade opened up Kinnunen's belly and Trigg felt his stomach muscle straining to push out of the gash. He wasn't gutted but it was close. Holding his ripped stomach in with one hand and the sap in the other, he took in a deep, breath trying to slow the nausea and panic he was feeling.

"That's two!" laughed Hatchet-face, menacingly. "You ready for another go?"

Only before Kinnunen could answer, the knifeman turned and rushed in with three more jabs driving him away from the protection of the building's wall. As he was back pedaling, Hatchet-face struck again, this time to Trigg's leading leg. The knife blade tore into the inside of Trigg's thigh. Kinnunen steadied himself against the wall to keep from falling.

"Hamstrung you, did I?" laughed Hatchet-face. Back to the others he said, "That's only three and the sorry ass looks like he's fixin' to drop."

"Quit playing with him, Tyrone. Hurry it up before someone else comes along," said the impatient freighter who was standing watch over the railroad man.

"Oh, shut the hell up, Jed!" barked the knifeman. "You just keep an eye out for his friends."

"What? You mean, friends like me?" Nyhavn said coming out of the dark alley. When Hatchet-face pivoted towards him the young soldier didn't wait for anything clever or threatening to come from the river man's mouth. He didn't wait to be attacked either. His pistol barked and the .36 caliber round punched the knifeman hard through the stomach, dropping him to his knees. He dropped the knife, tried to stand again but fell into the mud, groaning.

Bushy beard rushed at Nyhavn from his left, only to get backhanded across his already broken nose with the pistol barrel. Ben hit him again, this time with the butt of the gun, and the burly river man dropped to one knee stunned. With the third river man racing at him with a raised fish knife, the young soldier fired twice in rapid succession. The first round hit the man high in the chest and spun him to the right. The second shot tore through the attacker's ribcage and heart. He was dead as he fell.

"Ben, behind you!" yelled Kinnunen as Bushy beard's beefy paw grabbed at the pistol barrel, trying to yank it from the young soldier's grip. Ben pulled the trigger and the bullet blew off two of the man's thick fingers before it slammed into Bushy beard's upper lip. Close as he was, the muzzle blast set the man's mustache and grimy beard on fire, but the light in his eyes died out before the small flames.

Nyhavn had one round left in the chamber and turned the gun on the last remaining threat. Making his way over to Hatchet-face, he kicked away the knife that was still within the fallen knifeman's reach before going over to aid the injured railroad man.

Gaul was struggling to get to his feet. His face was badly bruised, and he seemed to be having trouble breathing.

"They...they waylaid me and dragged me back here," he said holding a hand over his left side of his chest. "That one there, took my stick pin and wallet," he said pointing towards Hatchet-face, "told the others he was going to cut my throat and dump me in the river once they got me downstream. Probably would have too, if you two hadn't come along," added the railroad man.

"You okay?"

"My back and head's a little sore, along with some of my pride."

"You need a Doctor?"

"No, a shot of whisky maybe, and some rest," said the railroad man and then eyeing the gut shot man on the ground. "I suppose we should notify the authorities."

"Maybe after we get you looked after," said Nyhavn. "He won't be going anywhere anytime soon."

"You…you best believe I'll…I'll find you, boy, soon as I'm able," hissed Hatchet-face, clutching the punctured hole in his stomach.

"Looking forward to the visit, mister," Nyhavn said, menacingly, "Unless you want it to be here and now? I can make that happen too." The young soldier cocked the pistol and held it on the river man's face, "Your call? And, it don't much matter to me."

"Leave 'em, Ben," said Kinnunen. "And give me a hand, will you?"

"You forgetting he tried to gut you, Trigg?"

Kinnunen managed a weak laugh. "No, not likely," he said, trying to stand on his own and slipping back down into the mud. The slide was comical and Kinnunen sat and shook his head chuckling.

"Winded, are you?" said Nyhavn, walking over to lend him a hand.

"Something like that," replied Kinnunen, and it was only then when the young soldier saw why his friend had fallen and realized there was another reason why he hadn't immediately gotten back up.

"You're hurt!"

"Yeah," Kinnunen said holding onto his leg wound with both hands trying to stem the flow of blood and failing miserably. The artery was nicked but even the small cut pumped out a burst of blood with each heartbeat. "The man keeps a sharp knife," he said.

Nyhavn yanked off his jacket and tied it over the leg wound. "Help me get him to his feet," he said the Railroad man who nodded and rushed over to assist.

Between them, they hauled Trigg up to his feet only to have him plead with them to stop. "No, don't," he said as bloody intestines pushed their way through his sliced stomach and into his lap. "Put me down. Jesus, please..."

They gently lowered him back down.

"Run and find a doctor," Ben said to Mister Gaul who hurried back down the alley yelling for help.

"Turns out I'm not much of a knife fighter," Kinnunen said in a weak attempt at humor as he stared glassy-eyed at the widening pool of his own blood beneath him.

"Help's on the way," Ben said as Kinnunen snorted a small laugh. "Hold on."

"What I'm holding is a mess," he said, "A bloody mess."

"You're gonna be okay, Trigg," said Nyhavn. "The doctor will be here in no time."

"Yeah, no time," echoed Kinnunen. "Ben?"

"What?"

"You ever gonna tell me what that French Joy thing is?"

"I'll tell you right after the doctor patches you up," said Nyhavn.

"You're a good man, Ben," Kinnunen said with a small nod. "Lord knows it took us long enough to get you there," chuckled Kinnunen as his head slumped to his chest and stayed there.

"Trigg?"

Nyhavn shook his friend's shoulder but didn't get a response. "Trigg?" he said again, but he would never get a response. Trigg Kinnunen was dead.

"Where's that damn doctor?" said Hatchet-face behind him. "I'm bleeding something fierce here."

Nyhavn wheeled around angrily towards the knifeman. The gun was back in the young soldier's hand and the knifeman realized he now had a new worry.

"Your friend was a Christian man," he said, realizing his mistake. "You... you heard him. He said leave me be."

"Yeah, well my friend was a better man than I am, you worthless son of a bitch!" yelled Nyhavn, backhanding him across the face with the pistol sending him back down into the mud.

Chapter 24

After statements were taken, Nyhavn's travel orders examined, and at Mister Gaul's insistence, the town Marshal, a tall, quiet man named Lamore, was satisfied that the soldier had acted in self defense.

"It's good enough for me but the judge will need to hear it again in the morning," said Lamore.

Ben nodded only Marshal Lamore wasn't done. "That being said, I'm afraid I have to lock you up until you see him."

"Is this really necessary?" asked Mister Gaul.

"It is, sir. The judge is a law and order man who tends to lean more towards the order side of things. Four men were killed and he'll want to sort it out." Back to Nyhavn he said, "Son, a warm cell bunk is better than sleeping on the cold boat."

"I'll be there for your appearance before the judge in the morning," promised the railroad man.

"That'll help speed things up with the judge," added Lamore. The Marshal knew that Gaul and the Railroad had considerable pull and the quarrelsome river men did not. "The judge though will more than likely want you out on the first boat."

"Oh, and in case you're wondering the man that killed your friend, his name was Rollins, Tyrone Rollins, a river freighter..."

"Was?" Nyhavn said to the Marshal.

"Uh-huh, the doctor said your bullet ripped up his insides. Nothing much he could do. Rollins died right there at the Doc's office," Marshal Lamore said. "Before he died though, he said it was you men who waylaid him and his people, the ones he said you murdered."

"That's preposterous!" cried an outraged Mister Gaul.

"Of course, it is," agreed Lamore. "But Rollins was too stupid to come up with anything better. He and his two first cousins the soldier killed…"

"Cousins, huh?" said Nyhavn.

"Yeah, it is one mean family, or was until you took out the worst of the bunch. Marshal Daley down river told me last month he thought the Rollins' were behind the recent disappearance of a German clockmaker who was on his way to meet his wife and daughter in St. Louis.

"Seems the clockmaker hired some river freighters to float his goods south, only according to the family, he never made it. The clockmaker was never heard from again. Shortly afterwards, Rollins sported a nice new gold pocket watch. Told Marshal Daley his father left it to him."

"And he believed that, did he?" protested Nyhavn.

"No, not really," said Marshal Lamore. "Marshal Daley was pretty sure that Rollins didn't know who his daddy was."

"Then why weren't they arrested?" demanded Mister Gaul.

"The wife couldn't say for certain if the watch was one of her husband's," explained Lamore, "And without a body or a witness, suspicion only gets you so far. Being caught with blood on your knife though is something else. I'd say you were lucky the soldiers came along when they did."

"Lucky indeed! They saved my life. Marshal, who can I see about having Corporal Kinnunen's body properly seen to and shipped home? The soldier died in my place. The least I can do is take care of the necessary arrangements for his family."

Gaul's tenor and tone were clear. A man of his position and status wouldn't be put off or ignored. "In the morning I would appreciate it if you would direct me to the town's Undertaker?"

"That would be Samuel Dunst and Sons," said the Marshal. "It'll probably take a few days though to make the preparations and get it done right."

"Then, I'll wait," said Mister Gaul. "If the judge can't be dissuaded from putting you on tomorrow's boat then I'll follow later with the Corporal's coffin and meet you in St. Paul."

Nyhavn didn't like it but knew it made sense. "Might be better if we met up in Winona," he said. "Winona's closer to New Tonder than the Fort, and the boat stops there too."

"It does, in fact," said the Marshal.

"That'll give me time to get our official separation papers from Fort Snelling I can meet you there in three days or so."

"Then it is settled," said Mister Gaul and Marshal Lamore agreed. "Who should I notify in New…"

"Tonder, New Tonder. Just south of New Ulm," replied Nyhavn. "His father is the Reverend Johan Kinnunen of the First Lutheran Church of God's Grace."

"Would you write it out for me, son?" asked the railroad man. When Ben searched for something to write with the Marshal handed him a pencil and a sheet of paper from his desk. Once done he handed the information to Mister Gaul.

"I will send a word to Reverend Kinnunen and you can rest assured that everything that can be done will be done for your friend."

Ben nodded unsure of what exactly to say.

"And I mean what I said earlier too about the job offer," added the railroad man. "If you need work, son, you contact me." He started to hand another business card over to Nyhavn, but Ben shook his head. It wasn't necessary.

"I still have the card you gave us in the cafe, sir," said the soldier.

"May I see it?"

"Yes sir," Nyhavn said and retrieved the card. The Railroad man wrote something on the back of it, and handed it back to Ben.

The inscription read: '*On my order: Employ this man immediately then send him to me- John Bishop Gaul.*'

"What time does he go before the judge?"

"I suspect it'll be about nine o'clock or thereabouts, not much later."

"Then I will be back here at half past eight."

"Good enough," said the Marshal. To Nyhavn he said, "Corporal, I'll need that pistol of yours."

Ben handed it over as the Marshal led him to the jail cell. "I got an extra blanket if you need it?"

"Thank you, sir. It's appreciated," said Nyhavn. "Marshal, could I trouble you to find my Sergeant? He's probably down on the dock waiting for Kinnunen and me to show?"

"I'll send one of my deputies," Lamore said, locking the cell door and then placing the pistol in a drawer of his desk. Retrieving the promised blanket he handed it to Nyhavn through the bars. "I'm sorry about your friend, young man," he said. "He deserved better."

The big German found Nyhavn lying on a bunk in the jail cell staring blankly at the ceiling.

"You okay, Ben?"

"Trigg's dead," Nyhavn said, sitting up. The words choked in his throat.

Frantzen nodded. "I know," he said. "The Marshal told me what happened."

"The riverman knifed him in an alley… after we left the café. We were on our way to the saloon up the street…the fog."

Nyhavn was working his way through all that had happened and struggling. "Trigg heard a commotion in an alleyway we'd just passed and went to check it out. I wasn't there. I was taking a piss…" His voice grew distant in the retelling as the pain outpaced his words.

"The Marshal said the river men waylaid the Railroad man."

"They did and they were beating on him something fierce until Trigg stepped in to stop them."

"He wouldn't walk away from something like that."

"He didn't. When I came down the alley he was in a fight with one of them, the mouthy one with the big knife. He was stabbing Trigg, so I shot him."

"The Marshal said you killed all three of them?"

"They didn't give me much choice," Ben said, "Wished I would have done it sooner."

Frantzen nodded, wishing too that he had been there to help but the wishing changed nothing.

"The Marshal also said that the Railroad man is making the arrangements with the undertaker about getting Trigg's body back home."

"Said it was the least he could do since Trigg died on account of him. The Marshal thinks it'll take a few days to see to Trigg and a few days more for the next boat to make it to Winona."

"Winona's closer to home," agreed the big German. "What time you go before the judge?"

"Early, I think. The Marshal says the judge will probably want me on the first boat out. You sleeping on the boat?"

Frantzen shook his head, "No, the Café," he said. "Frau Gonsenheim thought we'd be more comfortable there, laid out some quilts for you, me, and Trigg. Said she'd send us off in the morning with a good breakfast."

"That would have been nice."

"Yeah. You get some sleep. I'll see you in the morning."

Nyhavn nodded again. The conversation had run its course. There was little more to say. Like the aftermath of every battle they had fought, where their ranks had been cut down, and more friends had been lost in the fight, they could harden themselves with words and quiet resolve. But until time made a callous, the pain still felt raw and blistered.

Frantzen left the jail and trudged on up through the dark streets back towards the German café. For him the night carried a cold, numbing edge that went well beyond the swirling fog.

Chapter 25

The *Northern Belle* took them as far as Red Wing, before more fog upriver once again brought the boat dockside. When they finally reached Fort Snelling a day later and reported in, they expected to be chewed out for being late but instead were welcomed back with a rousing impromptu reception.

This was Minnesota and here were two more of the 'gallant lads,' the 'stout men from Plum Run,' who had brought high honor and recognition to the Regiment; something which they all could celebrate and share. Curious Officers and enlisted men came out of their offices and barracks to get a glimpse of the two returnees.

The few soldiers who had actually served in battle with the Regiment and remained on duty at the fort, along with a number of new recruits, came out to shake their hands, clap them on the backs, and offer them drinks. The new returnees had thought it would take an hour or so to officially sign out of the Regiment and Federal service; it took the rest of the day and most of the night. By then, neither the big German nor Nyhavn were in any condition to leave.

The next morning, the hung over two newly-minted civilians, made their way back down to the steamboat for the southbound trip to Winona. With a four hour wait before the boat left, they found a barber, and a place to eat before they went shopping for new duds. At a mercantile along the waterfront Nyhavn purchased a pair of dark wool trousers, a blue striped shirt, and a brown canvas jacket with a warm wool trade blanket for lining. He topped off the look with a black slouch hat which he promptly bent and shaped to his liking. With the addition of a Bowie knife with a wood and leather sheath, and a good pair of boots he was ready to go. As he waited for Frantzen to come out of the changing room, Ben worked his Two Corps trefoil badge into the lapel of his canvas coat and then spent a long, peacocking moment admiring himself in the floor length mirror. Being out of uniform would take some getting used to but the fact was, he liked the new look.

His once sparse mustache had filled in nicely and began to droop comfortably down and around the corners of his mouth. He had added a thin patch of stubble under his bottom lip to complete the look he was after, and since he hated shaving, this worked out nicely.

Frantzen emerged from the changing room wearing a brand new, black wool, suit and vest, white shirt, and black bowler hat. The barber had trimmed his beard in the shorter 'Prussian' fashion. His trefoil badge was on his left lapel, he carried a new Henry rifle in his right hand, but for the stern expression that said he was willing to use it, he could have been mistaken for a dandy.

With their grooming and shopping chores done, they made their way to the boat landing where they boarded the steamboat for the ride down river. When it left St. Paul a little after noon they were standing at the rail on the boat's upper deck staring out at the passing Minnesotan countryside.

"You're a little quiet this morning," Frantzen said to his friend.

"Wasn't expecting anything like that," Nyhavn said. "At the fort, I mean."

"Me neither," admitted Frantzen which surprised his friend.

"It bother you too?"

"What? The celebrating?"

"No, the 'gallant lads, stout men' talk, and them looking at us like we could do it all over again, if it came to that," Ben said. "The truth is I don't ever want to find myself on the wrong end of a cannon again."

"Me neither," said Frantzen, suspecting that a portion of Ben's uneasiness sprang from more than the reception they found at the Fort. The fact was the closer they got to home, the more quiet and somber Nyhavn had become. His war wasn't over. His battles, now, were personal.

"You given any thought on where you intend to stay when we get home?"

"No, not much," he said. "Mrs. Seely's boarding house or maybe Kelly's."

"The Roadhouse?"

"As good a place as any."

"Naw, no boarding house or saloon," Frantzen said. "The Frantzen's always have room enough for friends. You'll stay at the farm. Clubs are trumps."

"Clubs are trumps," echoed Nyhavn.

"You serious about going west with the railroad?"

"Good a plan as any," Ben replied, watching a farmer on the shore plowing a field. The man's son was trailing behind him planting seed. The boy, who looked to be about thirteen, had stopped to watch the steamboat pass and waved at the passengers who were standing on the boat's main deck.

Several passengers waved back while Nyhavn stared at the boy thinking that his brother, Jurgen, would've been about the same age had he not been killed. When he finally returned the wave he found that the boy had already returned to his work in the field, the gesture and significance lost.

At the Winona dock they were informed that the north bound boat from La Crosse had been once again, delayed.

"A problem with the boat's boiler," said the man behind the ticket counter. "Probably won't be here for another four days or so, a week latest. You expecting someone?"

Frantzen nodded.

"They know you're waiting here?"

"They do."

"It's possible then, they left a message. You can check at the agent's office in town. He might have word for you."

It was a good call. The agent did have a message for them from Mister Gaul. Because of this latest delay, the railroad man said that he would meet them in New Tonder. He'd contracted with a freight company to bring Trigg's coffin home, and had sent a telegram to Reverend Kinnunen explaining the situation.

With nothing more to do, the two veterans caught the next coach west to New Ulm. It was 140 miles away and the stage coach run took two and a half days. The coach ride south to New Tonder would take a little over an hour.

Near New Ulm Frantzen was wakened by the change in speed and pitch of the wagon as the coach pulled into the station. He nudged Nyhavn who came awake with his hand on the butt of his pistol.

"Stage stop," said Frantzen. This was the last night stop before home. They would eat dinner and then sleep on cots in the back of the stage station.

In the morning, after a breakfast of coffee and biscuits, they boarded the southbound coach home. Later, as the coach rolled into the outskirts of New Tonder, they caught their first glimpse of the town, and its subtle and not so subtle changes.

A new sawmill had gone up along the Cottonwood River. Whole logs were stacked in large piles in the lumber yard waiting their turn to be sawn. A plume of steam rose along with the pleasing odor of fresh milled timber. The new sawmill had brought progress to the once small settlement and turned it into a good size town. New homes and construction had gone up in place of what the Indians had burned out, along with the familiar buildings and store fronts.

The small settlement that once, only had one main street with a handful of businesses was now lined with bustling commerce. The town now was five blocks long and three deep. On both sides of Main Street there were competing dry goods stores, a haberdasher, a new and busy café, a butcher's shop, a solid, fieldstone bank and a brick jail house. A new addition had been completed to J. C. Allen's hardware store. Mister Staudt's Cobbler shop was still the same as was Dole's Feed and Tack store, but the Evans Tannery at the south end of the town looked like it had had recent renovations as well as a new owner. The sign painted on the side of the building now read: Scott's Tannery. Several back streets and cross streets had been added to accommodate the town's expansion telling everyone on the well travelled north-south route that New Tonder had a promising future. Named for the Danish town of Tonder from where the five original immigrant families had hailed, New Tonder, in Brown County, had grown into the thriving community that the farmers, mill workers, and townspeople called home.

After gathering their luggage from atop the stage, Ben said he thought he'd pay a visit to the town cemetery, before heading out to where his farm had stood.

"You need any company?" asked Frantzen.

"Naw, you go and head on home," he said. "I'll catch up with you later at Kelly's."

"You sure?"

"Yeah."

"Later it is," said Frantzen. He thought about going along with him, but figured Ben needed to handle it by himself. The big German also figured that it wouldn't hurt to have a few beers ready and waiting at the Roadhouse when they met up.

Ben was about to lose a little more of himself, and more of what he held close, and the big German didn't envy him one bit.

Chapter 26

Ben decided to pay his respects to Reverend Kinnunen at the whitewashed clapboard church before going around back to the gravesites. At the front steps of the First Lutheran Church of God's Grace he found a stooped older woman with one milky eye and a pronounced limp, sweeping down the front steps. When he asked for the Reverend she informed him that he wasn't in.

The woman he remembered as Mrs. Tom Evans, the Tanner's wife. Only what he remembered was a happier, more jovial woman with no limp then, and certainly not looking as old and worn as she did now. If she recognized him though, it didn't register.

"He went to the steamboat dock in Winona to bring back his son," said Mrs. Evans, frowning at a particularly dusty corner. "Killed in the war, don't'cha know."

"I was told the boat was delayed."

"Must have gotten it fixed. The Marshal went with him. Should be back in a few days," she added, pausing to face the visitor. "I'm sorry," she said, apologizing for her fidgeting. "We're trying to get the church ready for the funeral service. You knew the son, did ya?"

"I did. Trigg was a friend."

"The service will be this Saturday, noon."

"I'll be here," he said, adding, "I was told my family was buried here in the cemetery."

"Your family? I'm sorry, what is your name, young man?"

"Ben Nyhavn," he said. "My father was Johan, my mother Ileana Nyhavn…"

"Oh, from the troubles," she said placing one hand over her mouth and the second hand over her heart. It was a moment before the pain in her eyes eased and her demeanor softened. She searched his face with her good eye trying to recognize him but could only recall a small, skinny shy boy and not the square shouldered man standing in front of her. The three years had certainly changed him.

"Yes ma'am, the troubles."

"Lost my Thomas then too," she said. Her words were sad in their pitch. "He's back by your people. Once you enter the gate they're off to the left in back in the new section overlooking the river. It's pretty there."

"Are the Lundes markers back there as well?"

"They are," she said. "It's where those from the troubles are buried. The Lord is watching over them now."

Ben wanted to ask her why the Lord wasn't watching over them when the troubles happened, but let it pass. He thanked the old woman and left her to her sweeping while he made his way around the side of the church to the cemetery that was spread out behind it. The garden of the dead had grown considerably since he last seen it, but then it had reason to.

There are some moments that carry more weight than others, and Ben's burden grew as he moved from the grave of one family member to another and then, from those plots to the Lundes, only a short distance away. As he went, his pace slowed, his feet suddenly heavy.

Tears welled up in his eyes and he brushed them away with the back of his hand as he mouthed the names on the simple grave markers. But a wash of frustration rose up inside of him because the names and dates told nothing of who they really were, or what they had meant to others, let alone what they meant to him. Confined to the small corner of the church cemetery, in combined plots that were no bigger than a chicken coop, lay the roots of his past, this painful present, and a busted future.

Staring at Anna's grave he regretted the loss of the life he would have had with her. He wasn't foolish enough to think that there wouldn't have been hard or, even bad times, and maybe with a little of everything in between tossed in too, but together they would have worked through it. Young as she was she had been a strong, good woman who would've made a good wife. Nearly two years gone and it still hurt.

"Gonna head out to the farm," he said to her grave marker. "I'll come back later." He knew he was talking to himself, but he didn't care. On the way out, he stopped abruptly, noticing a newly dug grave next to Reverend Kinnunen's wife, Ruth. The new grave was for Trigg and was as dark and empty as Ben felt now.

At the town livery stable he found Micah Egan, the livery owner, mucking out a horse stall and depositing the fouled hay and manure in a fly infested pile out back. With Ben's new look, Egan hadn't immediately recognized the man standing in front of him. The Liveryman stopped his work to see what the stranger wanted.

"Can I help you, sir?"

"Yes sir, Mister Egan. I was hoping to do some business with you."

Before long though, Egan grinned, and held out his hand.

"The mustache and chin patch threw me for a bit. Looks like you grew some shoulders too," he said. "Good to have you back, son. You boys did us proud."

Nyhavn shook the man's hand and then got to the reason why he was there. "I'd like to rent a buckboard wagon, sir, if you have one available? I'm going out to the farm to..."

Egan raised a hand and cut him off.

"No need," he said. "I don't have one you can rent, but I have one you can borrow. Sorry about your family. Most of the town turned out for the services."

Nyhavn nodded again. "I'll have the wagon back before sundown," he said.

"Take your time. If I'm not here then leave it around back. Go ahead and take the horse and tack back inside when you're done. I'll leave out a feed bucket."

Ben said he would and thanked him.

"No thanks' necessary," Egan said, showing him where the horse and harness were kept. "Good to have you home."

The farm was four miles west of New Tonder on a twisting country track that eventually wound its way up to the town of Sleepy Eye. The wagon ride wouldn't take him all that long to show him what he told himself he needed to see. Time and distance had helped steel him to what he expected he'd find. But even so, it wouldn't be enough.

Three miles into the ride his stomach was churning and he could feel his pulse racing up when he caught sight of the tall, familiar alders and cottonwoods that ringed the farmhouse in the distance. The trees had been planted to shield the main house from the harsh winds, now they only conspired to hide the damage.

Steering the horse and wagon into the overgrown yard, he reined in, set the brake and tied off the reins. Then he just sat for awhile, taking it all in.

The farmhouse, the sod barn connected to it, and the lean-to work and wood sheds that had formed the U-shaped compound had all collapsed and fell into itself in the fire. All that remained besides a partial wall were burnt offerings. In the time since the Indian raid the Minnesota wind, rain, and months of snow only added to the overall despoliation.

Climbing down from the wagon, he paused at the leathery scrap of carcass, from a long dead animal, in the tall grass. Tufts of dark brown and cream colored fur, a sun bleached partial rib cage and spine lay where Loki had fallen close to what once had been the front porch. A broken arrow pinned the spine to the ground.

Loki was a mangy mutt that looked to be a cross between a goat and a hound. Dumber than a stump, he was all slobbering heart and tail wagging loyalty, and more than likely, dead where the marauding Indians had killed him when he had raced out to defend his people and property.

He shouldn't have been left like that, and as soon as he could find a shovel, Ben would bury Loki's remains. The trouble was, the more he walked around the homestead the more he realized that there was little to be found of any value or use. Indians hadn't hauled away the windmill pump, well buckets, ploughs or harnesses, let alone any of the tools or farm equipment his father had owned. Nor had Indians removed the window frame and glass panes from the only wall of the main house that had somehow remained standing.

Most likely scavengers had taken what they wanted or needed to replace what they themselves had lost in the Troubles. And since there wasn't anyone from the murdered families left alive to claim the items, they had become fair game before the banks stepped in to claim and sell off what remained.

Salvaging made good sense, even if it left him a little riled with those who had done it. What little they had was hard earned.

The Nyhavn homestead began as a simple, sod house that he and his father had literally carved out of the ground shortly after they had arrived from Denmark. That was eleven years earlier when the five family members, their one horse, and two cows had crowded into the slightly sagging three room sod home during the first Minnesota winter. Living conditions had stayed like that until they were able to scrape together enough money to begin construction of the wood framed home.

By their third year in America, a new wood framed house had gone up and the sod structure had become their barn. Lean-tos were added to serve as tool sheds and dry storage for firewood. With the addition of a chicken coop, and hog pen, the old country U-shaped compound began to take shape.

On the south side of the farm house, his mother and sister had planted a small but productive vegetable garden, along with four apple trees that were strategically placed to take in the most sun. The garden and apple trees eventually yielded more than enough for their needs, the rest they sold in town on market day.

Ben and his father, and even his younger brother, Jurgen, had spent weeks searching the river and surrounding fields for just the right size rocks and stones which they hauled back for the new fireplace and attached bread oven.

"A stone *vall* around a fireplace keeps *da vood* house from burning down, don't'cha know?" said his father as they set the heavy stones in place.

His father and mother spoke English haltingly with a thick, old country accent. Their 'walls' and 'woods' came out '*valls*' and '*voods*' and their 'ands' had a distinctive '*und*' sounds.

As the children of immigrants growing up in Minnesota, Ben sounded like any other of the local kids around town. The only accents this new generation carried had the characteristic lilt of the region, with a healthy dose of 'ya sures', ya knows' and 'don't cha knows' tossed into their talk.

His proud mother, with her heart happy smile, beamed when the two box-framed window casements were added to the new house. His sister, Saffi, had spent a week decorating flower boxes, intended for the new windows. Bright colorful red, blue, green, and yellow flowers and intricate Nordic designs covered the boxes.

His father had a cabinet maker in town build the windows. It was a costly purchase for the immigrant farmer, but well worth the investment, if the wife's grin was the real judge of the matter.

Ben chuckled recalling how his mother had so enjoyed the eight small panes of glass in each of the two casements, and how she carefully cleaned them with vinegar water and wiped them down with old newspapers every Saturday morning, and how she often stood back with her hands on her big hips, proudly admiring her work.

"My beautiful *vindows*," she said, maybe more to herself than anyone else.

The front door of the new wood house opened up to a sitting room and kitchen with a small bedroom in back for Saffi, and another just opposite, for his mother and father. A ladder with a support pole led to an upstairs loft that he and his younger brother, Jurgen, had shared.

The sawn lumber, nails, tarpaper, windows, five cows, two draft horses, crop seed, and most of everything else they had before he went off to war, came from a bank mortgage that depended on their corn and wheat crop, and any money made working other people's harvests. It had been a struggle, but by 1859 they were making it work. Mortgage payments were made on time, and the little farm had slowly expanded and prospered, until the Indian raid.

It was all gone now, what wasn't lost in the fire or salvaged, was now owned by the bank. As he made his way around the charred ruins, a gust of wind overhead rustled through the cottonwood trees in a ghostly whisper. Several crows, picking at rotten apples cawed at him, berating him for his proximity as he walked over to what was left of the front wall. They side-hopped away from him and nervously studied the intruder with craned heads.

"No need to squawk," Ben said to the birds. "It's yours."

He stepped on a few broken shards of smudged glass that shattered beneath his weight. Marks and scrapes against the remaining portion of one wall showed where someone had pried out one window frame. Several lines of rutted wagon tracks led back to the county road, marking the route where the farm site had been picked over, and then picked over, again.

Where the lean-to sheds had been, he found a broken shovel in the rubble and used it to bury his dog in the garden. Once done and with nothing more to see at the farm, he started towards the overgrown path behind the barn, following a well-remembered track to the small lake.

He hadn't noticed that he had picked up his pace as he headed towards a familiar shore on the lake and a favorite part of his past. The small familiar meadow and the azure water in the warm sunlight were still inviting as ever. At the water's edge his smile reflected back up at him from the memory it produced.

For the flicker of a better moment he saw Anna standing knee-deep in the lake, still playfully coy as she called for him to come in and join her. He bent down and scooped up a handful of water only to have it, like the memory, slip through his grasp.

The sound of hammering in the distance brought him out of his slump shouldered misery. What sounded like construction work was coming from the Lunde's.

After running lake water over his face and drying it with a sleeve, he headed towards the Lunde farm and the sounds of life. A few hundred yards on, beyond the brush and a newly ploughed field, he saw a man and a boy putting on a new roof on the main house. Two-thirds of the roof was done but it would take another full day to finish the job.

A canvas tarp covered part of the open rafters while the two workers were slowly closing the gap with roughhewn planks. A stack of shingles and a roll of tarpaper lay on several wooden planks as did a small wooden cask of nails.

The boy was hauling the lumber up the ladder while the father did the careful placement and hammering. A bone-thin woman sat on a straight back chair in front of a window shucking corn as two smaller children laughed and chased several worried chickens across the yard. Behind the woman a familiar looking painted window box rested on the kitchen window sill. Pink and white lady slippers were spilling out of the festively colored box.

It was the boy on the ladder who first saw the stranger approaching and called to his father pointing towards Nyhavn. The father stopped what he was doing, and after a moment studying the stranger, he climbed down from the roof. Stepping in front of his wife and children, he adjusted his tool belt and faced the visitor. Ben noticed that the man was still clutching the hammer.

"Hello the house!" Nyhavn called by way of greeting, waving as he came.

The man returned the greeting. "Afternoon," he said, warily.

"Afternoon," replied Ben. "You any relations to the Lunde's?"

"The family that used to own this farm?"

"Uh-huh."

"No," said the man. "We purchased it ten months back. Why, are you a relation?"

The question was simple enough, and guarded. After the Indian attacks, a number of the banks in the region had repossessed those farms whose surviving relatives could no longer make the mortgage payments. The bank's foreclosures left more than a few former owners resentful and bitter towards the bankers. Those hard feelings were sometimes passed on to the new buyers.

"Friend of the family. Bent… Ben Nyhavn," Nyhavn said. "My family has the next farm over. Well, we used to have it."

"William Dean Bascom," said the man placing the hammer in his work belt and offering a well calloused hand. Nyhavn shook it.

Bascom was a lean man in his 30s,' with a tonsured widow's peak and a soldier's bearing. His accent was British English, but slowly giving way to local colloquialisms.

"I was told that no one here had survived the Indian attacks, don't'cha know?"

"They didn't," he said. "I was off at the war."

"You're a soldier then?"

"Was. My enlistment is up."

"You plan on rebuilding?"

Nyhavn shook his head. "No," he said, glancing back towards the lake and the way he had come, "the bank took the farm last year. I just came for a last look around. Heard your hammering, thought I'd see if I knew you or your people."

The Englishman's eyes went from the young soldier back to his wife. "Would you like some fresh biscuits and coffee?" she said starting towards the kitchen.

"No ma'am, but I thank you for the kind offer. I borrowed a wagon from the livery and need to get it back to town."

There was an awkward pause as Nyhavn's gaze settled on the painted flower box on the kitchen window frame. "My sister painted the flowers," he said with a half smile.

"Pardon me?"

Nyhavn pointed to the gaily colored window box. "That was my sister's doing. She was so proud of the boxes she painted."

The Englishman's face colored. "We claimed it thinking it was abandoned," Bascom said as his wife, head bent low, remained silent, shamed with the admission.

A little girl of about four or five hugged her mother's legs and stared at Nyhavn from behind the simple cotton shift dress.

"Pretty frowers," said the little girl pointing to the window box.

Ben smiled. "Yes, they are pretty frowers," he said.

The Bascoms had taken the flower box from the ruined and deserted home. Unscathed as it was, he would have claimed it too.

"Just thought you should know is all," said Nyhavn.

"It livens up a house," said the wife.

"It does, don't'cha know," agreed Nyhavn.

"It's yours if you want it back," said the husband, as the wife almost succeeded in hiding her disappointment. Almost.

Ben Nyhavn shook his head. "No, let it liven up your house," he said. "Pleased to meet you folks."

He turned to start the walk back when Bascom's wife called to him. "What was her name? Your sister?"

"Saffi," Ben said. As the farmer's wife repeated the name.

"We'll remember it," said the wife.

Nyhavn nodded and turned back towards the lake and the ruined farm beyond. Remembering, at times, was enough.

Chapter 27

The big German was riding back into town when he spotted Nyhavn coming out of the bank. He rode over to him and reined up shy of the boardwalk.

"Thought I'd see if I could make some back payments and maybe buy the farm back," Nyhavn said by way of hello.

"What the bank say?" said Frantzen shifting uncomfortably in his saddle.

"They…well, actually he, Mister Aldon Stanhope…"

"Stanhope? Who's Stanhope?"

"The new banker."

"What happened to Mister Olafsen?"

"His bank closed after the Indian attacks. Some investors in St. Paul rushed in and bought it and a few more in Mankato. Brought in Stanhope to reopen it and straighten out the mortgage mess left by the Indian troubles. He sat me down in his office, lit up a big cigar, and informed me that unfortunately, I was too late; the farm had already been sold. Said it was a shame I hadn't been able to make the mortgage payments sooner…"

"You tell him you were busy fighting the war and all?"

"Something like that."

Frantzen glanced at the bank and spat, "And let me guess?" he said. "This Stanhope probably said there wasn't much he could do about it now?"

"Almost sounded sincere too," said Nyhavn. "However, he did say that there was another local farm that would soon be in foreclosure, and that I could put a bid on, if I'd like."

Frantzen's eyes narrowed. "Did he say whose farm it was?"

"Naw," Ben said. "He opened his records safe behind his desk, pulled out his ledger book and confirmed that it would be available soon. The greedy little bastard was damn near cackling."

Frantzen frowned at the bank. "How is it that a banker can figure out more legal ways to steal people's money and property with a notarized piece of paper, than someone else can with a pistol?" Frantzen said, and then went on to other matters. "I got a telegram I need to send, so why don't you go and hold down a table for us at Kelly's. I'll be along in a bit. I may have to walk. This saddle business takes some getting used to again. My ass is numb."

"Imagine how the horse feels?"

The big German chuckled thinking that was something Trigg might have said.

"You heading over to Kelly's?"

Ben nodded and said he was. "I could use a drink."

"I got a few quick errands to run here in town but I'll be along directly."

As Frantzen rode off, Nyhavn turned and found a young stern faced giant who was standing across the street in the doorway of the marshal's office studying him. The giant, whose head, damn near hit the top of the doorframe, was wearing a brass badge pinned to his well worn black cloth coat. He stood over six and a half feet tall and carried a good 250 pounds on a intimidating frame. Frantzen was nearly as tall, but nowhere near the size of this younker.

The Deputy looked vaguely familiar, but Nyhavn couldn't put a family name to him, and if the Deputy had recognized him or Frantzen, then he gave no indication of it. Nyhavn nodded and the deputy hesitantly, returned the gesture.

Marshals and Deputies were generally suspicious by nature, or from time on the job, and they were especially suspicious of strangers that suddenly showed up in their towns, standing in front of, and eying their banks. Ben guessed that the deputy was probably still watching him as he crossed the mud-covered street and headed south past Egan's Livery towards the Roadhouse. It was another route he knew well, as did most of the men and boys in and around New Tonder. If the deputy had something to say, then he should have no trouble at all finding him.

Rounding the southbound edge of town he smiled pleased to see Kelly's Roadhouse still standing, or more accurately leaning, in the distance. The Roadhouse had foundation problems. Kicking away the mud that had built up on his boots, he stepped inside the Roadhouse. The bartender nodded to him as he walked to the bar.

"What'll it be, friend?"

"A beer will do for now," said Nyhavn.

"Then beer it is," replied the bartender.

Ben didn't recognize the man, but given the growth of the town since he went away, it wasn't surprising.

"That'll be a nickel," said the bartender setting the beer on the bar in front of his new customer.

Nyhavn slapped a silver seated Liberty half dollar down on top of the counter top.

"You just passing through?"

"Probably," Nyhavn said turning to survey the room. Several mill workers were playing cards with two doves at a nearby table. One of the two doves at the table looked over and smiled at Ben, which annoyed one of the men she was with.

Figuring to avoid trouble Ben turned back to the bartender and said, "You still have rooms upstairs for the night?"

"A dollar a night," replied the bartender. "Twenty five cents more if you want a hot bath. $2, if you want one of the ladies to help you soak."

"Prices have gone up," Ben said. "Old Jake Kelly still around?"

"Caught consumption and passed."

"You the new owner?"

The bartender shook his head. "Nope, I'm just the hired help. She's the owner," he said, tilting his head towards the tall, full figured woman coming out of a small office in the back. "Hey Boss, this fellow here is asking for the owner."

The woman looked up and stared at the stranger at the bar who was staring back at her smiling. It took her a moment before she joyfully returned the grin.

Skinny Beth Traumen, it appeared, was no longer skinny.

Chapter 28

Inside the Roadhouse, the big German found his friend sharing a table with a comely, dark haired woman. Both were laughing and carrying on with a kind of shared intimacy that confused Frantzen. For someone who had been away from New Tonder for three years and had only recently gotten back into town, he was making himself welcome with the ladies. Apparently more of Trigg's traits had rubbed off on him.

The woman looked up as he made his way over to their table. Her lively eyes reflected the happiness of her smile. She seemed genuinely pleased to see him.

"Al, you remember Beth Traumen, don't'cha?" said Ben, gesturing to the woman as Frantzen took a chair.

The big German said he did, all the while searching his memory, but all that he could bring to his mind's eye was Ester Traumen, the oldest of five girls from the farm a few miles north of town. This Traumen girl had the same blue eyes as her sister and their German father. She also shared the same raven black hair and high cheek bones of her Sioux Indian mother. Moreover, she possessed the physical attributes and sensual charms that gave her a distinct commercial advantage in the Roadhouse.

"Good to see you again, Miss Traumen."

"Good to see you too," Beth replied before whispering something in Ben's ear that caused him to grin. Getting to her feet, she adjusted her flattering red crinoline dress. She said, "How about something to drink?"

"Beer's good," Frantzen said while Nyhavn reached for some of the change on the table.

"Oh, put your money away. It's on me," Beth said excusing herself as she went back to the bar for the drinks. Business had picked up, so she went to check on the handful of other customers as she went.

"She's working here now, is she?"

"Had to since the Indian raids. She lost everything too."

"Her family?"

Nyhavn nodded. "Everyone," he said.

Frantzen stared after her as Ben was talking. "Said she was answering nature's call in the outhouse when the raiding party swooped down on the farm."

"No warning?"

"Naw, nothing," said Nyhavn. "She couldn't get back to the main house, and with the Indians swarming around, she crawled down and hid in the glory hole."

"A smart move, all things considered."

"It was," agreed Nyhavn. "The Indians shot up the outhouse door and moved on. She stayed hunkered down in the pit until she was sure thay were gone. When she finally crawled out, she found her people dead and the farm in flames. She stumbled into town shell shocked, sobbing, and joined a host of others with similar stories."

"No other relatives?"

No, or at least none willing to send her any money to help out."

"No one else in town stepped up?"

Ben shook his head. "With so many families in town hurting, the churches did what they could, but some of the survivors were left to make due on their own," he said. "Her being half Indian didn't help."

"No, I imagine it didn't."

"After the troubles she tried to stay on the property, but couldn't make the mortgage payments, so with nowhere else to go..."

"She came to Kelly's."

"No, not at first," Nyhavn said. "Stanhope, the new banker, found charity, and decided to take her on a few days a week to keep house."

"You talking New York 'housekeeping' kinda work, are you?"

"I am."

"Ah!"

"She did it for awhile. Turns out though the banker fellow gets mean when he drinks, so after a black eye and cut lip, she quit him and came here. Said if she was going to be treated like a whore, then she might as well have some say with who she takes to her bed."

"This Mister Stanhope is a real stand up guy, isn't he?" sniffed Frantzen, wiping beer foam from his mustache and beard after talking a drink.

"The kind you'd like to knock on his ass, pick back up and then knock back down again," said Nyhavn, still holding an appreciative eye on Traumen.

"What was she then? Sixteen?"

"Naw, same as me then," he said. "Almost fifteen."

The response momentarily jarred Frantzen again. He snorted and slowly shook his head. Young as they were then, they were a whole world older now.

"Anyway, she came to work here and got good at it. When Kelly's consumption got the worst of him, she nursed him, and ran the Roadhouse for him. He was so grateful that he willed the business to her."

"He passed?"

"Last summer."

"So she owns Kelly's?"

"Uh-huh. Turns out she has a knack for business too," Nyhavn said. "Keeps most of her money in a New Ulm bank. Said she won't put a dime in Stanhope's bank."

Beth returned with several beer mugs and then excused herself a second time. "Sorry boys," she said, "but I have a few barrels of beer being delivered out back so I need to attend to my inventory. Enjoy the drinks. I'll be back once I'm done."

As both men watched her go it was Nyhavn who spoke first.

"Want to know what she thinks is the best part about owning the Roadhouse?"

"Sure, what?"

"The good banker, Mister Stanhope, wants to be a customer only Beth won't oblige and won't let her girls oblige him either. The fact is, she won't even let him darken the doorway. He's trying to get the Mayor to shut down the roadhouse as a public nuisance."

"Public nuisance, my ass! He's just trying to get even."

"Yeah, he is; it seems that he has to go all the way into Mankato for his eh…, entertainments."

"What a pity. So, is she gonna stay in whoring?"

Nyhavn shrugged. "Maybe, says it's mostly all that she knows and she's good at it. Also, she told me she likes the leverage it gives her to tell people like Stanhope to go hump himself."

"I bet it does."

"Said she's saving her money to eventually head out to San Francisco. Thinks she could do better out there."

"She's good looking enough to do better anywhere," admitted the big German.

They drank in silence for awhile before the conversation turned to other matters. Ben said, "How's your family doing?"

"Good, considering I've been gone for three years. My younger brother, Rolf is running the farm now." Old World traditions died hard even in the New World. Al was the older brother. By custom the farm should have been passed down to him.

"That sit well with you?"

"It does because I'm not really sure I want to be farmer anymore."

"Is that right?"

"It is."

"What do you think you'll do?"

Frantzen shrugged. "I don't know," he said. "I'm giving some serious thought to going back to La Crosse."

"The young widow woman?" said Nyhavn, not all that surprised. The big man was smitten with her. Any fool could see it.

"I figure they could use the help, probably head out next week, sometime," he said. "What about you? You staying here or are you still thinking about taking the railroad man up on his offer protecting the surveying teams?"

"The railroad work sounds promising."

"That promise holds danger too, you know."

"Don't really think it would be all that much different from what we've been doing over the last few years."

Frantzen reluctantly agreed. "No, I suppose not," he said, thinking back on the long road they all had taken. "They'd do well to have you."

It was the first real compliment the big German had paid him on his abilities, something not lost on Nyhavn.

"I appreciate your confidence."

"It's well earned," he said, holding up his beer glass. "Clubs are trumps."

"Clubs are trumps," replied Nyhavn.

"Have you heard anything about when Trigg's church service will be?"

"Mrs. Evans at the church…"

"Mrs. Evans?"

"The Tanner's wife, or was till the Indians killed her husband and made her a cripple."

Frantzen frowned. There was far too much of that kind of misery to go around.

"She told me that Reverend Kinnunen and the Marshal went to Winona to escort the body back."

"Escort it back? I thought the boat was broken?"

"Must have gotten it repaired. Anyway, she said the service will be around noon on Saturday."

"Then I suppose that'll give us time to take care of whatever business we have here in town before we go," said Frantzen.

With a habit he had picked up in New York, Nyhavn took a quick look around the Roadhouse and its small crowd of afternoon customers before he leaned into the table motioning for his friend to do the same.

"And speaking of that," he said, "There is one thing I'd really like to do before I leave and preferably before the Marshal comes back; something I could sure use your help with."

"Sure, you got it," replied the big German. "What is it?"

Ben Nyhavn lowered his voice to a half whisper. "I'm thinking that maybe we should rob the bank."

Chapter 29

"Rob the bank, huh?" Frantzen said, sitting back in his chair and staring at his friend like he was some kind of lunatic.

Nyhavn scowled as he looked around to see if anyone had overheard Frantzen's remark. Only when he was reasonably certain no one else had heard the big German did he offer up a slight nod.

"Good God! You're serious!"

"I'm not talking about taking any money..."

"Course not," said Frantzen, dripping sarcasm. "When someone says they want to rob a bank, the first I think is, what a hoot it would be for everyone involved, shooting up the place, scaring the living shit out of the employees, and anybody else who just happens to be in the bank at the time, especially and let me say this part again, *especially* when there's no money involved!"

"Keep it down, will ya?" pleaded Nyhavn. "Most of the money in the bank belongs to our friends and neighbors. We can't take it! Why would we do that?"

"Why is always a good question," Frantzen said, making his point. "As in, why do you want to rob the bank, if not for the money?"

"For the bank papers."

"Bank papers?"

"Uh-huh, loan notes and mortgages. From what Beth says Stanhope holds paper on damn near everyone in town."

"Loan notes and mortgages?" Frantzen said taking new interest in the proposition. It was still dangerously stupid. But it did have some merit, at least enough to hear him out.

"The truth is I'd rather shoot the smug son of a bitch instead, but figured this might work out better for everyone concerned, including me. Seeing how I don't wish to be hanged."

"Good point but you do realize, of course, if we walk in and ask for the loan notes at gunpoint we might as well take the money for all the jail time we'll get for it," said Frantzen.

"Uh-uh! And no guns, no money," Ben said adamant in his response. "I figure maybe we go in at night, get into the paper safe…"

"Paper safe? What paper safe?"

"Stanhope's got a good size stand-up metal cabinet in his office. It's about yea-big," he said using his hands to show that the cabinet was about five feet in height and three feet across. "It's a key lock cabinet with double doors, four shelves and a number of fancy wooden drawers. Kinda like a fancy pie cabinet."

"So we just go in and take it then?"

"Can't," Nyhavn said. "It's bolted both to the flag stone floor and stone wall behind it. It ain't going anywhere."

"Which, more than likely, is why he keeps his record books and papers in it."

"More than likely."

"Any idea what it weighs?"

"I dunno," Nyhavn replied, taking his best guess. "It's hefty. I'm thinking it could run at least five hundred pounds or more."

Frantzen blew air through his teeth. "Heavy safe, bolted to the ground and support wall," he said more to himself than Nyhavn. "You say it has double doors?"

"Uh-huh, with inside hinges."

"Which means it probably has a locking bar or two," Frantzen said. "A block and tackle with a good chain and rope should do it," he said, thinking it over. It was too heavy for them to try to lift out, and secured to the wall and floor as it was, it wasn't going anywhere. That only left the cabinet's double doors. "Maybe we could hook up some chains to the cabinet doors, tie the chains to a rope and wedge it in a door frame, and leverage it open. If the bolts are set in stone like you say then they should hold it in place while the block and tackle should be able to pry the lock bars enough to get at whatever's inside."

"That could work," said Nyhavn.

Frantzen sat back, pleased with his notion. "Yeah, it could," he said, liking the thought more and more.

Somehow the whole idea of stealing the mortgages and loan papers struck him as funny, and he started to laugh. The laughter soon died with consideration of another distinct possibility.

"You realize, of course, if we do this it would be more than a prank," he said, his voice and demeanor serious. "If we do this, it will make us outlaws."

"Only if we get found out and caught."

"So then, maybe we shouldn't get found out and caught."

"That's a big part of my plan too," he said.

"To that end I'd like to scout out the bank and maybe get a look at Stanhope's cabinet," replied Frantzen getting to his feet and finishing his beer. "Maybe get a better idea of what we're up against."

"What? Right now?" asked a surprised Nyhavn.

"Not at this moment, no," said Frantzen. "Probably wouldn't be too difficult to figure out who did it if we go waltzing in there and ask the banker if we could take a gander at his paper safe. No, I'll ask my brother, Rolf, if he'll accompany me to the bank in the morning to seek Mister Stanhope's counsel on money investments."

"Money investments?"

"Uh-huh, I doubt if there's a banker alive who'll pass up a chance to talk about what he would like to do with somebody else's money, and speaking of that very subject," said Frantzen holding his palm out. "I'll need what's left of your Army separation pay."

"Why?"

"I got to have something of interest to deposit with Stanhope that merits an invitation into his office."

Nyhavn brought out his money, counted out what he thought he needed for his stay at Kelly's, and then handed the rest over to Frantzen, who added it to his own. The big German tallied the count. "Between us we have close to $400. That should get his attention."

The big German also knew it would get him a good look at the layout of the banker's office. Breaking in at night with the right amount of stealth and tools might just work. Although, he'd only know for certain once he had a look at the office and cabinet.

Stuffing the money in his pocket he said, "My brother says you're more than welcome to stay with us. But let me forewarn you, Rolf's wife is kind of a stickler when it comes to being late for dinner, so we should probably be heading out."

"No, that's all right. I'm going to stay here in town. You can go on without me," Nyhavn said. "Thank Rolf for me. I'll see you tomorrow."

"You staying at the boarding house?"

Nyhavn shook his head and said, "Naw, Beth says she'll put me up here."

"Yeah, I'm sure she will," laughed Frantzen, thinking that the boy had learned more from Kinnunen than he thought. "Then I guess I'll meet you here about this time tomorrow and we'll talk more about our little plan."

"Clubs are trumps," said Nyhavn.

"Clubs are trumps," said Frantzen heading for the door.

The following afternoon under a dismal morning sky that threatened rain, and under the pretext of depositing his Army pay, the big German and his brother, Rolf, paid a visit to Mister Stanhope at the bank. Just as he had anticipated, after a certain amount of social pleasantries and inquiry as to how much the returning soldier intended to deposit, the gleeful banker invited them into his office.

The banker's office was surprisingly sparse. Besides a large oak desk there was the cabinet just as Ben had described it, two plain and straight back wooden chairs in front of the desk, an expensive, swivel chair for the banker, and a pot bellied stove. A closed and latched window with crimson drapes faced the alley.

"A cigar, gentlemen? They're from Spanish Cuba," said the banker offering the two brothers dark, thick cigars from a small cedar box after they were seated. Both brothers declined and patiently watched and waited as Stanhope went through a showy cigar lighting ritual. He removed an expensive cigar from the cedar box, clipped off the end of the stogie, and with a dramatic flair, he slowly lit it. The banker, who was in his mid-30s, of medium height, and leaning towards the portly side, held a Lucifer match just below the tip and rolled the cigar between his fingers working the flame until it glowed bright orange. Taking a deep puff on the cigar, he leaned back and blew a slow stream of smoke towards the ceiling before he spoke.

"You don't want to deposit your money," said Stanhope, in a patronizing tone that immediately annoyed the big German. Frantzen played along anyway.

"I don't?"

"No," said the banker. "You want to invest it and secure your future."

"I don't know. It's all the money I have and from what I understand, investing can be risky," said the big German. He rose out of his seat and walked back and forth in front of the window in convincing concern. The window faced the alley and had a small lock with a simple thumb swivel catch. Prying it open wouldn't be difficult.

"Mister Stanhope," the big German said turning back to the banker, "I hope you understand that the money I intend to put in your bank represents three very difficult years for me and its value far exceeds what is conveyed on the face of the notes."

"Of course, it does," said the banker, trying to placate him. "I don't mean to patronize you. But hard earned money always has more personal worth, especially for someone of your means. That's why I want to put it to work for you. And, if I may put it in terms you might more readily understand, you want it to grow for you. I want you to think of your funds as seed money, and my investment advice, as sound farming practice that will lead to a bumper crop."

"A bumper crop," echoed Frantzen smiling at the analogy; a smile that Stanhope misinterpreted as acceptance instead of amused resentment at the insult. "So how do you intend to do that, turn my money into a bumper crop?"

"Railroad stock," Stanhope said.

"Railroad stock?" the big German said, taking his seat and taking in the open records cabinet over Stanhope's shoulder as he pretended to be mulling over the banker's words. Ben was right. The cabinet was sturdy and well secured. There were four large bolts that attached it to the brick wall of the office and he figured there were probably an equal number securing it to the stone floor. Several metal locking bars were raised in the OPEN position and probably crossed both doors when the cabinet was shut.

"Railroads are this nation's future and its prosperity," said Stanhope going on with his sales pitch. "It won't be long before every settlement and town will have access to goods and services from the Atlantic Ocean to the great Pacific. The railroads are the foundation for that growth and success," he said, blowing smoke towards the ceiling and flicking more ash as he created a light blue haze in the confined office.

"Why, pretty soon you're going to see some exciting enterprise come to New Tonder. Your capital will help the railroad create that enterprise, and you will reap the benefits and financial rewards!"

"At a cost though, correct?" asked Rolf Frantzen. "I'm assuming there are associated transaction fees, as well as some risk?"

The banker dismissed the concern with a fluttering wave of his hand. "A small transaction fee," he said, "but very little risk."

The big German's response was slow in coming as though he was heavily weighing the decision. "I'd like some time to think it over," he said causing the banker's smile to fall, only to have it propped back up with the big German's follow up comment. "However, I'd still like to deposit the money today and let you know my decision about investing it by the end of the week? I mean, if it's all right by you?"

"Of course it is all right," replied Stanhope, still eager for the transfer of the funds.

"And the money's safe? I wasn't here during the Indian raids. But I know they burned down some buildings. The safe's fireproof, is it?"

"It is, and I can personally assure you that your money will be safe in my bank. The building is block stone and brick construction," said Stanhope, and went on to explain how the Chicago built vault with its twelve-inch thick steel walls and reinforced steel bars in the heavy door was installed after the Indian troubles. "It is not only fireproof," the banker added, "but includes the latest feature of individual safety deposit boxes."The banker knew that while most farmers didn't have all that much to put in the rented boxes before the Indian raids, many now stowed their most valuable possessions in the boxes for safe keeping.

If you are so inclined I can make one available for you for a small fee," he added.

"No sir, I won't need a bank box. But I thank you anyway."

Stanhope led them out of his office into the teller's area for a quick tour.

"As you can see the safe has been incorporated into the stone and steel reinforced walls of the building. The vault door rests behind a cage of steel bars that would make any jailer envious," he said.

The safe and its protective cage sat in full view of the plate glass window facing the street. "As you can see anyone trying to break into it would be on full and immediate display. Now, I ask you, sir. Does that meet your satisfaction?"

The big German said it did. Back in the banker's office, Frantzen deposited the $400 with Stanhope entering it into his ledger before handing the war veteran a deposit slip. Having what he came for, he thanked the banker for his time, shook his greedy little hand, and after parting with his brother, met up with Nyhavn back at Kelly's.

"Let's paper rob us a bank," he said, when he found Ben still occupying the corner table in the Roadhouse.

"Good enough," said Nyhavn, pleased with Frantzen's decision. "When?"

"I dunno, tonight," said Frantzen, surprising his friend.

"Tonight?"

"Yep, late. After everyone's fast asleep."

"You don't think maybe we should plan on it some more?"

"What's to plan? There's a storm coming in tonight that'll probably be in Iowa by tomorrow. And, like you said, the Marshal's out of town so I'm thinking this is as good a time as any to do what we need to do."

"Okay then," said Nyhavn, agreeing with his logic. "By the way, I think I know where we can find the block and tackle."

"Where?"

"Egan's Livery," he said. "He doesn't lock it up at night. And I'm sure we can find most of what we'll need. We can sort of borrow it and return it afterwards, and no one will be the wiser."

"When I was in Stanhope's office I saw that there is a latch window that opens to the alley. Wouldn't take much to pry the window or bust the pane to get inside."

"Well, don't you two look full of yourselves," said Beth carrying over a new round of drinks as she joined them at the table.

"Full of something," said Frantzen.

"Actually, we're just celebrating that we made it through some difficult times," Nyhavn said.

"Now that is something I can tell you is well worth celebrating," said Beth distributing the drinks and then hoisting her glass and holding it in the air. "To better days ahead."

"Hopefully beginning tomorrow," said Nyhavn.

"A good a time as any," laughed Frantzen.

Chapter 30

They slipped into the alley behind the bank and the Dortmunder Feed Store to avoid detection. Knowing that farmers and mill workers went to bed early and that the Town's Deputy didn't, they waited until he had completed his last rounds at midnight before setting out on their caper.

Frantzen set the iron bar, pulleys, and rope they had retrieved from the Livery down at the window before he went to stand lookout at the end of the alley. In the meanwhile the second burglar set down a bulky canvas satchel and brought out a small hammer. Ben was just about to break the bank office window when he reared back and chuckled.

"Hey Al!" he whispered over his shoulder to his friend.

"What?" Frantzen asked, still studying the street.

"You're going to love this."

"What?"

"The window."

"What about it?"

"It's not locked."

Frantzen turned back to face him. "You kidding me?"

"Nope, he didn't latch it," said Nyhavn, placing both palms flat against the sides of the window frame, and with a little pressure, raised the window several inches to demonstrate. "See?"

"So much for safe keeping our money," muttered the big German.

Nyhavn raised the window, used a wooden dowel to prop it open, and then slipping out of his boots, he shimmied on through. Down on all fours in the banker's office, he crab walked over to the open door that led out to the lobby, and slowly closed it. Once done, he padded his way back to the window.

"We're good," he said to his accomplice who retrieved the rope, bag and tools and handed them through to Nyhavn. Removing his boots Frantzen climbed through the window and closed the drapes behind him.

"Give me some light," he said as Nyhavn pulled a small candle from his pocket and lit the wick.

The candlelight illuminated the small office with a flickering yellow glow as Frantzen went to work on the cabinet. He ran a small chain through the handles of the safe's double doors, tied the chain to the rope, and then fed the hemp line into the pulleys. Pulling the rope through the pulley system he handed it to Ben who had braced the iron bar in the window frame.

After looping it around the iron bar he handed it back to Frantzen. Ben held the iron bar in place until the tension from the rope locked it against the frame. He pressed his hip against the shade to keep it shut and to keep the candle light from attracting any undue attention. Not that it was likely since the storm that was moving down from the Canadian plains and the high winds that preceded it, had sent the townspeople scurrying to shutter their windows until it passed. The heavy rain was a bonus because it would wash away any of their tracks.

Frantzen propped his feet against the base of the cabinet for better leverage. "Ready?" he said.

"Ready," replied Nyhavn.

"Then, let's open her up," said the big German getting a good grip on the rope. He began pulling the rope hand-over-hand until the pulleys slowly began to do their work. It wasn't long before the cabinet doors began to creak and moan and the taut rope trembled like a guitar string. Putting his back into it Frantzen gave a series of mighty tugs but to Nyhavn's horror the rope began to splinter and fray inches from the support bar.

"Al! Stop!" he said. "Stop! The rope is splitting! Ease up!"

Over his shoulder Frantzen could see that the rope was unwinding in spinning threads and seconds away from splitting. Frantzen scrambled to reverse the rope's direction as Ben grabbed the iron bar before it fell. Frantzen closely examined the rope and sighed. "The rope's done," he said and then ran a hand over the upper edge of the doors where he found a thin crevice, a sliver of an opening near the top of the cabinet, but little else. The steel bars used to reinforce the twin doors had served their purpose. The lock bars held.

"Any luck there?"

"No, not much. The block and tackle won't do it, not with this old rope anyway, and maybe not even with a better one. It's a pretty strong cabinet."

"All this for nothing?" said a dejected Nyhavn.

"Maybe not," said the big German as another idea sprang to mind. "You got a lantern in that canvas bag of tricks?"

"Yeah, a small one."

"Get it."

Nyhavn reached in the small carry-all and pulled out the lantern and handed it to his accomplice. "What are you going to do?"

"Improvise," Frantzen said. He unscrewed the fill cap of the tin lamp's well and retrieved a small piece of paper from Mister Stanhope's desk. He folded it into the shape of a small funnel and held it above the thin crack above the cabinet doors. He poured the coal oil into the crack until he emptied the lantern's well. He considered using the candle wick as a fuse, but dismissed it figuring it wouldn't do. He needed something more along the lines of a fuse.

"You have that pocket pistol of yours?"

"Yeah."

"Good," he said, "then give me one of the cartridges."

"A bullet?"

"Uh-huh."

"What?" You think you're gonna shoot it open?"

"Not likely," said Frantzen as Ben removed one and handed it to him. Placing the bullet between his teeth, he bit down hard on the soft lead bullet head, and twisted the brass cartridge until it separated. He hit a nerve on one of his teeth in the process and as he ran his tongue over the annoyed tooth he told himself that next time he'd use pliers. Even as he tapped on the cartridge and poured the gunpowder in the opening, he told himself there wouldn't be a next time. This was it, my one and only shot at being a bank robber.

"Stand back," he said to Nyhavn, but when he picked up the candle to the powder, Nyhavn nervously grabbed his arm.

"Hold on! You sure the cabinet won't explode?"

Frantzen shrugged. "Don't think so but there's only one way to find out," he said and lowered the flame. The powder sparked to life and disappeared into the crack. There was no explosion as Nyhavn had feared, nor was there any immediate flame or fire Frantzen was hoping for, either.

Nothing appeared to have happened.

Just as Frantzen was about to lean in for a closer look there was a muffled whoosh as the coal soaked papers and ledger books finally caught fire. "There it is!" said the big German leaning back and smiling.

A thread-like plume of smoke rose out of the crack in a sluggish stream as the contents inside the cabinet slowly began to burn.

"We're not gonna burn down the town, are we, Al?" Nyhavn asked. The question briefly made the big German pause.

"Naw, I don't think so," Frantzen said. "It's on a stone floor and set against a brick wall. Besides, there's not that much air getting inside to fan it. More than likely, it'll slow burn like coal in a stove until everything inside is ashes or it goes out. Either way, it's the best we can do. We might as well go."

Gathering up everything they brought in with them they moved back to the window. "You go. I'll follow," Ben said taking one long last look around the office before he blew out the candle.

Frantzen went out the window feet first and hurriedly pulled on his boots. When he was ready, Ben handed him everything they had brought in with them.

As he was going back the window his coat snagged on the window sill. He was momentarily stuck and as he twisted and worked himself free, he hit the wooden dowel that was holding the window open, and sent it flying out into the alley. The window fell with a resounding thud. The force of the lead counter weights inside the window casing slammed it shut.

To their astonished delight, when the window dropped, the locking bar swung back just enough to lock the window behind them. Better still, because of the howling wind and rain, no one seemed to take notice of the noise.

"Tis the luck of the Irish," laughed Frantzen.

"Aye, and their fookin' heathen country cousins," said Nyhavn as they slipped back into the dark night.

Chapter 31

A grim faced Marshal, and his just as dour Deputy, filled the Roadhouse doorway. Their targeted focus was aimed in on the two strangers who were seated at a back corner table. With their backs to the entrance, and as hung over as they were, Ben and the big German hadn't noticed the lawmen.

However, Beth Traumen, who was behind the bar talking to her bartender, did. When she started out from behind the bar, the Marshal motioned her back with the barrel of his shotgun and a slow shake of his head.

The sleeve on the Marshal's left arm was pinned up to the shoulder, the lower part of the arm long gone. His right arm was still in good working order as was the double-barreled, breached loaded shotgun he carried that more than made up for the stump.

The giant Deputy beside him had a serious grip on a Henry rifle. The Marshal motioned for the deputy to angle over to the bar while he cautiously moved to the two men at the table from their blind side. From their positions the Marshal and the Deputy had clear shots at the two strangers. The deputy also had full view of the entrance, the staircase, and the small hall that led out to the office and the baths in the back, so there would be no surprises, which is why the Marshal placed him there.

Halfway to their table the Marshal unexpectedly stopped, snorted, and then turned the gun barrel up towards the ceiling de-cocking the shotgun as he casually walked up on the table.

"Mind if I join you, gentlemen?" he said, leaning it against the wall where the big German had set his rifle.

"Heard there were some rough looking undesirables in town," he said. "But my Deputy didn't bother to say how damn ugly you were."

"Arne!" yelled Nyhavn jumping to his feet and enthusiastically slapping the Marshal on the back. The sudden jump startled the Deputy who brought up his rifle, but somehow managed to hold his fire. Confused by the friendly exchange, the Deputy wasn't sure what he should do.

"Good to see you boys, again," said Arne Hermansen offering his good hand. "When did you get back?"

"A few days ago," said Frantzen, shaking the hand. "Good to see you too, Arne! Really good! Sit down and join us for a drink."

"I believe I will."

Catching Beth's worried attention Frantzen gestured for another round of beers as he took in the rifle in the baffled Deputy's hands.

"I take it he's with you?" he said to the Marshal, who turned in his chair and waved the deputy's rifle away.

"Go on and lower your rifle, Justin. It's okay," Hermansen said to the large Deputy as Beth brought the new round of drinks to the table. Against their protests, Hermansen paid for the drinks and waited until their drinks were in hand before raising his glass.

"To Trigg Kinnunen, a good soldier, and a better friend," he said with the others echoing the toast. They took long, quiet pulls, each locked in their own memories of Kinnunen, the charge at Gettysburg, and its aftermath.

Three years earlier they all had eagerly marched off to war, fought in a number of the major battles, and bled enough in too many of them to form a bond between them that other onlookers might not initially understand, especially Hermansen's young deputy who was still struggling to figure out what in the hell was going on. He was a flinch away from shooting the stranger who sprang up to greet the Marshal.

"I heard the Marshal went with Reverend Kinnunen to Winona to bring back the coffin," Frantzen said to Hermansen who nodded.

"Met a railroad man there named Gaul who told me everything that had happened in La Crosse. Said Ben here saved his life and killed the men that murdered Trigg. Three of them in all."

"Wish I'd done it sooner," Ben said echoing the sentiments they all felt.

The Marshal nodded. He saw something in Nyhavn's eyes, a hardness and resolve, that wasn't there before Gettysburg. The look was easy enough to recognize because it was the same one that stared back at him each morning when he shaved.

"Said he was supposed to meet you there, but the riverboat got delayed. Sent Reverend Kinnunen a telegram saying he was in Winona arranging transportation. The Reverend returned it saying he would meet him there. The Reverend asked me if I'd accompany him. I told him I'd be honored. Mister Gaul is with Reverend Kinnunen now."

"We should head on over and pay our respects," Ben said to Frantzen who answered with a solemn nod.

"In a bit," replied Hermansen. "But let's visit a little first."

An awkward silence fell between them and it was the big German who broke it by pointing to the round, tin badge on Hermansen's coat.

"Town Marshal, huh?" Frantzen said. "When did this happen?"

"Four months ago," replied Hermansen. "You boys recall Marshal Denison?"

"John Denison, sure," said Nyhavn, remembering the tall and wiry old campaigner who had done just as much scouting and Indian fighting as Jim Bridger, Kit Carson, let alone anyone else he had ever heard of, and who had probably stood toe-to-toe with more real tough guys than all of them combined.

"Not long after I came back he came in here to roust out some hard case miscreants who were a little slow when it came to riding through. The Marshal had two of them pretty well convinced to leave town with a thump to their heads from the butt of his rifle and a boot up their asses, when a companion of theirs snuck up behind Denison looking to waylay him. I thought it was a chicken shit thing to do, so I tripped his legs out from under him and dissuaded him from trying it again with a boot to his ear.

"The Marshal thanked me for helping out as he kicked the bush-whacker a good one himself, and then inquired what kind of work I was doing. I told him that since I couldn't be a saddle maker anymore with only one arm, I was holding down a seat here at Kelly's on a pretty regular basis. No pay involved but I couldn't beat the hours."

"The man on the floor interrupted us by calling Denison's mother a few disparaging names and started swearing at me too, so I kicked him a good one again. Denison said that in his better days there was no way he would have let anyone sneak up behind him the way the bushwhacker had."

"That's true enough."

"Said he must be getting a little long in the tooth, so he asked me if I was interested in some part-time work, since it appeared he could use a Deputy. I asked him what it paid. He said, not much to begin with, but it was better than what I didn't make holding down a seat in a Roadhouse. Wasn't certain what he wanted a one-armed Deputy for, but I took the job anyway. Worked with him up until last January when I found him one morning sitting in his chair, feet propped up on the desk, and colder than the battered old coffee cup he was holding. His heart gave out while he dozed."

"There are worse ways to go, I suppose," said Frantzen.

Hermansen said, chuffing. "Don't we know it and haven't we seen it?"

"How old was Denison anyway?"

"Damn near seventy."

"That was one tough old man."

"Seeing how I was already in place, the Mayor offered me his job, so I took it, and then hired my nephew, Justin over there at the bar, to serve as my Deputy."

"Keeping it in the family, are you?"

Hermansen nodded. "The tall side anyway. He's my sister Bodil's boy from up in New Ulm." Turning to the boy Deputy he said, "Justin! Come on over here for a minute. There are some people here I want you to meet."

The family resemblance with his uncle was there close up. Mostly it was in the eyes and the determined way he moved.

"Justin, these suspicious looking characters you told me about are actually old friends of mine, First Minnesota boys, I served with in the war," said Hermansen as the Deputy's hard edge gave way to a reluctant smile.

"The Prussian General looking fellow is Aalderk Frantzen, Al to his friends and that one there with the new mustache and skid patch beard is Ben Nyhavn."

"Pleased to meet you," said the Deputy with an awkward nod, seeing how he almost shot him.

The Marshal saved him from any more embarrassment. "You can head on back to the jail," he said to his Deputy. "Everything's okay here, I'm gonna catch up with them on old times."

"Good to have you back, gentlemen," said Justin. The giant Deputy left grinning like the kid that he was.

"He's what? Seventeen?" said Frantzen.

"Soon will be," replied the Marshal.

"Kinda young for the job, isn't he?" said Nyhavn.

"What? Like you were much older when we ran off to fight? Besides, his family can use the money. My sister's husband took sick this past winter and is bed ridden. They had to sell their farm and move into town."

"Then, good for you for hiring him," said Nyhavn.

"And good for the town too," said Hermansen. "His size alone is enough to stop most disturbances from getting out of hand, and he's reliable. Got no quit in him, which isn't always the smartest thing, but he'll learn. We all did."

"Marshaling a good job is it?" asked Frantzen.

"Good enough," said Hermansen. "Pay's not bad for taking the oath to protect and serve the good, and not always so good, citizens, of the town. Not much trouble really, a few angry, drunk loggers or mill workers to haul in and lockup, other occasional law breakers, transients mostly, freight haulers or adventurers who are going west," he said. "Figured maybe, that's who you were when Justin told me about you."

"Transient might be a good description," said Nyhavn. "It don't feel much like home anymore."

"Small wonder. The town's about tripled in size since we left. Lots of changes going on too since the Indian troubles," said Hermansen. "There have been some rough adjustments. But give it some time. It'll grow on you again."

Ben gave a non-committal nod and took another drink. He wasn't so sure it would.

"So, where have you boys been? The Regiment, or at least what was left of it, came back to Fort Snelling a few months back."

"Philadelphia hospital after Gettysburg, then New York," Nyhavn explained.

"New York? I heard that the Regiment was only there for a few weeks, to put down the Copperhead riots or some such?"

"They were, and did, for a short time, but were gone by the time we arrived. New York had us rounding up conscripts and bounty jumpers with a Provost Company," Frantzen said.

"For the remainder of your time?"

"All seven months and thirteen days," Ben said, reeling off the time they had spent in Five Points.

"I didn't think they could do that?" Hermansen said, somewhat surprised.

Frantzen chuckled. "We weren't certain they could do it either," he said, "but they did."

"So how was it? Is New York all they say it is?"

"At times it was. Although where we were in the city wasn't always so nice," explained Frantzen. "Some good people stuck in some bad situations, some sons of bitches looking to take advantage."

"Speaking of bad situations, don't suppose you boys know anything about what happened at the bank last night?"

"Why? What happened?" asked Nyhavn. "It get robbed?"

"Not exactly," the Marshal said studying their faces, trying to gauge their reactions.

"Well, what exactly?" asked Frantzen.

"The damnedest thing. A bank safe caught on fire..."

"The safe?" said Nyhavn looking almost shocked enough to be believed.

"Don't tell me I lost my Army money!" said Frantzen with more than an alibi's interest in the answer. "I just deposited it yesterday."

"No, the money's okay. It wasn't the main vault safe that got ruined; it was just the small safe-like cabinet in the banker's office. Burned up most of the bank's important documents, mortgages, bank records, and such. No way now for the bank to know for certain who owns what."

"What do you mean, just the cabinet? You saying nothing else was destroyed in the fire?"

"No, only what was in the metal cabinet."

Frantzen asked, "How is that even possible?"

"Don't quite know yet. The double doors looked like they might have been pried at a bit, but then again, maybe it was the pressure from the heat inside the cabinet that caused them to bulge some. Hard to say, for certain."

"Any sign of a break in?"

The Marshal shook his head. "No," he said. "Locked windows and doors, no real sign of a forced entry. It's a bit of a mystery."

"What mystery?" said the big German offering his own assessment. "More like carelessness, if you ask me."

"Carelessness?" said Hermansen. "Why do you say that?"

"Well, when I met with Mister Stanhope in his office yesterday…"

"What time was that?"

"Late afternoon, two, maybe three o'clock. My brother, Rolf went with me."

"And where were you?" Hermansen said turning to Ben.

"Here," said Nyhavn, "holding down a chair."

Back to Frantzen, Hermansen said, "So, you and Rolf met with Mister Stanhope?"

"Uh-huh."

"Why was that, exactly?"

"To deposit my Army pay, only he seemed more intent on having me invest it, telling me all about the advantage of railroad stocks, all the while waving his big Spanish Havana cigar around, flinging ash everywhere."

"Your brother witness that too, did he? The ash flinging, I mean."

"Don't know how he could have missed it seeing how Mister Stanhope smoked the damn thing the entire time we were in his office as he explained some slow and simple bank terms to us. I guess he figured that with us being slow and simple country folk and all, we might not readily understand complicated terms like 'interest' or 'profit'…"

The Marshal chuckled. "Yeah, he's a little full of himself…"

"Or something," said Nyhavn.

"Some truth in that, too," said Hermansen. "He barged into my office this morning shouting about a robbery…"

"I thought it was a fire?" said Nyhavn.

"Deliberately set, according to him. Arson, he claims, which is why he's saying he was robbed, and why he reminded me, more than a few times, that he has some big and powerful friends in the state capital…"

"Is that so?"

"It is, which is why I'm looking into it. Point in fact; I received a telegram from the Lieutenant Governor's office bright and early asking me to do just that, which is why I'm here. So, you say he was smoking his cigar and flinging ash everywhere, huh?"

"Maybe not everywhere but he was waving it around a lot when he talked. I suspect if you talk to some of the people who work in the bank they'll pretty much say the same thing. Wouldn't surprise me if he flicked some hot ash in the safe by accident."

"Cabinet, you mean."

"Cabinet, right" granted Frantzen. "My God, that would be something, wouldn't it? The bank takes away our friends and neighbors' farms, and made their lives hell only to get a taste of its own flames. Now that's what I'd call divine justice."

"And all at the hand of the banker," said Nyhavn.

"Could be," said the Marshal. "People do some pretty dumb things," he added. "You boys were in town last night, were you?"

"Got a little drunk here early on," said Frantzen. "Celebrating our homecoming and all."

"Both of you?"

"I had nowhere else to be," said Nyhavn. "Beth! What time did you and I go upstairs last night?"

"About midnight," she said, walking back to the table and taking a seat next to Nyhavn. "Twelve thirty, latest. Right after I locked up, and right after we had to carry this one to the cot in the storeroom," Beth said to Hermansen who listened and nodded. It was true enough to a point. Both she and Ben had carried him back to the storeroom but it was a whole lot later than midnight.

"Afraid I might have a little too much to drink," said Frantzen, which was true enough too.

"It was more than a little, Al," said Ben.

"Oh yes, it was," added Beth

The alibis were convincing enough, even if the Marshal didn't believe them.

"So, you boys home for good?"

"Naw, I don't think so, Arne," replied Nyhavn with some regret. "There's not much left here for me anymore. Lost my family and the farm. Besides, Mister Gaul offered me a job scouting for the railroad surveying teams going all the way to California. Think I'll take them up on it."

"California, huh?" said the Marshal.

Nyhavn nodded. "They say there's gold and silver waiting to be found out west. Might as well pick some up once I get there."

"You know, you just may run into a few hostile Indians along the way?" said Frantzen.

"Yeah, I know. But I got me a good Smith & Wesson pistol and a knife. I'll pick up a good rifle too, before I go."

Frantzen reached back behind him, grabbed his new Henry rifle that was leaning against the wall, and handed it to Nyhavn. "This one tends to shoot a bit low and to the left, so remember that when you're down behind the iron sites, trembling as a whole shitload of angry Indians are racing at you."

"I can't take your rifle."

"Yeah, you can, and will!"

"Then, let me at least pay you for it."

"Put your money away, Ben," Frantzen said, angrily waving him off. "But I'll tell you what? You strike it rich with that California gold and silver you're talking about, then maybe we'll hold this conversation one more time."

"You have a holster for the pistol?" asked Hermansen.

Nyhavn shook his head and said he didn't.

"Stop by my office before you leave. I'll have one waiting for you," said the Marshal. "Ben ever tell you how he helped me out at Plum Run?" he said back to the big German.

"No, he didn't," said a surprised Frantzen turning to face the young Dane.

"Well, he did," said the Marshal. "A piece of rebel shrapnel had taken my arm off at the elbow at the Charge. When it did, I just sorta stopped and stared at the bleeding stump for a little too long, and didn't see the Johnny Reb coming at me with a bayonet the size of a fence pole. He was looking to finish the job but Ben here stepped up and shot him dead and then bought me some more time so I could get back to our lines."

"I guess that shouldn't really surprise me," said the big German nodding to Nyhavn. "The boy's got grit."

"He does indeed. And you, Al?" Hermansen said turning to the big German. "You staying on to help your brother with the farm?"

"No, maybe after what happened at the bank I think I might be better off taking my money out of the bank. I'm thinking about heading back to La Crosse anyway."

"Wisconsin?" said the Marshal. "Why? What's in Wisconsin?"

"A young widow woman who has poor taste in men," said Nyhavn. "There's a German mother and a busy café tossed in with the deal."

"They're on their own. They could use some help," Frantzen said.

"Good deeds don't go unnoticed, or unappreciated," said Hermansen, getting up from the table and straightening his coat. "Expect you'll be well received."

"Stay for another drink?" Nyhavn said to the Marshal.

"Can't, at least not right now," he said. "I've got to get back to the bank and have a little talk with Mister Stanhope."

"You might want to ask him about his poor cigar smoking habits," said Frantzen.

"I just bet that's what it was," said Nyhavn.

"Could be," said Marshal Hermansen, "that is, if cigars smelled like coal oil."

"Coal oil?" said Ben, haltingly.

The Marshal took in Nyhavn's reaction. "Uh-huh, coal oil. I caught a whiff of it when Stanhope opened the cabinet in his office. Although I doubt he noticed it since he had one of his stogies going at the time. Like I said, the only reason I'm looking into this is because he's steam pissing mad and reminded me that he has a lot of influential friends in St. Paul who'll demand to know the results of my investigation. To be honest, there's not much though in the way of any real evidence. Hard to say what exactly happened or say, who's really to blame."

"No clues, huh?" said Nyhavn.

"No, not many," replied the Marshal, appraising the two the way someone who's holding better cards might look over those with losing hands. Hermansen fished something out of his vest pocket and tossed it on the table top. "Here Ben, I think you might be needing this."

It was a small tin trefoil, the kind that both Hermansen and Frantzen each had on their lapels that identified them as members of General

Hancock's Two Corps. "I found it in the alley just outside the bank office window, his locked window."

The table went quiet. Nyhavn's eyes went wide as he quickly glanced down at his coat where the military decoration should have been. When he looked back up at the Marshal, Nyhavn found Hermansen staring back at him. The bluff was over.

"You probably lost yours back in New York or Wisconsin somewhere, so maybe this one can take its place," he said to Nyhavn and then nodded to Frantzen.

The one-armed Marshal raised his beer glass. "For Plum Run," he said.

Hermansen finished his remaining beer in one long pull and set the glass back down. "Now I have to go to the telegram office and let the Lieutenant Governor know that it just might be possible that it was Mister Stanhope's poor smoking habits that's the likely cause in this tragic affair. Clubs are trumps," he said.

"Clubs are trumps," they replied.

The Marshal retrieved his shotgun and casually strolled out of the bar in the kind of good mood he hadn't known in some quite time.

Chapter 32

Ben shifted in his saddle for the third time that morning trying hard to find the last place on his haunches that didn't hurt. His back was sore too and occasionally sent a clear message to his brain that maybe, sitting in a saddle, day after day, for the last seven or so weeks, wasn't such a keen idea after all.

No 'maybe' about it, he said chuckling to himself. He wondered how he somehow had missed that part of cowboy adventuring in all of the magazine stories he had read. Still, as he winced and stiffly climbed down out of the saddle, and walked his horse towards the crest of the knoll, he had no real regrets with his decision to take the scouting job.

He had been partnered up with Grant Lasnier, a veteran tracker and hunter, who cautioned him early on to walk and lead his horse from time to time, especially when cresting a knoll or ridgeline.

"It'll give your horse a rest and give you one too, for that matter," said Lasnier. "You'll want to keep him fresh if you need to ride off in a hurry but better still, it makes for a lower target in case someone's waiting or watching from the other side of the hill."

It made sense to Ben and helped to relieve some of the soreness in his lower back and legs even now as he followed Lasnier up a knoll. They tethered their horses just below the crest of the hill and prudently crept up to see what lay beyond. Lasnier's people a few generations back were French Canadian and Huron Indian and he seemed right at home being a scout.

"It's good work for a man," he offered when Ben asked what brought him to the job. "You get to see country that most folks don't get to see, hunt game for folks who appreciate fresh meat, and get paid well for doing it."

"What about protecting the surveyors?"

"What? From Indians, you mean?"

Ben nodded.

"Not much of it so far but when it comes to it, that's what else we get paid for."

Lasnier was right, so far they hadn't run into many Indians during their five weeks out of Iowa. What few they saw from a distance kept a curious distance.

On week six though, everything changed when a Pawnee hunting party rode up to within fifty yards of the surveyor's camp, and just stared at the railroad team. A senior surveyor, Willfred Josephsen, and a California scout named Roberto Martinez, went out to parlay with them. The Pawnee though, were in no mood to talk. They killed Josephsen with a lance to his chest, and as he scrambled to fight back, Martinez took an arrow in the ribs. He barely avoided being taken captive when the rest of the scouts ran out to help him. The Indians were driven off by the determined and better armed railroad scouts. Martinez survived, but just barely.

The Indians were armed with a few rifles and muskets, but most carried lances, bows or war clubs. The railroad, on the other hand, had provided their scouts with Henry 'shoot all day' repeaters and .36 caliber Navy Colt, hole punchers.

Because of their superior fire power, the war party attacks against the main camp became fewer during the following days. The Indians instead chose to keep a cautious distance. Nights though were another matter. Two nights after the initial attack, several bucks crept in and stole half a dozen horses from the surveyors' remuda. The scouts set up better guard schedules and kept their remaining horses closer to the camp. Caution became the watchword for the guard shifts and when the scouts went out on day patrols, foraging in their usual parties of two.

This time out, he and Lasnier were hunting game, searching for a fresh water source, and scouting out a site for the surveying party's next camp. They had ridden west, a few hours ahead of the survey team, when they figured they found what they were looking for just over the knoll. Less than a hundred yards below them there was a large, spring fed pond and flowing creek that ran out to the vast, grassy rolling plains beyond. A quarter mile out from their hide a herd of buffalo just south of the knoll filled the bill for the required game. Thanks to the veteran tracker and scout, the camp would eat well again tonight.

For going on two months, Lasnier had been teaching the new hire as they went, and he appreciated the fact that the former soldier had sense enough to listen to what he had to say and even better sense to learn from it. Dumb could get you killed and the boy wasn't dumb.

"We'll set up a hide here. Dinner will be here directly," the veteran scout said studying the surroundings. The hillside overlooked the pond, creek and much of the grass filled plains. "Might as well go fill the canteens while there's time. Set us up a good field of fire."

"Will do," Ben said.

Lasnier knew that the heat would drive the buffalo herd towards the water and both the spring and the pond would soon be muddied and fouled by the bison. As Ben rearranged some brush to provide them with a good field of fire, the veteran scout made his way down to the spring.

Out on the rolling plains Ben saw the buffalo herd meandering towards the creek. A big bull bison, weighing at least two thousand pounds, had his head in the air sniffing the cool water, and then lumbered towards it. Nyhavn smiled to himself as Lasnier made his way back to him with the filled canteens.

"Looks like we met up with a little luck today," he said, handing Ben one of the canteens as he sat down and settled into their hiding place.

Down below, the large bull, was still slowly ambling up the creek bed and turning towards the spring. The bull was followed by a dozen or so cows and calves.

"You take the first bison, I'll take the second," whispered Lasnier. "Wait though till it gets a little closer."

"How little?"

"Ten yards in front of the pond should do it."

Nyhavn nodded and relaxed behind the rifle. It would be awhile.

In the warm sunlight and with a pleasant breeze, Ben's thoughts drifted to Beth Traumen, and the last conversation he had with her the night before he left New Tonder.

They were in bed and she was propped up on one elbow, twirling a lock of his hair in her fingers.

"Thank you," she said.

"For what?"

"For helping me make up my mind. I'm going out to California."

"When?"

"June maybe. July latest. I talk about it but that's usually as far as I get. Now, thanks to you, I've decided to book passage on a Steamship from Boston to San Francisco, and see what awaits me there."

"Better business opportunities, I suspect," he said.

"And a better life," she said. "I want to go somewhere where I can start my own history, and maybe not be the half-breed whore, anymore. I have the money to open a café or saloon, so I'm going to do it. Maybe when you get to California, you can pay me a call, once I get settled."

"Of course, I'll pay you a call," he said. "I'd be a damn fool not to."

Beth brushed a lock of hair away from Ben's eyes and smiled. "By the way, where did you learn how to do that thing you did, that French Joy thing?" she asked.

"I took a lesson once," he said.

"Well, let me just say that you were a very good student."

"Thank you."

Beth shook her head. "No," she said, snuggling up against him. "Thank you."

The memory brought on a warm, comforting smile but the movement down below brought him back to the moment and why he was down behind a rifle on the knoll. The bull was lumbering up to the pond, maybe twenty yards out.

Nyhavn had the buffalo in his iron rifle sites. It would be an easy shot. He was just about to fire when Lasnier squeezed his arm.

"Hold on," he said, his voice barely above a whisper. "We got visitors."

Ben slowly lifted his head and searched the plains below but didn't see anything other than the meandering herd and rolling plains, until his eyes caught subtle movement on the far right of the spring. An Indian was on all fours and cresting a smaller knoll. He was crawling towards the spring, his eyes and attention focused on the bull and his loping followers. He had a bow and a handful of arrows in his hands while a second Indian, armed with a muzzle loader, veered off to the right. His attention was locked on the herd as well, and the old flintlock, muzzle-loader he was carrying would probably bring down the bull.

From the direction the first Indian was taking, he would soon come across Lasnier's sign. Worse still, the two scouts could see the rest of the hunting party of two dozen or more easing themselves up over the rise, positioning themselves for the hunt. There were maybe thirty warriors in all waiting for the signal to begin. The two Indians would shoot the lead buffalo and spook the line of the approaching herd and drive them into the main body of the hunting party.

"He's crawling right towards my sign. There's no way he's gonna miss it," whispered Lasnier eyeing the pressed down track that in the right angle was as clear as a dropped ribbon. "When he does, kill him."

Nyhavn nodded as he steadied his breathing with slow, deep breaths, hoping the Indian would somehow veer off and not find the track. But the Indian crawled on and, as Ben feared, came to a startled stop when he cut Lasnier's path. The bent grass path and boot heel depressions were clear and unmistakable to the Indian. He slowly lowered himself to the ground as his hunter's eyes cautiously traced the route back up the knoll, his face an angry mask.

He was just about to cry out in alarm to the others when a rifle shot from the second Indian tore into the big bull, signaling for the hunt to begin. The shooter slung the muzzle-loader over his shoulder and was running and yelling towards the downed animal with a drawn knife. He would cut out the heart while it was still beating, eat it, and the bull's strength would be his own.

The signal shot sent the once hidden warriors racing out, whooping and hollering as they rode towards the confused herd. Well shot arrows and practiced lances drove into the scattering bison as did the rounds from the handful of rifles that the hunting party had with them.

Nyhavn drew a bead on the Indian who had found Lasnier's sign and was up and yelling, trying to get the main party's attention. In the clamor and chaos of the hunt, the shot went unnoticed, as did the Indian that fell dead in the tall grass.

"Time to skedaddle," said Lasnier scurrying down the hidden side of the knoll and back towards their tethered horses. They scooped up the staking pegs, jumped into their saddles, and raced away, kicking their horses' ribs with everything they had. The dead Indian might not immediately be found by the others, but he would be found soon enough. Then another frenzied hunt would be on. The two scouts had to put some time and distance between them and the hunting party and they had to do it quickly.

"Ride!" yelled Lasnier but Ben didn't need to be told, because, if his horse could somehow manage it, he'd race all the way to California.

All he had to do was survive the places in between.

CPSIA information can be obtained
at www.ICGtesting.com
Printed in the USA
FSHW021950241120
76291FS

9 781432 776701